Lord of Druemarwin

by

Helen C. Johannes

Crown of Tolem, Book 2

Lord of Druemarwin

Cover Art by *Rae Monet, Inc. Design*

The Wild Rose Press, Inc.
PO Box 708
Adams Basin, NY 14410-0708
Visit us at www.thewildrosepress.com

Publishing History
First Fantasy Rose Edition, 2019
Print ISBN 978-1-5092-2855-3
Digital ISBN 978-1-5092-2856-0

Crown of Tolem, Book 2
Published in the United States of America

"Raell, now is not the time—"

Aye, it wasn't. They stood in torchlight on an open parapet while assassins stalked them, but this might be the only chance she'd have to press her case, to reach him across that precipice, to secure the future they were meant to share. Gathering her courage, she spoke what was in her heart, what had propelled her on this journey to this man to whom she'd given everything.

"Does *my* honor mean naught? When weighed with D'nalian honor, is mine lesser because 'tis a woman's honor? Or because 'tis a Tolemak's honor? Be honest and tell me that."

The world had gone silent, or so it seemed, because Raell heard nothing over the rush of blood in her ears, the terrible heavy beats of her heart while she waited, dizzy with fear, breathless with longing, for the man she loved to respond with a word, a look, even a blink. Even a shift of his gaze she'd take as a sign he'd at least listened, mayhap begun to consider—

"Yes, be honest, *Lord* Naed."

A voice she'd heard but once, a voice that raised all the fine hairs on her body. Her innards contracted into a cold, tight knot.

"Tell us both how much honor means to a bastard who's betrayed his countrymen and his blood."

Also by Helen C. Johannes

The Crown of Tolem series
THE PRINCE OF VAL-FEYRIDGE
(EPIC Winner)

~

BLOODSTONE
(Launching a Star winner)

~

Praise for *LORD OF DRUEMARWIN*,
2015 Pages from the Heart Winner,
Fantasy Romance

"*LORD OF DRUEMARWIN* is a deep and passionate love story set amongst war and chivalry, allegiances and betrayals, secrets and ancient myth....Romance readers will enjoy this fantastic adventure as Naed and Raell learn to trust each other while exploring the fiery passion between them."

~*Amy Sandas, author of historical romance*

Dedication

To my critique partner Steve Mitchell,
thank you for sticking with this book
through the long haul
and for catching me when it wandered off track.
To my first readers,
Mary Ellen, Andrea, and Amy,
thanks for finding
all those annoying inconsistencies and gaps.
You are the best.
To my WisRWA friends
for cheering me on
and keeping me sane in this otherwise lonely business.
I owe you more than I can say.
And to my husband,
Who's been my #1 fan since the beginning,
thank you.

See page 463
for a list of places and characters in this book.

Chapter One

Albon fortress, Western Tolemak

Sixty-nine, seventy, seventy-one... Naed counted the tower steps, gritting his teeth at every other one. His left leg held strong under the combined weight of weapons, shield and chest armor—even on the third climb.

Seventy-two, seventy-three... Never again would he be last up the stairs because of it. Never again would he fall.

Or fail.

Sweat dripped off his nose. *Seventy-four, seventy-five, seventy-six...* To make doubly sure, he would add his helm to the weight total tomorrow.

If only his patched-together thigh didn't still ache...

Naed emerged onto the parapet and halted, squinting. The winter sun glared off everything—snow, ice, stone. He raised a hand to block it, catching the attention of sentries left and right. *Good.* He expected no less of these Tolemaks. No one knew war better than those who waged it constantly. With their own kind if the Adanak couldn't be provoked. And against ever-neutral D'nalee if all else failed.

That was in the past now—or would be once the Kingdom was restored and the Prince took his rightful place at the head of it.

Naed bent with hands on knees while his breath smoked in the cold. That the Prince's motley alliance held together through these last, desperate, bone-chilling weeks amazed him.

That they'd followed *him*, a D'nalian, took his breath away.

Was it only two years ago he'd left home, stuffed with pride as a newly made Free Sword, and ridden south to aid his uncle at Druemarwin?

He stared at frost-flecked stone between his boots. *Sisters Three! Was I truly* that *naïve?*

The tower door banged open behind him, and the Prince stepped out. Naed took in the tall man's chest armor and weapons. The warrior prince who'd achieved the impossible—recovered the long lost Crown of Tolem—still looked pale, but seeing him once again dressed for battle was a blessing beyond measure.

Sisters, be thanked!

Mayhap the long Tolemak winter was over.

Arn, Prince of Val-Feyridge, crossed to the wooden rail overlooking the courtyard. He shoved a hand through thick black hair, clearing it from his forehead.

Naed's scalp prickled. The Tolemaks would hold their ceremony soon, hacking off handfuls of hair to feed the flames of war. A binding sacrifice had value—indeed, it was nigh a necessity for this unlikely alliance—but he drew the line at cutting his D'nalian queue or painting any part of his face Tolemak blue or Val-Feyridge red.

"M'lord, what brings you up here?"

Sweat, running in rivulets down the Prince's face, steamed as he surveyed soldiers sparring near the stables. "The same as you, I suspect. You test your leg, I test my lungs." The stone gray eyes glinted just before he seized an unlit torch from the wall and swung it.

Naed backed two steps, stumbled, and deflected the torch with his shield before his mind caught up with his reflexes. He knew all too well what that hawk-bright look signified and should've been better prepared.

"See!" Prince Arn swung again. "You still don't trust your leg."

Naed grabbed another torch and parried. *Damn the man!* This was a foolish game—and dangerous, too, given the rock-hard courtyard below and the tinder-dry railing shielding them from a fall—but he knew better than to give quarter. The guardsmen would already be watching, if not the entire sparring cohort too. They needed no more fodder for stories about 'the D'nalian' despite his status as the Prince's Second, despite the new alliances.

"M'lord, you should not exert yourself."

"Hah!" The Prince studied Naed over the rim of his shield. "I need to know my limits, and so do you. If I don't know what my body will do in any given situation, 'tis sure I'll be wondering when it will betray me." He swung at Naed's right.

To parry, Naed rocked onto his left leg. The force of his weight shook through his injured thigh, shooting fire into the bone. He stumbled, banged the stone at his back and spun away. Heat swept up his throat.

"Aye, 'tis true." Prince Arn advanced with the torch held at ready as if it were the longsword sheathed at his side. "You know you're still lame. Your eyes give you away. All I need do is follow that fear."

"Indeed? Mayhap I fear pushing *you*, m'lord." That

3

was true enough. "Your lady wife would have my head if I undid her healing efforts."

The Prince laughed. "My lady wife knows 'tis pointless to hold me back. And so do you. Come, test my arm. My enemies will do so soon enough."

"Very well." Naed reset his grip on his shield while assessing what his body had learned. "Your arm is weak, m'lord. I well remember your strength." He advanced a step, swinging his torch. "Now that I'm fully engaged, you'll be hard pressed to take me."

"So you think." The Prince charged, delivering a series of blows that drove Naed repeatedly onto his left leg. "A battle, my friend," he panted when he broke off, "is never merely about brute strength." He pressed his shield to his chest, rubbing fingers over what Naed knew all too well were fresh scars underneath.

Acid dripped into Naed's stomach. He'd been too slow that day, steps too slow, and all he could do was staunch the blood over the worst of wounds. *So much blood...*

He blinked away the memory. Knowing the man, the gesture had been an absent one, no more than the press of a hand to pulling stitches. *Nothing at all about blame...*

"While Aerid may accept your need to heal on your feet, m'lord, 'tis best you do naught to alarm her in her condition. And being newly wed, she may have kept her...*concerns* to herself. Having provoked her *concerns* myself, I know—"

The Prince laughed and struck again, a surprisingly weak stroke. "'Twill be spring ere the babe comes, but if you mean her stubbornness, be assured, I'm well acquainted with it."

Naed eyed the man who'd once defeated him with naught but a shield. He advanced with two solid strokes. If the Prince wanted to test himself, so be it. "Then I shall consider my duty to warn you as fulfilled, m'lord."

The Prince took the blows on his shield. He'd been backing, Naed noticed, toward the tower door.

"Ah," the Prince said, "you're thinking now, anticipating what I might use against you. Good. But I still know your weakness." He drove forward with a flurry of blows.

Gritting his teeth more against shame than pain, Naed fended off the strikes. He stumbled away from the wall and tried to regain momentum.

"D'nalian obstinacy." The Prince panted. "Makes you predictable. I'll keep coming back till you wear me down."

"Then I shall do so!" He unleashed a series of blows that forced the Prince past the tower door. He'd found his rhythm now, each strike precisely targeted, his legs working in unison with the power of his arm, his blood singing as he took out his frustration on the man who—

Naed pulled up short. The man was only telling him the truth. He jammed his torch into a wall bracket while his face burned. It was not the Prince's fault if the truth stung. He'd simply hoped, after all these months, his leg would've recovered. Pulling his arm out of his shield straps, he demanded, "What would you have me do?"

Breathing heavily, Prince Arn leaned his torch against the tower wall. "Acknowledging the fact is a good start."

The man's face had gone chalk-white, and the old scar that split the left from eyebrow to chin showed silver and tight. Naed flushed hotter. *Sisters!* He ought to have better control of his emotions than to take them out on a man barely back in armor.

"I have tried, m'lord. Each day…"

"You run the stairs, I know." Prince Arn crossed to the railing and glanced at the men gathered near the stables.

Under their lord's scrutiny, the soldiers bumbled into one another in a rush to return to sparring, or at least appear as if they were. Naed's flush deepened. They would murmur to each other, and when they finished their exercise, the whole fortress would know what had transpired on the parapet between the Prince and his Second. Would he never learn to avoid such public displays?

Prince Arn laid a hand on his shoulder and faced him. "'Twas your first serious wound. 'Tis like to make or break a warrior, how he comes back from it."

"How have you come back from so many?" He knew the man's history, had seen the scars, even tried to keep up as the Prince took to horse with broken ribs.

"I find my limits, as I told you before." Prince Arn took a deep breath, and his color improved. "If your leg refuses to dance as it once did, change the dance."

"Dance, m'lord?"

"Find what your leg will do, and change your stroke, your stance, even the way you approach the enemy. If you refuse to change, you'll lose. And I'll not lose my Second when I've barely begun to train him." His gaze shifted as if the cloudless sky claimed his attention, but Naed guessed where his thoughts had taken him. The Prince missed his previous Second, the man who'd ridden at his side, stood at his shoulder, and guarded his back for half a lifetime.

Naed missed the Tolemak bastard too. It was a pity he and Krenin had wasted so much time hating each other. "Krenin would be only too glad to spar with me," he muttered.

Those all-too-perceptive eyes returned to the here and now, and the Prince smiled. "Aye, 'twould suit him to pummel you. Demon knows you were a burr under his saddle. But your man Banir knows your need and will do the same—if you'll but ask."

"Aye, 'tis very like." Naed heaved a sigh. The dark-eyed Tolemak always saw more than he said.

A horn sounded far off. The guardsmen on the parapet hustled into position. One hailed the Prince, "The banner of Nye, m'lord. They approach under a white flag."

The exercise with torches had left Naed with a pent-up need to bash something, but he suppressed it. His emotions had ruled him enough for one day. He turned to the man who wore a considering look on his scarred face. "Might this be an offer from Roines?"

"Brought by Belac? 'Tis unlikely." The Prince signaled the men over the gate. "Let them come, but close the gate after them and keep watch." He again laid his hand on Naed's shoulder. "Tylus and I will see what he's about. I have another task for you. Indeed, 'twas partly why I came up here after you. Your man's packing as we speak."

"Packing, m'lord? Do I not belong here at your side as your Second?"

"Aye, in most things. But in this only a D'nalian

will do." Prince Arn rapped his knuckles on Naed's chest armor. "And, 'tis sure, only this D'nalian."

Startled, Naed searched the gray eyes. This was not just any tap on the chest armor such as one soldier might give another. It was a reminder of what both men knew lay beneath that armor, in a narrow leather cylinder against his skin and over his heart.

Dranoel's legacy...

He'd had months to come to terms with it.

If only I could.

His lips tightened. He'd demand the truth from his mother when next they met. She owed him that much.

While a fresh surge of acid dripped into his stomach, he said, "Is this the time, m'lord? 'Tis winter yet and you barely back in armor."

"'Tis precisely the time. Rally the D'nalian lords to our cause. If aught may move them out of that much vaunted but damned inconvenient D'nalian neutrality, it should be meeting the new Lord of Druemarwin." He placed both hands on Naed's shoulders. "'Tis time you took your rightful place among them."

"Aye." Naed inhaled the cold Tolemak air. Underneath his tunic and against his skin, the rise of his chest shifted something else that lay over his heart, a small gold charm whose chain seemed ever to tangle with the leather cylinder. The Prince was right, but—*By the Sisters!*—did the man know what he was asking?

Chapter Two

"Demon's Blood! Will you not *learn*?"

"Learn you can put me on the ground?" Flinging back her braid, Raell pushed upright, adjusted her helm, and reset her shield. "After five times running, 'tis sure I know *that*!" A season of blade-bearing and a twelvemonth advantage in age did *not* make her brother a sword master, however much Toth was acting the part.

He glowered through slits in a practice helm. "And I'll do it again till you learn to mind your eyes. A flick of them shows me your next stroke."

"Sisters!" Raell flashed her fiercest scowl. "I have to think or I'll not have a chance to win." Her tailbone ached despite straw padding the ground, but she refused to show Toth that sign of weakness. The cold air already betrayed her uneven breathing. "I have to know what's about me, too."

"Look about, aye, but think while your eyes are on me. Watch my sword, my eyes, and act upon what you see. Act as you've been trained, as you've practiced time and again till you've no need to think. Did you see them with the torches?" Her brother gestured to the two men who'd been sparring on the parapet. "Do you think the Prince and your—your lowland *lapdog* have the time to be thinking when the strikes come fast and hard?"

Toth was right, but only about swordplay. He'd pay for that slur on the man she loved.

"*Lord* Naed has my promise, and well do you know it, you overstuffed ass." Raell charged, enjoying a spark of satisfaction when he stumbled—before he knocked her down with his shield.

Toth leaned over and smirked. "At Druemarwin, so I'm told, the Prince defeated your *Lord* Naed with naught but a shield."

"He was but a Free Sword then and, so *I'm* told, disarmed the Prince first!" Spinning in the straw, she swept his legs from under him.

He landed with an *Oomph!* and she gained her feet before his face registered surprise.

Grinning, she pointed her sword at his helm strap. "Did you mark my stroke that time?"

Toth laughed. "'Twas no stroke to see, and well do you know it." He pushed her blade away and rose. "But you've put me down, 'tis true."

"Use whatever's to hand. Or to foot," she said as he dusted himself off. "Father's first lesson."

"Every Tolemak's first lesson. 'Tis why your D'nalian lapdog serves *our* Prince. 'Twould do you well to remember that, however much Father may seem to accept the man."

Raell opened her mouth to retort, but a horn blared at the gate and everyone in the courtyard froze. Would it be two blasts or three? A call to arms or an attack? When nothing more sounded, she lowered her weapon and breathed. "The scout returning?"

Toth threw off his practice helm and padding. Steam rose from matted sand-brown hair, telling her however much he'd seemed in control, she'd made him work for it. She savored the knowledge until he said, "Not by the look of it." He nodded toward men scrambling into position over the gate. "They've called up the archers. 'Tis more like to be a parley. And not with Roines or they'd have called us to arms." He shrugged into his chest armor. "Do up my straps, will you?"

She sheathed her sword and reached for his shoulder straps while he pulled the rib laces tight. As her fingers worked, she focused not on archers kneeling in place over the gate, but on the two men Toth had pointed out earlier. The Prince and Lord Naed had been sparring—with torches, no less—but now they stood in earnest conversation, the Prince's hand on Lord Naed's shoulder.

Prince Arn wore chest armor, the first she'd seen on him since the night Val-Feyridge fell and the folk rushed to safety in Albon. Lord Naed stood as ever she'd seen him, copper hair glinting red in the sunshine, the queue marking him as D'nalian dangling from his collar. He'd shaved the beard he'd arrived with more than a month ago on that wild night he'd saved the folk and rescued the Prince. Without it he looked as young as he was, scarce older than Toth, but she'd seen a strong heart in those rare green eyes. Aye, and a load of misery too, but—

"Clear up, will you?" Toth stuffed his practice weapon into her hands. "I must be finding Father."

"Aye, go. Play Second while you may."

"'Tis a man's task, Raell." He buckled his sword belt, then reached out and pinged a finger off her helm. "And well do you know it, you spoiled daft girl."

"Ass!" She flung her helm to the ground as he

11

jogged away. "'Tis sure, I polish his sword better than ever you will!'"

"Aye, and you do fight well, too, Lady Raell."

Raell started, surprised not so much that someone had opened the door to the living quarters behind her, nor that the voice belonged to a woman, but that it belonged to one particular woman. Though Raell had tried her best to be accepting of the Prince's bride, the young woman's Adanak accent still jarred. Too many generations of Adanaks had fought too many generations of Tolemaks for most of the folk, if truth be told, to dismiss the blood memory out of hand despite the new alliances, but she tamped the thought down.

"M'lady." She dipped her head to the small, dark-haired woman.

Raell had been sparring with her brother in an alcove off the main open area before the stables. The better, Toth insisted, to keep her from mixing with riff-raff among the common soldiers. Raell suspected another motive—to protect his reputation should she by some chance get the best of him, which she had. *Take that, you overstuffed ass!* Lest the Prince's bride mistake the meaning of her smirk, she kept her head down until it faded.

When she looked up, Lady Aerid had walked—waddled was more like for the woman was already large with child—into the sunshine and lowered the hood of her plain woolen cloak. Although entitled to finery, the Prince's bride dressed in simple, high-waisted working gowns such as the cream one visible beneath her nut-brown cloak's hem. And she carried on practicing her healing art.

While Raell picked up the sparring gear, she

scrutinized the young woman she'd once suspected of being Lord Naed's mistress, until evidence forced her to admit otherwise. That an Adanak woman had ridden halfway across Tolemak—in winter, no less, and thick with child—to bring the Crown and her healing skills to the Prince testified as much to her devotion as the looks Raell saw daily pass between the Prince and his bride. But Lady Aerid and Lord Naed were close in a way Raell still wondered about.

Not today, though. The woman had hardly come outside to watch Naed when the husband she'd spent weeks tending stood before all and sundry and declared himself healed.

"'Tis on the parapet you'll find the Prince, m'lady."

"Aye. 'Tis where he does belong." She shaded her eyes with a small copper-skinned hand.

Raell glanced at her own pale white one, and then chided herself for comparing their size and color. That she had half a head on the woman, and likely weighed more despite the growing babe Lady Aerid carried, further emphasized the woman's exotic looks. Skin prickling, Raell stacked the sparring equipment beside the wall and shrugged out of her practice padding. *Why isn't she leaving? Shouldn't she want a better view?*

When the silence stretched beyond her endurance, Raell blurted, "The Prince has put on his armor today," and grimaced. *Daft idiot! She can see that for herself.* She flung the padding onto the pile, grateful the woman still watched the parapet.

"'Twill not be long ere he does take to horse again." Lady Aerid turned, and the smile she'd bestowed on her husband faded. She indicated the sword Raell had just unbuckled from her waist. "Be it common among Tolemak women to carry weapons and fight?"

Ah, yet another difference between us. Raell bit the inside of her cheek. She had to stop thinking like that. Naed wore her charm and she had his promise. The woman had asked an innocent question, and she deserved an answer.

Raell contemplated the practice blade in her hand. Her father had given it to her when she was ten and had badgered him daily to let her learn swordplay alongside Toth and their older brothers. To her brothers' surprise, she'd not quit when they gleefully bruised her so badly she couldn't sit without a cushion. Her father watched with a twinkle in his eyes that told her she'd not surprised him at all.

"No, m'lady, 'tis quite *un*common." If the Prince's bride chose to be surprised, so be it. Raell raised her chin and met Aerid's gaze. "But the household of Tylus be a household of men, and though I've not your skill at healing, of necessity I've learned a fair bit. Just as I've learned a fair bit about keeping myself safe."

Lady Aerid stood with a hand on her belly as though soothing the Heir to Tolem within. "I did wonder. Krenin once did make me fight with a torch to help him. Aye, as those two atop the parapet did not so very long afore this." Her gaze turned pensive as though remembering the man who'd so long stood at the Prince's side—the man who, Raell was certain, must've raised the Demon Himself at the Prince's choice of bride. "'Tis not in my nature to be fighting, as you well do know."

She did. And, to be fair, she'd heard Krenin had

warmed to Lady Aerid in the weeks before he died. He'd even cursed the Prince for leaving her behind, or so Krenin's men had said. They'd been there at Druemarwin, so Raell had to believe them, much as she would've preferred not to. When she came out of her thoughts, Lady Aerid was studying her with those startlingly blue eyes everyone said matched the Kingdom Stone in the Crown. The folk may have had doubts about the common-born Adanak healer the Prince had wed, but those eyes of that color had gone far toward convincing them the Three Sisters had blessed his choice.

"And Lord Naed, does he know?"

Raell frowned. "Know, m'lady?"

"That you do fight as well as many a man."

Ah, yes. That. Stomach churning, Raell glanced at the two men still engrossed in their conversation on the parapet. In the scant month she'd known Naed, they'd had precious little time to learn anything more of each other than their hearts were linked. "No." She returned her gaze to the other woman. "And 'tis my wish that I be the one to be telling him."

Lady Aerid inclined her head. "'Tis not my intention to meddle. 'Tis only that...well, having lived among D'nalians, I do know 'tis unheard of among them to find a woman thus armed. And D'nalians be...aye, 'tis well known they do value propriety nigh as much as honor. Be that known to you?"

Not in so many words but, aye, she'd had an inkling or her stomach wouldn't have so readily curdled. What *would* he think? Living so deep in the west, she'd met but few D'nalians, and those had strutted about her father's court stuffed with self-importance. Until their lack of warrior skills properly deflated them. Raell cast another glance at the men on the parapet. No one who'd fought alongside Lord Naed doubted his courage, blade-skill or honor, and he was ever one for treating her as the lady she was. Not that he hadn't kissed her, or put his hands on her. Aye, he had the most wondrous hands…

The gate gears whined, drawing her attention. Raell stepped alongside Lady Aerid to watch ten armed men ride under metal spikes that were pulled just high enough the riders had to hunch over their horses' necks to pass. The spikes slammed shut behind the last rider's tail.

"Who comes? Do you know?"

Though Raell hadn't seen the man since she was a child, and his elegant beard had grayed considerably from the days when he offered her sweets and sat her upon his knee to marvel at the honey gold of her hair, she recognized the lead rider. "'Tis Belac of Nye."

"He does come on behalf of Roines, aye?"

"Mayhap." For years Belac and her father hunted together and fought side by side in the Northern Wars. But when the bastard Arn claimed blood right to the title of Prince and Heir to Tolem, Rolnar of Roines split the folk against Arn. Belac sided with Roines, and Raell hadn't seen him since. But her impression of the man with the kindly face and shrewd eyes hadn't changed.

"'Tis more like Belac plays his own game."

The rider alongside the man she knew had removed his helm and fixed his gaze upon her as they approached. He was young, of Toth's years, with dark wavy hair that brushed his shoulders, and an arrogant smirk that told her more surely than his features he was

Belac's son. She scowled. When last she'd seen Bennin of Nye, he was doubled over with laughter after having pushed her face first into the mud. She'd hated him then, and the insolent way his gaze now ran up and down her body, over the men's tunic and leggings she wore for sparring, told her neither he nor her feelings had altered a whit.

Chapter Three

In the crowded corridor near the kitchens, spotlighted by a series of high, narrow windows, Naed dodged sideways. Children of varying sizes darted around him, engrossed in a game of chase. If he hadn't played such games with his brothers, hadn't bedeviled his elders as only pent-up children in the waning days of winter can, Naed might have scolded them. But they and so many of their elders were here because he'd led them to Albon. His success at saving the folk of Val-Feyridge weeks ago made it nigh impossible to find in this throng the one person he sought. If only he had more time before he rode out.

If only I had the Prince's height.

Naed rocked up on his toes and there, bathed in a thin slant of winter sunlight, gleamed a long, honey-gold braid. His heart thumped, and he arrowed through the press of bodies to the slender figure who absorbed all his focus. She wore green today, a modestly cut gown she'd covered with a homespun apron. Six or seven servants attended to whatever she ticked off a list.

"Lady Raell," he said, when he caught her sleeve.

She beamed a smile that lit flecks of gold in her warm brown eyes.

Sisters! He would never tire of that smile. "I—I have news. Can we go…?"

"Someplace quieter?" Her gaze twinkled from

under her lashes.

He flushed, lost his tongue, and nodded.

Dismissing the servants, Raell took his hand and led him...somewhere. There were stairs. The dance of her hips as she climbed held Naed in thrall, and he truly cared not a whit where they went as long as her scent, that of white lilies and her own delicate musk, led him. When she stopped, he dipped his head and took the mouth he'd been thirsting for this past hour—and was never far from his thoughts these days. Raell came with a sigh and wrapped her arms around his neck. *Sisters Three!* He wished he'd not already put on his chest armor and traveling clothes. Still, her heat penetrated leather, plate, and wool.

Raell's skin tasted of paradise, and his tongue lingered at the base of her throat where her blood beat. She held him there with fingers twined into his queue. "You are going," she whispered. "Where?"

Aye, he was, all too soon. With a deep sigh, he captured her lips once more, drinking in all the memories he could hold. Who knew how long they would be parted?

When he straightened, he took in kiss-swollen lips a natural rose, eyes lashed with dark gold, languid with pleasure, and pale skin blessed by the sun. A man could forget his very name when a woman looked at him thus. He cleared his throat, forced himself to step back, to insert space between their bodies, to recall why and for what he should forgo the satisfaction promised in her company.

"I-I must go to D'nalee. To meet with the lords."

"So soon?"

"Prince Arn would have me away before the Lord

19

of Nye suspects."

Raell bit her lip, pinking it with even, white teeth. She slid her hands from his queue to his chest, anchoring fingers in his cloak. His news had chased the sensual fog from her face. "Aye, 'tis best to keep Roines from knowing more than he may."

Naed covered her hands with his. In the scant month he'd known her, she amazed him constantly. As the Lord of Tumin's least son, he'd grown up amid politics and war, watching his elder brothers and the lords of northern D'nalee posture, bicker, and maneuver for favors and influence. It was a man's providence, and none of the women he knew cared a whit. Even Aerid seemed content to stay out of such affairs. But Raell knew as much as any man, and more than most. He was not yet sure what to make of that. Now, though, was not the time to decide.

"I shall return as soon as I may. You may count upon that."

Smiling briefly, she opened her hands over his heart. "You wear the charm I gave you?"

"Always."

"'Twill protect you. You may count upon that." She kissed both of his hands and his mouth. When she leaned back, her eyes glinted with mischief. "And 'twill keep me ever in your heart when the ladies of D'nalee might otherwise throw themselves at your copper hair and fine green eyes."

He laughed and kissed her once more. "'Tis no one in my heart but you, Raell."

"See to it. We Tolemak women take such vows seriously."

Her scent, her warmth accompanied him all the

way to the frozen stable yard, where he found himself moments later being handed the reins of an unfamiliar horse.

Banir, his Second, glanced up from tightening the chestnut stallion's girth, surveyed Naed's face, and shook his head. "You should've wed her."

"I-we would not interfere with the Prince's joy."

"'Tis a fortnight since the Prince be wed."

"You know naught of how it is between me and Lady Raell!" That was bluster, and he wished once more he could keep his tongue firmly in his mouth. If anyone knew the truth in his heart, this dark-eyed tracker from Albon who said little but saw much was the one.

Banir shrugged. "I know 'tis best for a man to stake his claim to what he would have as soon as he knows he would have it."

Naed scowled, but the Tolemak who'd risked everything to side with a D'nalian was right. In the half year since Banir had appointed himself Naed's Second, he'd learned to trust Banir's judgment. Trusting it, however, did not make the receiving any less irksome.

In truth, Naed agreed. He should've wed Raell, but he'd hesitated once again, just as he'd hesitated to declare himself with Aerid the night she'd gazed at him with those summer-sky blue eyes and they'd had the corridor all to themselves. *Sisters!* Was it only last spring? The moment, the memory seemed a world away, a different lifetime entirely. He'd truly been as green then as Prince Arn told him he was. But there'd been destiny in his restraint. As the Sisters unfolded their tale for his life, and for hers and the Prince's, he'd been right to refrain then, though he could've done without the pain all that longing had engendered.

His heart, so sure of itself, had been wrong then. He was sure now, so sure his whole being ached with it, but—

The stallion shook its head, pulling Naed's arm up with the reins. "What horse is this? Where is my mare?"

Banir ran a hand over the animal's red-brown rump. "'Tis Firefall, Krenin's mount. Master of Horse Gorm thought he'd suit you."

Naed eyed the stallion, who eyed him back, nostrils flaring. It was taller than the Tumin mare he'd ridden for the last two years, and well-muscled, but it was scenting him now. Could it detect his D'nalian blood beneath the Tolemak cloak and tunic?

"Did Gorm consider Krenin's aversion to all things not Tolemak?"

"Have you no faith in my training, Lord Naed?" Master of Horse Gorm strode from the stable, his giant size and great height a match for the thunder of his voice.

Every time the huge Tolemak clapped a hand on his shoulder, Naed felt himself ten again and least among his brothers. He'd been least among Gorm's men once, not so very long ago—until the Three Sisters intervened and changed everything.

He regarded the big man with a sober look. "I have tremendous faith in your horse-handling, Master Gorm. However, for much of Krenin's and my association, he would have preferred seeing me roasted on a spit."

Master of Horse Gorm guffawed. "Aye, that was Krenin, to be sure." He cuffed Naed a good-natured blow to the arm that would've knocked him sideways had he not set his feet in anticipation. "But he trusted you in the end, and he'd want no one but you to have Firefall." Gorm grinned, a flash of teeth amid a beard that, if possible, had grown more bristly these past weeks. "Still, to set your mind at rest, I've been rubbing him with your gloves to make sure."

As if in confirmation, the stallion shook its head and butted Naed's shoulder. He resisted the urge to stroke its blazed muzzle. His leg already ached from the cold stone he stood upon, and the mare possessed a gait he could at least tolerate for the long ride ahead. "I thank you for your efforts, Master Gorm, but my D'nalian mare has served me well thus far."

"Aye, she has. A game little horse, that one, and you'll not be leaving her behind. The Prince's Second should always have a change of horse he can rely on." Gorm rubbed the stallion's ear. "But Firefall is faster, and you'll find he's smooth gaited too."

Gorm had witnessed the ambush, seen the arrow plunge into his thighbone. He ought to accept Gorm's consideration for what it was, an honest man's offering to a comrade, but Naed wished there was no need for such a gesture. If only his leg had recovered...

It had not, and he faced days of hard riding aboard a horse these Tolemaks seemed bent on making him accept from a dead man whose position he'd assumed half a year ago. He and Krenin had become comrades at last. Still, had the Sisters not cut Krenin's life thread when they did, Krenin and he would never have been friendly. They could respect each other, and play their roles with good grace and grudging cooperation, but Naed could never be easy with a man so different from himself.

Sometimes he thought it a mercy Krenin had died. With the Prince bent on reuniting the three territories, the world they all knew was changing, along with its rules. Even now he stood as a Tolemak Prince's respected Second and a lord in his own right in a place where scant months ago an untitled D'nalian Free Sword would never have survived. The Sisters had given him much, but they expected nigh as much from him as the Prince did.

Naed straightened his shoulders against the weight resting there. He would be old and stooped before this was over. "If Firefall is not as smooth riding as you claim, I shall hand him over to you when next we meet. In the meantime, I am entrusting the Prince's wellbeing to you and Lord Tylus."

The giant Tolemak grinned. "My life is his, as it has been since long afore you earned your sword, Lord Naed."

"We'll meet again soon."

"Sisters willing, you'll bring the D'nalian lords to us. I've some fine Eidvondin wine set aside to celebrate that."

"I shall look forward to it."

Aye, he would—if only he knew how in the Name of the Sisters he was going to accomplish that feat. It mattered not that the Last King ages ago had left his three sons to feud among themselves for the Crown, and the bloodshed had broken the Kingdom into three bitter parts. D'nalee territory, always in the middle, had suffered the worst for trying to remain neutral. And now he was being sent to convince his people the King had returned in the guise of this Tolemak Prince of Val-Feyridge—all because Prince Arn had found the long lost Crown.

Naed fit his boot to the stirrup and gritted his teeth for the effort his leg required to raise him into the saddle. Someday he would once again swing aboard as easily as Banir and the others. Now he grimly settled himself behind the shearling pommel as, under his tunic and against his skin, both the leather cylinder and the gold charm slid into place over his heart. It would be a long ride to D'nalee, and an even longer journey to success. Then, mayhap, he could think again of Raell.

Chapter Four

Prince Arn steepled fingers beneath his chin. The chair he'd selected in Albon's Great Hall offered solid support for his elbows and ample freedom for his weapons, should he be called upon to use them. Though he'd labored on his climb to the parapet, he savored being fully clad for the first time in weeks. Arn pushed his palms together, pressed hard, and eased them apart. Besides the all too familiar ache of deep healing, his chest muscles told him they'd needed the exercise with the torches.

"All in good time," Aerid assured him day after day, but he damned well understood Naed's frustration. Though they'd sparred more than an hour ago, his blood still ran hot and—*Demon take me!*—he half wished Belac had come itching for a fight. He couldn't wait to smash sword into shield again, to spin and strike amid the shouts and clangs of battle while the smell of fresh blood and hard-earned sweat filled his nostrils. Today, at least, he'd sweated like a warrior, and Belac could not mistake the scent.

"About time," Krenin would've said. He'd have greeted Belac with a drawn sword and belligerent glare.

Arn smiled, but his best friend would have also thanked the Three Sisters Arn had chosen this day to strap on sword and armor. The timing could not have served them better, but Arn doubted the Sisters took that much note of mortal affairs. Besides, Krenin the believer was dead, and Arn the unbeliever yet lived, not altogether unhappily.

Arn considered the compact wooden box he'd placed on the small table beside his chair. Of polished hardwood but bare of ornamentation, it seemed no more than the hinged box or casket a lady might use to store her jewels. Krenin had carried that box west from Vinvinnysee in central Adanak to Druemarwin fortress in D'nalee. Aerid had borne it—and the babe that was his heir—across half of Tolemak to bring it to him. Whether the Sisters had blessed him or not, Arn had regained the Crown that was his by right of blood.

Now all he had to do was remake the Kingdom.

Aye, just that...all.

He'd had no illusions when he set out to mend an ancient wrong, and he'd succeeded in more ways than he once dared imagine. Adanak territory was half his and Naed would soon bring D'nalee territory into play, but now was not the time to let down his guard.

Not when so many vipers lurked right here among his Tolemak brethren.

A trestle table separated him from the two men who approached. Lord Tylus stood at the right edge in the position the hawk-beaked warrior favored, one boot propped on a bench, sword hanging free to his hand. Tylus's youngest son Toth had been posted to the table's left. The youth had come into his blade after Arn left last spring. He knew naught about the lad, other than he'd inherited his father's glowering brows and distinctive nose, but Tylus trained good men. Arn would wager his life on that. In truth, he'd done so more times than he cared count.

The Lord of Nye's glance, and that of the youth following him, took in Tylus and Toth, swept once around the Great Hall with its rough-hewn beams and faded tapestries, and settled on Arn. The man carried himself as upright as ever, but his neatly trimmed beard was threaded with more gray than Arn remembered.

The Lord of Nye halted before the table and inclined his head. "M'lord."

Tylus snorted.

Arn suspected his long-time ally found the nod insufficient. Perhaps it was, but he'd never been one to stand on ceremony, especially when he was all too aware of Albon's limitations. There were other, better ways to impress than with furnishings.

"Belac," he said, lowering his hands to the chair arms, "what brings you to my humble home on such a cold winter's day?"

"If I may, m'lord, allow me to commend you for agreeing to see me and thank you for your hospitality."

Another snort, this from Belac's attendant. Toth glared at the man. They were of an age and, unless Arn was mistaken, recognized each other—and not with pleasure.

While he tucked that observation away for future consideration, Arn offered the Lord of Nye a bland smile. He'd made Belac and his escort wait where they couldn't count the defenders or note more of the defenses than a quick glance could have showed. He couldn't hide the fact the fortress was stuffed with more folk than it'd been built to handle, but that was no secret to his enemies. Tylus had managed to clear the hall—except for archers hidden among the rafters above—and that should suffice.

"It was the least I could do for someone who's come as *far* as you have." Was the Lord of Nye a messenger? Or a turncoat? Or the self-serving bastard both Tylus and Krenin always believed him to be? As if Arn had given the gesture no thought, he shifted a hand to the plain wooden casket.

Belac's gaze shot to the box. The eyes of his attendant—his son?—remained fixed on Toth.

Definitely something there, but not the matter of the moment. Arn trailed fingers along the box. Belac mattered. And the all-consuming focus he apparently didn't share with his son.

Self-serving bastard. Right, then.

The Lord of Nye dragged his gaze back to Arn. "M'lord, I'm glad to see you well. There have been rumors—"

Tylus's boot hit the stone floor. The bench it had rested on toppled with a crash. Both thuds boomed like thunder around the empty chamber.

"Aye, and no thanks to you! You can scuttle back to your *master* Roines and tell him the Prince is alive and well. Aye, better than well since we've all been dining on the supplies he so graciously *shared* with us."

"That was an audacious raid, I'll grant you." Belac rounded on Tylus. "And the sheer nerve of it—so like you, old *friend*—might have netted you some success even if—"

"'Twas not my doing, but 'tis sure—"

"No, 'twas the plan of the D'nalian, but you approved of it. Aye, you would've done it yourself if you'd had the nerve, but you've always been all bluster!"

The two men stood nose to nose like stags in full

rut. Belac, the taller, glared at Tylus, whose chin jutted out almost as far as the finger he poised to jab Belac's chest.

"So…" Arn leaned back as though making himself more comfortable. "We might have had some success even if…?"

Belac stepped back first. He flexed his hands as if reining in his emotions. His gaze, cooling as he turned, touched the casket on its way to Arn's face. "M'lord, may I speak plainly?"

Tylus rolled his eyes, but Arn merely said, "By all means."

"Roines anticipated the raid, and had your Adanak allies not arrived when they did, his forces would have hurt you badly. This point you must concede, m'lord."

"Bluster!" Tylus sputtered. "You would accuse me of bluster, and you—!"

"I concede naught." Arn stroked the box. "But, continue."

The gesture drew the Lord of Nye's attention, before he cleared his throat and looked at the floor. "I say again, your forces may have suffered badly, m'lord, had Roines' forces been at full strength."

Arn's fingers stilled. He resisted the urge to sit up and lean forward. *Well, now—self-serving bastard and a turncoat.* He lifted his hand to indicate Belac should continue.

The Lord of Nye grimaced as though he'd been served something bitter but had to choke it down.

Arn admired the performance while he sent Tylus a glance. Tylus read his cues nearly as well as Krenin had, and though the seasoned warrior glowered, he straightened away from Belac. Once more Arn gave thanks he'd brought Tylus instead of Naed to this meeting. While he trusted Naed as his Second, Naed wore his emotions too close to his sleeve to play the bully this task required. "If you are referring to the deaths of the lords of Ormo and Koth, that's hardly news."

"No, but the fact Roines killed them himself may be."

The pronouncement hung in the stillness while Arn's blood beat in his ears. He had not expected this.

"Here now, are you saying—?" Tylus sputtered.

Belac ignored him, gaze riveted on Arn. "As a result, some of us have decided we may...*choose* to play a somewhat...*less* active role in Roines' plans. Do I make myself clear, m'lord?"

As clear as your kind can be. "What do you want, Belac?"

31

Chapter Five

Northern D'nalee

Lady Vyenne of Tumin sat before her mirror and regarded the parchment lying on her dressing table. Her name was writ not in the flowing script she'd longed to see on a message from Druemarwin, but in careful lettering made by one who found ink and quill unfamiliar. Not Naed, though she could have expected a missive from her youngest son by now. No doubt her husband thought it was from the child she favored and had ordered the letter brought to her chambers straight away.

But he was wrong.

And so was she.

Vyenne traced the wax seal with fingertips. At least three hands before hers had touched it, the writer, the messenger, and her husband. But none had broken the familiar seal. Whatever lay within was hers alone to know.

Sisters, be merciful!

How she wished it were good news, but her heart had lain heavy in her breast for some months. Indeed, hearing a Tolemak army occupied Druemarwin had put all northern D'nalee on edge. Scant years before, they'd been the ones to suffer when the Northern Wars spilled from disputed borderlands. Now it was the south's turn to be victimized by the Tolemak/Adanak feud.

Vyenne closed her fist. Her husband and their eldest, Allyn, still bore scars earned defending Tumin from first Adanak then Tolemak raiders. Fennyn and Naed had been too young to go to war. But Elwyn— how proud he'd been to earn his sword. She sucked in a breath, steeling herself to remember her second son as she'd last seen him, waving as he rode out the gate. That was preferable to recalling the broken and bloodied body they'd laid to rest under mounded earth and stones.

And now her youngest had been caught up in this latest outbreak of their ancient feud.

All because she'd urged her husband to send the lad to Druemarwin.

She must have made some noise because her wolfhound Beauty rose from the hearth rug and padded to her side. The great gray animal sat beside her chair and looked at her with liquid black eyes nearly level with her own. Vyenne resisted the urge to comb through the dog's fur and absorb the comfort doing so always brought. She would need it soon enough, but first...

She forced open her fingers and once more traced the wax seal. Little news escaped Tolemak-controlled territories—save that Vinvinnysee, crown jewel and capital of Adanak, had fallen to the Prince of Val-Feyridge. Still, when last her family had heard, Naed was safely returned to his uncle's holding. Of that her heart was certain.

That meant...

Dread circled her heart, pulling icy fingers tighter.

Vyenne broke the seal.

Moments later, slow fat tears dripped on the parchment lying open on her lap. She stared at the glass, seeing not the reflection of her own upright bearing and still-auburn hair, but the bull-like shoulders and thick mane of the man she'd loved since she was sixteen. They'd met at her wedding feast in her father's Great Hall. While her new husband Alwyl of Tumin drank himself into a stupor, they'd looked long and hard into each other's soul. She'd have gone with him then, weak-willed as she was, but he'd held fast to his honor and taken her sickly sister as his bride. They'd seen each other but twice in the intervening years, first when she'd gone to Druemarwin to tend her dying sister, then here at Tumin when Naed was six and his cousin Dlaniger a sturdy twelve.

But now Dranoel, Lord of Druemarwin, was dead.

And Naed knew.

It would not be long ere her husband did too.

She folded the parchment, tucked it into her bodice, wiped her eyes and rang for her maid. The wolfhound whined, and she buried her face in Beauty's neck until she heard the chamber latch lift. "Elda," she said when the woman entered, "'tis time to pack."

****

As she did every evening, Raell set her father's mulled wine on the table before the fire. The chamber was small for the Prince's closest and oldest ally, but adequate, considering the limitations of Albon fortress. Toth had to quarter with their men, but she wasted no pity on her brother. Her tailbone still ached from sparring. Thinking about that was preferable to wondering how far Naed had ridden since he'd kissed her so thoroughly and left for Sisters knew how long.

He had a true heart. Of that Raell was sure, or she'd never have been drawn to him that night she'd first seen him, alone and dispirited in the darkened halls of Albon scant weeks ago. She'd been sent by her father to tend to the D'nalian's wounded cheek and settle him with food and clean clothes. Truly, her father had taken the man's measure aright. Lord Naed would not see to his own needs with the Prince's condition so heavy on his mind.

She'd expected to recognize him by his D'nalian queue, but someone said there was a hint of copper in his hair. More than a hint, she discovered in the torchlight. And beneath the grime, soot and blood streaking his face, she read misery in those rare green eyes, misery she longed to relieve.

None of the men who sought her hand—and there'd been more than enough—had garnered a second glance. They wooed her as the only daughter of the Prince's closest ally, thinking her a silly trifle they could bend to their will.

Silly trifle indeed! Raell punched up the cushion in her father's chair. *Asses!*

But it was the way of the world, and much as she wished to, she couldn't deny it. Even foolish Erodasi of Roines, the Prince's late betrothed, knew full well she was to be her father's brood mare. *That* girl had taken a lover to spite *both* her father and the Prince. Raell admired her audacity, if not her sense. At least her own father loved her enough to have thus far given her free rein to choose among those who sought her.

Mayhap he knew none of them would suit her any more than they suited him, but that was a dark thought and she dismissed it.

She picked up a poker and hooked a log fallen half out of the grate, shoving it back into the flames. Lord Naed suited her father well enough despite what Toth said. Her father knew full well she'd given her heart to the man even if he hadn't officially offered for her hand. Still, she wished they'd shared more than kisses and whispered promises before he rode out. It would be a long wait till midsummer—and then only if the campaign against Roines fared as well as everyone hoped. A crown, a king, and a new line of Tolem— more than enough to wish for amid the fragile alliances she'd known all her life. If only it would all come to pass....

Her father pushed open the heavy oaken door, entered, and latched it behind him. Usually Lord Tylus threw his cloak over any handy chair, unbuckled his sword and kissed his daughter's cheek while pressing the scabbard into her hands. Then he'd drop into his chair with a deep sigh and wait for her to pull off his boots. Tonight he simply stood near the threshold, watching her from under thick brows as she rose from kneeling by the fire. His face, peppered with gray stubble and creased with sun, wind, and all of his fifty-three years, told her more than the slump of those still formidable shoulders something was amiss.

"Papa?"

"Belac of Nye. He came today."

"I know." Raell held out her hands for his cloak and weapons.

Lord Tylus glanced at her upturned palms but dropped his cloak where he stood. When he headed for his chair without removing his sword, she stopped him. "Don't fuss, girl," he muttered, wrestling the weapon from his belt.

She laid it on the table and then plucked his discarded cloak from the floor. Of course her father was troubled. He and Belac had been friends, comrades since long before she was born, long before her father had even wed or risen to his title. Long before the Prince had come to part them so bitterly. She hung the cloak on a peg by the door. "Did you have words, Papa?"

He gulped his wine, coughed, and drained the cup. "Words, hah! The bastard!"

"Is he gone?"

"No. The Prince would keep him until Lord Naed be well away. Pfaugh! Clapped in chains would be my choice, but the guardsmen have cleared a chamber and packed them tight into it till morning. Toth and some of Gaelwynn's Adanaks be posted outside. 'Tis in the Prince's mind to show Belac no more than he knows of our alliance. 'Twere me, I'd give the Adanaks leave to carve a few afore we send 'em back. 'Twould be a fit message for that bloody bastard Roines!"

Raell knelt on the bearskin rug before the hearth, intending to remove his boots. "The Prince has a mind to winning good men, not carving them up."

"Aye, do you think I don't know that, girl?" He beetled his brows. "Don't fuss with my boots. 'Tis more wine I need." Slumping in his chair, he glowered at the fire.

Mustering patience, she sat on her heels. A volatile man in the best of times, her father was in a temper tonight, but she'd spent most of her nineteen years managing his moods. Narrowed eyes and clenched jaw warned her to tread carefully. Best to refill his cup.

Spices wafting from the pot warming by the fire were meant to soothe and settle. Tonight would be a true test of the mix.

Her father's gaze shifted to her. "Most times 'tis true, the Prince's vision, but damned if there be some men that'll ne'er come round."

"How do you know what man is which?" When he reached for the cup, she withheld it. "Don't gulp. 'Tis hot."

He grumbled, seized the cup, but sipped. "That's the rub, girl. You'll ne'er know till you die one day in your bed and not at the hand of one or more of 'em."

The fine hairs on the back of Raell's neck stood up. A leaden lump dropped from her ribcage into the pit of her stomach, and she shivered despite the fire. She'd expected he'd eventually tell what troubled him. She hadn't expected his fear to be this elemental. She rubbed her arms and stared into the flames.

All accounts of the night Val-Feyridge fell agreed on three points. The Prince had been betrayed by his bride-to-be and her D'nalian lover. Krenin had died at Erodasi's hand. The D'nalian lover had died too, but not before stabbing the Prince in the wild melee that started the fire and brought down Val-Feyridge. So much betrayal and so much bloodshed, and that was only what was known for certain.

Rumor had it the D'nalian lover was an assassin somehow connected to Naed's family. Those who'd served at Druemarwin insisted Naed was the nephew who'd inherited his uncle's land and title while others said the Prince had appointed him over a missing and disgraced heir. No one disputed his title or his right to it, but Raell wondered if the circumstances contributed to that air of misery following like a shadow after him. Naed had told her naught, but they'd had precious little time together between strategy sessions he spent with the Prince and his allies, and hours—sometimes full days—spent riding out with raiding parties or scouts. The Prince trusted Lord Naed, and Naed trusted the Prince. Her father trusted both men, and so did she.

Raell placed a hand on his knee. "What has Belac done to you now, Papa?"

His gaze shifted from the fire to her hand. Then he rocketed out of the chair and ranged the room. "Damn and blast! I'll not do it! I can't force you into this just because I made a foolish vow ages ago!"

The stone had infiltrated her body, stilling her blood and solidifying her limbs. *Bennin.* Was that why the son of Belac had looked at her with such a predatory gaze? *Sisters, let it not be so!*

"What…vow, Papa?"

Chapter Six

"Tell me and tell me true. What did make you think 'twas wise to agree to such terms? Aye, and from a man I'm told is not to be trusted!"

Arn regarded his wife with wary eyes. She didn't often spit fire at him, and he usually enjoyed the battle when she did. This time he more than deserved her wrath. Admitting it, however...

"I didn't agree." He attempted to divert her from pacing their chamber and into a chair. "'Tis Tylus who must agree. But such an alliance would be—*could* be— enough to weaken the resolve of others who side with Roines."

"And that '*could* be' does justify breaking the promise Lady Raell has made to your very own Second and my most dear friend?" Aerid spun to stand with arms crossed before the fire. "'Tis a love match, or mayhap 'tis as difficult for you to be seeing that as 'twas for you to see our own."

Firelight brought out the dark honey and cream of her skin and the exotic slant of her profiled eye. Thick with child—*his* child—she was as beautiful as the first time he'd seen her, kneeling at the foot of that ancient oak and bathed in an eerie green glow. He'd thought her a witch then, and though she'd proved to his rational mind she was nothing of the sort, she'd bewitched him that first moment they'd locked gazes.

"As I recall," Arn said, stepping behind her and sliding his hands under dark hair tumbling over her shoulders, "'twas just as hard for you to come to terms with it." He turned her gently, marveling again how someone so small the top of her head barely touched his collarbone could match him spirit to spirit, soul to soul. "You ran from me more than once."

Arms still crossed over the babe beneath her breasts, Aerid cast a glance up under her lashes. "Don't be forgetting, 'twas *you* who ran last."

So it was, but he'd never been one to dwell on past mistakes when the future was all that could be altered. He inhaled a deep breath, savoring scents that marked her—evenroot, tantalizing hints of other healing herbs, and whatever it was that infused her hair—even as he conceded. "What would you have me tell Tylus? Bear in mind, 'tis a matter of some consequence, this old promise Belac would hold him to."

She must've detected the slight wince accompanying his inhale because she unfolded one arm and smoothed her palm over his chest, over fresh scars beneath his tunic, wounds she'd knit together not so very long ago. He held her hand pressed to his heart. They stood thus for several heartbeats, until Aerid pulled down his head and brushed a kiss over his lips. Arn would've held out for more, enjoying the taste he'd not sampled since morning, but she trailed her hand down his tunic and gently separated them.

"I understand. 'Tis in your mind to protect your old friend even while you would ensure the Kingdom." She slid her hand from under his, and he sensed she'd come to a decision.

A scant year ago, he'd never have consulted a

woman regarding anything other than inviting her into his bed. Now this woman's insights, opinions, ideas mattered, and he waited for her to speak.

"Summon Lord Tylus. Aye, his son, too. Share some wine. Tell him 'tis best to delay his answer. After all, Lord Belac has been a long time in coming to collect. I will go to Lady Raell."

Arn eyed her as she turned out of his arms and lifted her healer's pouch from a hook by the door. "What are you going to do with that? Sedate her?"

Tilting her head, she raised one dark brow. "Do I question what you would be doing with your sword, husband? Then let me do what I must with the skills I possess."

His gut clenched at the intrusion of a vivid memory—a warm summer night in Adanak when he hadn't known her as well as he did now. Oh, aye, he understood all too well what *magic* she could work with the contents of that well-worn pouch. "Tell me and tell me true. Are you going to do what I think you are?"

"Aye, 'tis very like—if all is as I believe it to be." Aerid smiled as if to allay his concerns and took his arm.

Arn spared a thought for Naed, riding toward D'nalee and completely unaware. *Poor bastard.*

****

Vyenne paused at the foot of the stone staircase where guttering torches had nearly surrendered to the night. She'd come down from the living quarters with the wolfhound at her side and her winter cloak concealing her traveling clothes. With eldest son Allyn away inspecting Tumin's defenses, one last obstacle remained between her and the stables where her maid waited—the chamber in which her husband conducted affairs of court. She guessed he might be working late, and the occasional murmur of voices issuing from the open door confirmed that. Timed correctly, she'd traverse the pool of light thrown into the corridor before her husband noted her presence. Gathering her resolve, she strode forward.

The guard at the door straightened and dipped his head. "Evening, m'lady."

She nodded and sailed past, the dog's claws clicking on the stone. *Keep walking.*

"My lady wife, you're up late." Her husband's voice brought her to a standstill.

Vyenne schooled her face into a bland expression. The dog sat down beside her.

Alwyl, Lord of Tumin, stood by a parchment strewn desk. As was his habit in such a late hour, he wore a fur-trimmed robe over his tunic and dispensed with the thick belt that usually contained the paunch he'd accumulated in his middle years. In the privacy of his office, he'd relaxed his meticulously groomed appearance and unfastened his queue. The once oak-brown strands, now fading to iron gray, hung limply about his face. In the candlelight Vyenne noted how they'd thinned in the years since he'd last visited her bed.

To the right his scribe sat on a stool before a slanted writing desk. The quill in the man's hand fluttered with every stroke and flourish, but he spared her a respectful nod. From a table near the fireplace, the steward half rose and bowed to her over his ledger. Twin scents of melting beeswax and fresh ink told her they'd been hard at work for hours.

Only Fennyn was missing, although the silver fox-trimmed cloak thrown over an armchair suggested the middle son who shadowed his father in all things Tumin could return any moment.

A nerve jumped in her stomach. *Stay calm. Don't speak.*

Over the past fortnight, her husband had talked of naught else but tallying how Tumin had come through the winter and what needed to be planted, pulled out of storage, plowed, and so forth. He was a close and careful manager of his domain, and she'd always respected that about him. In truth, all of D'nalee respected Alwyl of Tumin. She'd married well, her father insisted—far better than her late sister—and she should remember that.

Aye, I have. Daily.

"Have you finished your household accounts, my dear?" her husband said, having planted his bulk squarely before his desk.

Is that all he wants? She nodded, allowing herself to inhale. "'Twas my intention to hand them over in the morning. Would you rather I gave them to you now?"

"No, no. Tomorrow will do." He scowled at the dog. "That beast keeps late hours. You know I don't approve."

Vyenne rested fingertips on the wolfhound's head. "None of the servants can manage her. We should be grateful Beauty took to me after Naed left."

"Humph! I should have been more grateful had he taken that beast with him." His gaze returned to her. "That reminds me—did you hear the news from Druemarwin?"

"That my sister's husband is dead? Aye." It took

all her willpower to speak those words without betraying the anguish vibrating along her nerves. Only the dog seemed to notice how her fingers tensed on its head because it looked up and whined softly. Vyenne stroked Beauty's ear, and the dog settled.

Apparently Alwyl had not yet heard *all* the news from Druemarwin. Part of her prayed he did not uncover it among the correspondence strewn on his desk; another part wished to throw it in his face. She held that part tightly in check. Now was not the time. Or the place.

"What a sorry affair," he was saying. "These Tolemaks bring destruction wherever they go. They had no business taking over Druemarwin as a pawn in their feud, either with each other or with the Adanak. Lord Dranoel may have had a paltry holding on nearly worthless marshland, but he was a brave and honorable man who didn't deserve to be murdered!" He tossed a parchment onto the desk and took a deep breath. "Despite this grave provocation, D'nalee territory *must* remain neutral. We cannot afford to surrender what has kept us safe for generations. I'll be sure to impress that upon the council of lords when next we meet."

Prone to high color when angered, his face was florid with it, but Vyenne expected him to rein it in. D'nalians kept their emotions in check, and Alwyl of Tumin was nothing if not a good D'nalian.

He rearranged scrolls as if looking for something. "I trust my nephew will manage the place to his father's credit."

"Aye." Her heart raced at his choice of words. "*Your* nephew should." She took hold of the dog's collar. "Beauty has been remarkably patient, my lord husband, but I must tend to her needs. Would you excuse me?"

He dismissed her with a wave of his hand and turned to the scribe.

Vyenne walked into the darkened corridor without a backward look. Four sons, two daughters, and well into thirty years she'd spent with this man within these walls, but she was done with all of it now. There would be no going back—for her or for Naed.

Sisters, give me strength!

Chapter Seven

Raell stuffed clothing into a pack and threw on her cloak. If her father and the Prince thought she'd quietly agree to this political marriage, they could bloody well think again! Her heart pounded. To slow the throb at her throat she clutched her mother's necklace. *Sisters, help me!*

She'd always prayed with her parents' twin charms, and although she'd weeks ago given Naed her father's half, the separation left her bereft now. She and Naed were *meant* to be together. She'd known it from the first she'd set eyes on him, and all his whispered endearments and searing kisses told her he felt the same. Besides, if a Tolemak prince could wed an Adanak healer—a commoner, no less!—despite a previous betrothal, surely a Tolemak lord's daughter could wed a D'nalian lord—after all, they were nigh equals—under similar circumstances.

She lifted the latch to see if she could slip out unobserved.

"Ah, good." Lady Aerid bustled across the threshold and closed the door before Raell could do more than stumble out of her way.

Flummoxed, Raell slung her pack forward, a shield against this...whatever it was. "M'lady, 'tis late, and—"

"Aye, but not so very late. 'Tis only midnight and

47

time enough to do what must be done to see you properly on your way."

Lady Aerid stood between her and the door, a battered leather pouch with many pockets slung over the small woman's shoulder and what looked like clothing bundled in her free arm. The blue eyes assessed Raell in the firelight, the gaze frank, direct, and clearly aware of her intention to flee.

Raell's stomach clenched, but she squared her shoulders. "M'lady, pardon me, but naught you can say will make me agree to wed anyone but Lord Naed."

"Aye, I know. Does your father?"

"No. Mayhap. I don't know!" She spun and slammed the pack into her father's chair. "He promised me to Bennin of Nye when I was a babe! And only *now* does he think to tell me!"

"'Tis sure, you've a right to be upset, but mayhap 'twas in your father's mind the Lord of Nye would ne'er come to collect, being as Nye did choose to ally with Roines."

Raell bit back oaths no proper lady should know, much less repeat. "Demon's Blood!" escaped anyway. "'Tis no excuse!"

"Aye, to be sure." Lady Aerid set her pouch and the bundle on the table between them. "But now, 'tis your charm Lord Naed wears, aye?"

"Has-has he shown it to you?" Why would Naed have shared something so private with another...*woman*?

Lady Aerid's expression softened. "Be assured, he has not betrayed your trust. 'Tis only that I have seen it tangled with something else he wears close to his heart."

Raell flushed, thinking how well the Prince's bride knew the man she loved that Lady Aerid was aware of the cylinder on the leather thong about his neck. Mayhap the woman even knew what lay within, a secret Naed had yet to share with her. She narrowed her eyes, wondering again what was between them and whether marriage to the Prince had laid it to rest. "What would you have me do? Wed that arrogant ass Bennin of Nye to suit the alliances when I've given my heart—and my promise—to Lord Naed?"

But the woman had opened the worn leather pouch and begun drawing out smaller pouches. "Tell me of the charm. What meaning holds it for you?"

"'Twas my mother's. She gave half to my father ere they were wed. 'Tis to protect and bind." Raell paced to the far wall and back. "What the Demon does that matter? I must leave afore my father returns!"

"Then tell me and tell me true, will you be running *from* this marriage or *to* Lord Naed?"

Raell stared at the Adanak woman who stared back, unblinking. For whatever reason, the Prince's bride seemed to be offering her...*help*? Lady Aerid still blocked her path, but nothing in the woman's stance suggested malicious intent. Instead, she seemed poised to take action. And that action, Raell understood, depended entirely on how she answered the question hanging in the air between them.

There was but one answer, and naught could change it. "*To* Lord Naed, to be sure."

"Do you love him?"

"Aye, with all my heart."

Lady Aerid acknowledged that with a nod, but her gaze remained unblinking. "Has he taken you to his bed?"

Raell gaped and then flushed to her toes. Her instinctive reaction was to tell the truth—*of course not!* But she hesitated. Mayhap, if her virtue were thought to be compromised, she could throw off this marriage. But to do so would call into question Naed's honor.

"No," she said, deciding on truth—all of it. Naught would likely shock this unconventional woman. "Indeed, I'd be sore pressed to refuse if he offered." The urge to slide into his bed that morning after she'd treated his wounds had nigh overwhelmed. No man had ever tempted her so, but when he'd blushed at knowing she'd seen him unclothed, she was all the more determined to win his heart.

She must have passed some sort of test because Lady Aerid gave her another nod. "I thought not." She smoothed a hand over her abdomen as though soothing the babe within. "Well then, be you prepared to do all that you may do in order to go to him?"

"Aye! Of course!" Raell ranged the room, wishing she had something to throw, but her father's cushion was wedged beneath her pack, and his pewter cup would do no more than clang on the stone floor. "'Tis where I'm bound if you'll but let me go!"

"Then I shall, but not alone. And not in the way you intend." She unfurled the bundle. "Put these on. 'Tis as your brother's young Second you'll be going."

"What? As a *man*? I'll ne'er pass—"

The small woman could command with a look, and Raell understood at last how this lowborn Adanak healer had won the regard of a Tolemak prince.

"Hear me and hear me well. For nigh onto two months I did pass as a boy in the Prince's army. Only

Lord Naed knew I was not. If I, who know little of weapons, may do so, so may you."

"Sisters! Did you say…for two *months*?"

"Aye, and 'tis yet such a well-kept secret that you may be equally successful. Besides, you'll not have an army to convince. 'Twill be but you and your brother until you reach Lord Naed. Keep to the forests and speak not to strangers."

Raell's head spun. The Prince's bride…disguised as a boy? Hidden by Naed? For *two months*, no less? Well, that explained much about their relationship—and yet nowhere near enough to process now. She fixed on the most practical thought amid the jumble. "Toth will ne'er agree. And my father will forbid it. 'Tis why I must leave now, and alone!"

"Your brother comes even now to fetch you. As for your father, be assured, 'tis in my husband's nature to be very convincing." She withdrew a small knife from the battered pouch. "Now, I have redroot paste here to darken your face, but as to your hair…."

****

Naed cleaned his sword with handfuls of crusted snow. What had moments ago been a pristine patch of white where trees thinned was now marred with hoof prints, crumpled bodies, and the snorting breath of a dozen riderless horses. The attackers had burst out of a cluster of fir trees just as moonrise deepened all shadows to black. While they'd charged with the ferocity of night-hunting wolves, they'd charged their last target.

"Roinesmen?" he asked of the man studying the maze of tracks.

"Koth and Ormo, mostly." Banir, his Second,

pushed up from his crouch. "Led by two Roinesmen."

"Waiting for us or for Belac?"

"They're all dead. Who's to say?"

Naed scowled. His men had been too efficient, but he didn't blame them. A fortnight without action made a man itchy. A little exercise to sharpen the skills and take the edge off would serve them in good stead for the journey. He'd been a bit overzealous himself with the two Kothmen who rushed him, but he'd finally satisfied that pent-up need to bash something.

"Send a bird back to Albon to tell the Prince what we've encountered." He dried his sword on his cloak hem, sheathed it, and caught his mount's reins.

Firefall snorted and stamped, but stood while Naed mounted. The battle energy surging in his veins rendered the motion easy and pain-free. His thigh would ache later, but for now he patted the horse's shoulder. In the suddenness of the attack, he'd forgotten his mount was new. Gorm—*Bless him!*—had trained the horse well.

An idea had been fomenting for the last hour— between distracting images of Raell. Her scent lingered on his garments, tempting him with every breath. Nonetheless, his life and the life of every man under his command depended on his ability to focus.

"Do you think Roines will be fooled a second time?"

Banir slung his shield over his back and mounted. "How so?"

"No one last spring expected the Prince to enter D'nalee through Myrinnen Marsh."

"Aye, but if he learns 'tis you who's left, he'll expect you to go that way to Druemarwin. Or north to meet with the lords."

"I'm of a mind to go south first. Farther south. Do you know a way?"

Banir flashed a grin. "Aye. Several."

"Let's be off, then." Going south would add days, mayhap a fortnight to their journey, but if Naed had absorbed one lesson from Prince Arn, it was to do the unexpected—as long as one chose it carefully, for good reasons, and with a solid expectation of results.

****

Prince Arn lounged in his chair and sipped his wine. Lord Tylus should've been well soused by the time Aerid let herself into their chamber, but the seasoned warrior's gaze fixed on her with undiluted clarity. All those times Tylus had refilled his cup, he must've merely topped it off.

You old fox!

Having done likewise, Arn tipped his cup to his friend, who responded with a slight nod while he rose in deference to the woman both men had waited nigh onto two hours for.

"Well?" Arn said as his wife took his hand before the fire.

"Gone, both of them. And together, though 'tis in my mind to wonder which of them will have at the other first o'er this whole affair." Aerid sank into the chair at his side, set her healer's pouch on the floor, and expelled a breath. "You've a fine pair of children, m'lord, but I suspect 'tis the Lady Raell who's first in your heart."

The hawk-beaked warrior sat and studied his cup. "She's the last, m'lady, and the only girl." He flattened battle-scarred hands on the table. "Just like her mother, she is. 'Tis why I've been reluctant to let her go—to any man."

Arn raised a brow. In all the years he and Tylus had fought and planned, sweated and bled side-by-side, his oldest ally had never revealed this much. But in the presence of an attentive and sympathetic woman, the grizzled warhorse opened his heart. A crack, aye, but a glimpse nonetheless. Arn squirmed.

As if he'd come to the same realization, Tylus's face darkened. Fists balled, he pushed to his feet. "I'm a tolerant man, m'lord, and 'tis sure I respect Lord Naed as your Second and a damned fine warrior, but if he's done...*aught* to my child—"

"Rest easy, old friend. Lord Naed has too much honor to compromise your daughter." If he knew anything of the young man who'd been willing to die to defend his uncle's holding, whose fearlessness and dedication to duty had won the respect of men predisposed to hate him simply for being D'nalian, Arn knew that. All the same, he looked to Aerid for confirmation.

She touched his old friend's sleeve. "Be assured, you have naught to fear from Lord Naed on that account." When Tylus grumbled and sat, she continued, "Though mayhap 'twould be better for all concerned if you had."

Arn shot her a startled look.

Tylus sputtered, "What?"

"The Lord of Nye may yet wish to recover her, aye? So long as she remains untouched?" Aerid folded her hands over the babe beneath her breasts and studied both men. "What will you be telling him?"

What indeed? Arn set his cup on the table. "As

little as possible, and no sooner than necessary."

Aerid was right, but damned if he didn't wish otherwise. If Naed weren't so obstinately upright, Tylus's daughter might now be breeding an heir and this whole issue would be moot. But as he'd often insisted to Krenin, he'd chosen Naed as his Second precisely because Naed could be counted on to uphold what was best about D'nalians: their sense of honor, obligation, duty.

And—*Demon be damned!*—if that didn't leave everything in a dangerous limbo.

He stood. "As my lady wife has so astutely pointed out, what touches Lord Naed is a matter of some consequence to our alliance with D'nalee and whatever the future there may hold. Now, 'tis late and we've done all we can. I suggest we take to our beds."

Tylus drained his cup—*finally*—and took his leave.

In a gesture Arn knew well, his wife fingered the birthstone at her throat. A Sisters' Tear, it marked her, the Crownkeeper had told him, as the gift to heal what had been so long broken among the three lands. She and the child they'd conceived would unite their two territories and begin to restore the Kingdom. Naed was to bring the final piece to the table. Arn would have to trust Naed—and he did, with his life and more—but by the Demon, he'd never been inclined to trust the whims of three fickle deities. Even if their prophecies had worked to his advantage.

His wife interrupted his dark musing with a stretch of both arms above her head. "To my way of thinking, 'twas in his mind from the start that if he but gave her a chance, the Lady Raell would run."

Arn met her gaze. "Tylus left her alone?"

"Aye, well before you did summon him."

"And was she about to run?"

"Nearly out the door she was."

Arn grinned. *Tylus, you old fox.*

****

"What do you mean, you've lost the trail?" Raell demanded. "There are tracks everywhere."

From his stance at the edge of the muddied clearing, Toth growled. Not words, she decided after receiving a stream of such responses over the last two hours. In Lady Aerid's presence he'd limited his displeasure to a few scathing looks cast in Raell's direction, but since they'd left Albon fortress her brother had done naught but stew and steam.

Well, it hadn't been *her* choice to saddle herself with a companion. She'd have bolted as soon as they reached the forest if she'd been sure he wouldn't follow, but since the Prince himself had enlisted Toth's help, her brother would see it through—no matter how much he hated her for it.

And despite the fact they'd now left their father completely alone.

A lump rose in her throat, and Raell choked it back. One or more of their older brothers could be summoned, but she doubted her father would think to do it. *Stubborn fool!*

She didn't want to leave him, but he'd given her no choice. She hadn't known about his promise, couldn't have. He hadn't told her. Hadn't told anyone! She'd given *her* promise to Naed in good faith. Her honor was as much at stake as her father's.

Aye, and my heart all the more so!

So she'd taken the only action she could think of

that might save them all, even if it merely delayed the day of reckoning. Her father couldn't hand her over if she wasn't there. 'Twould be an embarrassment, to be sure, but not the dishonor of a refusal. With the time she'd bought, she could reach Naed and—

Her breath hitched. Something warm trickled down her cheeks. *Demon's Blood!* Raell swiped at her face. She wasn't a child. She could manage this...*debacle* without tears, if only she didn't have to deal with her brother!

Visible through the treetops was a faint blueing in the east. Another hour and they'd have to take to the deeper woods. Toth led his horse forward a few steps.

"Well?"

"I'm *not* a tracker. If you wanted one, you should've taken yourself off with that turncoat Second of his and saved us all the trouble!"

Raell's face burned. "Aye, and I would've! If only I'd known I needed him afore he left with Lord Naed!" Her brother had no right to insult Banir when his anger should be directed at her. Banir had done naught but follow a man he trusted and respected, a man who just happened to be D'nalian. And the man she loved.

She yanked at the coarse men's leggings chafing her thighs. At this rate, she'd be rubbed raw before they reached the Arbez River, much less the D'nalian border. "Would you rather I wed Bennin of Nye?"

"Sisters and the Four Winds, no! I hate the bastard!" He twisted the reins, slapped the ends against his thigh, and spun to face her. "But you've landed us in it, Raell!"

"'Twas not my vow!"

"You can't blame Father! 'Twas what he thought

best at the time."

Raell cast her gaze skyward. Her huffed-out breath obscured stars, moon, clouds, everything but the thoughts vying for control of her mind. Toth was right—*Demon be damned!* The world had been a different place when she was a babe. Her mother lived, the bloodthirsty Yinnad reigned as Prince of Val-Feyridge, his murderous right-hand Rolnar was about to be rewarded with Roines fortress, and the Northern Wars had not yet begun. Tolemak, Adanak, and D'nalee were in balance then—if a constant state of unrest and frequent petty skirmishes counted as balance. She couldn't blame her father for making a promise to provide for her future.

But—*Sisters!*—how could she wed Bennin of Nye when her heart belonged to Naed? Her half-charm lay buried beneath layers of breast-binding, undertunic, tunic and cloak, but she pressed a hand to her throat anyway, willing the Three Sisters to hear her prayer.

"Just get us to Druemarwin. Can you do that? We know 'tis where he's bound."

Toth mounted. Moonlight and shadow turned the familiar features, so like their father's, into something stark and dangerous, particularly the way his eyes, under a ridge of brow, glowered. "In case you've forgotten, I've ne'er been east of the Arbez, but as I'm duty bound to do the Prince's bidding, to be sure, I'll do my best. For him and for Father, mind you!"

Raell rolled her eyes. "Aye, and you'll challenge Lord Naed if he but trifles with my affections. Do you think I don't know what's been stewing inside that thick head all these past hours?"

Lady Aerid had saved much of Raell's hair in a

D'nalian queue, but the loose strands had worked themselves into a prickly mass under her hood. She pushed at one side then the other. Her horse shifted with the fitful motions.

"Trust me—if you but say a word to Lord Naed afore I speak with him, 'twill be me you'll answer to! The Prince and Father will have to sort out the pieces!"

Chapter Eight

D'nalee territory

Snow-crusted meadows dissolved with the passage of long days into mud-filled clearings, foggy mornings thickened to constant rain, forests of bare trees opened to scrubby marshland dividing long, low hills topped with dense stands of birch and oak. Naed hunched in a cloak so thoroughly soaked it provided protection only from the pelting of a steady cold drizzle. For all the misery he'd endured during a Tolemak winter, D'nalee in spring was hardly a welcoming experience. A fortnight's growth of beard itched mercilessly where cloak met throat, and though Firefall's gait was as smooth as promised, days of hard riding had driven the ache deep into his thighbone and radiated it from ankle to hip.

He longed for a warm fire, a dry bed, and clean clothes.

And for Raell.

Her name conjured gold-brown eyes and a mischievous smile. Naed sucked in a breath. Despite rain, wind, and distance, her scent surrounded him. He pressed a hand to his chest, to the charm next to his skin. She'd given him her promise, and he had to trust the Three Sisters would respect that. If only the task the Prince had set for him were not nigh impossible. Well, he would know soon enough if his southern gambit would garner any support.

When he dismounted that evening in the courtyard of Kassi fortress deep in southern D'nalee, he could scarcely stand. Only Banir's ready shoulder held him up while the horses were led away to be stabled.

A thin, precise man with a neat, trim beard greeted them. Lord Wendelmyr's steward, whom Naed recognized from a year earlier, bustled about directing grooms.

"Begging your pardon, sir, but we'd not expected an entourage from Druemarwin till after the roads cleared. My lord well remembers his obligations and agreements with Master Dranoel, and supplies will be delivered forthwith, I can assure you."

"Of that I have no doubt." Naed bent to rub life into his numbed thigh. "But 'tis not the only matter at hand." When he rose, the man had gone preternaturally still.

The steward's attention, which must've skipped over Naed's attendants as beneath his notice, had settled on Banir. When Grodar and Morys flanked Naed, the man's gaze skittered between them. By torchlight, the men's Tolemak features shone milk-pale in contrast to their D'nalian garb and belied the Druemarwin banner flying over a cohort that was, at best, half D'nalian and filled out with Tolemaks of Vral, Albon, Val-Feyridge and a few of Gaelwynn's copper-skinned Adanaks.

The steward licked his lips. He'd allowed them entry on the strength of the Druemarwin banner, and now he stood frozen with the knowledge he may have fatally erred. Nearby guardsmen fingered their weapons, having caught the scent of something amiss.

Naed understood the reaction. He'd have shared it a year ago, even set himself to the forefront of any challenge they might have mounted. But tonight he was too wet, cold, and weary to diplomatically respond. He pulled off his glove and thrust into the torchlight the ring he'd inherited as Lord of Druemarwin.

"As you can see, much has changed in the world since I was here last spring with Master Dranoel."

The steward blanched, sucked in a breath, and bowed low. "My lord, pardon me! I shall take you directly to Lord Wendelmyr. But first, allow me to provide you and your attendants with dry clothes, food and drink." He snapped his fingers at servants hovering beside the door. "You there, alert the kitchen! The rest of you, take the lord's escort to the guardsmen's quarters and see to their needs."

When the steward turned his back, Grodar leaned toward Naed. He put all of his usual swagger into the movement, but his gap-toothed grin showed signs of tension. "M'lord, would you have me an' Morys stay with you or mind the others?"

"With me, I think." Naed tested his leg, decided it would hold his weight, and climbed the first step. He surveyed faces peering from fortress walls, doors and windows, noting a mix of puzzlement, suspicion and outright hostility. Well, he'd expected as much. "I think it best we show Lord Wendelmyr the faces of the new Kingdom."

****

Every night Raell mixed and drank the brew Lady Aerid had given her to stop her monthly bleed. When she'd counted five days, she reapplied paste that

62

darkened her pale skin to a D'nalian tan, something akin to what a soldier might acquire after months in the sun and weather. Each time she marveled at the woman's skill and cleverness. If they should meet again, Raell would ask to learn from her.

Endless gloomy days passed with naught but a grouchy bear for company. Toth forced her to corner him with the paste pot before he would apply one coat of redroot stain, and that only after they were two days deep into D'nalee.

"There's no one about to see us," he complained.

"Takes but one to see your white Tolemak face and sound the alarm. Besides, if I have to wear these bloody coarse leggings and bindings to hide my true nature, 'tis sure you can cover what's obviously Tolemak about you."

After more grumbling, he deigned to pull a plain cloak over his tunic emblazoned with the family emblem, a snarling bobcat. As if that were not enough to make her fume at being saddled with him, Toth got them lost twice, wasting a day each time. Worst of all, he decided to cross the spring-flooded and icy cold Arbez on a meandering stretch divided by two small islands and far from the main roads and fords. They managed the longest two stretches, but Raell's horse slipped on the last and she'd gone briefly under.

Eight days later the chill lurked deep in her bones, making her shiver at odd moments, even wrapped in blankets while a hare roasted over their campfire. She ought to be grateful for hot food and a dry day, but she was too saddlesore and tired, and her throat still scratched from swallowing river water. To add to her misery, the horse's churning hooves had bruised her calf.

She'd just nodded off when her brother dumped water on their fire. Sputtering, "What in the—?" she scooted away from an onrush of twigs, ash, and mud.

"Shh! There're men about!" Toth grabbed their gear. "Get the horses and follow me." He disappeared behind a horse-high blackberry thicket.

Daft fool! He's lost his mind. They'd meandered through this Sisters-forsaken marshland for days, and all the trails looked alike. As far as she knew, they'd gone in circles. Muscles stiff and protesting, she limped to the horses and untied them with a huff. She'd give him a bloody ear-lashing once she caught—

A distant neigh...

Raell's blood hammered in her ears. They'd met no one and seen naught but wildlife tracks for so long she must've imagined those voices carrying on the slight breeze. Until her horse lifted its head and snuffled. She clamped a hand over its nostrils, whispered, "Shush!" and led both animals into the dense vegetation.

****

"Stop!" Vyenne shoved her horse between three men on foot, separating her groom Humbert from two who assailed him with sword and club. "If I call off my wolfhound, will you leave him be?"

At her side Beauty snarled and snapped, keeping the other villains' horses in a squealing frenzy. One bucked off its rider and bolted.

Humbert picked himself up and shouldered her mount aside. "M'lady, please, get back."

Vyenne circled her horse around him. The stocky son of her children's nurse was an excellent groom, but his skill with the sword was as limited as that of these half-dozen savages. Pity she couldn't have taken a trained soldier or two as her escort, but only those devoted to her, not her husband, could be counted upon to keep her secrets. She unfastened her purse and threw it.

"There! Take what you came for and leave us be."

The apparent leader grinned. He had the look of a disgraced soldier, which made him far more dangerous than the farm and servant-class rabble he'd set upon her, her maid, and her groom, and far better able to control his mount amid the chaos.

"Aye, we came for that," he said, "but that's not all we came for."

Vyenne gave him her most regal glare. "You'll take that and be satisfied, or I shall not be responsible for the wellbeing of your throat."

"M'lady," her maid whispered, "'tis not good to antagonize them."

"They're a pack of slavering wolves, Elda. *Anything* we do will antagonize them." She'd raised sons, and she'd seen her share of bullies at her husband's court.

This pack would dissolve around its leader if she could expose a weakness. Beauty had already forced the unskilled lackeys to hesitate.

Under her breath, she said, "If they charge, bolt. I'll be right behind you."

****

Shadowy figures, some on horseback, some on foot, milled into the clearing. Voices sounded among the clatter of weapons and squealing horses.

"That's a *woman*! *Two* women!" Outrage tunneled Raell's vision. She drew her sword.

Toth grabbed her arm. "What do you think you're doing? 'Tis not our affair!"

Logic told her he was right; they couldn't risk being discovered. But logic had no heart, and she couldn't let these women be victimized by thieves and villains. The wars of her brief lifetime had made victims of too many women, women who knew little of how to defend themselves. Her father had allowed her to learn those skills, and if ever there was a time to put her blade-skill to use, this was it.

She spun out of his grip. "Stay back if you want, but I mean to even the odds."

Intent on the apparent leader, she dashed out of the thicket and into the path of a bolting horse. The animal squealed, rearing. Raell backpedaled, tripped, and landed on her rump. The horse wheeled away into the darkness.

"Daft fool!" A hand seized her tunic and hauled her upright. "*Think* first! And look!" Her brother tossed her a shield. "Unhorse the bastards and make sure they stay down!"

Raell's face burned. She'd committed them with her stupid, impulsive charge, and Toth would make her pay for it, but not now. Now he would do what any Tolemak would do, fight with all the skill he'd learned and make sure they won. Well, she could do that too!

She gripped her shield and rushed the first man struggling to his feet in the mud. A backhanded blow of her sword hilt sent him sprawling face down. She spun to the next target and came face-to-face with a huge gray head full of snarling teeth.

Wolf!

She froze, heart stuttering, while the beast—not a

wolf, an enormous, fierce dog—rumbled at her, ears laid flat and ruff raised.

"Beauty! Hold!" A woman atop a fine mare took in Raell, the villain at her feet, and the sword in her hand. The woman shifted her gaze to Toth engaging another villain a few paces beyond, and returned to Raell. For a heartbeat they looked at each other. Then the woman nodded, a slight dip of her regal head, and snapped her fingers. The snarling beast backed closer to her mare.

Raell breathed. She scanned milling horses and men, and spotted the leader pushing his horse through the melee, heading for the woman and the beast.

A quick glance revealed no more spooked horses, two men on her right with Toth, two men on her left with the woman's guard, no one between. She hurdled a stump, leaped a hummock, diverted around a fallen tree and rushed the horseman from the side. Her sword sliced the saddle girth in a clean cut before the horse could shy away.

With a yell, the rider slid sideways and down. The horse squealed, bucked, and bolted. The man rolled, gained his feet, sword and shield at ready. His hood slipped.

A shaved head. Disgraced soldier. Dangerous.

He grinned. Charged.

She'd sparred with Toth, but this man wasn't Toth, and he wasn't sparring. Her ears rang with the clang of sword on shield. His blows hammered her backward, landing with the weight of a smithy's hammer. Raell stumbled, wheezed, grunted. *Demon's Blood!* She tripped over something, dropped her guard, and his sword whistled past her ear. Fabric ripped. Flesh peeled back on her upper arm, pink and glistening with a bloom of blood.

Raell staggered. Her head swam. This was no practice session, no sparring with dull weapons and padding. She was bleeding! Damn it all, the son of a whore had cut her!

Her blood had drained to her core, leaving her lightheaded and stricken. Now it rushed into her head, arrowing straight to her face, throbbing behind her eyes, narrowing her focus to the man before her, grinning as if he thought he'd won.

"You bastard son of a Bedian goat!" With a wild shriek, she charged.

The villain was good. He met what she threw at him, but her strength had somehow doubled. Every blow she struck fell hard on his shield, pushing him back little by little. The grin vanished. He tried to hook her foot, pull her down while he danced away. She laughed, recognizing the move. She hadn't grown up with brothers for naught. They expected the two-step—sword, shield, sword, shield, mayhap with a spin. They never expected the three-step—sword, shield, and…she coiled her muscles

He deflected the sword, struck her shield, pushing up and away. Into the brief opening Raell leaped, left knee leading, right foot snapping out with all the power of her forward momentum. Her boot slammed into the villain's unprotected groin. His eyes crossed and he crumpled.

She hit the ground on her shoulders, tucked, and rolled backward, landing on her feet.

"Cut me, will you!" Raell launched herself at the prone man and kicked him again and again.

"Stop!" Toth yanked her back, held her shoulders,

stared into her face. "He cut you?"

Panting, she nodded while the red haze of rage receded.

Toth spun and plunged his sword into the man's chest. Bone crunched. Her brother snarled, features as fierce as the wolf-dog's, and twisted the blade. Planting his boot on the villain's neck, he pulled the blade out, unleashing a gush of blood. "You want to fight, Raell?" He faced her with his dripping sword. "Then you *kill* the bastards. Anyone who hurts you, you kill. Understand?"

The villain gurgled out his last breath. His staring gaze fixed on her.

Raell swallowed. She was Tolemak. She'd seen death many times, but not like this, not in a darkening marsh in a land far from home with sweat cooling on her body and something warm spreading down her arm. Not with the acrid tang of fear and violence filling her nostrils, not with her muscles shaking and her lungs rattling with breaths she couldn't seem to take in.

The bushes, thickets, grasses swirled around her, lit with sparkles of color. Sounds faded while her blood thundered in her ears. She couldn't breathe, couldn't think, couldn't reach Toth who leaned toward her with a look of consternation while she fell into darkness.

****

Vyenne called Beauty to heel and surveyed the carnage. A half-dozen bodies, a few milling horses, and two strangers who'd rushed out of the thicket. They'd helped her, and she'd made the snap decision to accept their aid, but now…

One had been wounded. The other knelt to attend his companion.

D'nalian clothes. Skilled. Soldiers, but whose?

"I thank you," Vyenne said, remaining astride. "My maid has some skill with healing. Would you like her assistance?"

The man had torn a strip from his tunic hem and pressed it to the shoulder of his fallen companion. "I'll tend my own, but if your maid has a water skin, 'twould be useful."

He hadn't looked at her, evidently didn't consider the maid and Humbert to be threats. He'd glanced at Beauty, but only as if to determine the dog's location.

Definitely a soldier, but why only two? "Humbert," she said to the groom who'd finally regained his breath, "see to the water skin."

Her groom leaned over the villain at his feet, nudged the body with a toe, and blanched. "Aye, m'lady," he said, then spun and vomited onto a hummock.

"Clean your sword," the stranger told him. "Get a handful of grass and wipe it down. Then fetch the water."

Humbert wiped his mouth and did as he'd been told.

Vyenne expected to see shame on his broad face when he collected the water skin from Elda but only relief showed. She'd seen that kind of exchange among her sons. *A good man.*

The stranger's companion tried to sit up. "What—?"

"Drink." He poured some water into the fallen man's mouth. "And don't move your arm."

"That's a lot of blood," Humbert said when the stranger returned the water skin.

The man swore, tore another strip of tunic. "Has your maid any skill with a needle?"

"Quite a bit. Elda will do what she can here in the dark and cold, but we're not far from Druemarwin fortress. A couple of hours at most. A fine healer resides there."

"Fetch a lantern," the stranger told Humbert.

As the groom rose, Elda approached the stranger with a wary look at her mistress. Vyenne made a shooing motion. She'd decided this fierce stranger posed no threat. Her count of the bodies suggested all villains had been dispatched, but the commotion and smell would soon attract scavengers, four-legged as well as two-legged.

"See to the lantern, Humbert. And then find your horse."

"Find as many horses as you can, Humbert." The stranger struck flint to a bit of tinder. His hood had fallen back, and the flare of light revealed a lean, blond-stubbled face, and loose, dark blond hair.

No queue. A finger of unease trailed down Vyenne's spine. D'nalian clothing but the stranger's hair hung freely at his shoulders—long or short, she couldn't tell. Not all D'nalians wore a queue all the time. His wounded companion wore a queue, though, clearly visible in the lantern light as Elda bent over the beardless youth, who'd passed out again.

Brothers. Or cousins, mayhap.

The man moved the lantern into place for her maid. "And collect these bastards' weapons, Humbert. No sense leaving them for other such villains." He cast a look in Vyenne's direction.

She stiffened and raised her chin. He could

command all he wished, but unless she was mistaken, she was the only one present with a title.

"I am Lady Vyenne of Tumin. We are bound for Druemarwin. I'm deeply grateful for your assistance, but I have no intention of remaining here any longer than necessary to attend your companion. If you would care to accompany us, I will be happy to see to your companion's continued care at Druemarwin fortress."

"Druemarwin?" He studied her from under prominent dark blond brows. Unlike his companion, a bold, hooked nose divided his face. "A couple of hours, you say?"

"We should arrive by midnight."

"Aye, then. I'll fetch our horses and we'll follow you."

He turned to help Elda, and Vyenne breathed. *Sisters preserve us! The lad's no older than Naed.*

She pressed a hand to her chest, soothing the ache that gnawed there whenever she thought of her son. How much had Naed changed since he'd been to war and back? Would she recognize him?

More importantly, how would he receive her?

She'd know soon enough.

****

Naed stretched his legs and savored warm toes and fingertips for the first time in a fortnight. The Kassi steward, as if to make up for his earlier slight, personally provided dry clothes, seats at a table beside a stoked-up fire, mulled wine and warm stew. Naed spooned some into his mouth.

Rabbit.

The taste propelled him back a twelvemonth. The Druemarwin cook had saved him such a meal when

Dranoel, he and fellow swordsman Yormoc had returned from this very place—the night before the world changed. He was chewing past the lump in his throat when Lord Wendelmyr entered and everyone at table stood.

A rotund little man, nearly as wide as he was tall, Lord Wendelmyr had changed little. Mayhap the man's bald pate shone a bit more between fewer strands of still dark hair, but neither his table, his furnishings, nor his fur-trimmed collar and cuffs showed signs the past year's unrest had touched his domain.

Sometimes 'tis a blessing to lay claim to lands no one else seems to want.

Something sharp and acidic burned his stomach. The same could've been said of Druemarwin a scant winter ago.

Banir, Grodar and Morys offered the nod expected of men who served at the right hand of a lord. Unmoving, Naed surveyed the man who, though he must have been warned by his steward, barely concealed astonishment at finding Tolemaks at his table. And not just Tolemaks, but Tolemaks who'd aligned themselves with a D'nalian.

Lord Wendelmyr blinked, remembered D'nalian rules of propriety, and offered his hand. "Welcome, Lord Dlaniger, to my humble abode. You must forgive my steward for not recognizing you. It's been nigh a dozen years since you visited with your father, and—"

Naed squeezed Wendelmyr's hand. Not hard, but enough to stop the man's blathering and garner a startled look. "I'm not Dlaniger."

Banir shot him a frown, and Naed released his grip. *Sisters!* He ought to have better control of his emotions. Wendelmyr could hardly be expected to know the messy details of Druemarwin's succession if he was ignorant of the critical fact of Dranoel's death.

He cleared his throat. "My apologies. I should've introduced myself before. I am Lord Naed."

Wendelmyr discreetly flexed his fingers. The man's hand was soft, pampered, and clearly hadn't held a weapon in years, if ever. Naed wished he could stifle the flush spreading up his throat. *Stupid!* He'd spent too much time with Tolemaks and forgotten how he'd been brought up. Best he remembered that now, before attempting to enter Tumin's court.

"Ah, I remember." Wendelmyr waved them all to sit. "You were here last spring with Master Dranoel. You're the nephew." He settled into his deerskin-lined chair and signaled his steward to fill his cup. "'Twas the beard, sir. Forgive me for not noticing, but you were clean-shaven last spring."

"We've traveled far and taken no time for vanities." He'd left off the 'sir' Wendelmyr would expect from an equal, but the man had to suspect from the Tolemaks present the order of things had changed.

The wine was warm and spiced, and the food delicious after a fortnight of camp food and months of limited rations, yet he couldn't stomach another bite until this was done.

"My condolences on your loss," Wendelmyr was saying. "When did you lose your uncle?"

Naed carefully set down his cup. The first time was always the hardest, so it was best to make no delays. He'd ripped enough bandages off scabbed wounds to know the shock would be intense and nigh overwhelming but nonetheless short-lived.

"My father," he said. "Lord Dranoel was my father. I am his bastard son."

Chapter Nine

Silence.

Lord Wendelmyr, after a flash of astonishment, steepled his fingers. "Begging your pardon, Lord Naed, but I never would have expected that of my good friend Master Dranoel. Apparently, he was a man of some surprises."

The cylinder under Naed's tunic shifted, reminding him of what lay inside.

You have no idea. He flattened his hands on the table. "I was unaware of it myself until I read his will."

"I knew, of course, he and Dlaniger had a falling out. Your...father and I visited frequently in the course of our trade." The man folded his hands across his ample girth. "How did your...half-brother take the news?"

"He's dead."

The rotund little man paled. Fear leaked into his expression.

"'Twas not my doing," Naed said, but the memory of that afternoon on the stairs at Val-Feyridge played anyway. He'd been too slow with his damned lame leg to save the Prince, too stubborn with his hurt pride to unbend and help Krenin when the man first asked. The Prince had been nearly killed and Krenin had died because Naed had waited too long to act.

"Mark me," he growled. "I'd have killed Dlaniger

myself had I been first to reach him that day. He betrayed his D'nalian heritage and sold himself as an assassin to the highest bidder. Whether he meant to or no, he was responsible for his father's death. For that, he deserved to die at the hands of any just and honorable D'nalian. A Tolemak killed him, to be sure, but I thank that Tolemak every day for avenging my father and my Prince!"

There. It was out—everything he needed to say to make Wendelmyr understand the new order. Everything that stripped bare the raw wound oozing in Naed's soul. How could he have grown to one-and-twenty without knowing—suspecting—the truth? Aye, he couldn't have known about the D'nal stone at the heart of it—no one had—but he should've known the burly bull of a man who welcomed him to Druemarwin with open arms was more than an uncle, mentor, guide. Blood should've known blood.

Why hadn't Dranoel told me?

Lord Wendelmyr cleared his throat.

Naed refocused on the man now squirming in his fur-lined chair.

"This prince you speak of…" Wendelmyr cast his gaze at the Tolemaks ringing his table. "Might he be the Prince of Val-Feyridge?"

Naed smiled. "Something tells me the lords of southern D'nalee are better informed than those in the north may suspect."

Wendelmyr colored. "Not to speak ill of the council of lords, but the prosperous and powerful look out for their own interests. 'Tis a fact of life."

"Aye, but that does not have to continue. I am the Prince's emissary to D'nalee and his trusted Second."

He leaned forward. "Hear me and hear me well, for what I have to tell you will be the first to fall upon D'nalian ears outside of Druemarwin."

Wendelmyr's eyes sharpened. When the lord leaned in, Naed knew his southern gambit would work. Too often discounted and outright ignored, the lords of sundry holdings making up southern D'nalee were in need of a leader. For years they looked to Dranoel, he who had wed into a northern family, and it was only natural they should look to his son. Especially the son who had allied himself with the soon-to-be king.

****

By Vyenne's reckoning, it was just past midnight when they dismounted before the stone well in Druemarwin's courtyard. There had been a brief delay while the gate guard summoned Ekwul, the late Lord Dranoel's personal servant, who verified her identity. And then the captain of the guard had to be roused to order the drawbridge lowered. Now both men stood at the steps to the living quarters surrounded by a handful of servants with torches.

"Ekwul." Vyenne touched a gloved hand to the grizzled old servant's sleeve. "Thank you for your letter. 'Twas a kindness on your part to inform me directly of your master's death."

Never a man of many words, the servant bowed his head, but not before Vyenne glimpsed tears in his eyes.

Forcing her voice to remain steady despite thickness threatening to choke it, she addressed the captain of the guard. "Please inform Lord Naed of our arrival. And be so kind as to summon Old Gam. One of my party has been wounded and is in need of her healer's gift." She indicated the young stranger gathering his companion into his arms. "You have thieves in the marsh, Captain. And naught but a few hours ride from here."

The captain, a solid man of forty-some years, withstood her scrutiny. "Old Gam be here, m'lady. M'lord thought it best she stay the winter within these walls, old as she be." He nodded toward one of the servants, and the man hurried off, presumably to fetch the healer. "But as to Lord Naed, he be not home."

"Not at home?" the stranger said. He'd come alongside Vyenne, carrying the wounded youth. The lad's pale face lolled against his shoulder.

She thought it a mercy the youth had remained unconscious then reconsidered. Mayhap he'd lost too much blood and would never awake. *Sisters, be merciful!*

The stranger looked from Vyenne to the captain, brows creased in a fierce frown. "How can Lord Naed be not here? 'Twas here he was bound a fortnight ago."

"You...know him?" Vyenne said.

"Bound from where?" the captain asked.

"Albon, in Tolemak, as well you should know, being your master serves as the Prince's Second."

Vyenne stared at him, but he'd focused squarely on the captain, who seemed not at all astonished. If anything, the answer satisfied the soldier.

"And who might you be, sir?"

"Toth, son of Lord Tylus, the Prince's oldest Tolemak ally."

Tolemak! That finger of unease scraped a talon down Vyenne's back. She shivered. *What in the Name of the Sisters is Naed doing in Tolemak?*

Neither man seemed to notice her consternation.

"Welcome, sir, to Druemarwin."

A servant arrived and spoke in the captain's ear.

"Old Gam'll see to your companion now. Follow the lad there."

The young man started up the steps. "I would speak with you later, Captain."

"As you wish, sir. M'lady, if you please, follow Ekwul here. He'll settle you and your maid."

Vyenne blinked and recovered her composure. "Thank you, Captain." She nodded to Ekwul, who preceded her up the steps. "Humbert, see to the horses."

Elda caught up to her mistress and leaned close. "M'lady," she whispered, "the wounded lad.... They think I didn't notice, but I did."

Vyenne scowled at the woman who'd served her for nigh onto twenty years. "Notice what?"

Elda chewed her lip, glanced about, then whispered, "I swear by the Sisters, m'lady, that lad…'tis a *woman*."

****

The small group of men hunkered around a campfire stirred at the rider's approach. Their light was well shielded by a shelter woven of evergreen branches, and the surrounding marsh offered few safe trails. Even though their hands went automatically to their weapons, there was no urgency in the motion.

The rider dismounted, tied his horse to a willow branch, and entered the firelight. He was clean-shaven, as were all the others, and his hair, when he lowered his hood, was fastened in a queue, like all the others.

The man deepest within the shelter, who had waited for all the others to rise before vacating his seat, came forward. His hair, pale blond and slicked back, gleamed like a helm in the firelight. "What have you seen?"

"A small party entered Druemarwin, sir. 'Twere four—mayhap five—riders. One looked to be riding double. They had extra horses, saddled."

"Saddled? Be you sure?"

The messenger shrugged. "There be little cover on the green. 'Twas a long way to see to the gate. Aye, and the mist be rising."

"They should've arrived by now," ventured one of the men around the fire.

"Aye," spoke up another. "Takes less'n a fortnight e'en if you don't come direct."

The blond man scowled, deepening lines of thirty-odd years scoring his face. When he had their attention, he spat into the fire. "They'd not come direct." He rested a hand on the intricately carved Adanak dagger sheathed at his belt. "The bastard of Druemarwin is hardly a fool."

Another rider approached, this one with speed. They all stepped out of the firelight, weapons drawn.

"Who comes?" shouted the man with the Adanak dagger.

The newcomer drew rein and leaped off. "Ax and his men are dead!" Panting, he hurried into their circle. "'Twas a slaughter."

"Who?" the blond man demanded.

"Four, mayhap five. 'Twas too dark to read the tracks. Ax and his men waylaid them, but 'twas a trap. Their weapons, horses—everything be gone."

"How long ago?"

"Hours."

The blond man swore.

"The same party?" said the first rider.

Hand caressing the carved dagger hilt, the blond man stared into the fire. "Not enough traffic in the marsh to be otherwise."

The men looked at each other. One said, "If we move, sir, 'tis best to do it now, afore they settle. Druemarwin's guard…their numbers be low."

"Aye," said another. "What if 'tis but an advance party an' more arrive on the morrow?"

"Then we move now." The blond man swung on them. He bared his teeth, and his eyes shone—just for a second—like a wolf's in the firelight. "Let's fashion a fit welcome for the bastard of Druemarwin."

****

Raell woke to the pungent scent of bearberry and the sting of a needle. "Demon's Blood! Who—?"

"Lie still, lass. 'Tis near done."

A hag's face full of wrinkles frowned over her. The old crone raised a needle pulling fine thread. The needle, the thread, and the crone's fingers glistened with blood. Raell gagged. She glimpsed her shoulder and saw a row of neat stitches fastening together a U-shaped slice in her flesh. Her vision sparkled. She closed her eyes, opened them again, and took in an unfamiliar chamber lit by lamps and a fire. "Who are you? Where am I?"

The hag's wrinkles reshaped themselves into a smile. "Ah, young folk. Always wantin' answers." The old woman hummed tunelessly as she stitched. "Old Gam's me name. You've come t' Druemarwin, you have."

Druemarwin. Naed! Raell pushed at the blanket covering her body, but her arm—her good arm—only twitched. *Sisters!* She was as weak as a baby. "Where's—?"

"Calm yourself, lass. Your brother be with the captain." The old woman chuckled. "In need of a good meal, 'e was, that one. Aye, t' be sure."

She retched at the thought of food. That and the pain firing along her nerves. A door opened and closed, and she flinched as a draft swept over her. "Lord Naed…"

"Is not at home," another voice answered, one she'd heard before.

The woman who approached her bedside wasn't tall, but she carried herself with an air of purpose and authority. *The woman from the marsh.* An image of snarling, wolfish teeth reared up in Raell's mind.

"Wh-where's your dog?"

"Beauty awaits me outside."

She wore the traveling clothes of a D'nalian lord's lady, and she gathered the skirts before she lowered herself regally to a chair beside the fire. She shifted her gaze to the old woman. "You haven't aged a bit, Gam."

The crone chuckled. "A dozen wrinkles or a hundred, m'lady. Once you've got 'em, no one notices more." She tied a knot and bit off the thread with a pair of crooked teeth. "You've changed but little, m'lady. The old master would've been pleased t' see you."

Auburn hair wreathed the woman's face and hung in a neat braid over her shoulder. With her back to the fire, her shadowed face revealed no more of her age than somewhere betwixt thirty and fifty, but that face had flickered with some emotion at the old woman's comment.

A mature woman with a face that must have set

men's hearts on fire, and mayhap still did. Clearly a lady of some note, the woman studied her.

Raell squirmed under the intensity of her gaze. "Begging your pardon, m'lady, but who…who are you?"

The woman folded her hands in her lap. "Mayhap the better question is, who are *you*? Wearing men's clothing, wielding a sword, disguising your Tolemak nature this deep in D'nalee raises far more questions than a D'nalian lady traveling through D'nalian territory on her way to a D'nalian stronghold."

Raell's mind flashed to her mother once catching her underfoot in the stable. Her mother had scolded her roundly for endangering herself. The shame she felt then rushed at her now, but she tamped it down. She was hardly a child. "I am Lady Raell, daughter of Lord Tylus of western Tolemak."

"Your brother claims no title."

"He is but fourth in line. I am my mother's heir."

The woman took a cup and held it to Raell's lips. "Drink. Gam will insist as you've lost quite a bit of blood."

The crone nodded and grinned while she spread a foul-smelling paste over her stitching. "Replenish the fluids, lass. Water be best."

The liquid was warm, slightly salty, and flavored with some herb. Raell wrinkled her nose, but she swallowed anyway. She hadn't the strength to fend off both women. "My disguise was a protection. 'Twas but the two of us, you see." She wanted to make that clear lest this woman consider them a threat now she knew their true nature. "We helped you."

"Aye, and I'm grateful to the Sisters for sending

you." The woman straightened and contemplated the cup in her hand. "Belike your...*skills* saved our lives." She set the cup aside and regarded Raell with startling and somehow familiar green eyes.

Where had she seen eyes of that rare color before? Mayhap she'd glimpsed the woman's eyes in the marsh, but twilight had already fallen and...

Raell's head buzzed with what could only be the effects of the drink, that herb within it, and she couldn't concentrate, especially when the woman was speaking again.

"Regardless, I am still determined to know why you were in Myrinnen Marsh and how you claim to know Lord Naed."

Naed! In the haze of weakness, Raell recovered the thread of their conversation. "Wh-where is Naed? And who are you to be demanding?"

The woman's elegant brows drew together. "*Lord* Naed," she corrected, "is my son. I am Lady Vyenne of Tumin, and I should like to know why you are referring to him in such a familiar manner."

Chapter Ten

Vyenne shut the chamber door and mastered her breathing. Beauty rose from her station in the corridor and shoved her nose under Vyenne's hand. She fondled the dog's ear while her mind churned. *Naed's intended!* A Tolemak slip of a girl whose father—*a lord, no less!*—let her roam barely chaperoned and leagues from home. Allowed her to wield swords, dress like a man, and fight!

Well, she would see about that—if and when her son was located. Pity she couldn't get more out of the girl than to confirm Naed had left Albon in Tolemak a fortnight ago. *What in the Name of the Sisters was he doing there?*

She slapped her hand to her skirt. "Come, Beauty." If the girl could say no more now Gam's drug had claimed her, answers would be found elsewhere.

****

Naed dropped his boots on the bearskin rug. Across the chamber, the bed piled high with quilts beckoned. He could stretch out for what remained of the night. No roots, rocks, or clods to shift from under his blankets. He exhaled a deep sigh.

Banir entered, carrying a flagon and a cup, and wearing a scowl.

Having filled his stomach with the first hot meal in weeks, he couldn't resist needling his Second. "Has

Wendelmyr no servants to spare?"

The jibe earned him a glare. "Grodar'll take the first watch in the corridor. Morys'll relieve him. I'll sleep here." He indicated a trundle bed near the door.

"Contrary to what you may believe, we are in a D'nalian fortress, not among your Tolemak compatriots or deep in Adanak. D'nalians do not attack those they've welcomed within their walls." When the dark-eyed Tolemak looked at him askance, he added, "They wait to do so until the guests have left and any ambush may be blamed on thieves or marauders."

"Tidy." Banir handed him a cup of what smelled like warm, spiced wine.

"If you do not trust our security in this place, what makes you trust this?"

"'Tis of my own making."

"Ah." Naed sipped. "Why are you Tolemaks so untrusting?"

"Why are you D'nalians so pig-headed?"

They grinned at each other. "Is this how the Prince and Krenin were?"

"Worse," Banir said, a twinkle in his eyes. "Krenin had a temper."

Naed laughed at what was private between them, how at their first meeting he'd bloodied Banir's lip before they'd saved the Prince and Krenin's lives. They'd been fast friends since. He drained the cup. "Have the riders gone out?"

"In three days' time, Sisters willing, there'll be an assembly at Druemarwin."

"Then we'd best alert Druemarwin."

"I've sent one of our own." He set the cup and flagon on a bedside table and crossed to the trundle bed.

"Wise choice."

Stripping off his breeches, Naed climbed into bed. Tonight he would sleep well. He pressed Raell's charm to his heart and closed his eyes, calling to mind her face, her form, the taste of her kiss. Tomorrow would be early enough to worry about his next gambit.

****

Vyenne found the Tolemak and the captain of the guard before a banked fire in the captain's chamber. Remnants of a cold meal—cheese, bread, the stripped bones of some kind of poultry, two cups and a flagon— littered the table. The scent of spiced wine wafted from a pot nested in the coals.

Both men rose at her entrance, and she allowed herself a moment to examine the stranger. The Tolemak and his sister had managed to darken their white skin to a D'nalian tan. Still, how could she have overlooked the distinctive angular features and high cheekbones? She'd not make that mistake again.

The captain assessed the wolfhound before returning his gaze to her. "M'lady, I would've expected you to be abed." He pulled out a chair. "Here be warm wine, if it suits your need."

"You are obviously unacquainted with me, Captain." She settled herself with deliberate care. "Otherwise, you would not offer me a nighttime draught and instead would be more forthcoming regarding the whereabouts of my *son*, Lord Naed." She enjoyed a moment's satisfaction when the captain dropped his gaze. Good. He would not overlook her concerns again. She indicated the men should sit.

The Tolemak gave her a half bow before he resumed his seat. "Forgive me, m'lady, for not introducing myself properly afore, but D'nalian propriety was not uppermost in my mind at the time."

Under the dark blond slash of brow, his eyes glinted. They were the same shade of brown as his sister's, but while the girl's had flared with righteous indignation before she succumbed to Gam's drug, his simmered with something darker.

Vyenne returned his gaze. She'd dealt with sullen young men before. Most of them, however, were hardly as skilled with a sword as this one. And most were not Tolemak. He would require more cautious handling.

"Your sister is resting comfortably, Toth, son of Tylus. Lady Raell is in excellent hands."

The sibling resemblance was strong, but mercifully the girl had inherited a smaller, more feminine nose. Among their own kind, they would likely be considered attractive—if anything Tolemak could be considered so. Vyenne inhaled. That was not where her thoughts needed to go.

"Please accept my thanks for interceding on our behalf with those villains."

He shrugged. "'Twas my sister's doing and none of my intention."

"I understand." She schooled herself to patience. "'Twas your responsibility to escort her safely here to join Lord Naed. Her *intended*."

His eyes flashed at that, confirming Toth may have escorted his sister, but he clearly did not favor the match.

Does Naed know? She would consider that later. She had more pressing concerns.

"As a result of the limited nature of communications between Tumin in the north and

Druemarwin due to the recent Tolemak and Adanak hostilities, 'twas only a fortnight ago I learned of Lord Dranoel's death and my youngest son's elevation to Lord of Druemarwin. This was, you understand, astonishing news since we had every expectation the holding should pass to Dlaniger, my late sister's son."

A bitter taste flooded her mouth as she spun words her husband would take pride in employing. Well, thirty-plus years of close association had taught her many skills Alwyl could scarce suspect she'd learned.

"I came at once since my husband, Lord Alwyl, could not be spared." Vyenne drew a breath. Alwyl would most certainly have spared the time—had he known it was Naed who'd inherited. When had he received that tidbit and the reason behind Dranoel's choice? Had he learned both at the same time he'd discovered her absence? Had he set out to retrieve her? Were his men even now dogging her trail? He ought to think himself well rid of her but for the scandal—

A log popped in the fireplace, jarring Vyenne from her rabbiting thoughts. Both men watched her.

The Tolemak said, "As the title has already been passed—aye, months ago, so I'm told—what did you hope to do here, m'lady?"

What indeed? Explain herself to Naed, certainly. Seek safe haven—if it could be offered. Find a way to reconcile with the child she loved best. The son of the only man she'd ever loved. The son who most certainly must be furious with her now. However, all that was no one's business but hers and Naed's.

She faced the young man whose impertinence hadn't shown in words or tone, but in the way he looked down his Tolemak nose at her. So, this was the family Naed had chosen to wed into.

Sisters, give me strength! She forced her hands to relax in her lap.

"To support my son, of course. At one-and-twenty, someone who has not been raised to expect a title is hardly equipped to handle such a responsibility when it is dropped upon one's shoulders. You, young man, as fourth in line must grasp that. Consider how it would be if you were only the nephew and a legitimate heir existed."

"Aye," said the captain, as though her answer satisfied him. "'Twas Dlaniger who should've had it, but he an' the old master fought, aye, all the time o'er everything." He stuck a thumb into his broad belt. "That Dlaniger was a right nasty piece of work, if you don't mind me saying, and Druemarwin's well rid of 'im." He leaned forward. "'Twas a good day for Druemarwin, m'lady, when your son came as Free Sword after Dlaniger left. He's done well by us since the old master died."

"But he's not here now." She steered the conversation to her own purposes. "He's in Tolemak, or so I understand."

"Was," said Toth, who continued his down-the-nose scrutiny despite the captain's testimonial. "He left Albon a fortnight ago to return to D'nalee."

Vyenne placed a hand on the table, palm perpendicular to the surface, fingers partially spread. It was a calculated gesture she'd employed many a time to invite assistance without the open palm of a plea. Men responded to it like the offer of a handshake.

"Gentlemen, I think it best you explain to me all you know regarding my son and his whereabouts. And what did you mean when you said he's the second to a...prince?"

"The Prince of Val-Feyridge." Toth leaned back in his chair. "Soon to be king of the three lands."

"He's found the long lost Crown, the Prince has!" The captain beamed at her, all soldierly demeanor gone. "'Twas here at Druemarwin for a time. Commander Krenin brought it from Vinvinnysee. The healer Aerid, the Prince's woman—"

"Lady Aerid now," Toth interrupted. "They be wed nigh a month."

"In truth?" The captain chuckled. "Aye, the little lass was always a good 'un. 'Twasn't her fault she was born Adanak." At Toth's pointed look, he flushed. "Takes some getting used to, these new alliances."

"You've some Adanak here, I understand. And some Tolemak?"

"Aye, some of Master Gaelwynn's folk and some of Master Illien's forces. We took the sick and lame among 'em and a few able-bodied to replace what went west with Lord Naed."

The men carried on as if she'd faded into the tapestry.

Vyenne asserted her presence. "I'm afraid I still don't understand my son's role in all this."

They looked at her. The captain scooted his chair forward. "Why, Lord Naed's at the heart of it, m'lady. He saved the Prince's life."

"Twice," Toth added, but his mouth puckered around the word.

"And helped to win Vinvinnysee from the Adanak."

"And is credited with rescuing the folk of Val-

Feyridge." Toth bounced a fist on the tabletop. "No one can deny his role, but if truth be told, he had Master Gorm and my father's help to do it."

The captain glanced at the young man, his soldier's eye assessing, before he returned attention to Vyenne and smiled. "Your son's distinguished himself, m'lady. Aye, to be sure."

Vyenne studied both men, absorbing the unexpected litany of praise for her son—and the attitudes with which it had been given. The door opened and Humbert entered, an unwieldy blanket-wrapped bundle clutched to his chest. Her groom shuffled across the chamber and deposited his heavy burden on the table with a clank. The blanket unfurled and a pile of mismatched swords and knives slid out.

"I had to settle the horses first, sir," Humbert addressed the Tolemak, "but here be the villains' weapons you bade me collect." Straightening, he noticed Vyenne, and his eyes widened before he bobbed his head. "M'lady."

She took the opportunity to remind him to whom his service belonged, but gently. "You've done well, Humbert. Have you eaten?"

"Not yet, m'lady."

"Then I suggest you do so…unless these gentlemen have another task for you." Vyenne directed her gaze at the Tolemak who'd risen to examine the weapons.

He met her gaze briefly before he pulled a longsword from the pile. "Good man, Humbert. Here's bread and cheese. Take what you will and tell the servants to find you a bed."

"Thank you, sir. M'lady." The groom stuffed his pockets and backed out of the chamber with a bow.

"You have capable servants, m'lady." Toth angled the longsword's hilt toward the fire and frowned over it.

Vyenne suspected he meant it as a compliment even though he didn't spare her a glance. She decided to receive it as one. "They've been with me a long time."

"'Tis a wonder to me that you took only two on this journey."

This time the young Tolemak pinned her with his dark, perceptive gaze. She raised her chin, returned the look. He could probe all he wished, but her secrets would remain her own.

Satisfied she'd made her point, she indicated the weapons. "I thought you wished only to collect them, to prevent others from scavenging them."

"Aye, that, to be sure." He laid down the longsword and pulled another from the pile. "But more so to confirm what I thought I saw." He tossed the weapon alongside the first. "These be Tolemak made. Ormo and Koth, mayhap Lede—eastern Tolemak. 'Tis against the Prince they align. Yet the men who accosted us were D'nalian, every last one."

"Be you sure?" the captain asked.

"I came into my sword against the Prince's enemies, Captain. I know a Tolemak when I fight one. Apart from their leader, these men were thieves and ruffians, not soldiers."

"Then how did they come by these weapons?" said Vyenne.

"An excellent question, m'lady, but as they're all dead, 'tis one for which we have no answer."

****

At the edge of a bearberry thicket, a half dozen

cloaked and hooded men dismounted, scattering night mist into ghostly threads. Two led the horses to a large willow and disappeared beneath trailing branches. The others entered the thicket, leaving one standing with drawn sword just inside the briars.

Deep in the thicket, operating mostly by touch and memory, the man with the pale blond queue pulled away cleverly woven branches and uncovered a trapdoor. He inserted a key into the rusty lock, held his breath, and turned. Nothing sounded but faint clicks as the bolt drew open. He pocketed the key, giving thanks the Druemarwin guard had thought to grease the lock. He hoped the hinges were coated too.

He motioned to the two men barely visible at his sides, and the door came up with only the suck of damp, cold earth surrendering its hold. Nothing wafted out of pitch darkness but stale air, a sure sign no one had used the emergency tunnel recently.

The blond man licked dry lips. He had no fondness for dark, enclosed spaces, but the end of this one took him where he wanted—*needed*—to go. He drew the intricately carved dagger from his belt and led his men down rough stone steps. At this hour, halfway betwixt midnight and dawn, the inhabitants would be abed.

Just where he wanted them.

Chapter Eleven

Raell shivered. A chill brushed her shoulders despite the banked fire at her bedside. She lay with lids half lifted, recalling where she was and why her tongue was furred like a cat's tail. They'd given her drugged water, that old woman who snored in the chair by the fireside. She and that other woman...

Naed's mother!

Her eyes flew open. Then she froze, a chill of a different kind alerting all her senses. Someone had entered the chamber. Someone who smelled of cold, stagnant water and rotting grasses, someone who creaked with the sound of heavy leather, the kind of creak that came only from trying to move with stealth.

Under the blanket, Raell slid her good hand down her side. The old woman had stripped off her tunic to tend her wound, but no one had removed her breast binding or breeches. Or the knife fastened to her belt.

Her heart raced and her muscles trembled, but she forced her hand to grip the hilt and draw it slowly under the blanket while a cloaked and hooded shadow paused to check the sleeping healer. Dim firelight showed a large man wearing a leather forearm guard above the knife in his fist.

Soldier! D'nalian!

He turned and thrust his blade at her face. "Where's your master, wench!" he hissed. "Where be

Lord Naed?"

Assassin! She glanced toward the chamber door. *Alone?*

At the flick of her eyes, he spun. "Ha!" Then flung his knife at the door.

Raell dove off the far side of the bed, hit the floor, and saw stars. Panting through the pain, she shimmied under the bed, shot out the near side and kicked the assassin behind the knees before he could slash his sword at the mattress she'd vacated. He crashed onto his back, toppling the healer's chairside table, pitcher and basin. Water fountained everywhere.

Gam snorted awake. "Here now—what?"

Sputtering curses and swiping at his face, the man rose on elbows, furious gaze intent on Raell.

Before Raell could scoot out of reach, the old healer seized a poker and whacked him across the face. Bone cracked, blood gushed. The body twitched once and lay still.

"Help! Intruder!" Gam struggled out of her chair, scooped up the fallen pitcher and bowl, and banged them together.

Knife in hand, Raell pulled herself up beside the bed. Her head spun, and she sat with a thump. Her injured shoulder burned. So did her forearms, where a quick glance showed she'd collected an array of slivers.

The chamber door burst open. Guards arrived.

Old Gam threw a blanket over Raell's shoulders and tsked at blood seeping through her bandage. "Half me pretty stitching gone, an' the edges all jagged now."

Toth rushed in, sword drawn, followed by a man she took to be the captain of the guard. Her brother made directly for her, pausing only to glance at the body. "Are you hurt?" He swayed a bit when she shook her head.

"Lord Naed. He wanted Lord Naed," Raell managed. "He meant to kill him."

Toth spun to the man who'd followed him, saw the knife embedded in the door frame, and paled. With jerky movements, he yanked the weapon out and waved it under the captain's nose. "How the Demon did the bastard get in? Have you no security in this Sisters-forsaken hole-in-the-marsh?"

Color rose on the captain's cheekbones. "Search the fortress!" he shouted at his men. "And bar the tunnel. If they came in that way, they'll ne'er get out."

The men rushed out. Toth and the captain of the guard remained.

The assassin's blood had spread to a seam in the floorboards, and a glossy trickle oozed toward Raell's bare feet.

Her stomach roiled. She scooted backward until her feet cleared the floor. "Is he dead?"

"Oh, aye." Gam sat and gripped her hand with knobby fingers. "Aim for the nose, lass. Hurts like the Demon, blinds 'em a bit an', Sisters willin', drives a bit o' bone into the brain." She grinned, exposing more gaps than teeth.

Raell shuddered but didn't draw away. They'd defended themselves, an old woman and a wounded one, and they'd taken down a trained warrior. She squeezed the healer's hand.

"This one," she said to her brother, "he was a soldier. I saw his armguard."

Grim-faced, Toth knelt, set the knife aside, and searched the body. "D'nalian. With Tolemak weapons.

Just like the others." Standing, he demanded, "How did they choose this chamber?"

"'Twas the old master's," the captain said. "The Prince and his lady stayed here, but Lord Naed—no. He'd not brung himself to take his uncle's chamber."

Not Naed's bed then. Though she'd not given conscious thought to whose chamber she'd been given, Raell's heart contracted anyway. No wonder she'd not caught his scent from the bedding.

"Fire!"

The shriek came from down the corridor. A guard dashed to the threshold, shouted, "Someone's put a torch to the master's bed!" and ran out.

"Sisters save us!" The captain raced after him, bellowing orders over the hubbub.

Servants with buckets hustled past the opening.

"Bloody hole-in-the-wall!" Toth stomped to the door.

"Oh!"

Raell turned toward the threshold. Two women stood framed there. Faced with Toth's unsheathed sword, Lady Vyenne had drawn up short, hand on her heart. She looked startled, but not afraid, unlike the maid trembling at her heels. No, the woman with the same copper hair and green eyes as the man Raell loved gripped that beast of hers by the collar.

"Is your sister…?"

"Safe," Toth growled. "Inside. All of you. I'm barring the damned door."

When he'd done so, he turned with sword at ready and focused on the wolfhound. With the heavy door muffling noises in the corridor, Raell detected the growl accompanying the beast's raised ruff and visible fangs.

"Can your dog track, m'lady?" her brother asked.

"Beauty is a guard dog, young man, not a hunter. She is trained to defend me and anyone else I direct her to defend. I'll set her at the door, if that suits you."

"Please."

She positioned the wolfhound where he indicated, released the collar, and faced him. "You wondered why I took but two servants, Toth, son of Tylus. Beauty is a more than adequate escort, wouldn't you agree?"

Raell caught the look that passed between Lady Vyenne and her brother before he inclined his head. Whatever they'd discussed while she was unconscious, Naed's mother had won at least a smidgen of respect from her hard-headed brother. At the thought of Naed growing up under the hand of this formidable woman, Raell's heart pinged. Mayhap she'd caught a glimpse into the mystery that was Naed—if only her head would stop swimming and her wound cease burning. She allowed herself to be pushed down on the bed, wincing only when the old healer pulled off her bandage.

"Elda." Naed's mother sidestepped the fallen table. "Fetch water for Gam. There's a pail by the fire." She gripped the bedpost and surveyed Raell. A tiny line appeared between her elegant brows. "Evidently, Lady Raell, your behavior in the marsh is not an aberration." With a nod at Raell's hand, she added, "I believe you can put that away. Your brother and Beauty can manage to keep us secure."

Raell flushed. She'd forgotten the knife. Her muscles jangled so violently, she didn't trust herself to sheathe it, so she let the blade drop to the bedding.

"He-he meant to kill Naed."

"So I gathered."

Was that disapproval in the woman's eyes? "I—I didn't kill him."

"I did." The healer beamed at both of them. Humming, she dipped a cloth in the bowl the maid held for her.

Lady Vyenne shook her head. "You've always been full of surprises, Gam."

The old woman cackled.

Toth stepped away from the door and kicked the dead man's boot. "Do either of you recognize this man? Or aught about him?"

Naed's mother lit a lamp and held it over the bloodied face.

Old Gam shuffled over and bent with a crackling of joints. After a moment's study, she shook her head. "Not from Druemarwin but mayhap one o' the villages along the marsh. A Free Sword, 'tis like."

Elda stole a glance at the body. She shuddered, and the bowl in her hands slopped bloody water onto the floor. "M'lady, is that…?"

Lady Vyenne straightened. Her face had paled, but she kept the lamp steady. "I'm afraid it is." She addressed Toth. "At some time or another, that man must have served at Tumin. He bears the colors."

"Tumin." Toth frowned. "But you're…"

"From Tumin," she said, features composed, chin held high. "Aye."

****

Two men clambered out of the tunnel into the bearberry thicket. Panting clouds of mist, they lowered the trapdoor, and the man with the Adanak dagger pulled out his key. Locking it both here and at the cellar entrance wouldn't fool the Druemarwin guard for long, but—*Demon be damned!*—he wouldn't make it easy for his pursuers. Let them tramp through the tunnel themselves to see if it'd been breached. The bastard of Druemarwin was too bloody lucky as it was. *Not at home, damn it!* The Sisters always smiled on golden lads like Naed with their lordly fathers and courtly training.

What about the rest of us who risk our lives to make our coin? He and Naed had stood side by side when the Lancers attacked the camp last spring. It was just bloody damned luck the Lancer they encountered chose Naed. *I'd have broken that lance too, if the Adanak bastard had come at me!*

"What happened?" said the guard at the edge of the thicket. "Where's—?"

"Dead—if he knows what's good for him. He must've been seen. Some hag raised the alarm."

"My chamber was empty," said the other man.

"As was mine." He'd assigned himself that one, certain Naed would've kept it. *Sentimental fool! If I'd succeeded to a lordship, I'd have taken the dead man's chamber in a heartbeat.* "I overheard the guards. The bastard of Druemarwin was *not* among those who arrived this night."

He sucked in a breath, held it, and blew out some of the frustration knotting his muscles. At least he'd torched Naed's bed. Now the upstart lordling would have to move chambers. Small satisfaction compared to slicing the man's throat, but he'd take what he could until the Sisters tilted the scales in his favor.

"What do we do now?" said one of the men.

"Hide our trail. Then wait and watch. He has to come home soon."

****

Vyenne would not allow herself to pace. Nor would she wring her hands. Elda was doing enough hand-wringing for both of them. No, as long as she was confined to this chamber and under the sharp eye of this young Tolemak, she would maintain the outward composure she'd perfected during three decades of marriage to the wrong man.

Alwyl!

Her husband *couldn't* have ordered the assassination of the babe he'd held in his arms, the youth he'd taught to hunt and ride and fight. He could not be that cruel to wipe out twenty years of close association.

But he was a man, and she was thinking like the woman she was.

Truth be told, after siring three elder sons and twin daughters, Alwyl had indeed held the babe, but he'd directed others to see to the hunting and riding and fighting. The last of six, Naed had always been an afterthought for her husband.

And now Alwyl knew. Naed was *not* his son.

Would he be furious enough to kill the lad who'd grown up believing he belonged to the Tumin bloodline? Who hadn't chosen to be born who he was?

She hoped not, but she had no way of knowing what a man faced with such provocation would be capable of doing—even a D'nalian. Mayhap, *especially* a D'nalian practiced at keeping his emotions in check. Vyenne flexed her fingers in her lap. Would Alwyl adhere to the tenets of logic, duty, and honor that governed all D'nalian society? Or would his outrage overwhelm him? Alwyl would certainly be furious

103

enough to kill *her*. He'd never struck her, but she dared not take the chance. Exile was preferable to whatever punishment he might devise for a wife who'd dishonored her husband and her vows.

A chill ran down her spine. Was *she* the intended target?

No. The man had demanded Naed. The Tolemak girl—*Naed's intended!*—had said so. Vyenne pursed her lips. Thinking of the young woman who wielded swords and knives as being in any way connected to her son left an unpleasant taste in her mouth, but she would deal with that later. For now, the girl slept after having her wound once more stitched up.

If only we could all get out of this infernal chamber!

Her eyes burned from too many hours without sleep. She itched to know what the Druemarwin guard had learned now the hubbub of the search had died down. Beauty's ruff had settled, and the wolfhound had stopped growling some time ago. That surely meant the danger had passed or been reduced.

How many assassins were there? And had they come for me too?

Stop that! Worrying did no good. She needed facts.

She rose, intent on convincing the Tolemak to open the door so they could find out what the Druemarwin guard had learned, when someone knocked.

Beauty stood, but the wolfhound didn't growl. Vyenne took that as a good sign.

Toth demanded, "Identify yourself!"

"Captain of the guard. We've secured the fortress."

"How many—?" Vyenne and the Tolemak both said as he pulled open the door.

They looked at each other. The captain darted a glance between them. Vyenne made a small nod. Much as she wished to control the situation, anything involving swords was best left to the men of the household. She shot a glance at the girl in the bed. If only her potential daughter-in-law subscribed to that notion.

"How many were there?" Toth asked.

"Six, according to tracks. As far as we can tell, three came in. One dead, one put a torch to Master Naed's bed. As to the third…" The captain licked his lips, leaned into the chamber and lowered his voice. "I don't mean to alarm you, m'lady, but 'tis like the third searched your chamber and threw your things about."

For the fourth time in this seemingly endless night, that finger of unease returned, and not alone. An array of ice-cold talons raked Vyenne's spine. Mayhap Alwyl *had* included her! She suppressed a stomach-rattling shudder.

"Sisters be thanked neither you or your maid were abed at the time," the captain said.

"How did they get in?" Toth asked.

Was he steering the captain's attention away while she recovered her equilibrium?

"The emergency tunnel. 'Tis like they had a key."

"That means you have a traitor amongst your folk, Captain."

The man scowled. "Either now or from afore. T'were a number who couldn't abide the new alliances." He pounded a beefy fist on the doorframe. "We've barred the tunnel, and I've set a guard. After sunrise, I'll send out a tracking party. 'Tis too dark to scour the marsh now." He signaled into the corridor.

"We'll clear out the body and clean the mess. Bring in some bedding. 'Tis best, m'lady, you stay here for what's left of the night."

Vyenne's whole being yearned to escape the combined scents of fear, blood, healing herbs, and death permeating every inch of this chamber. But her better sense told her to acquiesce. However much her D'nalian upbringing raged against sharing space with armed Tolemaks, the experiences of this night convinced her she was safer with these two than without them. Besides, Alwyl had controlled her life long enough. She would not allow him to end it, too.

"Of course. Thank you, Captain."

She stepped aside, and the Tolemak did so too, allowing servants to enter, but even as she waited with outward patience for the servants to complete their tasks, Vyenne sensed Toth's scrutiny.

Go stick your Tolemak nose into finding these assassins!

But she held her tongue. Mayhap that would lead him where she didn't want him to go.

Chapter Twelve

"Enough herbs and potions." Raell's shoulder burned and ached, but she refused another draught. Lady Vyenne and her maid had left the chamber, presumably to break their fast. Ravenous despite the night's events, she longed to do the same.

"Where are my clothes?"

Old Gam sighed. "You'll need a sling, m'lady. 'Tis best t' keep the arm still." Bending with a crackle of joints, she rooted in Raell's pack. "Have you no proper women's garments?"

Sisters! Waylaid by Lady Aerid and packing in a rush, she'd forgotten all but the essentials. "Give me what's clean. I'll not stay abed for lack of a skirt."

The healer tsked and held up a tunic and leggings. "Ah, well. Mayhap there be garments from the late mistress in a trunk somewhere. 'Twill be easy enough to alter them."

****

"I'm sorry, m'lord, but my horse fell in the dark. When I came to, the animal had run off." The muddied and bloodied messenger hung his head. "He must've scented home. 'Tis like we'll find the beast on Druemarwin's green."

Banir muttered, "Rode too fast, 'tis more like. All hot to be home. Bloody fool."

Naed huffed out a breath, his buoyant mood

squelched. Druemarwin had no idea they were coming. Well, they would be there themselves within hours. Half his cohort had ridden out from Druemarwin in the dead of winter, following their new master—him—into Tolemak territory none of them would've dared enter alone. He understood their eagerness to be home now they were on familiar ground. His heart had quickened too at the familiar sights and sounds, but his blood still sang for his birthplace.

Nonetheless, he tamped down the hum. This sense of hope brought by a teasing glimpse of sunshine after so many long, dark nights was an illusion. Hadn't he learned that lesson this past twelvemonth? He rubbed his thigh, massaging knotted flesh where an Adanak arrow had plunged to the bone. Under his tunic and next to his skin, Dranoel's legacy shifted with his movements, along with the small gold charm entwined with it. The Prince had set him upon a nigh impossible task. *Go back.* First to the inheritance he'd never dreamed would come to him. Then to his birthplace, where naught of what he'd grown up believing was true but the fact of his birth.

The men assembled around him, and Naed envied those who stretched their gazes, yearning to glimpse home beyond the next low hills. Where did his home lie? If only his heart were not as divided as the burdens hanging from his neck.

"Put him on a horse. Old Gam can tend to him soon enough."

He hoped the messengers sent to the lords had found better footing—and mayhap ridden with more care. The sooner the lords assembled, the sooner he could make his next move. Sisters willing, it did not lead to Tumin—but he knew down to his boot soles that it must.

****

Raell found Lady Vyenne and her maid at table in the lord's private chambers, the servant accumulating a neat pile of stripped poultry bones while the wolfhound sprawled at the lady's feet and gnawed something much larger. Naed's mother sat with a chunk of fresh bread gripped in her hand. The woman stirred at Raell's entrance, as if her thoughts—indeed, her whole being—had been elsewhere. But the green eyes sharpened as she swept Raell with a head to toe glance. That tiny line reappeared between her elegant brows.

"I'm pleased to see you up and dressed, Lady Raell." She nodded at Raell's sling. "Elda will fill a plate for you."

The maid shoved back her chair, but Raell shook her head. "My brother knows what I like to eat. He can do it."

Toth, following her, muttered, "I'll fetch, but I'm bloody well not feeding you," as he passed.

Raell ignored him. If he was going to dog her heels, she might as well take advantage of the situation. Besides, with Lady Vyenne present, he had to mind his manners. Sitting, she selected a hunk of cheese and bit into it. After a fortnight of drycake and scorched, half-raw game, the pungent flavor activated all her senses, and she almost moaned in pleasure. When she opened her eyes, she'd devoured the cheese.

Toth set a plate and cup before her and smirked. "Better than camp food, aye?"

She scowled. "You ate last night, didn't you?"

His grin widened. "I still had my wits about me.

You didn't." He filled another plate and cup and headed toward the corridor, nodding to Naed's mother. "Pardon me, m'lady, but while I've enjoyed your company these past hours, I think I'll break my fast elsewhere."

"You mean, Toth, son of Tylus, you can wait no longer to find what the captain of the guard has learned."

"Aye, there is that." Eyes twinkling, he hooked the door with his foot. "Fear not. 'Tis right outside I'll be."

Raell rolled her eyes and tore into a hunk of bread. The plain food—bread, cheese and meats—tasted so good, she cleared half her plate before she reached for her cup. She stole a glance at the wolfhound, whose great limbs and body covered nigh as much of the floor as a bearskin rug, and flushed. If she didn't mind her manners, she was no better than the beast. She drank and saw Naed's mother studying her. That tiny line between Lady Vyenne's brows had deepened.

"Forgive my ignorance in asking, Lady Raell, but is it a custom among Tolemak women to go about in men's clothing?"

Raell precisely placed her cup beside her plate. Her flush deepened. "No, m'lady."

The frown line eased a fraction. "'Twas for the journey, I believe you said last night, but—"

"The old healer promised to find proper lady's garments for me." There, that should satisfy the woman.

Lady Vyenne nodded, picked up her cup, and sipped.

Raell stabbed a sausage. She hadn't given much thought to how useful her left hand was until forbidden to use it. No cutting meat into smaller pieces. Should she bite off chunks from her knife? Was that better manners than using her fingers? Her brothers and her father sometimes did both. She was already wearing men's clothing. Might as well be damned for a sheep as a goat. She bit off a hunk.

"A bath." Lady Vyenne's announcement startled her into swallowing a half-chewed bite. "After as long a journey as you and I have both endured, Lady Raell, a bath is surely in order. Elda, see about organizing baths for both of us." She smiled across the table, a sympathetic woman-to-woman expression on her face. "A warm soak, a chance to scrub off whatever stain you've applied to your face, my maid to comb out your hair—doesn't that sound appealing, Lady Raell?"

"Aye, it does. Thank you, m'lady." What else could she say? *No, thank you, I'll see to my own bathing—one-armed and all?* Besides, her nose told her she smelled like a common soldier, and that was hardly the way to present herself to Naed whenever he should arrive.

She ought to be grateful to Lady Vyenne for her consideration—and was, truly—but the woman came from Tumin, the political and social center of D'nalee. She'd spent a lifetime moving in circles Raell had the barest knowledge of. And D'nalians elevated to an art the practice of holding in emotions. No, she'd do well to be wary of Naed's mother. She'd already seen how the woman regarded her skill with a blade.

Lady Aerid's words echoed in Raell's memory: *'Tis only that...well, having lived among D'nalians, I do know 'tis unheard of among them to find a woman thus armed. And D'nalians be...aye, 'tis well known they do value propriety nigh as much as honor. Be that known to you?*

Raell considered the remaining food on her plate. She hoped the Prince's bride had been mistaken—or limited in her observations of D'nalians—but Lady Vyenne's reactions dashed that hope. Any mother would be taken aback at meeting her son's intended without an indication he'd made such a choice. And any mother whose son had chosen an outsider would be additionally perturbed. Even allowing for all that, there remained that strong undercurrent of disapproval Raell suspected had nothing to do with the circumstances of their introduction or her heritage.

She crumbled a bit of bread between her fingers while her stomach churned and burned. *Sisters, please let me be the first to tell Naed.*

****

Naed rode onto Druemarwin's green in early afternoon when the sun revealed bare patches belying the name. It showed him, too, a collection of stone cairns ringed by a low, stacked-stone wall. Most cairns had settled, and mosses decorated the stones. One rose yet above the others, its stones raw and naked. Naed sucked in a breath. He'd expected the pain, but the deep, driving sharpness hit like an elbow to the ribs.

He must have made some sound because Banir looked at him. Naed waved away his concern. The Tolemak, for all his unwavering devotion, knew naught of the man buried there. Sometimes Naed wondered if he himself knew, even now. A hot surge of anger pounded behind his eyes. He balled his fists around Firefall's reins, riding it out. When the anger—*rage*, mayhap—came, of a sudden and sometimes without direct prod, it dominated his senses and he could do naught but *feel*, damn it!

He breathed, and redness faded from his vision. He would come back to this cairn he hadn't visited since the funeral. There was much he had to settle with the man he'd buried there—the memory *and* the truth—but not today. Not now when the horses' quickened pace alerted him to the fortress gate standing open, the drawbridge down, and the road before it churned into a muddy mess.

A horn sounded from the ramparts. One blast. Two. A call to arms. The gate gears whined and the bridge creaked up. Men hustled to the ramparts, shields and helms flashing.

Naed reined in. "Show the banner!"

The man bearing the Druemarwin standard swept it from side to side.

Halfway up, the bridge groaned to a stop. A figure stepped into the open on the ramparts and beckoned. Naed recognized the captain of the guard. He returned the greeting and led his men forward.

"What the Demon has them so spooked?" Banir said.

"Nothing good, I'll wager," Grodar said. "They've had the hounds out. Did you see the tracks?"

Naed had. He fisted the reins while Firefall danced in a circle. The drawbridge lowered by increments that ratcheted up his nerves. He was home again, but not *home*. When he'd last been wound this tight, he'd nearly killed Firefall's former master with his bare hands. *Sisters!* Would he never learn to contain his emotions? People depended on him. For their sakes, for the sake of the Kingdom to come, he had to focus on the matters at hand, the present dangers. Something had stirred Druemarwin into this state. He gave Firefall his head and the stallion trotted through the open gates.

****

"They're here!" the man perched high in the branches of a fir tree called.

As if in confirmation, muted horn blasts and muffled metallic groans drifted on the breeze to the men gathered below.

"Did you mark their banner?" demanded the man with the Adanak dagger.

"Aye, 'tis plain to see Druemarwin's crest. Two dozen armed men, at least, horses, an'...a bit of a motley."

"What do you mean?"

The lookout climbed down, dropping lightly the last several feet. He brushed winter-killed needles from shoulders and queue. "Their shields, armor...'tis not all of a kind. Motley."

"Like Free Swordsmen?"

"Mayhap. Soldiers, to be sure. Some of 'em from Druemarwin."

The blond man licked his lips. *Finally!*

****

Sorting through her late sister's clothing was less painful than Vyenne expected. She'd packed it away, alone, having nursed her sister through her last illness, having watched her linger and fade until everyone— *everyone!*—wished for the end. *Sisters, be merciful!* They had, finally, but by then Vyenne's grief had burned to embers, and the act of putting away her sister's belongings had seemed as much a burial as laying that withered body to rest. If only she hadn't sought to comfort the living afterward...

But she had. And she wasn't sorry. They'd been apart ten long years by then, loyal to their spouses. And Dranoel hadn't been the one to call on Vyenne for help. Her sister had written, her sister who knew, somehow, Vyenne's heart belonged to the Lord of Druemarwin. She'd gripped Vyenne's hand before delirium took her and said, "Love him. You always have," and she hadn't meant her son.

Beastly boy!

But Dlaniger was another matter for another time. Wherever he was, his father had disowned him.

In favor of the child we made.

Vyenne's eyes burned. She blinked away moisture and concentrated on the task at hand. She shook out garment after garment, noting cedar had protected even the wool but had done naught for the style. *Well, beggars can't be choosy.*

Vyenne assessed the young woman who'd emerged from her bath. Taller than her sister—they'd have to lengthen all the hems—and far less frail—they'd have to let out the shoulders and arms, too. Clearly, swordplay built more muscles than the labor most titled ladies endured. Vyenne frowned. Just how prosperous a holding did Lord Tylus rule? Certainly not comparable to Tumin. Was it even a match for Druemarwin?

She harrumphed and shook out a shawl. If there remained the slightest chance she could persuade Alwyl that Naed might be his son, this choice of bride would vanquish that possibility. None of *his* sons would wed anyone without a substantial dowry.

But *her* son might, if he chose for love.

As she should have done.

Had Naed?

Vyenne studied the girl, looking for signs she was with child. Had the son who'd grown up stubbornly idealistic and inordinately upright compromised himself? Doubtful. The girl, while attractive enough despite her overly pale Tolemak skin, hardly seemed the type to inspire, much less invite lust. Vyenne knew that type very well. There were more than enough predatory females at Tumin court. Besides, of all her sons—*and* twin daughters, if truth be told—Naed was the least likely to be caught tumbling a lover in the hayloft. But if he had, he would be the first to own up to it.

She cast another glance at the girl who was now being fitted for appropriate underthings. Mayhap Naed hadn't known the girl long enough for such signs to show, even to one who'd birthed six children.

"Indulge me, Lady Raell. How and when did you meet my son? I was not aware he had journeyed to Tylus."

The girl turned. She had lovely hair, Vyenne had to admit, a honey-gold color that fell in waves halfway to her waist. What a pity concealing her identity required shortening it. And the same brown eyes as her brother. Was she as perceptive? So far her face had been easy enough to read. One advantage of dealing with a Tolemak rather than a D'nalian or an Adanak.

"'Twas after Val-Feyridge fell, m'lady, mayhap two…" The girl paused, eyes cast upward as if calculating. "Aye, nigh onto two months now. Lord Naed led the folk to Albon, the Prince's old stronghold. My father…" Those brown eyes shifted to Vyenne and sharpened. "How much do you know of Tolemak, m'lady? The alliances? The politics?"

"Only that the entire territory seems perpetually in turmoil. Tumin trades with many in the northeast but, as you are well aware, D'nalee territory remains steadfastly neutral. Those who visit with us at Tumin know that and behave accordingly."

The girl glanced at a dress Elda held, nodded, and allowed the maid to measure her waist. "Aye, well, belike that needs must change, what with the Prince finding the Crown and taking an Adanak to wife."

Vyenne started. *The Crown of Tolem?* She'd heard that news last night but not grasped the import. After generations of separation, of outright enmity, the three lands were to become one again? With a Tolemak for a king and—and an *Adanak* for a queen? She dropped the trunk lid and sat down hard upon it.

At the double thump, the wolfhound jerked awake by the door.

The jolt shook sense into Vyenne. Did Alwyl know? How in the name of the Sisters had Naed found himself in the midst of this? She pulled herself together. "You—your father's role in this?"

"When Prince Arn decided to seek the Crown, he put my father in charge of his Tolemak holdings. The Prince knew if he left Tolemak his enemies would move against him. So he and my father and his allies planned all the winter to fight on two fronts. They expected Rolnar of Roines to attack Val-Feyridge. They didn't expect the assassin that nearly killed the Prince." She paused with a faraway look, then stepped into a skirt Elda held for her. "Your son was there, m'lady, the day Val-Feyridge fell. He pulled the Prince out of the fire and led the people to Albon. Father's a clever man. He'd left Toth and me there to mind the place, thinking all might not go well. Sisters be thanked he did so."

"Aye, Sisters be thanked," Vyenne murmured while her mind absorbed the news this Tolemak slip of a girl—a *wildling*, no less—was an experienced lady in charge of not one but two holdings. Even so, the girl looked no older than Naed. Mayhap appearances could—*should*—be considered deceiving in this case. "So, you were at Albon..." Vyenne rose to hold together a seam for Elda to stitch.

"Aye. Father sent me to tend the wound upon Lord Naed's cheek and to settle him with fresh clothing and food."

"Naed was wounded?" Vyenne's hand shook.

Elda shot her a glance.

The girl's gaze had gone into the distance again. "A scrape. 'Tis well healed." She sighed. "Father took his measure aright. A man with that much courage and heart would not see to himself when others needed tending."

Vyenne's heart thudded. Aye, that was her son, always thinking of others, rushing to someone's defense, heedless of his own safety. How many times had she found the boy bloodied and scraped, eyes full of fire and lips sealed? His brothers were merciless, even Elwyn the otherwise gentle, and she knew better than to interfere. Somehow Naed had survived, apparently even thrived since he'd left Tumin, if these reports were to be believed.

"So, he came to you as a hero," she said. "I can see where that might be—"

"No, *not* as a hero." The girl's gaze locked on Vyenne. "You think I saw him wrapped in glory. Aye, 'twould be a powerful thing and, to be sure, I've seen him that way, shining in victory." Her breath hitched, and she gripped the charm at her throat. "But not that night."

Vyenne retreated a half step before the intensity in those brown eyes, the emotion thick in the girl's voice. She cleared her throat. "How did you see him then?"

"Mayhap he came as a hero to some—aye, to most of those he led to safety—but I...I saw him as he was that night, a man who'd lost all. Who thought everything he'd fought for was gone, whose friend was dying and there was naught he could do to prevent it. I saw him, m'lady, when he thought he'd failed everyone who depended on him." Though she cradled her injured arm, she stood tall and her gaze, fierce and full of challenge, never wavered. "I saw his heart, m'lady, and I loved him for it."

Naed has found himself a lioness.

A tidal wave of emotion swamped every other coherent thought. The girl expected a response, but Vyenne stood speechless for so long Elda nudged her. She opened her mouth, hoping the Sisters would provide her with some platitude when a horn sounded outside.

With a scramble of claws Beauty stood, nose in the air.

Toth opened the door. "Stay in here and bar the—what the Demon?"

The wolfhound threw herself into the gap. The heavy door crashed into one wall, Toth banged into the other, and Beauty sped down the corridor, a deep rumbling *Woof!* echoing in her wake. Glowering, Toth rubbed his elbow. "Where's the bloody great beast going?"

Vyenne's heart stuttered. How much more could she endure? Her emotions were already at the breaking point, and her body not far behind. She would not curse the Sisters—they never gave anyone more than he or she could bear—but did they have to push her to the very edge? Well, there was no going back now. One had to take trials as they came.

She squared her shoulders. "Last night you asked me if my dog could track, Toth. Well, I suspect she's caught a scent she recognizes."

Chapter Thirteen

Naed dismounted beside the stone well in the middle of the courtyard. While his pulse beat at his temples—too fast—he fixed his gaze on the captain of the guard descending the gate stairs. He had no reason to look at the base of the well where Dranoel had died. Winter snow and spring rain had certainly washed out the bloodstain. What shadow remained, however slight, would fade under the summer sun.

Morys stepped to his left and held out a hand. Naed unclenched his fist and passed over Firefall's reins. He yanked gloves off clammy hands while Grodar directed the rest of the men to the stable with their horses.

Banir appeared at Naed's right. "If it suits you, let me deal with Ekwul, alert him to the lords soon to arrive."

The offer shook Naed out of himself. Banir and the old servant detested each other. He acknowledged the gift with a glance. "Good thinking. He'll know how to prepare the grounds."

"I'll take this sorry excuse for a horseman to the healer, too." He and the injured messenger headed toward the living quarters, past a blackened heap littering the paving stones.

Naed frowned. That looked like scorched bedding. A faint scent of charred linen teased his nostrils before the sweet odor of drying blood arose and swamped it.

Sisters! He twisted his gloves, stuffed them into his belt, and choked back a cough. The blood was just a memory, a ghost. He had no time for ghosts. Not when the captain of the guard squared up before him.

"Sisters be praised you're home, m'lord!"

It took no skill to read relief on the man's broad face, or a measure of chagrin. Naed inhaled, and the pulse slowed at his temples. "What's the situation, Captain?"

"Intruders, m'lord." He toed the paving stones. "Three men came in through the emergency tunnel afore dawn. We killed one, rather, Old Gam did. Two escaped, but not afore one of 'em set fire to a bed." He indicated the blackened heap. "Your bed, m'lord."

Naed willed himself to remain still. He'd anticipated something of this nature. Men had tried to kill him outside of Albon more than a fortnight ago—if those men had indeed known who he was. That was still open to debate. The fact he'd made himself a target for Roines and his cohorts was not. Nonetheless, a part of his brain rebelled, shocked his enemies had come into his *home*, however much he still didn't believe it belonged to him.

He cleared his throat, unwilling to leap to the conclusion his emotions screamed at him to accept. The ghosts fed those fears, ghosts he had to overcome. "Who were they? What do you know?"

"D'nalian. Leastways, the dead one was. He had Tolemak weapons, him and the thieves what attacked some travelers in the marsh yesternight."

This was news, though not unexpected. Myrinnen Marsh was largely a wild place. "D'nalian thieves? With Tolemak weapons?" That didn't mean the incidents were connected. Thieves and soldiers alike scavenged weapons. Still, they could be assassins. Or mercenaries, like his traitorous cousin—*half-brother!* Naed's stomach churned. He would never accept sharing that much blood with Dlaniger. But Dlaniger died months ago, and he needed to focus on the man before him.

"Aye." Thumbs in his belt, the captain rocked on his heels. "They picked the wrong target. Got 'emselves killed for it. We collected the weapons and some of the horses. Mayhap you'll want a look at 'em later."

"Thieves? Not soldiers? You're sure?"

"Aye. Leastways, that's what the young Tolemak says."

Sisters! The man was as difficult to pull sense from as Grodar and Morys. "What Tolemak, Captain?"

"The travelers, m'lord. They came here round midnight with one of 'em wounded. The Tolemak was telling me about the ambush when Old Gam raised the alarm. The intruders had a key, m'lord, an' three men outside, too. We sent the hounds out at dawn but the marsh—M'lord, look out!"

Naed stumbled back a step. With a deep-throated woof, a great gray beast skidded to a halt at his feet. Tail wagging furiously, the wolfhound whined and licked his hand.

He blinked, saw the collar buried in the whorled fur, and knelt. "Beauty?"

A giant tongue slathered his face. The wriggling body bowled him back on his heels.

Pushing the massive head aside, he gave himself a heartbeat—or three—to press his cheek to wiry, warm fur. Let the observers think he was reclaiming his balance after the beast's assault. They would be at least partly correct.

"Stop, Beauty. Sit."

Whimpering, the dog obeyed. Her tail swept the paving stones, and she leaned into his leg when he stood. Soulful black eyes tracked his every movement. Naed fondled the dog's ear, more to calm himself than the wolfhound.

"When did my mother arrive?"

The captain had the grace to redden. "Yesternight, m'lord."

Perfect. As if he didn't have enough on his plate with the lords about to convene, assassins—*potential* assassins—in the marsh, and ghosts lurking in every stone and stain.

"Brick up the tunnel, Captain. The southern lords will be gathering here within a day or two, and I'll not have any of them assassinated within Druemarwin's walls. I want to know who's been in or out of the fortress since I left, and I want to see this Tolemak."

****

Naed! Heart pounding, Raell jerked free of needle and thread and bolted for the door. "It's him, isn't it?"

Toth blocked her, arms spread, voice low. "Mind yourself! 'Tis D'nalee, Raell."

"Aye, I know that!" She danced around him, feinted to duck under his arm, and drove her good elbow at his ribs.

Grunting, he caught her in a bear hug. "These be the folk you'd live among, aye?" He jerked a nod at the women in the chamber. "What would you have them think of you?"

She glared at Toth, desperate to see the man she'd

endured a fortnight in the saddle to reach, to breathe the same air, bask in the same sunlight, sense the warmth of his hand on her arm. Instead, her brother generated the heat burning through her thin garment. The damned obstinate fool stood between her and her goal.

"Stand aside!"

He dragged her into the corridor. "You have a title, Raell. Act like it!"

She would've stomped his toes, kicked his shin, even bitten his arm. But gall rose in her throat. The thick-headed, uncouth brother who had no love for the man of her choice was right. She'd seen what he wanted her to see—the maid on her knees poised with needle and broken thread, the old healer grinning with open interest, Naed's mother by the window, an aloof column of propriety.

Heat rushed up her face. "What would you have me do?"

"Dress yourself appropriately." He plucked at a half-stitched sleeve. "And 'tis no need to meet him in the courtyard. Let him come to you."

"But I've come this far—"

"Without him knowing! Would you make a fool of yourself before all and sundry? What if his feelings be not what you believe?"

"Aye, 'tis what you'd wish!" She twisted in his grip. "'Twould prove you right for him to disavow me now!"

"I'd kill him if he did, and well do you know it, Raell!"

That stilled her. She looked at Toth sideways, but he met her gaze full on. He meant every word. Her cheeks burned anew. She wanted only to wound him, to vent her frustration, anger, fear that mayhap he was right and Naed's feelings had changed. They were a fortnight past their last embrace and Naed was deep into his mission for Prince Arn. What if he'd given no thought to her even as she'd dreamt every night of him and longed all day to reach him? What if all his fine D'nalian words were empty promises? That fear nagged at her whenever she woke after midnight and tossed in her blankets.

Her heart was sure. Was his? Her stomach curled into a tight knot.

****

Vyenne noted the girl's return to the chamber without moving her head. No childish tantrum would divert her gaze from the mullioned window and the wedge of courtyard visible through it.

The need to lay eyes on her son gnawed like an empty belly after a too long winter. The girl had seen Naed but a fortnight ago. Vyenne had lost two years.

Movement from below. Horses and men. More men, some in Druemarwin colors, some white-faced Tolemaks.

Fear lanced through her, ingrained and automatic, but she tamped it down. Her son was known to have Tolemak companions. *Sisters Three!* He served a Tolemak *prince*! Vyenne pressed a hand to her heart, wondering how the world—*her* world—had so quickly fallen apart.

Then she saw him.

He'd filled out. She'd not considered him thin before, nor was he bulky now. Mayhap he weighed no more than when he'd left Tumin, but it had gone to his shoulders, wider under his cloak than ever she could remember. His face had thinned, the contours had lost their youthful roundness and what remained were hard planes and angles. He'd always been a serious lad, not one for smiles and silly banter. That appeared not to have changed, nor did she expect it to. He'd been to war and back.

And everything he believed had proved false.

If only I could have saved him that.

Vyenne rubbed at her breastbone. The gnawing had spread. She'd not meant to drop the world from under his feet. In truth, she'd given no thought all those years ago to the possibility of a child or the consequences. She'd seized a moment in time, she and Dranoel. And she was not sorry. For what they had was beautiful, the one bright moment in her life. If Naed could not accept that, then so be it. But she would try to make him understand...

That he was a child of love.

She drank in the sight of the familiar stranger below. He walked like the lord he'd become, confident, self-assured, in command, but—

Her brow furrowed. Was that a hitch in his gait? She narrowed her eyes. Yes, most definitely a hitch. Her fingers dug into the cloth over her breast. The girl had mentioned only a wound on his cheek, a slight one.

A chill shivered through her. What else had the barbaric child omitted?

****

Naed surveyed the intruder's body where the servants had dumped it outside. Beauty growled until he soothed her with a stroke of his fingers. The weapons collected from the marsh had been spread on the paving stones. In full sunlight, the Tolemak markings could be seen without bending.

Lede. Koth. Ormo. Enemies of the Prince.

He'd last seen such weapons scattered in a snowy, bloodstained clearing a fortnight ago in Tolemak.

Where they belonged.

He straightened, saw Banir approach, note the wolfhound, and change course to put the captain between himself and the beast.

Beauty, pressed so close her paw rested on Naed's boot, watched the Tolemak with her ruff raised.

"Friend." Naed tapped the dog.

She looked at him, quivering, and her tongue lapped out.

If the wolfhound weren't so well trained, she'd knock him to the ground so she could slather his face again. He supposed he had his mother to thank for the training. That thought left a bitter taste in his mouth.

"This is Beauty." He had much to explain to the Tolemak who studied him with those dark, unreadable eyes, but not now.

He indicated the body and the weapons. "Tell me what you think." The dead man wore Tumin colors and his hair was just long enough to gather into a queue. A disgraced soldier turned out not many months prior. How had a northerner and outsider gotten into the tunnel?

Banir bent and performed a careful examination while the captain stood alongside and fidgeted.

Partly to distract the captain and partly to distract himself from the man's edginess, Naed said, "Does Ekwul still keep the keys?"

"Aye, m'lord. Won't let 'em out of his sight."

Ekwul undoubtedly slept with the keys under his

pillow. Dranoel's long-time personal servant was so territorial about his duties he wouldn't unfasten his fist for his own mother. Naed had refereed more than enough disputes between Banir and Ekwul to know.

Another key must exist.

"I would speak with Ekwul."

But not merely about the keys. Where there was one emergency tunnel, a honeycomb of all-but-forgotten passages might lurk below Druemarwin. It wouldn't do to have them discovered by those with evil intentions. Not before he could see where they led.

Banir stood. "D'nalian Free Sword. Been living rough in the marsh." He toed the man's boot sole. "Tamarack, black spruce, marsh grass, bearberry seeds in the muck there."

"Aye," said the captain, thumbs in his belt, "'tis what we found when we followed the tracks."

"Till your hounds lost the trail," Banir said.

The captain reddened. "You know the marsh, m'lord. It swallows everything."

Naed did, but Banir could track a flea across a pack of dogs. Still, by now the villains had either moved camp or departed the marsh entirely.

"Call back your search parties, Captain. We'll need every man to secure the grounds these coming days."

When the man had gone, Banir stepped closer. He'd opened the dead man's purse and the contents glinted on his palm. "Paid in gold. Vinvinnysee coin mostly."

"Adanak gold?" He picked up a disk and turned it over. All gold was accepted currency no matter where it was minted. The Adanak coins likely meant nothing.

Banir looked at him steadily. "Master Gaelwynn

said 'twas a plot amongst the Vinvinnysee masters to kill the Prince, aye?"

"Months ago, but 'twas foiled when the city fell and the masters all captured." He rubbed the coin between thumb and forefinger. Why did the sensation fail to soothe?

"Mayhap only their part in it."

"Sisters! You don't think—"

"They paid Master Dlaniger, aye?"

Naed slapped the coin into Banir's hand. He used too much force, but the cursed thing burned his fingers. His traitorous cousin—*no, half-brother*—had left a poisonous trail from Adanak to Tolemak and back. The man was *dead*, damn it! Why hadn't everything he touched died with him?

Beauty whined and licked his hand. The warm, wet touch reminded Naed a few coins in one man's purse proved nothing.

"What of the Tolemak weapons?"

"Not his."

"Do you think those men in the marsh and this one are connected? The captain does."

Banir glanced at the sun overhead. "If it suits you, I can be back by nightfall."

"Good. Take Grodar. Leave me Morys." Banir would find the bodies. Whatever was to be learned from them, the Tolemak would learn.

Naed hoped the situation was not as he feared, but he skirted the well on his way back across the courtyard. Just because it was there didn't mean he had to look at it.

Damned ghosts!

Chapter Fourteen

Raell had bitten the inside of her cheek bloody. If she had to stand still for another garment adjustment, the curses rampaging through her brain would pour out of her mouth and pelt her damned, obstinate brother. He deserved to be hurt. She imagined seizing the maid's needle and jabbing him everywhere.

Dressed appropriately, indeed! She huffed out a breath.

The maid stood, stepped back.

Raell's heart raced. "'Tis done?"

Toth came away from the door. He'd allowed no one in, and only the healer out when she'd been summoned.

That had been ages ago. Raell tapped her foot.

He unfolded his arms, surveyed her, and nodded. "We'll go down together. Greet the master." Instead of offering her his arm, he pivoted toward the window. "Lady Vyenne, may I attend you?"

Naed's mother started. She'd been watching Naed in the courtyard. Raell was certain of it. A viper's tongue licked along her nerves. Why couldn't she have been the one to set eyes on him?

Shame heated her face. Naed's mother had the right to see and greet him first. Raell was only the betrothed, not the bride. That would change. Soon.

It had to, or all she'd endured was for naught.

Raell pulled off the sling and handed it to the maid. She'd keep her injured arm still like the demure young lady these D'nalians expected, and Old Gam would be none the wiser. Besides, she would be damned if she'd appear before Naed in any way diminished. She'd shock him enough just by appearing.

Touching her charm, she prayed he'd be pleased.

****

"They be staking out what look like pavilion spaces on the green," the lookout high in the fir tree called. "And the search parties be coming in."

The men lounging on logs stood. Several grinned, and their shoulders relaxed.

"I thought we'd ne'er fool the dogs," one said.

"It pays to know the marsh," another said. He looked at their leader. "Pavilions?"

The blond man had been sharpening the Adanak knife he carried in his belt. A kill prize, he'd made plain to them, won months ago in the battle for Vinvinnysee. The men gave him a wide berth whenever he unsheathed the wicked blade with the intricately carved handle.

He laid aside his sharpening stone. "A gathering of the lords, 'tis like." Plucking a blade of grass, he sliced it into pieces. "So that's where the bastard of Druemarwin's been."

The men looked at each other.

"What now?" the first man asked.

He stroked his chin where stubble had accumulated. He didn't like stubble. This living rough in the marsh was not at all to his taste.

"T'will be much coming and going and new men to swell the ranks. We'll slip in among them, three of you with me, and we'll wait. Before he went west, the bastard was wont to walk the parapet after nightfall. Belike he'll do the same tonight."

And then I'll gut the traitor!

****

Shadows darkened the Great Hall after bright sun outside. Naed's gaze locked on his mother at the end of a double line of servants and guardsmen. He was dimly aware of the press of bodies, vaguely surprised at the crowd's size. He'd forgotten how many served at Druemarwin, and the failure shamed him. He would amend that fault straight away. But first he would confront the woman he hadn't expected to see so soon, and certainly not here.

D'nalian protocol demanded the guest greet the lord, and she'd always been a champion of protocol. His lips compressed. How did she square her conscience with having broken the most basic rule?

Leaving Beauty at the door with a firm "Stay," he strode forward, acknowledging those who served him with a nod and a glance. They smiled, most of them, and many murmured, "Sisters be thanked, you're home, m'lord," and "Bless the Sisters you're safe," as he passed.

Naed's heart swelled. He hadn't been born here, but he'd been conceived in this place, and the folk seemed genuinely happy—and relieved—he'd returned.

Mayhap it was home, after all.

He reached the end of the long line and halted.

His mother wasn't tall, her forehead barely even with his chin, but she'd always managed to look him in the eye. It was the way she carried herself, ramrod straight as if she had every right to her pride.

Hypocrite! He squared his shoulders, raised his chin a notch.

As she was his mother and a lady in her own right, Naed had learned to nod respectfully and offer a kiss on hand or cheek. He schooled his body to resist its training. He was lord now, and this was his home.

Something flickered in her eyes.

Acknowledgement? Acceptance? Annoyance? She'd never been easy to read.

She stepped forward and offered him her hand. "My lord son."

"My lady mother."

He intended to grip her fingers long enough for her to register the ring marking his lordship, but the contact sent a spark through him. In its flash, he was a child again. Those fingers ran through his hair, soothing nightmares, taming wayward strands before a state occasion, absently stroking while itinerant storytellers filled Tumin's Great Hall with legends and heroic tales. But that was a lifetime ago, another Naed entirely.

Another woman, too.

Odd how she hadn't outwardly changed save for a few new crinkles around the eyes. Yet everything about her was not as it had been. He released her hand. *Who was she, really?*

The coals banked in his heart ignited. He'd lived among plain-speaking Tolemaks too long to resist scratching that cool, contained surface. "How fares your *husband*?"

A hint of color bloomed on her cheeks, but she held his gaze. If anything, her chin rose a fraction. "He was well a fortnight ago when the news of Lord Dranoel's death reached Tumin. He expressed his wish that his *nephew* will do better by Druemarwin than the previous master."

Naed made fists. The Lord of Tumin no doubt meant Dlaniger, being ignorant of the details of succession, as unexpected and unlikely as they were, but the insult to Dranoel, the man who loved him, rankled. He forced his fingers to uncurl. Alwyl, the man he'd long thought of as father—now his uncle—was a matter for another day.

"How did *you* learn the title had passed to me?"

"Ekwul sent me a letter. He kindly thought I should know what had become of my son."

Another issue he would discuss with Dranoel's old servant. "And Lord Alwyl?"

She gave a delicate lift of shoulders. "A matter of time, I should think. He had a packet of letters from Druemarwin in his possession when I took leave of him."

He could imagine how she'd 'taken leave of' her husband. She'd always been decisive. While Alwyl, her husband—*not* his father—pondered a matter for days, weeks even, Vyenne acted. "Who accompanied you?"

"My maid, Elda, and Humbert, your old nurse's son. And Beauty, of course."

"Of course." A timid maid, a green youth of a groom, and a large dog. Well, she'd made it unscathed. He ought to thank the Sisters for that, but he wasn't sure it was a blessing.

"I trust Ekwul has seen to your comfort despite the…less than pleasant circumstances of your arrival. Those circumstances require my immediate attention, Mother, so I'll take my leave of you. We'll speak more at dinner."

As he turned to seek out Ekwul, she laid a hand on his arm.

"Are you...well?"

The mask had slipped and she looked at him with open concern. Almost like the mother he thought he knew, almost like a mother who loved her son. She was studying his cheek, the months-old scrape he'd forgotten once it ceased to pull. He covered her hand, squeezed it.

"Yes, Mother. I'm fit and well."

Her gaze flicked to his leg, and a tiny line appeared between her brows. "Indeed?"

Beneath tunic and leggings, the puckered flesh on his left thigh crawled. He ought to have known she'd notice the limp, no matter how slight it had become, how determined he was to overcome it. He leaned forward a fraction, lowered his chin, and returned her frown. He would not discuss it now. "Indeed, Mother."

She held his eyes a moment before disengaging her hand. A cat's smile flitted across her lips. Naed's frown deepened. He had the sinking feeling he'd won a move only to lose a gambit.

She extended her arm in a beckoning gesture. "Then, mayhap, you could spare a moment to greet your betrothed."

Chapter Fifteen

Naed looked thunderstruck.

Raell pasted on her best smile. She'd expected no less, hadn't she? But Lady Vyenne needn't look so pleased.

Casting a prayer to the Three Sisters, Raell offered her hand. Naed reached for it like one spellbound, the hazel eyes she so adored wide and unblinking.

Until skin touched skin.

A thrill ran up her arm. She sucked in breath at the tickle of it, at the sudden darkening of his eyes, at the clasp—*so tight*—of his fingers.

"Lady Raell." The huskiness of his voice set all her body to tingling.

"Lord Naed." Had that throaty whisper come from her mouth? Raell flushed.

If possible, his grip tightened. He stared as if he couldn't quite believe she stood before him. "When…how…why…?"

He blinked, and his expression shifted from astonishment to bewilderment to a darkening comprehension. "Something has happened. The Prince—"

"Is well, so far as we know," Toth said, stepping up to her shoulder. "Leastways, he was when we left him a fortnight ago, m'lord."

Raell shot her brother a daggered stare. In truth,

he'd saved her from fumbling for an answer, and she was grateful, but she'd never tell him so.

Naed looked from Toth to her, brows quirked. She could see more thoughts clicking into place, more questions.

"He sent you, then."

"In…in a manner of speaking," Raell said before her brother could respond. She stroked her thumb over Naed's hand, hoping he'd understand now was neither the time nor place for explanations.

Those hazel eyes darkened again, like shade covering a pond. "I see."

Raell swallowed. How she loved this man for reading her need, mayhap even for that D'nalian propriety that kept private things private.

He held her gaze, and her body heated with it. *Sisters be thanked, he loves me still!* She licked her lips, flushed, and ducked her head, lest he read too much hunger, too much relief in her eyes.

His thumb brushed once, twice, three times across her knuckles before, with a deep breath, he directed his attention to Toth. "The captain of the guard has been singing the praises of a Tolemak who was of great assistance to him yesternight. You must be that Tolemak."

Her brother offered a respectful nod and a shrug. "'Twas a difficult night, m'lord. I merely did what I could."

The two men eyed each other. She'd been parted from Naed for a fortnight, but she read his mood as well as if they'd kissed only yesternight. The tension in him crackled, so she squeezed his fingers again. His gaze returned to her and warmed. He bent, touched his lips to her knuckles, and sent shivers down her spine.

"You will tell me all, aye, Lady Raell? At dinner, or after, as it suits you."

Releasing her hand, he stepped back, as if mindful of the crowd that watched avidly. He was D'nalian, after all, but her heart still pinched to see it.

She gave him the slight nod expected in public. "As you wish, m'lord."

"In the meantime, I would have your brother attend me. I'm given to understand he may shed some light on the events that unfolded yesternight."

Toth flicked a glance to her before he nodded. "Glad to be of service, m'lord."

Her brother could be a right bastard, but his look promised he'd keep her counsel. Not that he'd do so out of love. He'd take great pleasure in watching her squirm her way out of the mess she'd landed them all in. What the Demon would she say to Naed later?

The truth, aye. But how best to tell that truth?

She chewed her lower lip. Three hours till dinner, according to the sun slanting through high windows. Might as well be minutes. She'd had a fortnight to consider, for all the good it had done. Her mind still churned like a whirlpool, sucking every idea down as soon as it formed.

Naed moved away, and Toth with him. The folk parted, nodding to each other. Naed had won their hearts.

But as for her...

She straightened her shoulders. The folk would be buzzing as soon as they cleared the Great Hall. They'd had their first look at the future Lady of Druemarwin, and she hoped she suited them. *Sisters Three!* She'd never thought to find herself so completely out of her element, so far from all things Tolemak. Well, her heart had made its choice, and she had to accept all that came with it.

If only Lady Vyenne hadn't looked so pleased.

She turned to accompany Naed's mother back to the living quarters and stopped.

The woman stared after her son, a look of consternation on those fine D'nalian features.

Raell's mood lifted. *You didn't think he loved me. Well, now you know.*

****

Naed yanked his mind into to the present. These last hours had been a tug-of-war between what he needed to do and decide and what his body and heart wanted.

Beauty had whined piteously when he left the Great Hall. Liquid black eyes tracked him with the intensity of one who couldn't bear to be parted again. Naed understood, so he brought the wolfhound to heel. After a fortnight without Raell, minutes in her company were not enough.

His hand still tingled with Raell's touch, the taste of her skin lingered on his lips. He wanted to catch her in an embrace and hold on till the hours—*days!*—melted away.

He *needed* to pay attention to what Toth was saying.

Toth and Humbert and Beauty against six? Naed had no notion of Toth's blade-skill. He'd fought side-by-side with Lord Tylus, but knew this son only as the father's attendant and the one whose clothes Naed had been lent upon arriving at Albon. Lord Tylus had shown himself to be a fierce warrior. Was his youngest son already that skilled?

And what the Tolemak was *not* saying.

Why in the Name of the Sisters had he and Raell come to Druemarwin? What Toth had told him about the last days was concerning enough without considering the risks they'd undertaken.

Sisters and the Four Winds! Naed's head ached. How did the Prince manage so many disparate thoughts and threats? The man deserved the Crown for that ability alone.

Together they'd quizzed Ekwul, who'd shown Naed the keys. If any had gone missing, Ekwul insisted, it had to be the former steward's doing. That fool had let the Tolemak spy into the kitchens last spring, hadn't he?

Wullauf had. Naed had uncovered that betrayal himself. But that spy was a Tolemak and loyal to the Prince. These intruders and thieves were D'nalian. With Tolemak weapons, to be sure, but belonging to the Prince's enemies.

Will the thieves in the marsh be carrying Vinvinnysee gold too?

Banir would have answers.

Naed needed answers. Thus far all he'd encountered were questions.

"The intruder was after you, m'lord," Toth said after they rounded a bend in the corridor. They were alone for the first time, Morys having lagged behind to attend a messenger.

Naed halted. Toth had the look of a man who'd waited for just such an opportunity to speak, but Naed would've preferred another moment, *any* other moment.

The Tolemak's attitude, though not overt, kept him bristling. They were *not* equals, however close in age, build and height. This was D'nalian territory and, while allied with the Prince, was not under any Tolemak thumb.

He huffed out a breath, schooling himself to patience. Toth and he were soon to be family, after all. "And?"

"Why would a man from your father's holding seek to kill you?"

"He's *not* my father!"

Naed flushed, wishing he could cut out his tongue. It had been a knee-jerk response, an impulse boiling too near the surface to be contained on a day when emotions assaulted him from all sides, but he should never have given it voice.

Toth regarded him with eyes so like his sister's Naed's heart sank. Raell would look at him thus, with astonishment, mayhap censure, when she realized she'd pledged herself to a bastard, that he'd withheld the truth about himself from her. It didn't matter he'd not wanted to face that truth or there'd been no time in all the hurly-burly of war to share much more than kisses and promises. He should've been honest with her.

But Toth was merely nodding now. "Lord Dranoel and Lady Vyenne. I see." He cast Naed a measuring look. "'Tis more to you than I'd have guessed, m'lord."

The cylinder beneath Naed's tunic and chest armor slid across his heart. *More than you think.* He resisted the urge to press his hand over it. "Your sister and I have much to speak of." He hoped Toth would give him the chance to do so.

The Tolemak surprised him with a grin. "Aye, that

you do." He chuckled. "That you do, indeed."

Seeing no reason for humor, Naed fished for a response and came up with what he should've said earlier, despite the Tolemak's attitude. "Thank you for seeing to my mother's safety."

Toth shrugged. "'Twas not all my doing." He indicated the wolfhound.

"Even so." He stroked Beauty's head and tried to relax his shoulders.

"As to Lord Alwyl, 'twas in my mind to wonder why it should matter when he received news. Now I see you believed him ignorant of your true parentage."

"Sisters Three! I was ignorant myself till I read Dranoel's will!" Naed flushed again. Bouncing a fist off the wall, he cursed his mother for the coloring that made him prone to it and himself for a tongue without restraint.

Despite the good humor of a moment ago, Toth had earlier displayed the natural suspicion of an older brother toward a sister's suitor. That the suitor was D'nalian no doubt multiplied suspicion. In the space of heartbeats, Naed had thrown in bastard and a fit of temper to boot. He needed to rein in the energy coursing through him or he'd thoroughly ruin his standing with Raell's family, not to mention shame himself as a D'nalian.

He faced Toth. As long as the Tolemak knew this much, he might as well know the rest. After all, Lord Wendelmyr was no doubt spreading the word among the southern lords. "Until these letters were dispatched, no one outside Druemarwin, save the Prince and Lady Aerid, knew the truth. And they discovered it when I did." He drew in a long breath and placed the blame where it belonged. "Apparently, my mother excels at keeping secrets."

"So I've gathered."

At the dry tone, Naed frowned. There was no censure in Toth's expression. Instead, the gold-brown eyes glinted with something suspiciously like sympathy. Then it vanished, replaced by the Tolemak's previous glower.

"Nonetheless, is it possible Lord Alwyl's behind this? He must've guessed where Lady Vyenne was bound."

That a man who'd sheltered him from birth, who Naed thought he knew, might turn so quickly to murder was a conclusion he did not want to entertain. He shook off the chill of it. "The man Gam killed was a disgraced soldier. Mayhap he had a grudge."

"I'd have pegged this attack to enemies of the Prince, given the weapons in the marsh. Now..." Toth crossed his arms. "Mayhap we're meant to think that, m'lord."

The man was like a dog with a bone. A Tolemak trait, no doubt, as Banir possessed it too, but Naed refused to leap to any conclusions. His emotions had ruled him enough for one day.

"The weapons imply planning. The timing is short if the letters are a true catalyst. Do not forget that." If Toth read admonishment in his reply, so be it. The Tolemak needed to know whose home he was a guest in.

Morys trotted around the corner with news Banir had returned. Glad of the interruption, Naed directed them to the courtyard. He took the rear, waiting till they'd reached the first landing before he tugged at the leather thong digging into his neck.

Tonight, he had much to say to Raell, but this burden he had to carry alone.

Chapter Sixteen

Dinner was a small, awkward affair in the lord's private chambers. Raell sat at Naed's left and his mother sat at his right with Toth beside her. Banir filled the seat beside Raell. Naed's Second was a man of few words and Raell appreciated that tonight. He also clearly made Lady Vyenne uncomfortable. Sharing a table with three Tolemaks from the 'barbaric' West had to be an ordeal for a woman used to the highest D'nalian society. And the furnishings, while comfortable, undoubtedly didn't meet Tumin standards.

They suited Raell just fine. The tapestries, though faded with age, muffled the lingering chill of the stone better than those in Albon. Tables and chairs hewn from some kind of oak—*marsh grown, belike*—were worn smooth with years of use but padded with fresh deerskin cushions. Pewter utensils and cups graced the table as they had this morn. Since then, someone tried to bring up the shine, mayhap to honor the lord's arrival. Raell ran a finger over her cup. Their effort, heartwarming as it was, hadn't managed to hide the stains, nicks and dents of heavy use. Clearly, Druemarwin was not in the mainstream of D'nalian society. Equally clear was the lack of a woman's touch.

How long has Lady Vyenne's sister been dead? A long time judging by the garments Raell had been given. She would have plenty to do here as mistress, but she'd not interfere with the kitchen. The food, although plain, smelled delicious, as if the cook had a gift with spices. She closed her eyes and inhaled. This was a place well lived in, and her mother would approve.

If only the master hadn't somehow switched skins with another person entirely.

Raell cast a narrow-eyed glare at the man who'd made her heart weightless and her hopes soar mere hours ago, the man she'd ridden a fortnight to join. But Naed continued to push food around on his plate and ignore her despite all his earlier attentions. That stung like a slap to the face until she realized his preoccupation excluded everyone.

Apparently unaffected, Banir and Toth attacked their meal with the enthusiasm of the recently deprived.

Raell rolled her eyes. *Men—all stomach and no emotions.* How else could they miss the tension radiating off Lady Vyenne? Glances she darted at her son fairly prickled with annoyance. Or was it frustration? In the Great Hall they'd greeted each other like adversaries anticipating a duel. Hardly the mother and son reunion Raell had expected, even considering the D'nalian penchant for restraint. Mayhap that explained some of the misery always shadowing Naed's eyes. Certainly it prompted his uncharacteristically rude behavior now.

Whatever the issue between them, it was prudent to hold her tongue, however difficult. To distract herself, she stabbed a chunk of some kind of vegetable. At end-of-winter storage, all vegetables looked alike—wrinkled, withered, and dry. She hoped it wasn't parsnip, but she would choke it down if it was. Her mother had drilled into her during barren early spring no one refused what was put before her. Food was life and all folk, even the lord's children, starved or survived together.

She chewed and swallowed what proved to be a tasty morsel, before shifting her attention to Naed. He looked thinner, as though the fortnight of hard travel had taken a toll. Had he encountered enemies beyond the skirmish where Toth lost the trail? The few glimpses of his eyes showed them more haunted than usual—even considering his mother's surprise appearance.

Her indignation faded. He had reasons aplenty for being preoccupied, troubled even. Raell hoped she could soothe him. Indeed, his expression mirrored her father's when last she'd seen him. Her heart contracted, and she picked at her food. In the turmoil of the past days, she hadn't thought of her father. She sipped wine and sent a prayer to the Sisters for his continued health and well-being.

Dark copper brows drawn together, Naed pushed away his barely touched dinner. "Within the next days, the southern lords will gather here."

Lady Vyenne started. A tiny frown marred her fine brow. "You called an assembly."

"I did."

The tension level in the chamber spiked. Even Banir and Toth put down their knives. Raell chewed her lip. Were D'nalian assemblies risky? A Tolemak assembly, aye, as it involved shouting, insults, and duels, both public and private. Deaths occurred, sometimes. She hardly expected such from D'nalian masters of self-restraint. Mayhap the risk was because they would be discussing war, something D'nalians studiously avoided.

Lady Vyenne pursed her lips. "Alwyl will hear of it."

"Indeed."

"You expect him to come?"

"I expect him to take note, as perhaps he has already done, since he must have noticed your absence by now."

This was news. Raell hadn't given any thought to why Lady Vyenne had been traveling with so few attendants, but she'd barely been in a condition to think about much until this morn.

Across the table, Toth flicked her a glance.

You know something, don't you?

He smirked.

Ass!

A tilt of his head to mother and son redirected her attention.

Although Lady Vyenne's cheeks had pinked, she maintained her ramrod straight posture. "What did your...*inquiries* this afternoon lead you to discover?"

Naed rotated his cup between thumb and fingertips. He studied the wine swirling inside for so long, Raell wondered if he'd mesmerized himself. He'd nearly mesmerized her as she waited for him to respond.

"Mother, I need you to think carefully. Did Dlaniger visit Tumin at any time in the last twelvemonth?"

Dlaniger? That was the missing and disgraced heir, wasn't it?

Lady Vyenne's mouth puckered as if she'd tasted bitterfruit. "Since Dlaniger was well aware of my feelings toward him, I doubt he would've called upon me if he had come to Tumin. If he met with Alwyl, he might've done so privately." She fixed her son with a withering glare. "Why? What does that have to do with recent events?"

"The man Gam killed was carrying Vinvinnysee gold. So were the men who ambushed you in the marsh."

"I fail to see the connection." She deposited her purse, which Banir had recovered from the marsh, on the table. "Gold is gold. I very likely have both Adanak and Tolemak coins here."

Raell considered her own purse. His mother had a point. What could possibly be the significance?

"Dlaniger was paid in Vinvinnysee gold."

"For what?" Frustration poured off Lady Vyenne in waves. "Speaking of my wayward nephew, where is he? A man of his nature can't have taken the news of your inheritance without contesting it."

Naed raised his head. The skin stretched tight over his cheekbones, and his eyes fairly blazed. "Dlaniger is dead."

Color drained from his mother's face. Her sharp intake of breath echoed in the chamber.

Raell gaped. *The missing and disgraced heir is dead?*

Across the table, Toth's eyes widened.

A tiny spurt of satisfaction shot through her. Clearly, he hadn't known *that*. Not that she had, of course, but...

At her elbow, Banir sat as still as ever, dark eyes watching.

Before the hearth, the wolfhound raised its great gray head.

Clearing her throat, Lady Vyenne broke the silence. "You...you didn't kill him, did you?"

"Do you think so little of me, Mother, that I'd kill my own blood for a title?"

He'd spoken softly, but Raell had never seen Naed look so dangerous, or so angry. Like fire contained—barely—in the stillness of ice. She swallowed. And shivered.

The wolfhound whined and sat up.

Lady Vyenne pressed a hand to her heart, but she held her son's gaze. "'Tis a fair question, given the circumstances. And others will ask it."

He made fists, knuckles whitening, and then flattened his hands on the table. "Dlaniger had a plan to kill the Prince. When I learned of it, I rode like the Demon to stop him. But I was seconds—*seconds!*—too late, or 'tis sure I would've done the deed." He met Lady Vyenne's aghast stare. "Dlaniger was an *assassin*, Mother. He hired himself to whoever offered the gold, and he dealt in death. My kin, *my blood relative* was a murderer for hire!" He shoved the cup away, where it teetered but didn't fall.

"I...see." Lady Vyenne smoothed hands over her purse.

That the assassin hired to kill the Prince was related to Naed was not news. Raell had heard that tidbit within days of Val-Feyridge's fall. But his *cousin*? She glanced from Naed to his mother. Lady Vyenne's own nephew? As much as Raell knew of D'nalian society, that kind of scandal ought to rock its foundations. No wonder the chamber crackled with emotion.

Lady Vyenne looked shaken but not cowed by the

news. "Even so—"

"He killed Dranoel, Mother. Whether it was his arrow or that of his minion, he caused the death of my father. May the Sisters curse him for that! He killed his own blood and mine! Demon *damn* him!"

****

Vyenne must have said appropriate words when she left the table, but her mind was a blur. Somehow, she'd climbed the stairs to the living quarters because she found herself standing alone in the middle of her chamber. Her body had moved of its own accord, as in a dream.

A nightmare.

She was ruined. They all were.

Except Alwyl.

She grimaced. He could recover from the scandal of her infidelity if he repudiated her and her son, if he shunned all connected to Druemarwin. That, done quickly enough—*Perhaps already!*—would be enough to salvage the reputation of the most influential lord in D'nalee and, mayhap, shield his legitimate children.

Though her heart ached for them, she needn't concern herself about the twins. They were securely wed, each having produced at least one heir for their fine, upstanding husbands. Allyn and Fennyn—well, they were their father's sons and would align with him.

But Alwyl...

Bitterness flooded her mouth. If she hadn't hated her husband before, she could—*must*—hate him now. *If* he were guilty of what Naed implied. All the more damning that she'd considered the possibility herself mere hours ago. And that was before she'd learned about Dlaniger.

Dlaniger and Alwyl?

No. There'd been no sign in all these years Alwyl suspected anything about Naed's birth. She'd have known. Her life, and Naed's, depended on knowing.

If Alwyl and Dlaniger worked together, conspired, it had to be political, not personal.

Vyenne sat on the bed she'd not slept in yesternight and weighed the gold in her purse. Vinvinnysee gold. Tumin colors. Betrayal of the worst kind.

How could you kill your father, Dlaniger! Tears ran down her cheeks. *Dranoel, my dear one!* She stuffed a fist into her mouth, but racking sobs escaped anyway.

Bastard! Bloody damned bastard!

Her throat burned, her breath came in ragged gulps, but she huffed at the irony of it all: that a bastard-by-heart should escape society's judgment, but a bastard-by-birth should suffer as Naed so clearly did.

You have nothing to be ashamed of, my son.

Standing, she paced to the mantel and held icy hands close to the flames. In the flickering light, bones beneath her flesh glowed red. *Sisters, forgive me, but I would've killed Dlaniger too!*

Despite the heat radiating from the hearth, she shivered.

I'll never be warm again.

She straightened and hugged herself. No one else would. Not in the way that mattered.

Naed had to be saved. He'd done nothing wrong but be born.

He must not suffer!

She would see to it, however she could, Alwyl be damned.

Chapter Seventeen

Raell cornered her brother at the foot of the Great Hall staircase. "What are you not telling me?" Even though Lady Vyenne had disappeared into the living quarters above and the stairs looked deserted, she kept her voice low. This was between the two of them. "Naed's father—the Lord of Tumin—lives, aye? They speak of him—all day they've spoken of him as if he does. I don't understand. What does Naed mean? 'Tis Lord Dranoel who's dead, aye?"

Toth stared at the chamber they'd exited, as if the light spilling from a still open door required watching. "You were there. Piece it out for yourself."

When she grabbed his sleeve, he shifted his glare to her.

"'Tis for Lord Naed to explain, not me. Just as 'tis for you to tell him why we've come."

"Ass!" She could pummel him with her fists as she'd done when they were children, but he'd keep his secrets. Flinging away his sleeve, she focused on the lord's chamber. "I mean to."

If only she knew what to say.

I've come so you can wed me and bed me afore the man my father promised me to can find me.

Gah! How stupid the truth sounded when stripped of all heart and put bluntly.

And she couldn't shake a niggling fear Naed would

balk if she used the word *promise*. He was D'nalian, after all.

Sisters, help me! The words would come. They had to. She could delay no longer. The need to touch the man she loved nigh overwhelmed her. She'd traveled a fortnight through unfamiliar territory, endured cold, hunger, a twice-stitched upper arm to reach him. To be this close without threading her fingers through that unruly copper hair was too great a yearning to suppress.

Banir exited, leaving the door ajar. Naed would be alone now. She stepped away from her brother.

"Have a care, Raell."

He'd merely closed a hand over her forearm, but her wound throbbed. *Damn and blast!* He knew exactly what he was doing, but she refused to give him the satisfaction of a wince.

Instead, she presented him with her most imperious look. "Why? What troubles you?"

"Adanak gold. Treachery among blood. 'Tis more here than mayhap even the Prince knows." He squared up before her, brows lowered. "I was sent to protect you. To do the Prince's will and hand you over to a husband, not land you in a blood feud."

"A runaway wife is hardly a blood feud."

"See what you think when you hear the whole of it." Another glance at the spilled light, then his eyes glittered down at her. "For all his pretty words, your Lord Naed's but a man. 'Twould do you well to remember that."

"Aye, 'tis sure, he's a *man*!" She twisted free. "Do you think I'd fall in love with aught less?" She spun away before he could make some ill-mannered retort about D'nalians—and saw Naed. He'd thrown on his cloak and was striding away across the dimly lit Great Hall.

"Thank you, dear brother," Raell growled over her shoulder. "Now I have to chase after him. Again."

She hurried away from Toth, thinking fast. Naed was no doubt headed into the damp night, but she had no cloak. To fetch one from her chamber would take time, and she'd lose sight of Naed. Her knowledge of Druemarwin's layout was limited to the Great Hall, the lord's private chamber, and the living quarters. To go beyond that and not become lost, Raell needed to follow him. If only she weren't already chilled…

****

The hooded and cloaked man had waited for hours while the bastard of Druemarwin ate a fine dinner and drank good wine before a fireplace throwing warmth into all the dark, cold places.

In *there*, that chamber where the door remained firmly shut.

Not out here in the Great Hall where shadows had darkened to ink and winter-long chill gripped the stones. That chill had seeped into his feet, numbing his toes faster and more thoroughly than the worst snow and ice he'd endured in the marsh. The bastard would pay for that. If only the man would move, be done with dinner and depart the chamber so he could move too, get out from behind this tapestry and shake some blood into his limbs.

He'd slipped into Druemarwin late in the afternoon, he and his men folding into a caravan of supplies from Kassi fortress. That had been a blessing. He knew some of the Kassi guardsmen, had cast beads with them over the years. They clapped him on the back, vowed to win back what they'd lost to him last spring. He laughed, made promises he wouldn't keep, and joined them as if he'd never left the employ of Druemarwin. It was a gamble, but a safe one. *Lord Naed—the bastard!—*was unlikely to admit what lay between them.

Honor—hah! The old master had been a fool for it. And so was the new one.

Master Dlaniger had the right of it. A man could make his way in the world with honor, as D'nalians had done for generations, or he could play the honor-bound for gold. He grinned. Playing them for gold was so much more satisfying.

The chamber door opened. People poured out, actors in the little drama he'd observed earlier.

There was a bride and her apparent guardian.

You've been busy, my lad, courting a Tolemak after losing the Adanak witch to the bastard Prince. He tugged at his tunic neck, remembering Naed's hands at his throat. Nigh a year ago, but he hadn't forgotten. He'd never forget. *If I'd known the witch mattered that much, I would've tumbled her when I had a chance. Then there'd be no bastard for the bastard Prince!*

Or is it yours, after all, my lad? Is that why you're back so soon? Your lord and master suspects?

But that was wishful thinking. And unlikely, given the man he stalked turned up his nose at willing—and lush—kitchen maids. Saving himself for something better, was he? *Mayhap I'll have a go at your soon-to-be widow. Console the poor thing.* He shifted, adjusted himself as his cock came alive. He'd scratched that itch once already, having found Gert alone below stairs. He preferred Elthred, or both together, but up against a wall Gert was as good as any. At least she knew to keep her mouth shut.

Unlike the mother he'd observed, a proper D'nalian lady.

That one looked a right bitch. He'd almost feel for Naed—if he didn't hate him so much. *I'll put you out of your misery, my lad.* He fingered his Adanak blade. *You'll die thanking me.*

Last were the three Tolemaks who went everywhere with Naed—the braggart, the halfwit, and the tracker. The white-skinned riffraff had attached themselves to Naed sometime after the bastard made a hero of himself in the Lancer attack. He knew little of them except they stuck to Naed like a frog's tongue to a fly. The braggart and the halfwit had been sent off on some errands. All that remained was—

The tracker walked out.

He straightened, flexed his fingers on the intricately carved hilt while his heart kicked up. *Not...quite...yet.*

The bride and her guardian lurked by the staircase. And the chamber was too public. He needed someplace with more dark corners, more escape routes.

Patience...

The door opened again and Naed strode out.

Licking his lips, he stepped forward only to freeze mid-stride. The damned bride trotted after the bastard. She'd see, raise the alarm if he followed.

Not to worry. He backed off, changed direction. *You know where he's like to be going.*

****

Drawing even with the lord's chamber, Raell paused. Banir had left without a cloak. Mayhap his remained in the room whose door stood partly open and leaking light.

Raell slid inside, saw the cloak hanging near the hearth, and darted across the chamber. She plucked the garment off the peg and froze.

The wolfhound had come to its feet in near silence. Unblinking, bottomless black eyes fixed on her.

Would it attack? For breathless heartbeats, Raell hugged the cloak. The great gray animal wasn't vicious. Well, it hadn't *yet* been vicious to her or Toth. It was a guardian, Lady Vyenne said. It had guarded all of them yesternight. It must be guarding Naed now. Raell shifted her weight onto her back foot, slowly.

Then why did he leave it here?

Not something she needed to think about now.

Eyeing the beast, she edged away. *One step at a time...*

The animal whined, softly, and glanced toward the door.

When the liquid, soulful gaze returned, Raell's heart thudded—hard—and blood rushed back to her extremities. "He left you, aye? You've just found him again and now he's gone off and left you here alone." Lowering her arms, she blew out a breath. "I understand. Aye, I do." She threw the cloak over her shoulders, wondering how many other hearts Naed had laid to waste in his wake.

She offered her hand to the dog, who sniffed it delicately. "He doesn't deserve us, you know. Come. You find him and we'll tell him that."

"Raell?"

She and the wolfhound turned as one.

Naed stood framed in the doorway. He looked

puzzled, wary.

Her heart leaped, and then stuttered. He hadn't expected to see her, hadn't been seeking her. Did he hear what she told the dog? She didn't think so, or he would've looked contrite.

Straightening, she said calmly, coolly, as if she had every right to be found in his private chamber, "I thought you'd gone out."

"Aye, but I forgot—"

"Your dog?" That was waspish, but justified. And she could hardly call it back.

He colored. "My gloves."

Her chin shot up and her eyes narrowed. *Wrong answer!* Exchanging a look with the wolfhound, Raell stepped beside the animal's shoulder. "She loves you, you know. 'Tis sure, you're breaking her heart to swoop into her life and then leave her like this." This anger, this frustration was not at all what she should be feeling to finally be in the same room, alone, with the man she loved, but it fired in her cheeks and shot words out of her mouth. "She's come all this way to find you and you can't—"

Naed lunged across the room, knocking aside a chair, and seized her face in both hands. She caught a glimpse of his eyes, stark and full of need, before his mouth came down on hers and she stopped thinking altogether.

She gripped his arms as momentum shoved her against the tapestry. Hard stone hit her back, stinging areas she'd bruised the night before. She sucked in the taste of him, wine and dinner spices and his own tangy flavor. She licked into his mouth, hungry for more.

Stubble grazed her chin as he came up for air,

gasping. "Sisters, Raell..." Then he thrust his fingers into her hair and ravished her mouth again.

Her fingers curled into his tunic, digging into muscles that flexed and rippled. With a groan, she pulled him closer, wishing she could tear off garments that prevented her from running her hands over hard, smooth flesh beneath. She'd seen him half naked once, the night they'd met and she'd treated his wound. His shoulders were freckled, and a narrow dusting of curly, copper hair crossed his chest. She groped for his tunic laces, desperate to uncover, touch, taste.

He released her face, bumped her against the tapestry again, and blazed a hot, wet trail of kisses down her throat. One hand found her breast, the other snaked around her waist and pulled her hard against him.

Raell yelped.

Naed stilled. His breath panted across her cheeks, and he looked at her with dazed, drugged eyes. "Did...did I hurt you?"

He'd jarred her wounded arm, and it hurt like the Demon. *Pain be damned!* She couldn't—wouldn't—have him stop. Her body hummed with want, with all the hunger he'd awakened in mere seconds.

"No," she whispered, and tried to straighten, to crawl back into his embrace.

Still breathing hard, Naed put her at arm's length. A frown creased his brows, and some of the green returned to his eyes in the firelight.

Beside him, the wolfhound sat at attention, watching.

Raell blushed. She'd forgotten the dog. Some of her ardor cooled, and with it, the burn of her wound intensified. In automatic response, she cradled her injured arm.

Naed looked crushed. "I'm a beast! Naught but a beast!" He pounded both fists on the tapestried wall and then dropped to his knees. "Raell, forgive me, please. I wanted you so badly, I—I didn't think. I was too rough."

"It's not your fault." She touched his face, eager to absolve him. "Last night…in the marsh…"

What to tell him? How much to admit just now when she didn't want to distract him? But he leaped up before she could decide.

"Sisters and the Four Winds! The captain told me someone had been hurt, but I never once thought—" He guided her to a chair and made her sit. "What happened? How could your brother let you be injured?"

"I-I fell."

That was true enough. Naed's face had darkened to such a dull red, she feared he would storm out to challenge Toth if she told him more.

"The horses spooked. One knocked me down in the melee." She eyed him. Was that enough for now?

He inhaled, held it, and exhaled with a scowl. "I still shouldn't have been so rough."

"I love you," she said as the wolfhound laid its head in her lap. "I wanted to be with you."

He choked, knelt at her chairside, and kissed her gently, as if she were the most precious thing in the world. Then he pressed his forehead to hers. "I love you, too, Raell. But you shouldn't have taken such a risk to come."

There it was, the perfect opportunity to tell Naed all.

Raell opened her mouth, but words refused to come. She could blame her blankness on pain still throbbing up and down her arm, or on passion still vibrating through her body, but that would be lying. She was afraid, plain and simple.

Would his honor bind him to her or force him to step aside to Bennin of Nye?

She couldn't bring herself to take that chance.

Someone knocked, cleared his throat. Naed and she turned to the door.

Banir stood there, half inside. "If it suits you, the servants wish to clear away."

Naed's flush deepened. "Of course. Thank you." He stood. "Give us a moment."

Nodding, Banir withdrew.

Raell's cheeks burned. "He was smiling, wasn't he?"

"Him? The man never smiles." He picked both cloaks off the floor, but his lips quirked. "I was going to walk a bit. Would you—would you like to join me?"

Chapter Eighteen

At Naed's order two guardsmen vacated the segment of wall between the tower door and a guard shelter. They likely went no farther than the other side of the warming house, but he appreciated the measure, mayhap illusion, of privacy.

If only he knew what to say, how to begin when his mind was fogged with Raell's kisses, her scent. To clear his head, he gazed over the battlements and breathed.

As usual, following a warm spring day, the earth exhaled what it had stored all the long winter—a cold, damp mist. Like the tattered banners of long forgotten armies, the mist undulated in feathery streamers across Druemarwin's green. Soon, it would all but solidify, rising slowly so that by midnight the fortress would seem adrift on a pale sea. Naed shivered. He was not unacquainted with foggy nights. They came often enough to Tumin, where he'd grown up. But here in the south, ghosts walked. And not just because of the land's ancient roots. Or the burial cairns obscured in the mist. History lived here. And it weighed like a millstone on the cord around his neck.

He'd failed Dranoel there, out on the green, failed to take down the Prince after stripping the man of his sword. A bit of acid leaked into Naed's stomach, burning as it always did when he numbered his failures.

You'd not be where you are now if you hadn't failed there.

The voice of reason spoke the truth, and that diluted the acid burn. The Prince had spared him, the action at first heaping shame upon shame for losing to a man armed with only a shield. But it had opened a door too, where respect could grow and honor could live and a dream might take root.

A kingdom reunited. A land at peace...You'd not have the woman beside you either, if you hadn't failed that bright spring day nigh a year ago.

Another truth. Another burn, sharper, more incisive.

I don't deserve her. What can she possibly see in me?

Raell's hair gleamed in the torchlight as she looked out over the fortifications. They'd gone a few steps from the tower door, far enough the torch affixed to the structure threw steady light but not heat. Deep shadows, too, or he might've divined her thoughts as she shifted away from a barrel of torch oil tucked into the corner. She'd said little on their climb, staying close behind while Beauty bounded ahead.

The wolfhound snuffled around the vacant guard shelter. The animal was fond of hunting rats, killing what she found and presenting him with the carcasses. Naed sighed. He'd forgotten how much he missed his dog.

He hadn't forgotten how much he missed Raell.

Even now his blood pounded so heavily in his ears he thought she might hear it. The bright spots had faded from her cheeks, leaving them pinked with her natural color and the cold. He wanted to kiss the chill out of them, bring the passion flush up in her face, darken her eyes so the honey-gold irises nigh disappeared as they had not so long ago.

He'd never known want as much as he did in her presence. He thought he loved Aerid, desired her kiss, but she'd never once made his blood run so hot with a mere whiff of her scent. White lilies and musk—he could detect it now wafting from Raell's hair, from the cloak collar where it gapped alongside her throat.

To resist seizing her again, Naed dug gloved fingers into the stone. The beast living inside his flesh had merely tasted, sampled what it hungered for. If he let it rule him, he was no true D'nalian. But—*Sisters, help me!*—how could he contain it when she was the one his heart wanted?

He broke out in a cold sweat. What if she rejected the bastard he was?

Leaning forward, Raell placed a hand beside his on the stone. Not touching.

Did she sense his disquiet? How to tell her what he must, what she had to know?

"I like this place." She lifted her face to his gaze. "'Tis a fine, fair holding, Lord Naed. One to be proud of."

Not what he expected to hear. "You—you've seen but little of it."

She smiled and glanced up beneath thick lashes. "If I were a man, mayhap, but a woman looks at a place with different eyes." She turned fully and laid her hand over his heart. "A woman looks to make a home."

Her hand, for all its gentle pressure, pushed the cylinder containing Dranoel's legacy into his skin. His hopes deflated with the movement. "Raell…"

"I didn't understand at first, but I think I've pieced out why Lady Vyenne is here."

"Forgive me, please. I didn't intend for you to meet my mother this way. She can be…"

"Intimidating?"

The humor in her voice prompted a check of her expression. Aye, there it was, that cat's smile accompanied by twinkling eyes. He sought the twinkle, but she'd lowered her gaze and her smile faded.

"No more intimidating than mine, were she alive. You know my father. 'Tis sure, it took a strong woman to manage him." After a moment, she shrugged. "Besides, your mother is here for the same reason I am. She loves you in her proper D'nalian way."

"Raell, were you not at dinner—?"

"To hear you imply you were born a bastard? Aye, I heard that, finally, when my brother insisted I give what was said some thought." She cocked her head and shot him a severe look. "How does Toth come to know it before I do?"

"I-it came up this afternoon. He's only looking out for you."

Her response was a distinctly unladylike snort. "Mayhap among your kin that would be true. Mine lives but to torment me."

He gaped at her retort and blurted, "That would be my mother's role." Then flushed. He hadn't meant to disparage his mother, but the words had formed without thought.

Her eyes twinkled, and his whole body heated. Heart racing, he licked his lips. "Raell…"

But she wound her fingers into his tunic and he forgot how to form words.

"So, 'tis true then—Lord Dranoel and your mother? 'Tis the real reason you inherited this place?"

"I...uh...I didn't know until after...after I read the will." His tongue was thick, unwilling to do anything but taste the air wafting up from her face, her body.

She'd drawn so close her stomach brushed his tunic. His blood pounded. Without the armor he'd lived in for months, the armor he'd removed before dinner, he could've been naked for all the protection his clothing afforded. Half a step more and she'd know how much he desired her.

Beauty erupted in a barking, snarling rage.

Startled, Naed lifted his head. Had the wolfhound cornered something larger than a rat?

Raell stiffened. "One of the guards is coming."

Naed turned, frowning. Hadn't he told them to keep their distance?

The man approached with purpose, hand on his sword. Not the left hand resting on the pommel, but the sword hand gripping the hilt. Alarm buzzed along Naed's nerves. Behind that man, another turned away from the guard shelter, the door of which shook as if a body battered it from within.

Beauty!

"Get behind me!" He seized his sword. "Guards! Intruders on the wall!"

Where the Demon were the guardsmen?

"The door, Raell! Get into the tower and run down. I'll hold them off."

"Not without you!" She clung to his cloak. "You have no armor! They'll cut you to ribbons."

"There're only two of them." *I hope.* They were taking their time, setting shields. Why had he come up here without his? *Stupid!* He yanked off his cloak and wrapped it around his forearm. Layers of heavy wool would be harder to slice through than a bare tunic sleeve.

There was a clatter behind him.

"Here!" Raell shoved something round at his left hand. "If you won't go, use this!"

He grabbed the handle, smelled oil, and recognized a barrel lid. Wooden, weathered, but better than nothing. Warmth shot through his veins, an absurd little jolt of pleasure. *By all that's holy, I love this woman!* He flashed her a grin. "Clever girl! Now go!"

He didn't look to see if she obeyed. There was no time. With a roar, he charged, hoping to push the intruders back, to startle them with a show of aggression, to give himself room to maneuver.

To give Raell time to escape. *Sisters, help me!*

****

Raell flinched. The ferocious roar curdled her skin and she turned. The assassins broke stride too, and Naed was on them in a rush of flashing steel.

Hand at her throat, she backed against the tower wall. He'd told her to go, but she couldn't. Not yet. Not when—

The tower door creaked open, slowly, stealthily. Raell spun, panic skittering along her nerves. The tip of a sword emerged.

More assassins! She had to bar the door. If she threw the bolt and pin, they'd be locked inside the tower and Naed would be safe.

"Help! Help! Up here!" She flung her body at the door.

Thud! A howl of pain. A falling sword.

"Get back!" Raell fumbled for the bolt, cursing the dainty slippers that gave her no purchase on the stone. *No! No! No!*

The door plowed into her. She sprawled backward two steps and sat down, hard. Her skirt rent. Pain shot through her bruised backside. *I'll never sit again.* Breath hissed between her teeth.

A man charged onto the parapet, holding his wrist, face full of fury. "It's the Tolemak wench!"

"Leave her! You have your orders!" echoed from deep inside the tower.

Demon's Blood! There were two more at least! Naed would never fend off that many. She scrabbled for something, anything to use as a weapon.

"She broke my arm, the bitch! I'll teach you!" The man lumbered toward her.

Raell leaped to her feet, nerves jangling, every muscle prepared to bolt.

Her heart thudded. She had nowhere to go.

****

Naed swung and blocked, swung and blocked. The parapet was narrow and the second assailant hadn't worked up the nerve to dance on the inner edge so they could come at him side by side. From the look in the man's eye, though, he'd be trying it soon.

Run, Raell, run!

Wood shards peppered Naed's face. The makeshift shield splintered with every blow, cracks running deep, endangering the handle. Another heavy blow and he could lose fingers.

Not if I make the cracks work for me.

With a growl, he caught the first man's blade high, wedging it in a crevice. Wood groaned, the blade

170

squealed, stuck fast. He glimpsed surprise in his attacker's eyes. *Good.* Then he wrenched the barrel lid out and down.

Get inside.

The Prince had taught him that—the hard way. He pulled his sword arm in and spun, trapping the man's shield against his body. They careened into the wall. The assailant fetched up hard enough to *oomph* out a breath before Naed rammed his shoulder into the man's jaw.

That should put you down.

To be sure, he delivered a backhanded hilt to the head as he spun out in time to meet the second man's charge.

And his leg faltered.

He'd been running on adrenaline, on the battle blood surging in his veins. On the desperate, driving need to protect Raell, to defend himself and her, to give her time to get to safety in the tower.

Now he went down, crashing into the stone while his attacker's blade whistled over his head. He rolled and scrambled to his feet, as startled as the man who stared at him.

Face aflame, Naed backed up, old wound throbbing, and raised his makeshift shield. He had no time for shame. Not if he wanted to survive.

Get under the opponent's skin.

Another hard-learned lesson from the Prince.

Naed straightened, flashed his teeth. "I like the odds much better now. How about you?"

The man swallowed, circled. A stranger. D'nalian, or he'd have been more aggressive.

Shouts from the courtyard below.

Beauty attacking the door to the guard shelter, barking and barking, the wood shuddering under her weight.

"You're running out of time." Naed matched the man's steps, wary, watching. He rotated the splintered barrel-lid shield, flaunting it. "Did they tell you this would be easy?" Sweat ran down his face. His thigh burned and trembled. How much longer would it hold up? "Either engage or flee."

A clang, a shriek, two figures illuminated beside the tower.

Raell! Dear Sisters, no!

Chapter Nineteen

Think! Her brother's words echoed in Raell's brain. *Watch and think!*

She gave herself a beat, a breath. And her panic receded.

The man was big, angry, *not* thinking. Empty-handed.

Her eyes narrowed. *Bitch, eh?*

She stepped into his charge and rammed the heel of her hand upward at his chin. Bone met bone with a crack, crunch, snap. The impact shuddered all the way to her shoulder, stinging every nerve between.

Damn and blast! She'd only practiced that move, never used it full force. It bloody well *hurt!* She sucked in breath, wanting to shake life back into her hand, but now was not the time.

Yowling, the man staggered back, hands to his face, blood spurting, and banged into the tower door.

She surged forward, got caught in her skirt, and cursed. Grabbing the rent part with both hands, she ripped. Pain shot through her wounded arm, stitches pulled, strained but she had to free her legs.

Her attacker still staggered against the door while someone battered it from inside, yelling. One more push and they'd be out. Who knew how many more there were?

She threw her body at the door, heedless of the

man floundering there, blood and tears streaming down his face. The door thumped into something, bounced, then clanged shut. She drove the bolt home and stuck in the pin.

"Sisters!" She gasped and pushed away.

"Got you, bitch!"

Her brothers had grabbed her by the braid too many times. When the man yanked, she threw her weight into him. He staggered. She pulled his knife and plunged it into his thigh. He went down with a shriek, and she tumbled free, weightless for an instant before she smacked, wounded shoulder first, into the tower.

The parapet swam. A hundred torches sparkled before her vision cleared and all those damned torches ignited in her arm. It lay by her side, a throbbing, useless appendage just when she needed it most.

She'd only wounded the blind beast clambering to his feet in a snarling blood rage. But she had his discarded sword. Gripping the hilt with her good hand, she braced the pommel against the wall and raised the blade tip as he charged.

Shock spread over his face. He backed away, dropped to his knees, and keeled over.

Raell stared at the blood running down the blade and onto her hand. It was warm, slick, and metallic smelling. Her stomach heaved. She rolled to the side and vomited. Then she pulled her knees beneath her and vomited again and again until every last bit of the fine dinner she'd eaten overlay the blood splatter.

****

"Damned Tolemak bitch!" She'd knocked him down ten steps at least, ass over crown, shield caught in his cloak, spinning in the pitch dark till he'd clattered onto a landing and planted his feet. Cursing, he fought free of his cloak, rage pounding behind his eyes and checked himself.

He'd heard the snick of the bolt, locking the tower door. The game was over for tonight. Now to get out before the Druemarwin guard trapped him. Already he heard men below, saw the flicker of a torch.

Not to worry. Some of them knew him as one of their own. He'd trade on their ignorance of his real role as long as he could. Composing himself, he fixed the proper mix of consternation and alarm on his face. Then he launched himself down the stairs, yelling, "They've locked us out! Hurry! We've got to find another way! The master's up there by himself! Hurry!"

The guardsmen took him at his word. They turned with much shouting and poured back out of the tower. He trailed behind, watching them swarm up a nearby open staircase before he slipped into deep shadow beneath it.

Master Dlaniger would be pleased at his ingenuity.

He would *not* be pleased by his Second's continual failure.

He spat blood. The Tolemak bitch cracked his lip with that damned door. She'd pay for that, but he had his primary score to settle first.

Good thing he wasn't out of ideas.

The idiots he employed were expendable. Outsiders all, they knew nothing.

He cast another glance at the parapet, confirming his target still lived. *I know this place better than you do, my lad. And I have friends.*

****

Naed functioned in a blur. Guardsmen, stairs,

corridors and torches shuttled past the fringe of his focus. He had one goal. Get Raell to safety. His leg would not falter, no matter how much it shook under his burden. He would not fail her. Not this time.

"'Tis-'tis not mine. The-the blood's not mine," she insisted as he strode toward the living quarters with her body cradled in his arms.

Sisters and the Winds! How could it not be? Her hands and skirt were soaked with it. She was shivering so hard her teeth clacked.

"Let Gam be the judge of that."

"No! Don't tell Gam. She'll have my head for this." She burrowed into his chest, bone to bone, as if she would crawl inside his skin.

Under his tunic, her charm bit into his flesh. It stung, a tiny cut when the sharp gold edge should've gouged out his heart. He ground his teeth.

"'Tis my head she ought to be having." He'd been stupid. *Stupid!* He should never have taken her to the parapet alone. Not when he knew there had been attacks and intruders in the fortress.

"'Twas another man…or more…in the tower. I-I locked the door."

"I know. You said so afore. Banir will see to it." He hitched Raell closer and suppressed a shudder. He'd barely been able to dispatch two. What if she'd not stopped the third? He dared not think about a fourth. But his mind ran to it anyway, and the shudder rattled his teeth.

She'd killed a man.

The woman he loved had been forced to kill a man, all because he'd acted the fool. He'd put Raell in danger and then failed to protect her. Bile rose up in his throat, but Naed welcomed the burn. He deserved no less.

His mother met him at the top of the stairs to the living quarters. "Sisters, be merciful!" She firmed her lips and opened the nearest door. "Take her in here."

"'Tis not my blood," Raell insisted when Naed lowered her to the bed. She fisted his tunic, holding him awkwardly sprawled across her.

Her scent called to him. Despite mingled odors of fear and fresh blood and his own sweat, her unique scent teased at his nostrils, arising from her hair, her throat, the delicate shell of her ear. For three heavy heartbeats Naed surrendered, covering her with his body, infusing her with the heat venting from his skin, wanting nothing more than to wrap his arms about her and quiet her shaking.

But Lady Vyenne pushed a blanket between their bodies, murmuring, "Aye, we can see. But you've had a shock. Lie back and rest a bit." She separated them with a well-placed arm and shoulder.

At least his mother hadn't been so crude as to yank Raell's hand from his tunic with her not-so-subtle maneuver. And he had his feet under him again even if he had to brace his knees on the bed, but Naed still stabbed a glare at his mother.

Her demeanor radiated calm—the mask he knew so well had slid into place—yet a face drained of color belied her manner. Nonetheless, her voice was brisk when she addressed the maid who hovered at the foot of the bed. "Elda, pour water. In a basin and a cup. And find the cloths Gam didn't use yesternight."

Instead of scowling at her, he ought to give thanks she'd taken charge. Raell needed a woman's help to tend something as intimate as stripping off clothes. Having delivered her to safety, he was useless here, but she clung to his tunic. He needed to go, do…whatever, as long as it got him upright where his injured leg would cease trembling before it turned to mush and he crumpled. Again. His face burned. At least the witness to that incident was dead.

Prying off Raell's fingers was like prying off icicles, slick, red-drenched icicles. His hands shook, but he succeeded in freeing himself and straightening until he became aware of what had soaked into his tunic.

"But the blood…" His head swam.

"I see no gashes in her clothing." His mother shoved a chair behind his legs. "Sit before you fall down."

He sat with a thump and she slapped a cloth into his hand.

"Your head, you're bleeding." She scowled, pointing to her forehead. "Belike, 'tis some of your own blood you see on her." A line had appeared between her brows, and her eyes snapped. "Your arm too. What were you thinking? No armor!" With a huff, she snatched a cup from her maid and bent over Raell. "Take some water," she crooned.

Naed blinked. What had gotten into his mother? Did two different people inhabit her body? Something trickled into his eye. He swiped across his forehead and discovered a fresh red smear. No pain there, but his left arm burned above the elbow where torn fabric glistened.

So, he'd been cut.

He assessed the blood as though it belonged to someone else. Scratches, belike, or he'd have passed

178

out by now. A stitch or two and he'd be fine. If only his mind weren't so muzzy.

There was a cloth in his hand, and he stared at it. He was to press it to his wound. Probably the arm. That was more like to keep bleeding. With an extreme effort, he placed the cloth over the stain.

"I'll not be drugged," Raell mumbled. "Not again."

"'Tis but water. We'll leave the herbs for Gam to decide."

Limbs weighted with lead, mind churning with disjointed thoughts, Naed sat holding his arm while the two most important women in his life eyed each other. They'd had hours together before he arrived. Hours to come to whatever terms they'd negotiated that he was not privy to, terms that allowed Raell to sip from the cup, lie back with a sigh, and allow Lady Vyenne to minister to her.

His heart skittered in his chest, and not merely as aftershocks of battle blood. No, whatever was between them raised alarm bells, and he ought to pay attention to the signals, yet all he could focus on was to repeat, "But the blood…"

His mother shot him an exasperated look. "Belike, she's torn her stitches. Again." She set the cup aside, drew her eating knife, and opened Raell's sleeve to the shoulder.

The scent of fresh blood, warm and sticky-sweet, assailed Naed's senses.

Dots speckled his vision. He swayed in his chair, caught himself, and swallowed. *Sisters!* He was nigh bathed in it, his own and that of others. But this blood was different. It seized him by the throat and dropped the world out from under him, catapulting him into a memory, a moment on a staircase in Tolemak where the stones ran red and his fingers could do naught to staunch the Prince's blood oozing between them.

So much blood, so many wounds...

Glancing at the beamed ceiling, he forced himself to breathe, in and out, until his mother's words penetrated. "Stitches? What stitches?"

Lady Vyenne peeled away the sleeve, and Raell sucked in a breath. "Gam will ne'er forgive me," she groaned.

"Hush now and rest."

His mother turned to take a cloth from her maid, and air fled Naed's lungs. One glimpse of the wound, the stitching, and he knew. This was no injury made by a fall. *Sisters and the Demon!* He'd been too late to protect the Prince, too late to save Krenin, and he was too late for Raell now.

Red hazed his vision, and his words came out in a strangled hiss. "She was cut yesternight, aye? In the marsh? By the bastards that attacked you?"

His mother jerked around, hand going to her heart. "Dear Sisters! Were you not told?"

Raell's blood stained her fingertips. His stomach twisted like a knife to the gut. If he'd wed Raell when he should have. If he hadn't hesitated—*again!*—mayhap she wouldn't have set out to join him. And with naught but her brother as escort!

His pulse hammered at his temples. Rocketing to his feet, he knocked the chair back on two legs. "Where the Demon was her brother? Where was Toth when she was cut?"

"Naed, stop!"

He'd spun toward the door, but his mother

launched herself into his path. Her speed aroused a fresh surge of fury. Even she could move faster than his game leg allowed. A growl escaped his throat.

She whitened but didn't give ground. "Wait. You don't understand. She was dressed as a boy. And armed. No one knew she was...*who* she was until after."

Brows lowered, he glared at her, noting how the mask had slipped, how those eyes, so like his own, glimmered with concern. *For whom, Mother? Whose secret would you protect now?* Fresh acid surged into his stomach. He was done with secrets. Well and truly done.

"Her *brother* knew," he snarled and stepped to the side.

She matched him, first one way then the other, until he growled again and put his hands on her. If she wouldn't give way, he'd hold her in place while he moved around her.

"Naed, listen!" She gripped his arms. "There were half a dozen of them, the villains. That we survived at all 'tis a blessing." Extending a hand, she pressed it to his chest—as if that puny gesture would hold him back. "'Tis no one's fault. Do you hear me? *No one* is to blame."

He heard, but chose not to listen. What did she know about blame?

The room narrowed, the door frame tilted. A hum filled his ears, growing louder. That red haze returned to his vision. He welcomed it, recognizing it from months before, knowing while it terrified him then, it gave him strength. It overrode pain and weakness and gave his body power to do what it wanted—*needed*—to do. He simply had to relinquish control, turn off his mind and let the haze fill him.

So simple...

Bodily moving her aside, he strode from the chamber.

Raell's brother met him halfway down the corridor. The Tolemak had been running. "Raell," he gasped, "Is she—"

Naed lowered his shoulder and body slammed Toth into the wall. "What the Demon kind of brother are you?" He grabbed Toth again and hurled him against the other wall. "How could you let her be hurt? You were supposed to *protect* her!"

The smack of flesh on stone fed his fury. Twice was not enough. Not nearly enough to satisfy the demon raging inside him. With his bare hands, he would drag the Tolemak to the floor, bash his head against the stones, if he could just get his fingers on the blasted man's throat!

A mighty shove bounced Naed against the wall. He saw stars until he shook them away.

Toth stood in the middle of the corridor, fists raised, feet braced apart, eyes blazing. "I could say the same to you, you damned D'nalian bastard! I gave her into your care and look what's happened! She's attacked in your own bloody fortress!"

The words struck like slaps to the face. Like a knife to the heart, twisted. The truth of them staggered Naed back, gasping, before the red haze flooded his body and all he could do was roar and fling himself at the man who dared to make him *feel*!

They crashed to the floor, rolling and grappling, first one on top then the other. The thud of his fists on flesh filled Naed's ears. The impact of his blows shuddered up his arms. The need to pound, pulverize, exorcise *everything* drove him on and on.

Banir pulled them apart. Grodar and Morys grabbed Toth while Banir pushed Naed against the opposite wall. "Leave off, Naed! Leave off!"

He'd been here before, hauled out of a raging fight, Banir holding him back, talking him out of fury trembling to be spent. A memory flitted at the back of his mind: Krenin on his knees, retching. The all-too-familiar sound of panting breaths, his and others, and the scrape of boot soles echoed in the corridor.

"I see you two cannot resist pummeling each other. Pity."

Naed flinched. Not because his mother had shouted. She didn't shout. She employed carefully measured, icy disdain that scraped like needles along his nerves.

"'Tis no one's fault Lady Raell's been hurt." She glared at them from the chamber threshold. "But 'tis sure, you're both to blame for behaving like this!" And she shut the door with a resounding thud.

Naed's face flamed. He shoved out of Banir's grip. He was a grown man. And a lord! How dare his mother chastise him like an unruly child! Heat burned his ears because she'd humiliated him before his fellows—before *Tolemaks*, for Sisters' sake!—not because she was in any way right.

Toth shrugged free of Grodar and Morys. "Back away, lackeys."

Grodar and Morys exchanged a look.

Grodar stuck thumbs in his belt. "What's that you said, young sir?"

"Leave it." Banir centered himself in the corridor. "We've had blood enough for one night."

"Have we?" Toth shouldered past Grodar. His nose bled, and his upper lip had ballooned under it. "Mayhap *I* haven't."

He squared up before Naed even as Banir stood between them, tense and watchful. Toth dragged a bloody-knuckled hand across his mouth, smearing his chin with red. He looked at both hands, then leaned toward Naed and held them out.

"Tell me. Does it make you feel any better, having my blood?"

The red haze had receded, and the aches had begun. He'd bounced up against stone more than once this night, shoved by more than one hand, and the blood spattered on his clothing belonged to…he'd lost track of how many. He ought to have had enough. But his fingers still curled into fists.

"What do you think?" he growled.

Toth searched his face in the torchlight. A muscle in the Tolemak's jaw ticked. Finally, he lowered his arms and stood like a man facing execution. "Then hit me again. Mayhap 'twill make *me* feel better."

Chapter Twenty

Vyenne leaned against the chamber door. She needed a moment to still the trembling. If she could contain it within her body, where her insides quaked like jelly, she could maintain the outward composure the situation demanded.

Dear Sisters, the blood!

She closed her eyes, just for a heartbeat, long enough to suppress the shudder. But the image of Naed bleeding, covered in blood, wounded, flashed behind her eyelids. A memory of Elwyn—poor, gentle Elwyn, his body broken and lifeless—followed. She'd buried one son. She could not—would not—bury this one. And certainly not now, so soon after the death of his father, dear, beloved Dranoel.

Sisters, be merciful! She pressed a hand to her heart, soothing the ache there. The ache that had become a breath-stealing burn.

"Have Toth and Naed hurt each other?"

The girl's concern reminded Vyenne she had no time for these fears. She pushed away from the door and composed her face.

"Not so much as they'd like, mayhap." Anger spiked through her. *Men, hah! Overgrown boys!* She had no power to change that, but she could deal with what had set them off.

She righted the chair Naed had upset and

repositioned it beside the bed. "Why did you not tell Naed the truth of your wound?"

"I meant to. 'Tis sure, I tried." The girl dropped her gaze. "But I feared...I feared..." Her fingers worried the blanket.

Bloodstained fingers. Vyenne gagged. She signaled Elda to bring the basin. With brisk movements, she dipped a cloth and wiped away the offending stain. Action helped, but the smell of blood permeated the room. They would have to burn the girl's gown and wash all the linens. But that was a matter for later.

Why was everything with this girl so difficult? "He should not have discovered the truth this way."

The girl's eyes snapped. She'd been deathly pale before, even for a Tolemak, but a hint of color rose in her cheeks. "Aye, I know, but I have brothers."

"And I have sons. What of it?"

"Well then, 'tis sure you know what *fools* men can be when they think someone they care for has been hurt or wronged or threatened. Demon's Blood!" She flung out her hand, scattering water drops. "I could see it in Naed's eyes, all evening I could see it. You've only to look at my brother to know Toth's the same. Mad, passionate, and too proud to resist bashing someone's head in!" Her tirade spent, she collapsed onto the pillow and closed her eyes. "I knew this would happen if I told him."

With three fingers, Vyenne wiped moisture from her cheek. The droplets were water, no more. Even if they did smell of blood. Without looking, she dried her fingers and handed the bowl to her maid. Calm, control, discipline, with these she would spill nothing, reveal nothing.

Raell was right about her brother and Tolemaks in general. Were they not ever the first to raise sword or wield knife? But as much as the girl professed to love Naed, she apparently knew naught of D'nalians.

"Passion is not valued as a D'nalian trait. Nor is bashing heads in."

The girl's teeth had stopped chattering. For several heartbeats, she studied Vyenne with gold-brown, considering eyes. "Mayhap that's why Naed's so unhappy. He has a great and passionate heart. Your values make him an enemy of himself."

Vyenne reeled. The girl couldn't have stunned her more if she'd reared up and slapped her. "How dare you! I nearly lost my son tonight. Do not lecture me about values you know naught about."

"Values? 'Tis *fear* you should be thinking of. Aye! You're terrified. Or you should be. 'Tis sure, I am." She shuddered, and color bled from her cheeks. Her voice fell to a whisper. "I killed a man tonight. So much death in so few days..."

Her legs moved restlessly under the blanket as she rolled to her side and curled up. "'Tis sure, both Naed and I could've died. But I did what I had to, and so did he. And now we're alive, both of us, and there's blood on our hands...so much blood... Oh, Sisters!"

The sound of dry heaves spurred Vyenne to action. She snatched the bowl from her maid and held it while the girl brought up nothing but gall. When she collapsed, spent and sweating, Vyenne pressed a damp cloth to her forehead.

"Sleep," she urged.

When the girl's breathing evened out, Vyenne sent her maid to see what kept the healer. The door latched, and she waited until the footsteps faded before she leaned forward, buried her face in her hands and sobbed for the second time this long and terrible night.

****

They'd emptied the wine stocks in the lord's private chamber, he and Toth and the others, and Naed sent Morys to the cellar for more. It seemed the thing to do, drown their shared misery in flagons of the stuff.

Naed contemplated the dregs in his cup. If only it could wash away the shame. Banir slipped in and out, bringing the captain of the guard one time and Beauty another. The wolfhound whined, licked Naed's hands and lay at his feet, only to watch him with dark, soulful eyes.

He understood. They'd both failed. Miserably. His gut clenched when he thought of Raell and how close she'd come to being killed.

The captain of the guard reported three attackers were dead. Banir had found blood on a tower landing, and the guardsmen reported someone—no one could say who—had rushed down to head them off. Banir had set the guardsmen to search for anyone with a fresh injury.

Old Gam had come. With much tsking and considerable rough pulling, she stitched Naed's wounds and applied unguent. The healer put a few stitches in Toth's head, too, but she refused to mix pain-deadening powder with the wine they'd drunk.

"Boys." She cackled when she left them.

Ears burning, Naed cringed. *Boys, indeed!* He was full grown and a D'nalian. He ought to have mastered his temper by now. But the evidence he hadn't was writ all over his knuckles and Toth's face.

That evidence sprawled in an armchair. The one eye Toth could open fully was glassed over, but he raised his goblet in Naed's general direction. "I'll give you this, Lord Naed. 'Tis clear to me now, you're a fool for love."

Seven times a fool for all the damage I've done this night.

Not so much to Toth, though. Tolemaks were surprisingly forgiving of physical violence. Whatever the grievance, a mutual bashing, followed by shared aches and the consumption of spirits usually cleared the air. Both Krenin and Banir had taught him that. Another hard lesson, useful in the long months he'd served the Prince, but one mayhap not to be applied so generally in the heart of D'nalee, where D'nalians did not behave like Tolemaks, nor were they expected to.

Rousing his D'nalian sense of decorum, he cleared his throat. "'Tis your sister we're speaking of."

"Aye, and she's a handful, she is." Toth slopped a toast. "You'd best wed her ere I have to beat you again."

"Beat him?" Grodar scoffed. "From where I sit, young sir, you're a sight more bloodied."

"Only…" Toth blinked at the wine dribbling into his lap, then recovered his train of thought. "Only 'cause he fought a few D'nalians afore me. They warmed him up."

Naed wished he had a head for wine. Two cups and he could barely keep his eyes open. Of course, the night's exertions had played their role. He ached, but thanks to the wine, not as much as he would tomorrow.

"'Tis sure, he has the right of it," Banir said.

Naed focused on his Second, the man who insisted

he wash and change clothes when all he wanted was to sleep. And forget.

He blinked. Mayhap he'd already forgotten. Just as he'd lost track of this conversation. "The right of what?"

"Lady Raell." Banir filled Naed's empty cup with what looked suspiciously like water. He wrapped Naed's hand around the stem. "She followed you here with naught but her brother as escort. 'Tis sure she would have you wed her. And soon, else she'll be compromised."

"I mean to wed her."

"Aye, you've said. 'Tis time to do so."

Naed frowned. Something niggled at his brain. He turned toward Toth. "The Prince...he sent you?"

"D'you think I'd have come otherwise?" Toth expelled a long, loud belch. "D'you think I want my sister wed to a D'nalian? To live in this fog-bound pile of stone? No offense, m'lord, but to my way of thinking..." His eyelids drooped until a log popped in the fire. He flinched, winced, and hugged his cup to his chest. "At least you've some powerful good wine in your cellar."

"But the Prince...it was his express wish—"

"Aye, and Lady Aerid. Daft girl was going to bolt. I was ordered—ordered!—to keep her safe." He grimaced. "Look how that's gone." He lifted his cup, found it empty, and groaned. "Bloody, stubborn healer. More wine! I'm not numb enough yet."

Morys arrived lugging a small cask. Toth cheered, and Grodar got up to pour another round.

Banir waved him away from Naed's cup. Leaning forward, he set a splintered circle of wood on the table.

The smell of torch oil wafted into Naed's nostrils, and his eyes widened. How in the Name of the Demon had he fended off two attackers with something that small and brittle?

"Good thinking." Banir rotated the barrel lid as if testing the weight, the maneuverability. "Belike it saved your life."

"'Twas the Lady Raell's idea." How she'd thought of it, and under such circumstances, still amazed him.

Banir cocked an eyebrow, but the dark eyes betrayed no surprise.

Weariness and wine fogged Naed's brain. He was missing something here, and he'd lost track of the conversation again. "What?"

"Your lady...'twas not luck she killed her attacker. I saw the body."

He longed to drop his head onto his arms and sleep where he sat. But the Tolemak regarded him with those steady eyes that meant this was important. If only he could make sense of it.

"What?"

Banir sighed. Setting down the barrel lid, he gripped Naed under the arms and led him to a padded bench along the wall. Folding a cloak for a pillow, he made Naed lie down and covered him with another cloak. "Wed her. And soon."

"Aye," Naed murmured. "I mean to." But whatever he intended slid away as quickly as consciousness.

Chapter Twenty-One

Raell stood before the looking glass and considered how to conceal a sword beneath her skirt. Whoever claimed D'nalians were peaceful, trustworthy people was a fool or a liar. She'd not be taken in again, not after yesternight's events.

At least in Tolemak she could arm herself openly.

Midmorning light filtered through east windows in the late Lady of Druemarwin's chamber, illuminating Raell's reflection and the garments spread on the bed and draped over every available chair. Turning this way and that, she tested the fall and heft of the fabric.

She'd woken just after dawn, sweating and heart thumping, with Old Gam snoring softly at her bedside and Lady Vyenne gone. Images burned behind her eyelids, some frighteningly realistic but, once she was awake, wholly untrue. Naed was alive. The attackers were human. And there'd been but four. The best way to banish lingering fears was to arise and greet the day. Nothing encountered in the sunshine could possibly terrify her as much as the vivid imaginings of sleep.

She'd called for a bath, some broth and bread to break her fast, and summoned Lady Vyenne's maid. Together with Old Gam they'd gone to forage once more through the late mistress's clothing in search of additional garments to alter. After ages of bending, draping, dressing and pinning, Raell blew a wisp of hair from her face and scowled at her image. If she'd thought to pack some of her own things instead of fleeing Albon like the Demon Himself snapped at her heels, she wouldn't be playing the beggar now.

What was done was done. Today was what mattered. Today, her arm throbbed dully under a new bandage, bread and broth settled her nausea, and she'd accumulated a new array of scrapes and bruises to add to the vivid purpling of her backside. She could sit, just barely, and only on a cushion. She'd wear the sling Gam insisted on, but that was a small inconvenience as long as she could find a place for her sword.

That sword, still sheathed, was grasped at arm's length—as if its very nearness could slice flesh—by the woman kneeling at Raell's feet.

"The hilt, m'lady," Elda pleaded, "'tis too big to hide. And the weight too...'tis more than these fabrics will bear."

Damn and blast! She'd feared as much after pawing through the garments. Despite the damp climate, these D'nalian ladies insisted on going about clothed in entirely impractical fabrics. That troublesome lock of hair returned to tickle her nose. She blew it away and stared down the woman in the mirror.

Never again would she be caught without a weapon. Never again would that unreasoning panic paralyze her and push her against a wall. As long as she carried something with a blade anywhere on her person, she could stand up to it. She'd prefer the comforting weight of her sword right at her hip, but she could make do. For now.

"Very well, but I'll have some kind of dagger in the left sleeve and this long knife beneath the right pocket here." Raell held out her hand, and Gam passed her the sheathed blade. "If the fabric will not bear it, I'll fasten it to my leg like a trapper's knife and reach it through a slit in the pocket. And no more slippers." She kicked away dainty footwear Elda had pushed toward her. "I want boots, something with a solid sole. Decorate them however you wish, but I want something hard enough to kick with."

The maid blanched.

Old Gam chuckled.

Lady Vyenne opened the chamber door and halted. For two heartbeats she stood thus, before she squared her shoulders and stepped inside.

Raell watched with narrowed eyes as Naed's mother picked her way around garments and took a seat on the now empty trunk. Surely the woman had something to say. But she merely folded her hands in her lap.

When the silence lengthened, Raell raised her chin. "I'll not be caught unarmed again."

"Events yesternight would seem to support your concern."

That was an unexpected retort. Head cocked, she studied the woman who sat primly on the trunk, much the same as she had the day before.

Beneath her bland expression, Lady Vyenne's face was pale, drawn. Sunlight revealed fine lines and crinkles Raell hadn't noticed in the softer light of torches and candles. And her eyes were bloodshot, as if she hadn't slept.

Raell huffed. No one in Druemarwin had slept. Except mayhap herself, and that had been filled with nightmares.

Dark circles marred those fine green eyes, so like Naed's, and a lump thickened her throat. The woman had more than enough cause to worry. She'd had her own life threatened, found her son consorting with Tolemaks—both politically and personally—and nearly lost him to assassins. All within two short nights. A flush crept up Raell's throat. If only she'd held her tongue yesternight. What she'd said was truth, and it needed to be said, but mayhap not just then.

"I would like to apologize for…how I spoke to you yesternight. 'Tis a failing of mine to say what I think when I think it. I should've been more considerate."

Lady Vyenne's lips curved a fraction. She made a small movement with one hand. "'Twas an…eventful night. Mayhap we both spoke…truth…in less than diplomatic words." She smoothed her skirts and met Raell's gaze. "I lost a son in the Northern Wars. Naed's second eldest brother, Elwyn. If truth be told, I loved him nigh as much as Naed. However—" She held up a hand to stop Raell's response. "—intruders have never entered Tumin, and I have never had to face such violence in my house as you have done these past days. Clearly, your skills, however uncommon, have proved their value. More than once."

Heat rushed up Raell's face. She bit her tongue and accepted the compliment with as much grace as she could muster, understanding the effort Naed's mother had made in offering it despite her evident disdain of all things Tolemak. This fiercely proud, self-contained woman had unbent herself—before witnesses, no less!—and met Raell's apology with something similar.

Similar, but not the same.

How had Naed survived in such a cold household?

Where had his heart come from?

Mayhap from his father—his *true* father, not the one in whose house he'd been raised.

Turning to the mirror, Raell angled herself so she could watch Lady Vyenne's face. "Tell me, if you would, what was Lord Dranoel like?"

Naed's mother shot her a sharp look.

Gam laughed. "Proud. Loud. A bull of a man."

"But honorable," Lady Vyenne added, studying her hands.

"Aye, true t' his word he was. Always."

"And kind. Accepting."

Naed's mother still hadn't raised her gaze, but Gam nodded and mused, "He'd take in strays, he would. Gave me that Adanak orphan when he saw I needed help. She what's become a lady now. Come up in the world, she has, wed t' the bastard prince."

Raell blinked. This was news. "Lady Aerid—*you* trained her?"

"Aye. A true gift from the Sisters, that one."

Lady Vyenne looked up at this. "You both know this woman?" A line appeared between her brows. "Does my son?"

"Oh, aye," said Gam. "Friends they were. When the master wanted her safe from the bastard prince's army, your son made it so." The old woman tilted her head. "Though he's ne'er said how 'twas done."

A frisson of awareness tickled Raell's spine. *I know how. She told me.* Her stomach curled into a knot. *But Naed hasn't.*

The old woman laughed. "'Tis all well now. She's wed an' he's the new master."

So he was, and he and Lady Aerid were leagues

apart now. And yesternight Naed had kissed her as if he were as starved for her taste as she for his. Raell mentally shook herself. Lady Aerid had helped her come to Naed. The woman *wanted* Raell and Naed together. So did the Prince. Her fears were foolish imaginings inspired by yesternight's emotions.

A subtle shift in Lady Vyenne's posture drew Raell's gaze to the woman's reflection. If possible, she sat even more upright, and the knuckles of her clasped hands shone white.

Something we said has upset her. Mayhap about Lady Aerid?

But when Lady Vyenne spoke, she said, "Tumin seems to be quite out of touch regarding this prince and his plans. Mayhap both of you could enlighten me since my son has yet to do so."

Uh-oh. Raell's heart pinged, both for Naed and his mother. Much as she was ignorant of Naed's previous life, she at least knew who he'd aligned himself with and why. "The Kingdom, m'lady," she said gently, "'tis to be remade and the lands brought together."

"Aye, that much I understand from what's been said these past two days. That and the Crown being found. What I fail to understand is my son's role. How in the Name of the Sisters did he come to be attended by Tolemaks and acting as Second to a Tolemak prince?"

Lady Vyenne's voice hadn't risen, but she'd compressed her lips to a white line. Raell's heart throbbed again. The world was changing, shifting right under their feet, and Naed's mother bore the brunt of it.

Tapping the sheathed long-knife against her sling, she considered how best to help Lady Vyenne come to terms with the changes. "Prince Arn will not wear the Crown afore he wins sufficient allies in all three lands. To his way of thinking, the folk must *want* the new Kingdom and join it willingly. Druemarwin, and your son, be central to his plan for D'nalee. Your son's mission be to bring the D'nalian lords into the alliance."

She shifted her gaze to the windows, to sunlight sparkling off dozens of dust motes stirred by their activity. Change had come to this long neglected chamber with the passing of the title to someone unexpected and unforeseen. The Kingdom's coming, equally unexpected and unforeseen, had likewise stirred the hopes of the folk, whose needs and wishes had been ignored far too long. Eyes closed, Raell sent a prayer upon the Winds. Sisters willing, the folk would have the change they desired. The world had come too far to go back to what was.

Opening her eyes, she focused on the woman reflected in the mirror. "I know but little of what brought the Prince and your son so closely together, but I know they both be bound heart and soul to the Kingdom."

Her carefully considered speech was received with a scowl. Not the tiny line between Lady Vyenne's brows she'd learned indicated displeasure, but a full and fierce frown that took Raell aback.

"Again." Naed's mother leaned forward. "You are telling me what I've already surmised from all and sundry, some of whom are far more forthcoming than courtiers at Tumin, where I have spent more years than your life span absorbing such information from minute hints and implications. Pray, employ some of your Tolemak directness and provide me with clear answers to these questions regarding my son." She straightened, folded her hands once more in her lap, and waited.

Raell shut her mouth before something hot and ill-considered escaped. Let her cheeks reveal how she'd been blistered for being kind! Deciding that wasn't obvious enough, she glared her irritation before she allowed herself to admit—*mayhap*—she'd been equally condescending. Only an astute and determined woman could have kept hidden such secrets, explosive and life-altering as they were, for as long as Lady Vyenne had in Tumin. Indeed, the woman would likely be keeping them yet if Naed hadn't learned the truth. Raell cast another glare at the woman who would be her mother-in-law. To underestimate Lady Vyenne again would be folly, especially when a small part of her admired the woman's tenacity and willpower.

Nonetheless, she must stand her own ground. Making an effort to soften her expression, she said, "Please, ask *direct* questions, m'lady. My Tolemak nature prefers it." That had the woman reddening. *Do not underestimate me.*

Lady Vyenne's lips thinned, but she paused as if to consider before responding. "Very well then, answer me this: why is Naed not attended by D'nalians? Why are his closest companions not men of Druemarwin? The folk here seem genuinely to respect him. Pardon me if I offend, but I find the situation odd at best."

Ah, so that's the issue. Raell studied the woman in the mirror. *She insists she wants bluntness, does she?* "Yesternight you told me I fail to understand D'nalian values. Mayhap, for your part, you fail to understand what Tolemaks hold dear."

As expected, Lady Vyenne's gaze snapped to hers.

"'Tis not my intention to offend either, m'lady, but to speak plainly—as you requested—so we both may understand. Your son has brought us together, unexpectedly and unaware, in a place where neither of us is at home. He himself has come here with a difficult mission to perform. 'Twould be better for Naed's sake if we were allied rather than at odds."

The silence stretched. In the periphery of her vision, Gam and the maid waited with avid attention. Neither seemed prone to let secrets slip to the household. Nevertheless, Raell offered up a prayer. *Sisters Three, let us settle our differences in private.*

Finally, Lady Vyenne made a small, stiff nod. "Very well. Enlighten me about Tolemaks." She drew her ramrod posture even straighter. "Then, mayhap, you will also enlighten me about this *mission* to which you refer."

Raell unclenched her fingers. Her wound throbbed from the tension. She lifted her shoulders to relieve the ache and marshaled her thoughts. "As I've told you before, my household be a household of men, where lads learn to wield a wooden sword as readily as a spoon, where peace be merely the interim betwixt this war or that."

Where any man may die betwixt this moment and the next.

Her stomach turned in upon itself. She never knew which of her brothers—or her father—would come riding home alive and which they'd have to bury. That was a dark-of-the-night fear, but yesternight's events brought it up, raw and palpitating, to seize her throat before she swallowed it down.

Now was the time to explain, not cower beneath

covers. "Therefore, I may have more intimate knowledge than most women of how such a man chooses his closest attendants." *Good.* She'd sounded confident, in command. "Will you concede that, m'lady?"

"Of course. Your skill with weapons is evidence enough. Pray, continue."

She could do that now fear had been contained, shoved back into the shadows where it belonged. "To be a man's second is a bond unlike any other. Among Tolemaks, 'tis more unbreakable than vassal to lord, husband to wife, ally to ally. A man and his second trust each other with their lives. Banir and the others, they'd stop a blade for your son. And he would do the same for the Prince." She gave herself a beat, a breath, before asking, "Be that the case among D'nalians?"

"You are going to tell me it's not."

"Naed must believe so, for he has chosen these men and they have chosen him."

Lady Vyenne arched a brow. "So, you are asserting Naed is safer now than ever he was?"

Raell hesitated. There was no other way to say what had been left unsaid since a man wearing Tumin colors had bled out on the floor at her feet. "Mayhap, if the man who is your husband would seek to kill him."

A shudder rippled through Lady Vyenne's frame. She must've tried to suppress it with her rigid posture, but the tremor ran its course anyway. A haunted look darted across her expression before she expelled a breath. "*Someone* has sent these villains. If not Alwyl, or someone acting on behalf of Dlaniger, then who?"

That's the rub, girl. You'll ne'er know till you die one day in your bed and not at the hand of one or more of 'em.

Raell's heart stopped, stuttered, and beat again, hard and heavy, while a chill curdled her skin. The well-loved voice echoed in her ears, as if she'd been transported in both time and place to Albon, to her last night with her father, and then yanked back to the present. She leaned a forearm on a high-backed chair, steadying herself.

"The Kingdom and the Prince have many enemies, m'lady," she said as much to dispel her own sudden terror as to comfort Naed's mother. "'Tis not necessarily a personal act."

Lady Vyenne snorted. "Do *not* tell me you subscribe to that manly *twaddle*! 'Tis a cartload of *excrement* men use to excuse any and all killing! Any harm done to anyone I love is of necessity a very personal act. And I will not forget it!"

Raell stood, dumbstruck, by the coarse, inelegant sound that had erupted from the very proper D'nalian lady's mouth. Two heartbeats later, when she'd processed Lady Vyenne's words, and the emotion with which they'd been delivered, she turned away from the mirror. What she had to say required being said face to face. If only her voice would obey her need and speak past the lump lodged in her throat.

"Mark me well, m'lady, for we are allied on this. No harm shall come to those I love so long as I may prevent it! 'Tis assured you may be of that!"

Silence.

A slight softening of Lady Vyenne's stern expression, a flick of her eyes downward, then back to Raell's face. "Indeed, Lady Raell. I have never doubted that. Your passion has been abundantly clear since I first beheld you."

What the Demon is the woman smiling at?

Raell glanced at the mirror.

Damn! The knife. Somehow during her tirade she'd flung off the sheath. With her flushed cheeks and fierce stance, she looked ready to gut whoever stood in her way. Eyes closed, she stifled a groan. All day she'd tried to prove to these D'nalians she could be calm, logical, rational, even ladylike.

A knock sounded at the door.

"Enter." Raell seized the interruption to regain her composure. *Sisters!* Could she make herself any more ridiculous?

"Banir," she said, and flushed again, though why she did eluded her. Mayhap because he might bring news of Naed? "How fares your master? After yesternight, I mean."

"Breaking his fast, m'lady." He glanced at her hands and quirked a brow.

Bloody hell, the knife! Her flush spread. She handed the weapon to the maid, who fumbled it to the floor with a clatter.

Elda blushed furiously and shot sidelong glances at Banir as though being within inches of a Tolemak warrior terrified her more than handling the weaponry.

Foolish woman! Banir was a good man, hardly one to fear. Unlike the D'nalian assassins from yesternight.

Clearing her throat, Raell reiterated her concern. "Lord Naed, is he…well?"

"He and your brother shared some wine yesternight. 'Tis as well between them as can be, m'lady."

"Oh." The fight she'd heard down a stone corridor

and through an oaken door. *So they'd settled their differences with fists and drunk themselves into a stupor, eh?* She pursed her lips. If only wars could be settled so quickly. "Thank you."

Banir inclined his head. "There be another matter, m'lady and m'lady. Lord Wendelmyr of Kassi approaches, the first of many southern lords. Will either, or both, of you wish to attend him? Or would you be wanting to stay above stairs?"

Raell hesitated. In all the turmoil of the past hours, she'd forgotten the assembly Naed had called.

"Both of us shall attend the lords." Lady Vyenne stood and surveyed the faces in the room. "If my son's alliance is to be the future of the land, 'tis best we show the truth of it. However—" She gestured to Raell's unfinished gown. "—as you are not yet properly attired and—" She indicated the sling. "—somewhat indisposed, I suggest I receive Lord Wendelmyr." She smiled. "Does that suit you, Lady Raell?"

Well, it had to, didn't it? She couldn't very well refuse such an artfully composed suggestion. It was logical and practical and most definitely covering some ulterior motive. Raell forced a smile. Two could play at this game. "An excellent idea, Lady Vyenne. Thank you."

As Naed's mother departed with Banir, Raell watched in the mirror. *What are you up to this time?*

Chapter Twenty-Two

Vyenne hurried down the staircase from the living quarters. She had a small window in which to set in motion the plan she'd conceived while pacing her chamber in the predawn. Reviewing it over bread and cheese in the sharp morning light, she'd had doubts, but no more. This past hour in her late sister's chamber had squelched any lingering qualms.

She paused on the final landing and glanced back. The arrival of the Lord of Kassi meant she had to act now. Sisters be thanked Naed's man had been accosted by Ekwul, leaving her free to continue alone.

Near the Great Hall, she found the lord's chamber door shut and Beauty lapping at a bowl of water. *Good.* Naed was still inside. She snapped her fingers. With one low whine, and a soulful glance at the closed door, the wolfhound obeyed its training and trotted to her side.

"Good girl." She didn't usually praise the dog, or fondle the soft ears, but she couldn't stop herself. One day without the beast's silent comfort and she'd all but fallen apart. Lifting the animal's chin, she met the liquid dark eyes. "You'll be back with him soon, I promise. But I have need of you now."

Lord Wendelmyr of Kassi was precisely as Vyenne remembered, short, stout, and entirely too friendly. He showed surprise at finding her at Druemarwin, said all the right words, but that familiar gleam in his eye noticeably brightened, confirming he knew of her infidelity. Well, she'd expected as much. She introduced Wendelmyr to the monstrous wolfhound, and watched with covert satisfaction as he stepped back.

That should cool his immediate ardor.

Henceforth, she would treat him with her usual courteous distance and ensure he never found her alone. If Naed didn't need him, she'd happily suggest one of these ever-present Tolemaks castrate the aggressive little toad.

Sisters Above, but I've become bloodthirsty. It must be the influence of these Tolemaks.

Or mayhap she was shedding all those layers of polish that had kept her confined for so long. Either way, she had the freedom to act, so she put on her most impersonal smile and set about doing what needed to be done.

****

Every inch of Naed's body ached, and if Toth's face was any reflection of his own, no wonder Lord Wendelmyr started at the sight of them. At least Wendelmyr had the good grace to cover his shock with a quick grin and a clasp of hands.

If only that didn't hurt, too.

Naed flexed swollen knuckles. He would keep this greeting to the minimum protocol demanded and then discover how Raell fared. She had to be better. No one had told him otherwise. He managed a painful imitation of a smile. "Welcome to Druemarwin."

The round little man laid a hand over his heart. "At your service, Lord Naed. It seems you've more need of me and mine than I'd assumed. Was it only two days ago?"

"Hard to believe." From Wendelmyr's expression, the lord assumed there'd been an attack on the fortress, and Toth and he had been injured defending it. *Good.* The attacks were truth. What was between Toth and himself could remain there.

He flicked a glance at the Tolemak to alert him and then addressed Wendelmyr. "If you wondered at the viciousness of the Kingdom's enemies, be assured, this is but a small taste. Best to see it now when you still have time to change your mind and go home."

"I'll consider that fair warning, sir. That and the bodies on display outside the gates. Are you sure you want to greet the lords in that way?"

With sunlight spearing him in gritty eyes and the clatter of Kassi horses and men hammering at his skull, Naed's willingness to mince words reached its limit. "On our advance to Vinvinnysee, the Prince hung the stripped bodies of Lancers in the trees." He let that image sink in. "That much brutality is not to my liking, but the message is plain enough. They invaded my home, sir. These villains are fortunate I'm letting them keep their clothing."

Wendelmyr shuddered. "I concede your point, sir. But..." He leaned in and lowered his voice. "Were those Tumin colors I saw on one of the bodies?"

Damn the man. Of course he'd notice that. Well, let him draw his own conclusions. Naed had no definite answers, only a host of questions. "Indeed they are."

Wendelmyr paled, but after a quick glance at how his entourage was dispersing to their duties, his expression brightened. "Now, on to better things, m'lord." He clapped a pampered hand on Naed's shoulder.

The little man's touch had practically no weight, but laid upon flesh beaten against stone, even that much pressure shot fire along Naed's nerves. He fought the urge to wince and recoil, belatedly noticing Wendelmyr continued speaking.

"—delighted, simply delighted to be of service at such a happy time. So it's to be tonight, is it? I can see why you'd want to settle the business before the assembly convenes." He beamed at Naed and his eyes twinkled. "Your mother—delightful woman—explained it all."

What the Demon is he babbling about? Naed exchanged a stupefied look with Toth.

The Tolemak quirked a stitched brow and winced.

A frisson of alarm ran up Naed's spine. "My...mother explained it...all?" *When?* He'd been alerted to the Kassi contingent's arrival only minutes ago.

"How your bride's arrived and there's no one of status who's not related to either of you to give witness to the joining, of course. 'Twas before your time, but your mother will tell you I was a witness at Lord Dranoel's joining ceremony, and he stood in attendance at mine." Wendelmyr swept his gaze over Naed's expression, smiled benevolently and tutted. "A few nerves, I see. Well, I shouldn't worry, Lord Naed. 'Tis a fine, fair thing to be wed when one is young and full of...*stamina.*" He winked. "A little happiness before we talk of war won't go amiss, will it, sir?"

Another clap on Naed's shoulder, more enthusiastic, and the little man leaned in. "Mayhap you'll breed yourself an heir tonight, eh?" He rubbed his hands together. "When shall I meet your intended? I do so love a good wedding feast. How fortunate I thought of including wine and ale among the supplies I sent over yesterday."

****

With one brusque knock and no pause for permission, Toth stalked into the late Lady of Druemarwin's chamber.

Elda gasped, stuck Raell with the needle, and gasped again.

Raell flinched away, rubbed her shoulder, and glimpsed his face. "Demon's Blood!"

"Don't you like it?" he snarled. "'Tis no worse than your *intended's* face."

From her seat beside the mirror, Gam chuckled. "At least the master has two eyes t' see out of."

Toth growled at her. Then he pulled the quivering maid toward the door. "Go, both of you. Leave us a moment alone."

While Gam slowly rose, and Elda stumbled to help her, Raell stood stock still and stared at her brother. Her skin had gone clammy at the sight of him. Now her fingers tingled too. She'd heard the fight—how could she not for all the clamor and shouting?—but she hadn't imagined, hadn't considered they'd have done this much damage to each other.

When the door closed behind the women, Toth rounded on her.

"You-you pig-headed excuse for a Tolemak! What the Demon were you thinking? A fight, to be sure— you're a man after all, though a sorry excuse for one— but to batter each other senseless!"

209

"He let you be *hurt*, Raell! The damned bastard—and I mean that in every sense of the word—let you be hurt!"

"So you pounded him, did you? Thought it would somehow even the score? Ass!" She hauled back her fist and punched him in the chest. "Blinder-eyed, stones-for-brains ass!" Another punch. And another. "Did you ever consider Naed did the best he could? That there were four of them?"

"Bloody hell, Raell!" He blocked her fist and backed out of reach. "Your precious D'nalian bastard pounded me too! For the same damned reason! For letting you be hurt in the marsh." A pained expression crossed his face and he turned half away. "We've settled it. They'll be no more pounding."

"Oh, I see." Panting, she glared while her knuckles smarted. "He did as much damage to you as you did to him. Now you can be friends."

"Relatives," he muttered, avoiding her eyes, "by marriage."

She snorted and flung up her hand. "Men! Be thankful I understand you better than most women would." Hadn't she just told Naed's mother as much? She hadn't expected to be tested so soon.

Well, that was over and she'd passed. Leaning toward the mirror, Raell inspected the half-stitched shoulder seam for any blood from the needle prick. None, thank the Sisters.

"Now, what the Demon brought you barging in here?"

"Marriage."

"What?" Her gaze snapped from Toth-in-the-glass to Toth-in-the-flesh. For some reason his expression in

210

both places set her heart to galloping.

"Lady Vyenne's arranged it. The Lord of Kassi will witness a joining ceremony at dinner tonight." He faced her squarely. "You'll be wed, Raell, and I can go home."

To Father.

He left those words unspoken, but she heard them anyway. They echoed in the throb of her blood—until the shock of Toth's actual words rose like a tidal wave and swamped every other thought.

"Tonight?" Raell squeaked. "A—a joining?"

If she couldn't catch a breath soon, she'd collapse into the clothing puddled on the floor. Head spinning, she groped for the chair and tumbled toward it, remembering at the last minute to sit gently. Still, as her bruises contacted the hard surface, she hissed out what precious little air remained in her lungs.

Toth cocked his head, studying her with the one eye he could open fully. "'Tis what we came here for, aye? You should be happy."

Aye, it was. And she should. But—

Tonight?

With Naed's battered face and her stitched-up arm, wearing a beggared gown and standing before a host of strangers? In all her wildest imaginings she'd never once conceived of this as her joining ceremony.

And she'd not yet told him about Bennin of Nye.

Chapter Twenty-Three

Naed concentrated on the door of his private chamber, willing his mother to appear. He'd summoned her nigh an hour ago, and paced for most of that time, alternately fuming at her impertinence, her audacity, her high-handed *interference* and panicking at the possible consequences of what she'd set into motion.

Marriage…the wedding night…Raell would expect him to…

Blood rushed to his groin. *Sisters and the Four Winds!*

He flung himself into a chair and tried to breathe.

Tonight?

The thought increased constriction in his breeches. Face aflame, he shifted, tugging at his sword belt to free more of his tunic. He was well past the age when a mere glimpse of a female breast or thigh should give him palpitations. Just because he'd not done this before didn't mean he couldn't. The act was as natural as breathing, wasn't it?

He panted like a fish out of water and focused on who'd triggered this state of affairs.

What in the Name of the Sisters were you thinking, Mother?

Without announcement, Lady Vyenne swept into the chamber and shut the door. "I have but few moments to spare, so let's be direct, shall we?"

Surging to his feet, Naed choked out, "I demand to know—"

"Do you intend to wed Lady Raell or not?"

He blinked. She was glaring down her nose as if he were ten again and had attempted to lie to her. "What—?"

"I don't have time for you to hem and haw. We need to settle this at once. Are you or are you not betrothed to that young woman?"

"Aye, but—"

"Are you attempting to explain yourself with that utterance, or is that sound an 'aye' of assent?"

This was *his* home and she had no right to interrogate him. Naed leaned over her, emphasizing his height advantage. If he had to grit his teeth against the protest of his bruised body, the better to convey his fury. "What do you think you're doing, Mother?"

She'd been standing within inches, hands on hips, when her fierce demeanor altered. A smile ghosted across her lips. "Answer my question, and I'll gladly answer yours."

Feeling as if he'd been top-spun, he clenched his fists and motioned her to a chair. He could concede this first round. The answer was simple. "Aye, I am betrothed to Lady Raell. I love her, in case you haven't noticed."

"Oh, I have. Yesternight was most convincing." Sitting, she smoothed her skirts. "Which is why you should be thanking me instead of accusing me of interference."

Her cat-with-cream expression filled him with dread. "What, exactly, have you done, Mother?"

"Arranged a wedding that will absolve both of you

of any breath of scandal. If Lady Raell stays here a day longer without a joining ceremony witnessed by an unrelated individual of equal status—in this case, not just any lord but one well known and long established—you risk having your marriage called into question by both Tolemak and D'nalian society. As a bastard—yes, I take responsibility for that, so don't throw me that injured look. I'm not sorry for it, but that's a matter for us to discuss another day. For now, we have your political future to protect."

Naed reeled as if a load of logs had rolled over him. He dropped into the chair he'd vacated moments earlier. It was still warm, a detached part of his mind noted, while what remained of his focus splintered like yesternight's barrel lid under her verbal assault.

"As a bastard your inherited title already comes with attached questions, some of which you've undoubtedly encountered when soliciting the Lord of Kassi's support. If you intend to properly serve the man you've apparently aligned yourself with, you cannot afford additional questions." Folding her hands, she speared him with her most direct gaze. "Do I make myself clear?"

Naed gripped the chair arms so hard the wood creaked. He'd like to throttle her, but she was daring him to do just that, to lose his temper, rage at her, behave like a child. With a mighty effort, he suppressed a growl, refusing to give her the satisfaction. His emotions lived too close to the surface these days, but that didn't mean he couldn't contain them, as she had clearly done with hers, even if white knuckles and rigid posture betrayed her effort.

So, she has feelings. Interesting.

Thinking now, he recognized she'd thrown down the gauntlet in more ways than one. She wasn't sorry, eh? He'd poke that beast under her skin, but not now. She'd challenged him to set aside his emotions, to behave like a true D'nalian and consider the logic behind what she'd done.

Wonderment crossed his mind first. When had his mother become so politically astute? Never in his life at Tumin had he heard her express an opinion, venture a word of advice, or demonstrate any interest in the affairs of court. She simply presided over dinners, festivals, and assemblies as the perfect hostess, ever gracious, ever polite, entirely inoffensive. And all the while she'd been thinking these thoughts, watching and observing. *Sisters and the Four Winds!*

"Very well, Mother. You've made your point." That would be the last, if he had aught to say. "What I fail to understand is why you felt you needed to act independently. Why, for instance, you did not consult me." He shot her a glower, emphasizing she'd overstepped.

A wave of her hand deflected his censure. "These are not usual times. Clearly, you have a great deal to occupy your attention, and the opportunity presented itself to settle this one issue before the assembly convenes and your duties expand. In addition, anyone can see Lady Raell came—or was sent—all this way with the express purpose of completing your betrothal. Arranging the details of joining ceremonies is something typically done by the women of the household. Therefore I have done what any mother would do for her son."

Naed's mind whirled. She was as slippery as the

best Tumin courtier, and when had she time to consider all these contingencies? She'd arrived only the night before he had.

He was drowning—*again*—under her onslaught of logic when one idea surfaced and his heart grabbed onto it: Raell had come—*or been sent*—to join him. They'd had barely a moment to themselves, had spoken of hardly anything but the attacks. He'd left her at Albon with the promise of his return, and she'd seemed content. Now, so soon after, she was on his doorstep, accompanied only by her brother. *Sent by the Prince?* Either she was in danger or the Prince required their marriage now.

His mother smiled as though she'd read his thoughts. "Since you intended to wed her anyway, why object to the timing?"

Why indeed? Raell was who he wanted, needed, and, though he'd tried desperately to suppress those thoughts, *desired* in his bed since he'd first encountered her. Not since his early teens had his urges driven him so strongly. Even Aerid, when he still thought he loved her, hadn't inspired such...*lust*. Raell, on the other hand...

Heat swept up Naed's throat. Hadn't he dreamed—nightly, if truth be told, sometimes twice before morning!—of uncovering that lovely white skin inch by inch, of unbraiding that honey-gold hair and cascading it through his fingers?

Ears burning, he squirmed in his chair and hoped his mother hadn't read that thought, hadn't noticed his body's all-too-prompt reaction. It was unseemly for a D'nalian, and certainly not appropriate to discuss with his mother. His movements jogged the cylinder and the fine gold chain he wore against his skin and over his heart.

Raell's charm.

He'd pledged himself to her, freely and with every intention of fulfilling that pledge *at some time in the future*. He hadn't expected it to rear up and smack him in the face mere hours before the event. Certainly not before he'd had a chance to prepare for the most important day—and night—of his life. His heart skipped a beat, hammered hard another, rattled off a few more.

Demon be damned! He'd not been this wound up since his first battle. Mayhap not even then.

His tongue had dried to cotton wool, but he forced a swallow. Belike, being a virgin herself Raell wouldn't expect expertise from him. The thought allowed his heartbeat to settle, although sweat trickled down his ribs.

Whatever the reason for her journey, Raell was here now. The luxury of time was gone. The only motive he could think of to delay the marriage was to frustrate his mother for her audacity. While the idea tempted—if only to teach her a lesson, not because he was in any way nervous—giving in would be both petty and dishonorable.

Apparently taking silence for assent, his mother said, "Very well, then. Now, as to the matter of a ring— I suspect you haven't had time to provide for one, so you may use mine." She pried at the band on her finger.

"No!"

Her turn to blink. And cock her head in question since he'd all but shouted.

"No," Naed repeated in a more measured tone, glad

to speak of something less intimate although no less important. "I'll not signify my marriage with a ring that's been tainted."

He hadn't meant to score, only to assert control over a future rapidly being decided for him. But the color painting her cheekbones gave him a measure of satisfaction. At least his mother understood she'd done wrong, even if she claimed she wasn't sorry.

She returned her hands to her lap. "Very well. Mayhap your father left you my sister's ring. We did not bury her with it."

"No."

The familiar line appeared between her brows. "That one is not 'tainted.'" Her lips puckered on the word, as though it tasted foul, but she pressed on. "Your father was ever faithful to my sister. Dranoel was an honorable man. He honored his vows. 'Twas only after she died that you were conceived." She straightened. "If we must discuss this now, I was the one who broke a vow, not Dranoel. Never Dranoel."

"He told me otherwise, in the letter he left with his will."

"Did he now? Well, he should not have taken the blame. 'Twas not his to take."

Naed stared at her, and she stared back, entirely unrepentant. He folded his arms. If she were this fiercely protective of Dranoel's reputation, even now, he understood in part why she'd come to Druemarwin. Not so much to save herself from an angry, cuckolded husband—although her journey certainly accomplished that—but to protect Naed from the consequences of her actions. It was a brave choice, and he looked at her with new eyes.

How had he been so wrong in so many ways about this woman who'd given him life?

Not that he forgave her. Not by any means. Mayhap, though, he was parsing out precisely what he held against her. Leaning back in the chair, he decided he could be magnanimous this time and postpone their reckoning.

"In any case, Dranoel's effects contained no such ring."

Her lips thinned. "Mayhap the Lady Raell has brought something suitable with her." She rose. "I have a great deal to organize before dinner, so you'll pardon me if I take my leave."

Resisting his training, he stayed sprawled in his chair and offered a dismissive nod. A small gesture, and probably petty, but she needed to know who was master here.

Her face betrayed nothing. At the door, she turned sharply, and ran a critical gaze over his entire body. "You require more suitable clothing."

Naed flushed, conscious of travel stains on his second-best tunic and breeches. His best had gone to be laundered and mended after yesternight's battering. What little he'd accumulated in the short time he'd been a titled lord lay in a trunk upstairs, and Sisters knew where it had been taken after his bed had been burned and his chamber cleared. Presumably, his mother was aware of that. He shot her a glare.

She ignored it. "The servants are preparing you a bath. I shall have Ekwul deliver your father's finer garments. Among them, your man should find you something appropriate to wear." She added, "Pity he can do naught about your face," before she swept out

the door, trailing that icy disdain he loathed.
Damn the woman!

Chapter Twenty-Four

The slim gold band disappeared into Lady Vyenne's pocket. Resisting the impulse to snatch it back required all of Raell's willpower. The ring and charm were all that remained of her mother, and she'd borne them together about her neck since her mother's last day of life.

"You'll have it back soon, though it will sit this time upon your finger." The woman had undoubtedly noted Raell's expression, for a look of sympathy crossed her elegant face.

Was it real?

Disgusted with her train of thought, Raell removed her hand from her throat. Though the ring weighed hardly anything, and Gam had refastened her charm necklace about her neck, she couldn't help feeling naked and alone. Surely Lady Vyenne understood those feelings.

She cast another glance at the woman who fussed with the drape of her skirt. She had no reason to doubt the woman's perceptions, only her motives.

"Why did you arrange this joining ceremony?"

Lady Vyenne's adjustments paused over the right pocket. She straightened slowly and arched a brow. "Dare I assume you found a place for that long blade?"

"I said I'd no longer go about unarmed, and I meant it. If that troubles you so, why would you wish for me to wed Naed?"

"Why indeed?" Myriad tiny expressions flitted across her face.

Two days of close association had schooled Raell in reading them well enough to detect the chief one: resignation. Her heart pinged. Not exactly what she'd hoped for, but what could she expect? Her own brother regarded Naed with something similar. For a moment, she envied the Prince and Lady Aerid their lack of relatives. But then, neither she nor Naed were alone in the world, and that was better, wasn't it?

"You would prefer to have your son matched with one of your own kind. I understand, m'lady. Truly, I do—"

"No, you do not." Lady Vyenne reached for her shoulders, hesitated as if remembering Raell's wound, and gripped her hands instead. "Naed needs a champion. My own circumstances are, to use his exact words, 'tainted,' as well you are aware. I can do only so much for him until he and I resolve what lies between us." She stepped back and assessed Raell from head to toe. "You are not what I would have chosen for him, but mayhap you are precisely what he needs."

"Is that a blessing, m'lady?"

The woman pulled her into a brief embrace, cheek to cheek, while the scent of expensive dusting powder wafted to Raell's nose. "You may consider it so...daughter."

As quickly as they'd come together, Lady Vyenne set them apart. Raell could've sworn moisture glinted in those fine green eyes. Assuming, of course, she saw properly out of her own welling eyes. This woman was not her mother, could never be anything like the woman who'd given her birth, loved her father, and set her on the path to womanhood, but Lady Vyenne's gesture was the closest to that of a mother—or sister—Raell had experienced in years. Of course, it would thicken her throat and send a jolt of warmth into her chest.

While she stood confounded, Lady Vyenne crossed to the door, followed by the wolfhound.

"As to what is expected of you in the bedchamber tonight, Gam will explain. I ask only that you refrain from turning that knife on my son and instead save it for his enemies."

Gam guffawed. Raell gaped. That pleasant warmth in her chest ignited like embers on which oil is poured. The conflagration scorched her face into her hairline.

"As if I would," she growled to the door closing behind Lady Vyenne and the dog. *Maddening woman and her D'nalian prejudices!*

****

Vyenne gave thanks for the dim corridor and the wolfhound at her side. The dimness allowed her to compose her face for the next task in her campaign. Beauty's silent presence reminded her at least *someone* trusted her completely.

Sisters, but this day will drain me.

The previous fortnight's challenges had proved trivial compared to those of the last two days. But she was a fool if she thought her trials would end on the morrow.

Alwyl.

She shivered. Would he come himself or send someone to fetch her?

Best not to think of that now.

Nor did she intend to probe the emotion she'd just

expended. Tomorrow would be soon enough to consider why she'd said what she'd said to Naed's bride. Today—tonight—she had limited assets to command, but command them she would. Stiffening her posture, she faced the girl's ever-present watchdog.

The Tolemak lounged against the wall in the shadows, a pose Vyenne did not mistake for unpreparedness. Everything about the young man suggested a coiled spring, or a set trap. Not a whit of that energy seemed spent despite yesternight's brawl and the violence that left Vyenne shaking for merely overhearing it.

She sucked in a breath, containing the quaking before it returned. She'd managed the sight of her injured son without betraying how much it dismayed her; she could manage the sight of the man who'd tried to beat him senseless. "I should like you to attend me tonight, Toth, son of Tylus."

He uncoiled from the wall, and her stomach betrayed her. *Sisters Above!* He looked terrible, worse than Naed. *Good!*

The gold-brown eyes, so like his sister's, studied her. "I should've thought you'd prefer someone of rank to escort you, m'lady."

Her heart thumped. Had her face revealed that wholly inappropriate—but justified—stab of satisfaction? Regardless, she had her answer prepared. "You and I represent the families being joined. 'Tis only fit you should be elevated tonight."

"And the Lord of Kassi? He'll not object?"

"He is to preside. That should suit him quite well."

Hand over his breast, he inclined his head. "Then I shall be your escort for the night, m'lady. And your guardian."

If he referred to Lord Wendelmyr, however Toth could've guessed, she required no Tolemak interference. "Beauty is perfectly adequate in that function."

"Indeed. I shall welcome the beast's assistance *under* the table, m'lady. However, 'twill be a long night of revelry, and much about your circumstances remains unsettled."

Her cheeks heated, but Vyenne refused to look away from that challenging gaze. *Been listening at the door, have you? Insufferable, arrogant Tolemak!*

Beauty nudged her elbow, and her hand descended to stroke the dog's wiry fur. A measure of calm infused her body. The young man with the ready sword intended to be vigilant; why not let him?

She forced a smile. "Your service is much appreciated."

"We're soon to be family, m'lady. 'Tis my duty to serve the women of my family."

There's so much more to you than duty. If he saw that thought in her eyes, so be it.

With a brusque "Come, Beauty," Vyenne headed for the stairs. Despite yesternight's fistfight with Naed and the impending marriage Toth had been sent to witness, the young man radiated barely suppressed anger. Not at her, or she'd never have asked for his help. Nor at Naed. She was fairly certain their brawl had settled that. Something deep lurked there, but she judged it unlikely to surface tonight.

Tonight Toth was the one person she trusted to play his role to perfection. To be, as it were, her Second.

Her lips quirked. Did he appreciate the irony of their joint purpose?

She considered that while heavily laden servants clogged the stairwell. The fortress was all astir, the folk attending to preparations for tonight's festivities, ones she'd set in motion mere hours ago. Sisters be thanked, all was going well.

A moment later, alone on the landing before the Great Hall, she paused to marshal her wits, her energy, and her composure. She needed to be at her best tonight. *Dear Sisters, but I'm so tired.*

Eyes closed, she rubbed her hand over her breastbone, soothing the ever-present ache centered there. *Get through tonight and then think about tomorrow.*

Gathering her skirts, she headed downstairs with the dog at her side.

Chapter Twenty-Five

Humming tunelessly, Banir applied a plaster to Naed's cheekbone.

"Does it have to stink?"

The stuff was making him gag, but if the vile mix worked, it would show his mother he could indeed do *something* about his face. *If* they had time. The bath had taken long enough. While warm water had soothed some of his aches, for which he grudgingly gave thanks, his bruises bloomed.

"Belike, my face will still be purple," he grumbled.

"More like 'twill be yellow and green by dinner." Banir wiped his hands on a rag. "'Tis meant to draw out the blood, the purple. As to the stink..." He pinched Naed's nose.

"Ow! What—!"

"You're breathing better, aye?"

The dark eyes were as serious as ever, yet Naed swore he'd seen the flash of a grin. He scowled.

"You're enjoying this. I can tell." But the foul stench *had* cleared his nasal passages. "I won't stink before the Lady Raell, will I? You'll clean this off before the ceremony, aye?"

Ekwul chose that moment to enter, followed by two boys bearing Dranoel's trunk. The boys, wide-eyed in the presence of the new master and his Tolemak Second, stumbled over their own feet but managed to set the trunk down intact. Shooing them out, the old servant unpacked what garments he deemed suitable and left.

Banir cleared away his plaster makings, humming all the while.

A long, low rumble sounded. Both looked at the high window, where gray light did nothing to brighten the chamber. Until the flash.

Naed rolled his eyes. *Perfect!* A heavy rain would turn Druemarwin's barren green into a muddy mess for the soon-to-arrive lords.

"Spring in D'nalee," Banir said, grinning. At Naed's glower, he added, "'Tis not all bad. If it lasts, mayhap 'twill keep the villains hunkered down and the festivities safe."

That it could. Spring storms tended to go on all night. Only a fool or a desperate man would be out in one. That was precisely why the Prince would advise him to be extra vigilant tonight.

"Put Grodar and Morys on the guards. I don't want to underestimate the threat."

Heaving a sigh that welled up from his soles, Naed contemplated the darkening window. Rain streaked the glass. If the storm lived up to spring's promise, thunder would rattle the plates during dinner. He and Raell would be fortunate to hear their vows, much less Wendelmyr's blessing.

To the best of his memory, this was not how his siblings' weddings had gone. True, Allyn the eldest had suffered the ceremony with a hangover, and prior to the festivities, there'd been some set-to about a goat, presumably instigated by third-in-line Fennyn, but his mother settled that with her usual firm hand. That the marriage dissolved after two unfruitful years was not to the point: No one else had stood before all and sundry with a battered face and borrowed clothes in a place where he was the surprise bastard heir.

With a fortifying breath, he shoved his aching body upright. Best to simply get on with it. The Three Sisters would have their way regardless of what mere mortals wished.

Holding the plaster in place, Naed stepped beside Banir and considered the garments draped across the table. All were too big, for Dranoel had shoulders like a bull, but a dark green tunic trimmed in silver fox fur looked promising. Some artful tucking and belting made it fit, mostly, over dark green breeches.

Silver thread glinted on Naed's sleeve, a pattern of fine stitches barely visible in the dimming light. *What the Demon are those things?* He squinted.

Deer—dainty, leaping deer—cavorted all the way down his arm.

Sisters! He'd forgotten how to wear such frippery. In two years of soldiering, sleeping in the rough, and washing in streams, he'd never once missed it. Prince Arn had his scarlet cloak, which he used to great advantage, but Tolemaks put far less stock in appearances than D'nalians, especially the Tumin sort of D'nalians.

A loose bit of fox fur tickled Naed's nose. He sneezed and winced. Mayhap it was an affront to his bloodline, but the Tolemak practice seemed eminently appealing.

"At least you were of a height." Banir studied the ornately stitched, double-tanged wide belt they'd employed to gather in the tunic. Despite the gathers, they'd had to punch another pair of holes to accommodate Naed's narrower waist.

The belt impeded his ribs. It rubbed up against every bruise on his torso. If only he had a plaster for those injuries. Raell would get an eyeful of blue and purple when at last they retired to their bridal chamber. He flushed from head to toe. Mayhap he could put out all the candles before disrobing and disappointing her.

Not that I won't disappoint her anyway.

His throat seized, his head spun, and he dropped into the nearest chair before his legs gave out.

"You've gone all pale." Banir reached for the belt. "'Tis too tight—"

"No!" Naed deflected the Tolemak's hands before he undid all their efforts. "I'm…" he panted, wishing for once he'd followed his brothers' example to 'scratch an itch' as they called it whenever a willing maid caught their eye. Even the Prince scoffed at his naiveté when they'd fought over Aerid. But he wasn't like his brothers—*half*-brothers now—who'd more than once forced him to watch their exploits until he'd grown strong enough to fight his way free. Mayhap that was why he'd always shied from turning something intended to cement the marriage bond into mere sport. It was debauchery, plain and simple, and not the behavior of a true D'nalian.

His nostrils flared. Ironic, considering his mother's infidelity had spawned him. But he was not like her either and, however he'd come by it, his strict adherence to the rules left him a panicked mess now. His stomach wrung itself into a knot. He could keep silent and muddle his way through tonight, or…

He slid a glance at the man who'd stood beside him

for months, who'd risked everything to follow a D'nalian, the man he trusted above all others. Even so, heat crept up his face and he focused on the rain-shadowed wall as he forced out, "Banir, tonight...what do I do?"

"Truly?" It was the Tolemak's turn to redden and look away. "There's been no one afore...to teach you?"

Slumping in the chair, Naed closed his eyes. "I have brothers. I know how 'tis done, but I don't want to be...clumsy. I love Raell. I want to please her."

There was a thump and a metallic clunk—a man dropping onto a chair, a scabbard banging floorboard.

Naed opened one eye, the other. Both widened.

The Tolemak who'd fearlessly faced four-to-one odds in an Adanak wood, who'd single-handedly escorted Aerid across war-torn territory—in winter, no less!—pulled at his collar and sweated. His gaze flicked to Naed, flew around the chamber like a trapped bird, and landed on his hands. He cleared his throat, coughed, and finally managed, "'Tis but one way. Put her pleasure first."

"How...?"

Banir steadfastly refused to look at him. "Touch her. Everywhere."

"Everywhere?"

Face entirely scarlet now, he nodded. "Use your mouth, your fingers."

Images of precisely where on Raell's body he could use his mouth, his fingers flooded Naed's mind. His cock twitched as if eager to be let loose, to serve its purpose. *Sisters!* If any blood remained in his face after so much had rushed to his groin, his cheeks had to be as red as Banir's.

"Take your time. 'Tis important to a woman."

Take my time? His body could hardly wait, but his head wanted to bolt. *Breathe. The first time is not the last.* Nor would it be the best, he'd been told more than once. "I don't want to disappoint her. Or frighten her."

Banir met his gaze and held it long enough to say, "Your lady's a Tolemak. Don't be a D'nalian with her."

The message was as clear as Banir could make it: *Don't be a prig in the bedchamber.* Raell would be his wife. Whatever they did together was sanctioned by their vows. Besides, she'd never been shy about...*anything.*

Heat scorched Naed's ears. Images of stolen moments in dark corridors shuttled through his mind, her breasts filling his hands, her teeth tugging his earlobe, her body pressed sinuously to his. He inhaled, pretended to study the ceiling beams.

Banir was right. *Stop thinking.*

If only he could put aside twenty years of D'nalian training and let his body lead.

****

In the Great Hall torchlight danced as merrily as the folk of Druemarwin. Ale flowed. Lightning cast wild, gyrating shadows across the crowded room. Thunder competed with the musicians, adding its rumble to their hand drums. Rain pelted the high windows, but that was outside. Inside smelled of roasted meat, burnt oil, and a multitude of sweating bodies. Along the walls large fireplaces, each manned by a pair of servants, roared like bonfires.

Vyenne discreetly fanned herself. Beneath the table, Beauty lapped at her second bowl of water and panted. Clearly, the local folk had been starved for festivities, considering how they'd thrown themselves into tonight's celebration. From what she'd gathered, a year of war, the murder of their beloved master, and the upheaval caused by old alliances broken and new ones made had taken its toll. Yet they'd given their hearts to Naed, and for that she was grateful. They'd even welcomed her despite what they knew of her 'circumstances.'

Her spine stiffened. Now was not the time for such thoughts. *Get through tonight and then think about tomorrow.*

The food, plain fare pulled from winter storage, tasted better than Vyenne expected. Mayhap that was why she ate the morsels Toth persisted in placing on her side of the plate. She'd told him not to feed her, she wasn't hungry, and he'd clearly understood. She considered slapping his hand with the flat of her knife, but that would reduce her to behaving like a Tolemak.

Not that it wasn't tempting.

Get through tonight.

Sisters Above! Had she turned those words into a chant?

Certainly not! She was fully capable of enduring another few hours with her dignity intact. Laying aside the knife with great care, she flicked her most imperious glance at the young man in question.

Toth's gold-brown eyes smiled even if his battered mouth didn't. At least they did so when he wasn't surveying the crowd like some predatory animal who'd been fed but wasn't full. Mostly, he watched the Kassi men and the lord himself.

That exalted personage had beamed his way through the ceremony, moderating the giving-away with all due gravity, binding together Naed and Raell's hands with a flourish, and pronouncing the blessing in a booming voice. Now he sat glassy-eyed, florid-faced and gesticulating, next to Raell in the place of honor to the right of the newly joined couple. Her new daughter-in-law managed to keep a polite distance, but Vyenne elbowed Naed anyway.

Her son had been staring into space with a dazed expression. Beneath the bruising, which had inexplicably faded to a mottled green-yellow, the face he turned to her was nigh as pale as a Tolemak's.

Those tasty morsels Toth had foisted upon her turned to acid and chewed at her innards. Her heart stuttered. She hadn't meant to bring all this upon Naed so suddenly, but he would thank her soon. For reasons known only to the Three Sisters, he loved this Tolemak wildling, and the girl loved him. They would be happy. And safe. But they had to complete this joining.

"You should retire soon. 'Tis long enough to satisfy propriety." She didn't say Wendelmyr was well past soused or that Toth would soon crush the little man's wandering hands. Raell was still his sister, and the Tolemak could hardly undo years of training in one night. Instead, she shifted her glance in Wendelmyr's direction.

Despite the toasts offered in his honor, Naed's eyes sharpened. His man, who stood at his shoulder, had been discreetly watering his cup. Vyenne, who'd been sipping herself, approved. That Tolemak now tensed, like a hound on the scent.

Naed pushed back his chair. "Can you manage, Mother?" He didn't look at her but extended a hand to his bride. The girl took it with an undisguised look of relief.

Vyenne gave thanks for small blessings. With this Tolemak bride, Naed would never have to guess his wife's emotions. "Go. Everything will be fine." She signaled Elda to escort the couple to their chamber.

Accompanied by a chorus of bawdy toasts and lewd suggestions, from Tolemaks *and* D'nalians, the newly joined couple climbed the stairs, waved, and departed.

Naed's men would guard their privacy and the joining would be declared complete by morning. Vyenne exhaled. The burning beneath her breastbone subsided somewhat. She reached for her cup to wash away what lingered when all the hairs on her body stood up.

The air sizzled.

CRACK!

White light flared throughout the Great Hall. Stones rumbled and shook. Dust glittered down from the rafters.

Folk cowered, musicians stilled, everyone waiting for the crash of something falling from roof or battlements. When nothing punctuated the collective hush but pelting rain, exclamations of "Sisters, be thanked!" rippled through the crowd.

Toth turned to a servant. "Go and see—"

But his words were drowned by the jangle of armor and tramp of boots.

"M'lord, they insisted—"

Vyenne's blood chilled.

Alwyl!

Chapter Twenty-Six

Naed hadn't paid attention where he and Raell had been led as long as it was away from the hubbub in the Great Hall. Too many people, too much noise, and nothing to do but smile and nod. The chaos of a battlefield held more appeal. At least there he could act and dispel the tension stiffening his shoulders.

Raell walked silently at his side. Eyes forward, her expression was pensive. She'd clearly been relieved to escape Wendelmyr's attention. Was she as nervous as he? They'd done no more than speak their vows, offer each other food and drink—which Naed couldn't remember tasting—and accept congratulations. What in the Name of the Sisters was she thinking?

Before he could ask, their escort halted and the maid in the lead opened a door.

The chamber glowed with soft light, candles all about and a fire in the grate. The table had been laid with a basket of bread and cheese, a wine jug, and two cups. Fresh linens decorated the bed, the largest in the fortress and curtained with heavy green fabric.

Naed saw all this peripherally, but his focus arrowed to the well-worn, deerskin-padded chair before the fire. *Dranoel's chair.* His pulse beat heavily in his throat where his heart had pushed it.

They'd been brought to the lord's chamber. The one he'd been reluctant to take.

While Raell and the maid entered, he hesitated on the threshold. A spark of anger fired through his veins. Hadn't he endured enough this day, what with all his mother's machinations? He was about to consummate his marriage, something that had him wound tighter than a spring. He did *not* need to deal with this too.

"This chamber, why?" he whispered over his shoulder to Banir.

"Ekwul arranged it."

"And you let him?"

The Tolemak shrugged. "'Tis the lord's chamber, aye? And you be the lord."

Ekwul and Banir, acting in concert for once—how the Three Sisters accomplished that miracle, Naed had no idea—must've decided he'd spent enough time dithering. He glowered at Banir. He'd already accepted the full responsibilities of his lordship. Why couldn't everyone be satisfied with that? Why did they think he needed to confront the ghost who lived in this room?

Banir made a half bow and gestured inside where the maid had begun taking pins from Raell's hair. The challenge was plain: *Make a fuss before your bride or deal with it.*

"I ought to have your hide for this!" Naed's heart beat in triple time. "And Ekwul's too."

"You'll thank me on the morrow." With a nod toward the chamber, he added, "Would you keep your lady waiting?"

Damn the man!

Inhaling against the weight crushing his chest, Naed stepped over the threshold.

Time slowed, reversed. It seized him with thorny vines and dragged him through a tunnel until he stopped, here, on this very spot where he'd stood nigh a year ago after the fortress had fallen to the Prince's army.

A dark night—indeed, a dark time—all in Druemarwin had been virtual prisoners, unsure of their future. He'd come upon Dranoel sunk deep in that chair, shoulder bandaged, stockinged feet stretched toward the coals, brows so low Naed thought the man asleep.

But he wasn't. "You have your mother's coloring," Dranoel told him. "When I look at you, 'tis her I see."

Naed closed his eyes while time blurred past into present, present into past. How little he'd known then, about the man, his own mother, the Three Sisters' plan for his life. How confounded he'd been when Dranoel opened his hand and offered a leather cylinder. "Take this and keep it safe. 'Tis my will."

"Your will? But-but I am more like to die," he protested, stunned. "Go I not with the Tolemak army tomorrow? Does not their Second, Krenin, want my blood?"

"Silence!" Dranoel had bellowed. "Am I yet your master and are you yet pledged to do my will?"

Aye, he was, then and now. He pressed a hand to his chest, to the cylinder resting next to his skin and over his heart. If only he'd known what fulfilling that pledge and carrying that document would entail. If only he'd had an inkling, months earlier, about their true relationship.

His throat swelled and something prickled at the back of it.

If only he'd had a chance before Dranoel died to call him by his rightful title.

Father.

Naed heaved a sigh as the present returned, grounding him in the world of regrets and lost chances. His emotions were still a tangle, but there was no going back. There was but one direction for him, indeed, for all of them: Raell, his mother, the folk of Druemarwin, even the Prince's still-so-fragile alliance. Crossing the chamber, he laid a hand on the empty chair.

Sisters bless you, Father. I accept that I am your son. And heir.

****

The man leading a group of soldiers into the Great Hall was not Alwyl.

Sisters, be thanked! Or mayhap not.

It was the man who'd grown up to look like his father in all things. Allyn, her eldest and his father's heir. A very wet, very fierce looking Allyn stalked into the center of the hall and demanded, "Where is your lord? I would speak with him."

Vyenne breathed, but shallowly. Her ribs seemed unable to expand.

Toth gripped her arm. He'd risen with her and supported her. "Tumin colors," he said at her ear. "Come for you?"

Dear Sisters, why else would Allyn be here?

"My son," she managed.

Allyn spotted her. He strode through a crowd that parted before the heavily armed intruder and his attendants. She had to head him off before he made more of a scene. What they needed to say had to be said in private.

Toth tsked and clamped her arm firmly to his side. "Patience, m'lady." When she gaped at him, he had the gall to look down his bold Tolemak nose and smile. "This affair's been a bit too tame for my liking. Till now, that is."

"You'll not—" but he was already leading her forward in an entirely unhurried fashion.

With a scrabble of claws, Beauty clambered from under the table to accompany them.

"See here!" boomed someone above the murmuring crowd. A round, little man planted himself in Allyn's path. "I am Lord Wendelmyr of Kassi and I am presiding at this function. Who are you to come barging in here?"

"I am Allyn, eldest son of Lord Alwyl of Tumin, and I've come for my mother." With a perfunctory nod, he sidestepped and confronted Vyenne. "My lady mother, you're safe. Thank the Sisters!"

"Of course, I'm safe." Her voice worked! Vyenne strengthened it. "Why would I not be?"

"You left without…" Gaze shifting, Allyn noticed he'd gathered a crowd.

He'd never been the brightest of her sons, charging straight ahead at all times. Blessedly easy to read. Dawning on his face now was the realization some of the faces surrounding him were not D'nalian. Nor was the battered and bruised one at her side.

His expression darkened. At his signal the half-dozen men accompanying him fanned into a defensive circle.

Tolemaks in the crowd were armed. So were Druemarwin guardsmen. Ale-infused or not, they overwhelmingly outnumbered Allyn's small cohort. Women, children, and elderly faded back behind the warriors. The wolfhound's ruff rose.

Vyenne held her breath and Beauty's collar. *Sisters, please! Let no one draw a blade.* Allyn might be reckless, but she'd never known him to be a fool.

With a curl of his lip at the growling beast, he faced Vyenne, brows lowered. "I've come to take you home, Mother."

"Mayhap the lady does not wish to go." Toth spoke softly, but the look his sister had so vividly described yesternight was all over his face, the look that said, *Come on. I dare you.*

Vyenne cast her best quelling glare from man to man, but they had fixated on one another.

Toth released her arm, presumably to allow him free access to his weapons, so she angled her body between the men. "You will both stop now." When they shifted to outflank her, she moved again. "Stop. Now. Both of you."

Sullen-faced, they glared at each other, dogs squaring off over a bone.

She was not about to be their bone.

"Hear me and hear me well. We have much to discuss, Allyn, but we will *not* do it here. Or now. Is that clear?"

He flicked her a glower, returned his daggered stare to Toth. "When?"

A growl, but she deciphered it. Vyenne pulled from her diaphragm the voice her children never ignored.

"Tomorrow, Allyn. I shall see you tomorrow at the time of my choosing. Is that clear?"

Another glower, but accompanied by a grumbled, "Aye. Very well."

"Stand down! Stand down!" Lord Wendelmyr pushed through the crowd, checking his progress only to sidestep the wolfhound. He'd paled, as if the tension sucked all the ale from his veins, but frowned with the full force of his lordship. "This is a wedding celebration, Allyn, son of Alwyl. We welcome you in the spirit of D'nalian hospitality if you would care to join us. Put your weapons down and the servants will find you and your men a place at table." He drew himself to his full height, a fraction above Vyenne's. "If not, mayhap 'twould suit you to go back out in the storm."

Allyn, the fool, weighed the choice: comfort versus male pride.

Vyenne considered smacking him—a Tolemak mother would undoubtedly do so—when he bowed.

"We accept your offer of hospitality, my lord." With a mighty effort, he contorted his snarl into something resembling a polite smile.

The effect was truly frightening. It set Wendelmyr on his heels and sent a shiver through Vyenne. Toth, who'd reclaimed her arm, arched a brow as if to say, *Is that the best you can do?*

Vyenne dug her fingernails into his forearm. Wendelmyr recovered his voice.

"Excellent! You've missed the ceremony, missed the happy couple, but 'tis sure the night is young and ripe for more revelry." He clapped his hands. "Music! We'll have more music!" As the musicians complied, he reached for Allyn's arm. "Come, join me at table and tell me the news from Tumin."

Allyn planted his feet, a solid, immovable, still dripping object. "I will, m'lord, gladly, but first I should like to know one thing." He raked Vyenne and the man beside her with a smoldering gaze. "Forgive me if I offend by asking, but why are Tolemaks in attendance?"

Blinking as though the question were unexpectedly easy, Wendelmyr chuckled. "Why, the bride's a Tolemak, and a delightful one too."

"Indeed." Allyn allowed himself to be led away, but not before sending another, clearly murderous glare at Toth.

As soon as the Tumin contingent trailed away, Vyenne spun to the man still glowering after the 'enemy.' "You!"

The word made him start.

Good. She had his attention. "You will not—I repeat—*not* brawl with another of my sons. Is that clear, Toth, son of Tylus?"

He took his time responding, breaking eye contact long enough to stroke Beauty's head and murmur, "Ah, my pretty lass. You're a right good judge of character, you are."

The wolfhound, inexplicably, accepted the touch with a thump of her tail.

Vyenne refused to be distracted by the dog's betrayal or Toth's assumptions about her eldest. "You will *not* brawl with Allyn. Do I make myself clear?"

For heartbeat after heartbeat he stood silent for so long she wondered if he considered her demand unworthy of a response.

Then he cocked his head and said, "Would you rather have him think what he is thinking now, that you and I are lovers?"

"*What?*" It came out as a strangled sound.

"Consider this, m'lady, your son has come to find you, to fetch his unfaithful mother back to his father."

Toth's gaze was full of patience, a parent explaining something to a child. "Were I he, 'tis what I would think to find you with another man."

"But-but you're *half* my age!"

"'Tis not unheard of among titled folk." He pulled her hand from her burning breastbone and tucked it into the crook of his elbow. "But, aye, your Allyn's a fool to think that's what's between us. 'Tis sure, I need to set him straight. Nor will he take you away, m'lady, if 'tis not your intention to be going. Not if I may do aught to prevent it."

Vyenne suppressed a shriek. Barely. She ground her teeth to hold her jaws shut until the urge subsided. For once she understood why women tore their hair out.

Bloody, stubborn men and their ridiculous codes of honor!

Chapter Twenty-Seven

Raell shooed the maid toward the door. The woman wanted to plait her hair and dress her for bed, but she'd been fussed over enough. Because she refused to wear the sling—trussed up and injured was *not* how she wished to appear before all and sundry for her joining ceremony—meant her arm ached. In truth, it throbbed. Nonetheless, she and Naed could manage just fine on their own.

That was the point of a wedding night, wasn't it?

Spending time together…

Alone.

Her stomach jittered, but it was a good jitter, an *I-can-hardly-wait* kind of jitter.

In the corridor, guardsmen murmured, laughter gusted, and "I'll take that bet," rang clear enough Banir, standing on the threshold, scowled at the men.

The maid, who'd edged toward the door, seized the opportunity to sidle past. He turned, their bodies brushed, and Elda, blushing furiously, ducked under his arm and ran like a rabbit.

"That maid's daft enough to be back at dawn," Banir grumbled after watching her flee. "Lock the door behind me and I'll see you're not disturbed."

Was that a glint of interest in Banir's eye? Raell allowed herself a grin as she shoved the bolt home. *How will you manage* that *pairing, m'lady mother-in-*

law?

CRACK!

A stone-shuddering rumble.

Brushing plaster dust from her sleeve, Raell turned to Naed, who stood by the fire, looking at the ceiling.

"Do you need to—?" she said when nothing else broke the silence.

"They'll sort it out."

He'd been slow to enter the chamber, the one in which she'd been sleeping. The one in which she'd been attacked. She cast a discreet glance at the floor near the bed, but a thick woven rug had been laid there. If any bloodstain remained, the rug concealed it. She shuddered and approached the fire. If there was naught to see, there was no reason to think about it. Tonight was about the two of them, alone, together. *At last.*

Naed stood with his hand on the deerskin-lined armchair Gam had slept in. Brows lowered and glinting red in the firelight, he looked deep in thought and far away.

She moved closer. "What are you thinking?"

Rousing with a sigh, he ran his palm over the well-worn skin. "This was my father's chair."

Of course! No wonder he'd been reluctant to take the chamber. If she'd learned her father was not her father but her uncle…

The idea was inconceivable. Her heart pinged, knowing he'd grown up thinking the same—his kin were who he'd been told they were—only to have his world turned upside down.

"If 'twill discomfit you to be here tonight, we can move."

"No. I need to accept it. All of it. Whether it

discomfits me or not."

A brave choice. Her throat thickened. "'Tis more than enough you've had to accept, Naed of Druemarwin, formerly of Tumin."

When he raised his head, firelight shone on bruises marring his cheekbone. *Bloody, stupid men!* He *did* look better than her brother, and for that she was grateful—not to mention proud at having her choice of husband vindicated. Still...

"I'm sorry about my brother—"

"I'm sorry about my mother—"

They eyed each other, grinned, and the tension in the chamber dropped to a low hum.

Raell's shoulders relaxed. "Did you see Toth steaming? 'Tis sure, I thought he'd break the Lord of Kassi's fingers."

"My mother would terrify even the Prince. She's more devious than Rolnar of Roines."

"What a pair they make! Sisters be thanked, they only want what's best for us."

"Even...even when we might not want it?"

The temperature of the room plunged, and Raell froze despite the fire. Her heart stumbled. Had she heard correctly?

What are you asking? Her pulse pounded out the question, but she dared not give it voice. If she spoke, he'd have to answer, and she feared with all her heart what he might say. She steeled herself to meet his eyes, to wait.

The flash of humor had gone from Naed's face, and he took her hand between his. His touch was warm, palms calloused, knuckles bruised and freshly scabbed. Her body sang, as always, at the contact, but she held herself still.

"Raell, are you in any way being pushed into this marriage?"

Oh, that. She blinked, laughed, blurted, "Of course not," while blood returned to her fingers. *Mayhap it's come a little sooner than expected because of Bennin of Nye, but...*

He studied her so earnestly a curl of doubt tightened her stomach. What if she'd misjudged? What if she and the Prince and Lady Aerid had all misjudged the depth of his affections? What if he thought a Tolemak bride was too much trouble now he was home among his own kind?

"And you?" Speaking took enormous effort, and her voice came out husky. "I know Lady Vyenne sprang this on you—on all of us—only this morn. Is it—is this what *you* want?"

Those rare green eyes she loved didn't blink or dodge but held her gaze as Naed moved closer, toe to toe.

The firelight revealed a scattering of gold, brown, and blue flecks throughout what she'd thought of as a solid band of eye color. That colorful iris shrank to a narrow ring as he touched fingertips to her cheek, pools of warmth that shot delicious tingles along her nerves.

"Ah Raell, I've wanted you from the moment you accosted me in Albon, telling me I needed tending, ordering me about."

Heat flooded her body, dissolving fear and doubt and replacing them with another kind of tension, the kind induced by the way his voice had gone all gravelly. Confidence restored, she lifted her chin, looked him in the eye. "'Tis sure, someone had to. You weren't going to care for yourself."

Her left arm ached, but she raised it anyway. Demon be damned if she'd forego touching him now they were alone. She traced two fingertips along the cheek she'd cleaned and patched not so long ago. Amid a day's growth of copper stubble, and barely visible beneath green-blue bruising, a tracery of pale lines remained of the scrape.

"'Twas a fine bit of work, you know, for one who's not a healer."

"You're a woman of many talents, Raell. I look forward to discovering them." Naed moved closer, knee to knee, and released her good hand, clearly intending nothing to impede his progress toward what she suspected would be a kiss.

Clunk.

"What's that?" He pushed back half a step.

Bloody hell! His sword hilt had thunked up against her pocket, against the weapon concealed there. She rolled her eyes. Now was *not* the time to explain *everything*. Best to keep it simple.

"After yesternight, after the attacks, 'twas in my mind I needed something to defend myself." Reaching between their bodies, she carefully withdrew the long-bladed knife from its sheath beneath her pocket. He needn't know about the dagger in her left sleeve or the footwear she'd ordered made to conceal a knife.

Saucer-eyed, he blinked once, twice, before he coughed out a chuckle. "Banir tells me I must remember I've wed a Tolemak, not a D'nalian."

"Be there that much difference?" This was the crucial question. She held her breath, dreading his answer.

"Among titled ladies with regard to weapons, aye." With great care, he took the knife and examined it. "I doubt my mother has ever touched a blade, or my sisters either. Nor have they ever had need to." He tested the edge with his thumb, found it mayhap sharper than he expected, for he shot her a glance. "From the armory?"

"Ekwul is accommodating."

Naed's brows winged up. "Ekwul? Truly? That man is never accommodating to aught Banir and I require." He laid the knife on the table. "If you've charmed him, Raell, I'll be eternally grateful."

In truth, she'd stunned the old servant with her request, and Gam had bullied him into action, but when she'd additionally asked for the dagger and the boots to be made, he'd readily complied. She wasn't sure if the old man was charmed or frightened, but if the result pleased Naed, mayhap he wasn't as put off by her blade-bearing as she feared.

"You are not disappointed...that I might be...unafraid to handle a weapon?"

"Hardly." In confirmation, he once more closed the space between them. "Your quick thinking saved both of us yesternight, Raell. Thank you."

He'd taken that well. Mayhap she could unburden a little more.

She ran her good hand down his arm, finding a bit of raised stitching under her fingertips. The green tunic was clearly not his and definitely out of fashion, though she approved of how it set off his eyes and fiery hair. What was that silvery pattern along his sleeve meant to depict? *Sisters!* If those were deer, someone needed a lesson in embroidery.

Blinking, Raell refocused. If she were to broach this subject, she needed her wits about her. She traced a finger along the silver fox trimming Naed's collar. "Yesterday you wished to know why I came so suddenly and without notice."

"The Prince sent you, aye?"

His breath stirred her hair. Spices in the wine he'd drunk pleasantly flavored the air. She'd rather taste the spices in his kisses. If she rose up on tiptoe and touched her mouth to his, belike he'd forget what she'd started to say, but that would be cowardly. And no one in the house of Tylus was a coward.

"Aye." She curled her fingers into his collar, anchoring her gaze on his chin. "But 'twas because of the Lord of Nye."

Above her focal point, his face pulled into a scowl. "He arrived just before I left. Sisters, I should've waited to see what he wanted."

This was the delicate part. How much to tell...

"Lord Belac proposed an alliance. I know naught of the details, other than a request to wed me to his son Bennin."

Not a *request* so much as a calling due on a promise, but she dared not be that blunt. As it was, her news had Naed's expression darkening.

She gripped his arm. Muscles had already bunched there. If she didn't cling to him, he would likely break free and pace. "Be assured, the Prince meant to protect you—and us. 'Twas why I left in such a rush. The Prince ordered Toth to accompany me, and Lady Aerid provided my disguise. 'Twas why I was injured in the marsh. No one could know I was a woman."

"If I had waited but an hour or two more—"

"You could not have known. No one could have."

There, she'd told him—at least as much as she dared for the time and place. Now to pull him from his dark thoughts and bring him back to this chamber, this moment, their impending union.

With a deep sigh, Raell ran her hand along Naed's sleeve, smoothing, soothing, kneading at the tension beneath her fingers. When the muscles loosened a fraction, she slanted a glance upward, coaxing his gaze with a flutter of her lashes. "But all is well, aye? We are here now, together, wed as we wished to be—mayhap in circumstances other than we'd foreseen but wed nonetheless."

She stepped closer so their bodies brushed. Her reward was a sound so low in his throat she doubted he knew he'd made it and a different kind of tightening of his muscles. The delicious kind that set all her womanly parts humming in response. She leaned in.

His scent wafted around her, a blend of leather, wool, and something…pungent. Her nose wrinkled and she sneezed.

"Damned poultice!" He'd jerked back a step and was scrubbing both hands over his cheeks. "Banir swore he washed it off, but…"

That blush she loved spread up his throat. Between the rubbing and the blushing, he'd be delightfully red-faced soon. Laughing gently, Raell approached and laid a hand on his chest. "Mayhap 'tis the tunic."

Naed stilled, and his hands fell slowly to his sides. She had his full attention. Those beautiful eyes, dark pools now, watched her intently. His heart hammered beneath her hand.

Smiling with womanly power, she regarded him

from under her lashes. "My gown be borrowed too. What do you think we should do with them…husband?"

Chapter Twenty-Eight

Tear them off. Now.

Naed gulped. Wire-tight, it was all he could do to stand still and resist his immediate impulse. Raell didn't really want what she was suggesting. Did she?

All evening when he hadn't stared at the crowd, dazed and overwhelmed, he'd snatched glances at the vision in blue beside him. The color set off her hair, and the gold trim ignited her eyes. The fitted bodice, while modestly cut, emphasized her breasts, neither too large to be vulgar or too small to ever be mistaken for a boy's.

How in the Name of the Sisters had she managed to conceal such perfection?

He swallowed, knowing from yestereve just how perfectly those breasts fit into his hands. At the memory, his fingers flexed.

Breathe.

Mayhap that was a mistake, for the inhale teased him with her scent, white lilies, some kind of fragrant soap, and whatever infused her hair. Of its own volition, his hand gathered up locks trailing over her shoulder and thumbed strands across his fingers. He'd not paid attention to hair except as it identified a person. He gave little thought to his own except to tie it back from his face and occasionally curse the color for making him stand out.

But these strands…they slid across his skin like silk, some dark gold, some nearly white, most the color of honey. In Vinvinnysee he'd seen finery and furnishings made with golden thread. Not a strand of it compared to the glory shimmering in the palm of his hand. Eyes closed, he brought the locks to his face and inhaled.

Sun. Earth warm with it. Grass…tall, thick, and freshly pressed under their bodies. They'd not yet shared a summer, but Raell surrounded him with the sense of it.

"Naed?" She gazed at him expectantly. "Will you kiss me?"

"No."

He'd startled them both, but his mind asserted control and amended, "Not yet. If I kiss you now, I fear I won't be able to stop and-and things will happen too fast…for both of us."

"Ah, but I'm not afraid. I trust you, husband."

There was that word again, the one that undid him, that wound him into a quivering mass of desire, want, need.

Husband.

They were wed; she wore the ring he'd placed on her finger; they'd had their hands bound and their lives forever linked. Raell was his in word. All that remained was to make her his in deed.

If only he could bring himself to move, act.

Breathe.

Her hand lay over his heart, a warm gentle weight atop every bang and thump rattling his ribs. Grasping it, he pressed the palm to his lips. When her eyes darkened, Naed flicked his tongue and tasted her skin.

He blinked, startled. What had impelled him to do that? But when she sucked in a breath and her pupils grew enormous, lightning shot through him. It took all his control to not yank her into his arms and crush her mouth beneath his. He'd done that yesternight and caused her pain. He would not act like a beast again.

'Take your time. 'Tis important to a woman.'

He licked his lips, tasting her on them, wanting more, wanting to know all the flavors of her skin.

How much time?

If only he weren't wound so damnably tight.

If only he knew what in the Name of the Sisters to do next.

Mayhap, be honest?

Seizing the idea like a rope tossed to a drowning man, he blurted, "Raell, love, I've not done this before and…"

"What? Be wed?" Her eyes glinted with mischief. "'Tis sure, I should hope not."

Not the reaction he expected. Mayhap she misunderstood? "I've not…I'm as much a virgin as you are."

Sisters Three! The flush raced to his hairline, a full-body flush made longer and hotter for wishing it away. Why the Demon hadn't he confessed to being *untried*? That sounded so much better than…what he'd said. What would she think of him now?

Oddly, those expressive gold-brown brows, darker than her hair, hadn't risen in shock or surprise. Instead, her lips curved up at the corners, as though he confirmed what she knew.

"Well, then, we'll discover this together, aye?" Raising their still-linked hands to her mouth, Raell pressed a kiss to his bruised knuckles. "To be sure, I'd have it no other way." Holding his gaze, she trailed her tongue across the back of his hand.

Trailed fire was more like. He stood rigid while every nerve ending in his body burst into flames and his cock stood at attention.

She regarded him with that cat's smile he knew all too well, the one that told him he was entirely in her thrall. "I'll not be sharing you, Naed of Druemarwin. Ever. 'Tis best you know that now."

Though she smiled, steel laced her voice. He recalled the blade she'd withdrawn from her gown and understood he'd wed not just a Tolemak but a daughter of Tylus, a man who held to loyalty as fiercely as he fought.

Well, he would meet her expectations—exceed them even—with the steel of his fidelity. "I-I'll not be sharing you either, Raell. Be assured, I'm not my mother. Or my father. On my honor, my heart is yours, and has been since the day we met."

"Good. 'Tis settled then." She released his hand, and some of the tension spooled from his body, only to rewind tight when she tossed her hair over her shoulder and said, "What would you like to do first, husband?"

That word again, the one that gave him license to know her body as no other man would, to uncover every delicious curve and valley, to put his cock where it yearned to go, to mate and become one with the woman he loved. To do to each other and with each other whatever they could conceive that would give them both pleasure. For hours he'd thought of little else; now his mind had gone blank, except for three words—*Take your time*—pounding in time with his pulse.

How much time?

His throat worked, trying to swallow, but all moisture had evaporated from his mouth. He ran a dry tongue over dry lips. "Mayhap, 'twould be best if you begin, Raell."

She nodded, smiled, and Naed released a breath. Sisters be thanked, he'd stumbled upon a response that pleased her.

"Aye, then." She touched a forefinger to her lips while she considered.

If she'd meant to make him rock hard, she'd succeeded. Blood thundered in his ears, and he focused on her mouth, *not* on the finger she tapped against her teeth, *not* on images crowding his brain, trying instead to hear what she wished, hoping he could fulfill it. Sweat bloomed along his hairline before she spoke.

"'Tis my wish to see you—" Her eyes twinkled. "—without your tunic."

That was easy. Before she could change her mind, he unbuckled his sword and thumped it and his knife on the table. That infernal belt of his father's clattered down next. Relieved to breathe again without impediment, he yanked his borrowed tunic and undertunic over his head. He was wondering where to put them when Raell took the garments and tossed them over Dranoel's chair.

A glimpse of Gam's three neat stitches closing the wound he'd forgotten as soon as he'd discovered it yesternight, and heat again crept up his throat. "Mind you, I'm all purple and green."

She flashed a thoroughly wicked grin. "Not everywhere."

Toe to toe, she flattened her palm on his chest and sighed. Running her hand from nipple to nipple, she paused only to thread fingers through the patch of hair between.

He sucked in a breath. Her gentle tugging set his skin on fire. Every hair she brushed across lit up a nerve that arrowed straight to his groin. "You saw me once before without my tunic," he managed, remembering a morning in Albon.

"Aye," she said, grinning like a minx, "but not to touch." She slid her hand up to his shoulder, sculpting all the planes and ridges between, and circled behind him.

He bit his lip while fingers trailed down his spine. When she pressed a kiss between his shoulder blades, he shuddered.

"My turn." Catching her arm, he steered her to stand before him.

She came with a pout that made his cock twitch. Without his tunic covering his breeches, nothing could hide his arousal. He flushed as her gaze took it in.

A D'nalian woman would be offended, or at least pretend to be. Raell smiled like a cat offered cream. She raised her gaze to his face.

"And what is your wish?"

"These." He cupped her breasts with both hands. "You've no idea how long I've wished to see and touch and...taste."

Her eyes darkened at the contact, and her intake of breath pressed those perfect mounds into his palms. "Then you must help me," she said, her voice husky, "for the gown fastens all in the back."

He gulped and nodded while she turned ever so

slowly and drew her hair over her shoulder.

Breathe.

If only he could. He'd never been confronted with a woman's gown before. There was a dizzying array of laces and ties and small knots, and his fingers felt thick and clumsy as he plucked at the top one. Her scent wafted from each inch of skin he uncovered, and her finely curved bottom teased him with a new thought. He'd never held her from behind. Now the image of her naked, his hands cupping her breasts, his cock pressed into that space just hinted at by a shadow below her waist gripped him with such clarity, sweat trickled beside his ear. His hands trembled, but finally the gown fell away, and she stepped out of it, leaving her clad only in a sleeveless shift and slippers—and a tightly bandaged upper arm.

"Your wound," Naed said as she gathered up her gown and draped it over Dranoel's chair. "Does it trouble you?"

"Only when I think of it." With a mischievous glance over her shoulder, Raell added, "Have a care to distract me and I'll not think of it." Then she toed off her slippers and pushed them beneath the chair. When she straightened and turned, firelight silhouetted her body within the shapeless garment.

Curves. Valleys. Rosy nipples tenting the thin fabric. A shadowy triangle at the apex of her thighs. He swallowed. "Take it off. Please."

"Would it not please you more to do it yourself?"

Aye, it would. The beast within agreed. With a feral growl, Naed seized her hips and pulled her against his body with so much force, he tumbled backward into the chair. He made to rise, but the breasts he'd waited so long to taste brushed his face, so he opened his mouth and suckled fabric and all. His hands swept her back before bunching in her shift to hold her in place when her body bucked.

Shifting to the other breast, he left a damp circle around a perfectly peaked nipple. The dark aureole outlined by thin fabric invited him back, this time to tongue the peak and then suck even more of soft, warm, yielding mound into his mouth.

She moaned, a breathy sound deep in her throat. Her fingers ran rampant through his hair until she grasped his queue and pulled his mouth away. "Take it off, please!"

Her words, her meaning, penetrated the sensual fog induced by tasting her, and Naed tilted his head. Inches above, her face was flushed, eyes half closed, lips parted.

Resisting those enticingly moist lips took all his control. Instead, he grasped the front of her shift with both hands. "Is that *your* wish now, Raell?" came out as a rasp. "Because you've not yet fulfilled mine."

Her lids lifted enough to show him dark pools circled by bright gold and sparkling with fire. "'Tis my wish to be naked with you, Naed of Druemarwin. Is that not clear enough?"

Oh, aye, it was. So clear the shift tore between his fists, rent to her navel. He'd startled her so much he had time to shove the garment down her arms, turn her, and pull her back atop his lap before she protested, "But I want to touch you…"

"Shush, now, I'm having my wish." From behind, he cupped her breasts, testing the weight, the soft, resilient pliability of the treasures resting in his palms.

Kneading gently, he nipped at her shoulder, skimming little bites up to her hairline. This close her skin glowed like pure cream in the firelight, and the delicate fuzz beneath her ear tickled his tongue.

Moaning, she covered his hands with her smaller ones, splaying pale, slender fingers over knuckles he'd bloodied in defense of her, of himself, of his right to hold her and touch her like this. A growl rumbled up from his chest. The sight, the sensation was more erotic than anything he'd imagined.

So was the heady realization that, for the first time this night, he'd gained control, and not merely of her body—although this position *did* put him in delicious contact with almost every part of her he yearned to explore. Still, she'd had her way—not that he hadn't enjoyed it—for long enough; now it was his turn to take her where he wished to go.

Naed flattened one palm on her belly and anchored her against his throbbing cock. Her scent surrounded him, warm naked woman and more, the earthy musk that was hers alone wafting from beneath what remained of her shift, wafting from that thatch of dark golden hair visible at the bottom of the rent. His nostrils flared and he bit down, then soothed the bite with his tongue.

Take your time.

"You are so beautiful, Raell." Catching her earlobe, he sucked on it while she squirmed and pushed at his hand on her belly. "Tell me what you wish, love, what pleases you."

"Have-have you had your wish?"

He rolled a nipple between finger and thumb, and she panted. "Aye, for now. 'Tis your turn."

In truth, he was barely clinging to sanity. Thank the Sisters she'd not insisted he drop his breeches. That thin barrier kept the beast at bay. That beast could smell how she wanted him, how ready she was to take him inside her, but he had a plan. He kneaded that taut, tight little belly and inched fingertips beneath what remained of her shift. "Would you like me to touch you...lower?"

He would see to her pleasure first. Even if it killed him.

****

The blond man sat at the far end of the Great Hall and sipped ale. He'd filled his belly with the finest dinner he'd eaten in months. He'd laughed with the Kassi men and drunk toasts until some of them slid under the trestle table. Fools they were who couldn't hold their ale. He, on the other hand, enjoyed the pleasant numbing of aches inflicted by yesternight's tumble down the tower stairs. This morning's deliberate collision with a servant's tray cost him a tooth, but it served to explain the split lip the Tolemak bitch had given him with that damned, heavy door. He'd considered starting a fight instead, but that would've drawn too much attention when the guardsmen were already searching for someone with a fresh injury.

So he sat now in the shadows, surrounded by snoring and ale-addled Kassi men who sang snatches of the same song over and over again. Their voices had dropped to a low hum, easy to ignore while he stared at the table raised above all others at the opposite end of the Great Hall. If he had a few pinches of shepherd's bane, mayhap he could've persuaded Gert to slip it into a pitcher headed for that table.

But he had none. So he hadn't hailed Gert except to

nod in passing. And that table raised above all others sat empty as the festivities wound down. He itched to make use of his Adanak knife, but Dlaniger had advised patience. He was a great teacher, Dlaniger was, for one so young and so dead.

He scowled. The bastard of Druemarwin would pay for that death, but not tonight. If only he and his bride weren't guarded by Tolemaks...

Tossing down the rest of his ale, he leaned against the stone wall and contemplated the drama with the Tumin contingent that had fizzled all too quickly. An emissary from D'nalian power and authority in the north, a pack of uncouth Tolemaks far from home, Kassi and the soft southern lords...and all these weapons at the belts of men too stupefied to notice how or when they might go missing.

He pushed away from the table. Mayhap an opportunity would arise to make a little mischief.

Chapter Twenty-Nine

Naed had slid his fingers into her woman's hair, found her wet and throbbing, and touched her...*there*. She'd convulsed around his fingers, mayhap even screamed—a little—while he'd bitten her neck like a stallion dominating a mare. And she'd thrilled at it.

Then he'd lifted her, deposited her on the bed, and stripped off his breeches and boots. Before she could properly see him erect and proud, he'd found her slick sheath and pushed his way into it. There had been...not pain but discomfort...until there wasn't, and he'd taken her soaring again. He may have shouted too, when the hot rush of his seed filled her. Now he lay atop her, heavy and damp with sweat, and all Raell wanted to do was kiss him. She could reach only his jaw, so she scraped her teeth over stubble.

He stirred, pushed up on his elbows. "Forgive me, Raell. I thought...I meant to be gentler. Are you...are you all right?"

His expression, as if he feared he might've broken her, triggered a laugh. "Silly man. You've made me tingle all the way to my toes. I love you." She palmed his face and pulled his mouth down, offering her tongue, sucking his when he responded.

They were still joined, and his cock twitched inside her. She purred at the sensation, the sense of feminine power.

"Now, that was a proper kiss." She gasped when they broke apart. "Why did you not kiss me sooner, husband?"

He rolled to his back. His cock slid out of her, leaving her oddly bereft. But the tender way he pulled her onto his chest and stroked down her spine more than made up for the loss.

"Because, wife," he said, eyes twinkling, "your mouth is more temptation than I, poor soul that I am, could handle just then."

"Humph. Poor soul, indeed." She flattened palms on the planes of his chest. Bone overlaid with muscle, solid yet resilient under her fingertips, a brown nipple she'd touched but not tasted. She licked her lips and slid one knee between his thighs, relishing the prickle of coarse leg hair on skin sensitized to all manner of contact. "And now?"

Naed chuckled. "A few kisses, my love, might be in order."

She gave him one, open mouthed and wet, then sprang up on her knees. "I want to see you. You had your look at me. 'Tis my turn to see what I'm getting in a husband."

"Mind you, I didn't see nearly enough. But go ahead, have your look." He lay back and grinned.

"Tell me, why do you look like a cat that's dined better than he should?"

"Because I pleased you. Twice." Grin widening, he fit his hand to the dip in her waist. "'Tis more than I expected I could give you when I wanted you so badly."

He looked happier than ever she'd seen him, that persistent air of misery banished—temporarily, at least—his body fully relaxed. A sudden lump pushed at her throat. Loving her, making love with her, had done that for him. She lifted his hand and kissed each fingertip, tasting herself on his skin. Her nostrils flared at the musky scent, and a little thrum vibrated low in her belly where his cock had stretched her, broken her barrier and claimed her body. Muscles she didn't know she possessed felt pleasantly exercised.

"'Twas wonderful, both times. And 'twill be wonderful again, for I'm not near done with you this night, husband."

"You're an insatiable little minx, but I'll do my best. I love you, Raell." He pulled her in for a wet, open-mouthed kiss of his own. "Have your look while you may before my strength returns."

"Be that a promise? If 'tis, I'll hold you to it." The candles had dimmed, draping the bed in more shadow than suited her purpose. "Stay but a moment. I need more light." Well aware of her nakedness, and reveling in his avid attention, she slid off the bed and winced. Her legs, it seemed, protested having been spread wide to accommodate his body. Well, a few twinges were small payment for such pleasure. Padding to the fire, she threw on a log and stirred up more flame.

"Your bruises...Sisters, Raell! Did I do that to you?"

Bloody hell! She'd forgotten her purple backside. "'Tis a wonder what a fall on stone may do, aye? Be assured, you've done naught to make me ache. In truth, I'm feeling no pain."

Indeed, their lovemaking had banished all thought of her wounded arm and multiple bruises. He needn't apologize for the few new aches such activity had created.

Touching a finger to her lips, she shaped them into the pout he'd responded so strongly to earlier. "Have I done the same for you, husband?"

Naed's grin returned and widened, confirming she'd made the right move. Sisters, but she loved the way he smiled, the way he devoured her with his eyes.

"Can you not tell, my lady wife?" He laced both hands behind his head. The position showed off his biceps and corded muscles wrapping his ribs. Exposure to the sun had darkened his arms and chest, making his skin glow like warm gold in the renewed firelight. Freckles dusted his shoulders and arms. Below his waist his skin was a rosier pale than hers, a color mayhap that came with fiery hair and a D'nalian bloodline.

What would their children look like? Rising from her crouch, Raell passed a hand lightly over her belly. Mayhap she was breeding one now, a girl with red-gold hair or a boy with bright green eyes. Her throat thickened again and she paused at the table, both to recover herself and pick up a chunk of cheese.

"I thought 'twas me you were hungry for." Naed's gentle chiding pulled her from her reverie.

Flashing a grin, she broke the cheese, put half in her mouth, and climbed onto the bed. "Aye, but I mean to make the most of this night. That requires a bit of sustenance. Would you like a bite?"

"I fear I cannot move yet. Will you feed me?" He gave her an uncharacteristically wicked look, full of mischief and such heat it stirred answering warmth in all her womanly parts.

She attempted an aloof expression, but her voice

betrayed her, coming out husky. "If you insist. Open, please."

He did, and sucked her fingers.

All the secret spaces attuned to his body's use clenched and moistened. She enjoyed a delicate shudder while her body sang. Two could play at this game. With wet fingers, she tweaked his nipple.

He sucked in a breath.

"Oh, you like that too, do you?"

"You surprised me. Try it again and we'll see."

"Later. 'Tis looking I wish to do." Sitting on her heels, she ran her gaze down his body. His belly was concave and corded. More dark copper hair like that curling on his chest circled his navel and then arrowed a thin line to his cock, which stirred in its crinkly nest at her scrutiny. She glanced up, saw a blush spreading up his throat and grinned. "Fear not, husband. All I see pleases me."

She was well acquainted with lines scoring his cheek and small nicks that marred his face, arms and hands, injuries common to a man who'd grown up handling blades, common among brothers who played rough and fought. She'd had a glimpse, twice now, of the silvered patch along his ribs. What she'd not seen but knew by his gait had to exist was the puckered mound surrounding a gouged area on his thigh. No wonder the injury pained him. Even her untrained eye could see it was deep and still healing.

He shifted under her examination. "'Tis ugly, I know." He pulled a bit of bedding over the wound, but she stopped his hand.

"No more ugly than this will be." She lifted her bandaged arm. "Twice Gam's stitched it."

Leaning forward, she ran her hand gently over Naed's wound, conscious of how his thigh muscles trembled, how he tried hard not to flinch. With fingertips, she absorbed how the skin's texture changed, from bristly body hair to stiffened bare scar, tracing her palm over the uneven surface, locating as she bent closer the tiny, even stitch marks that had begun to fade. "Gam does fine work, but these be even better."

"Aerid—Lady Aerid—did her best. She saved my leg."

Ah, so there was that *between them as well.*

The spike of jealousy struck as keenly as a thin, sharp blade. Raell held herself still until it passed. *Don't be daft. He's lain with no other woman but you. He loves you. D'nalian honor will keep him true.*

Besides, Lady Aerid was a gifted healer. Of course she would've saved the man who saved her beloved Prince.

Relaxing her shoulders, Raell took a breath. Best not to open what was clearly a painful memory for him and a sore point for her. She transferred her attention to his torso. Careful not to tickle, she rested her palm on the scarred patch over his ribs. "What of this? How came you by it?"

"'Tis naught. A bit of missing skin, no more."

He dodged her eyes. Belike, her interest in his scars made him uncomfortable. She exhaled a small, exasperated sigh. While Naed's reticence was usually refreshing, considering she'd grown up listening to innumerable retellings of each injury suffered by her menfolk and their comrades, that modesty she so admired could sometimes prove a trial.

Placing a forefinger on the cleft in his chin, Raell

turned his face to hers. "'Tis a part of you, and I would know all that I may of the man I love. Will you not tell me? Or must I guess? Bear in mind, 'tis many a wound I've seen among my brothers." *And heard recounted till I thought my head would burst.* She looked at him expectantly until he squirmed and confessed.

"If you must know, 'twas from a lance."

"Vinvinnysee Lancers?" She sat up straight. "You fought them? Tell me."

His blush deepened. "I tried. 'Tis a fool who goes at one on foot bearing only a sword."

"But you did well, aye?"

He shrugged. "I broke the weapon of one of them, but a second one gave me this."

"Splendid!" She beamed. "'Tis sure that must be how you caught the eye of the Prince."

He'd gone scarlet from chest to hairline. "No. I caught his eye weeks before, here on Druemarwin's green. He gave me this." A flick of his eyes indicated a whitened line on his upper arm.

"Oh, I heard. You disarmed him."

"Aye, until he flattened me with his shield before all and sundry." He stared into the canopy above, clearly embarrassed.

How D'nalian. She snorted, unsympathetic. "A man flattens another man, they get up, share wine or ale, and all is forgotten but the next day's headaches. 'Tis true, aye?"

He gaped as if she'd sprouted two heads.

Heat infused her cheeks. He shouldn't be startled; everything she said was true, even for D'nalians. When it came to brawling, a man was a man, regardless of his bloodline. "Toth assures me all is well between you two," she explained. "'Twas the same for you and the Prince, aye? Else you would not be his Second."

Silence.

Those green eyes she loved shrank from wide open shock to something more assessing. Naed studied her so intently she jumped when a log popped. Had she somehow put her foot in it?

Put her foot in what? He was D'nalian, after all, and she was not. She was chewing her lip when he uncurled an arm and placed his hand on her hip.

"I've never before met a woman who comprehended that."

He spoke softly, and his thumb traced lazy circles toward her belly, toward that spot between her thighs that came alive with anticipation. The merest look, the least touch and her body vibrated like a finely tuned instrument.

"How did you become so wise, Raell?"

"Belike, it comes from having naught but brothers." She'd tossed off the retort as though his comment hadn't mattered, as though his look hadn't conveyed admiration. But her heart bloomed with the praise and her face warmed. To hide the blush, she tilted her head toward the canopy and plowed fingers into her hair.

He chose that moment to rear up and catch her about the waist. Before she could squeak a response, his mouth was at her breast and she tumbled onto her back. "I'm not near done looking," she protested as he pressed her into the bedding.

"You took too long." He shifted to her other breast, tonguing the nipple, then sucking it into his mouth. "Is this what you planned to do to me?"

She ran a bare foot up his calf while her body hummed. Every stroke of his tongue, every nip of his teeth triggered an answering pulse in her secret spot. Could she do the same to him? It would serve him right if she could.

Thrusting her fingers into his queue, she pulled his head up. "Aye, if you'll but let me."

With a lazy smile, he licked her nipple once more as she hadn't pulled him far enough. "Very well." He rolled to his back, hauling her fully atop him. "But I might not last long. I mean to have you again this night."

In this position his intention was clear, firmly pressing into her belly. She slid a little lower, enjoying the velvet heat against her flesh, thinking about how his cock would feel in her palm if she dared reach between their bodies. If her touch there triggered the kind of response his touch...*there*...did, mayhap she should direct her attention elsewhere, for now, or he'd flip her onto her back again. A little thrill rippled through her belly. He was gentle and considerate, but when he used his strength...

His fingertips dug into her back, and he must've read her body's cues, for his pupils had grown enormous.

Murmuring, "Patience, my love," she flicked her tongue over the nipple she'd been tempted by earlier. The nub stood up straight under her ministrations. Beneath her splayed hands his body tensed as though he held his breath, waiting for what she would do next. Encouraged, she shifted to the other nub and circled it with her tongue before sucking it into her mouth. His chest hair tickled her nose, and his skin tasted pleasantly salty, so she licked and nipped her way toward his belly before a rumble beneath her lips stopped her.

"So you *do* like that." Grinning, she levered onto her elbows. "What else do you like?"

"I like to feel these—" Reaching between their bodies, he thumbed a nipple. "—wherever they touch me."

"'Tis pleased I am you find them so pleasurable."

His touch made her shiver, but she concentrated on what she'd not taken the time to examine before. Grasping first the leather thong about his neck, she untangled the cylinder from the fine gold chain before pressing a kiss to the charm she'd given him.

"I've not taken it off."

"Good." She placed both charm and cylinder side by side over his heart. "'Tis a powerful gift from the Sisters. And a mate for mine. See?" She located a slender chain beneath her hair and pulled its charm forward. "Alone, they be but two crescent teardrops, aye? But together—" She flipped his charm upside down and fit it into the spaces of hers. "—they become one whole piece. See how this chain of rings around the edges was broken but now the chain becomes whole again?" She demonstrated, and he nodded. "These belonged to my parents. Now they be ours."

"Raell, I'm honored." His serious expression confirmed he understood her gesture's significance.

Sighing, she rested her chin on hands folded over his breastbone and stared into those eminently honest green eyes. "Now you must tell me what resides in that cylinder you wear close to your heart."

A shadow flitted across his face, too fast to read.

His body tensed slightly before he heaved a great sigh. The inhale lifted her as though she were a feather upon his chest. While she grasped his biceps with a startled little hiss, his gaze went into the darkness above her head.

"My father's will is in there. He gave it to me nigh a year ago—to hold, mind you—while I went to war with the Prince. His gesture, the timing, made no sense, but he made me swear to carry it, so I did as he insisted. I had no idea I was his heir until after he died."

Ah, so that emotion she'd glimpsed was sadness. Or was it bitterness? Mayhap both, so tightly interwoven as to be inseparable. Sighing, she pressed a kiss to his breastbone. As for the will, she'd suspected he carried something of that much import close to his heart. She'd wanted only to confirm it, not return him to that persistent state of misery.

Mayhap, if she slid down and rubbed those breasts that so fascinated him on his belly, she might distract him. It was his turn to hiss when she dipped her tongue into his navel. Smiling, she grazed his cock with first one nipple, then the other, relishing the silky heat on her sensitized skin.

His eyes went dark and he gripped the bedding. "Raell…what…"

"Shush now." She ran her fingertip down his length. "I'm having my wish."

His body bucked and, fearful he'd throw her off and stop her exploration, she wrapped her hand around his cock.

Hot. Silky. Thick. And so, so strong, it pulsed in her hand. His musk enveloped her, urging her to squeeze and stroke and pull all that hard, hot thickness into herself. She levered up and straddled his hips.

"Raell—" he rasped as she positioned herself, "do you, do you know what you're doing?"

"No, but I want to do it." Tongue curled between her lips, she concentrated on lowering herself by increments, head thrown back, eyes closed, focusing on how her body adjusted to his size, sliding down when it did. "Do you…want it?"

"Sisters Three, don't stop."

Naed's fingers ground into her hips, pulling her down even as he thrust upward.

I'll have more bruises. Then her body took control of the age-old dance of love, and she stopped thinking altogether.

Chapter Thirty

Naed awoke to the curious sensation of having overslept yet having slept barely at all. Thin morning light filtered through high windows and revealed a gray-ashed fireplace, a clothing-strewn chair, and guttered candles. That pleasant heat glued to his back possessed a nose pressed to his shoulder and an arm draped over his ribs.

Raell.

Smiling, he grasped her hand and drew it under his chin. He could get used to waking like this, comfortably wrapped in warm, naked woman. All the soft parts of her fit so perfectly into all the hard parts of him. His cock twitched, reminding him of all the ways their bodies had so recently fit together. Sisters, but she'd surprised him with that last maneuver. No shy D'nalian, his clever Tolemak bride.

If he turned over now, he could have her again before the day intruded. In truth, he'd gladly spend the day abed—at least the whole morning—simply exploring, taking their time with each other. Anything to extend this bliss, remain in this delicious cocoon, this intimate world of sensual delight. Sighing deeply, he kissed her fingers.

Her scent surrounded him, the subtle white lilies of her hair, the musk of their love-making, and—he sniffed—something subdued but still pungent,

277

especially when it contacted the back of his throat. He frowned. What the Demon would she be wearing that would—

Gam's unguent!

His eyes sprang open. There it was, wafting from the tight bandage practically under his nose on the arm he'd tucked beneath his own.

Immediately he freed her and eased to his back. She exhaled a protest but snuggled into his side. He scanned the bandage for any sign of blood seepage. Nothing, thank the Sisters. Considering how she'd used—and abused—her arm yesternight, it was going to hurt like the Demon when she woke. He smiled, and his cock pulsed, remembering precisely how she'd used her arms on that last maneuver. They were definitely going to try that again.

Facing her, Naed folded one arm beneath his head and studied the woman who'd flabbergasted him by her wholly unexpected appearance at Druemarwin. Even now he could scarce believe she'd arrived before him. Accompanied by naught but her brother, no less. Much as he wished to avoid disturbing her, he couldn't suppress his head shake. Wonderment, chagrin, and a dose of humility scattered all thoughts but one.

Sisters Three, how completely she's changed my life.

Two—no, three—days ago he'd awakened in Kassi fortress, surrounded by his men, with no thought but of the hard road home and then on to Tumin. Here he was, scant days later, wedded to the woman of his dreams. His grin widened. Last night, together, Raell had opened his eyes to a whole new set of dreams involving his body and her body and all the ways they could pleasure each other.

Wayward hairs lay across her nose. He carefully gathered them and thumbed the strands across his fingertips, absorbing the texture, the shimmer of gold.

Treasure. Mine. Aye, that she was, and more. So much more Naed's heart stopped, kicked hard, then triple-timed until dots speckled his vision. Panting, he gripped her hair, clinging to the fragile, precious threads as to an anchor while the world shifted beneath him.

Now—*now*—he understood why, months ago, if Prince Arn had been armed that night in Vinvinnysee when Naed dared to confront him over Aerid, the Prince would've killed him, and done so without a qualm. Friendship, alliances, mayhap even family could go to the Demon when a man found the woman he wanted. The Prince was willing to risk everything he'd fought so long and hard to gain solely to keep Aerid in his bed.

Having found a woman of his own to love and cherish, Naed at last understood what his naiveté had allowed him to only partly grasp then. What he'd disdained as a purely animalistic, physical need was the glue that set the unbreakable bond.

His heartbeat slowed, his breathing evened, and the world—on its new axis—came into focus. Now he'd bedded *his* woman, now she belonged solely to him and he belonged solely to her, he'd cut his heart out before he'd yield her to anyone else. Raell was *his*, irrevocably so.

Belike, that was how his father had felt, and his mother, but—

He scrunched his eyes shut, blotting out *that*

image, *that* train of thought.

Inhaling deeply of scents that would forever fix *this* moment in his memory, he allowed himself the luxury of studying *his* woman. Dark gold lashes fanned her cheekbones. In the thin light, he counted eleven small freckles decorating her nose. Rosy color infused her cheeks and plumped her lips. They looked delicious enough to kiss, and he was sorely tempted, but he didn't want to wake her just yet. Smudges beneath her eyes made clear neither of them had slept much the past two nights, and Raell was still healing.

Opening his fist, he considered the strands of hair he'd crushed. They sprang back with surprising ease and, relieved, he gently tucked the strands behind her ear.

With his movement, the blanket slipped down. Dark purple marks stood out starkly against her pale skin where shoulder met neck.

He'd made those. With his *teeth*.

Flushing, he raked a hand through his hair. He'd let the beast loose, after all, and apparently it liked to bite. His good D'nalian morals ought to be offended, but his cock begged to differ, standing and pulsing at the memory—the salt-sweet taste of her skin on his tongue, the silk-soft texture beneath his lips, the firm resilience of muscles, tendons between his teeth, the eager, breathy sound of her pants as his fingers found that sweet little nub and stroked it.

Sisters! He wanted her again. How would he function when they left this bed? All he could think of was Raell's hand wrapped around his cock, how he'd practically crossed his eyes with pleasure when she'd squeezed and pulled and drawn him into herself.

Mayhap if he slid his hand lightly from her shoulder to her hip, he could nudge that silky little belly closer and—

Rap. Rap-rap. Rap.

Naed stiffened, recognizing Banir's knock. If ever there was a more inopportune time, with him hard as rock and the means of relief mere fragrant inches away…

He closed his eyes, wishing—wanting—to ignore the summons, but the Tolemak wouldn't disturb him unless it was important. With a heavy sigh, he eased out of bed, taking care not to dislodge the bedding. He plucked his breeches from the floor and pulled them on before sliding back the bolt. Though he opened the door a mere hand's span, a draft rushed over his bare feet and raised gooseflesh on his torso.

"What is it?" His voice came out hoarse.

Standing sideways, the Tolemak wore an apologetic expression but those sharp, tracker's eyes completed an instant's assessment. "The southern lords, their outriders be near."

Naed frowned, wishing he could read Banir as well as Banir read him. "And I should be dressed to receive them, aye?"

"As you say."

"Very well. Give me a moment."

Shutting the door, Naed thrust both hands through his hair. Sometime during the night his queue had come undone. So too, at this particular moment, had his will to see the Prince's mission through. His mind needed to shift to matters greater than the wishes and desires of one man and one woman, but it was exceedingly reluctant to do so, especially while he remained in this chamber. Sighing, he sat on his father's chair and pulled on his boots.

Remembering what he and Raell had done on this chair heated his cheeks. He'd made peace with his father's memory, for the most part, and he was fairly certain Dranoel would have approved of his bride, after he'd growled at her, of course. Naed smiled. Despite his gruff exterior, the man knew what love was. All Dranoel's actions spoke of it, even, mayhap, Dranoel's actions with his mother.

He heaved a sigh. That subject still rubbed him raw. Standing, he tugged on his undertunic and eyed the fur-trimmed dress tunic with distaste. Mayhap at this early hour he could go through the corridors carrying it and that damned belt. Banir had no doubt arranged for a shave and fresh clothing to be laid out in his private chamber near the Great Hall. Belting on his sword and knife, he flung the green tunic and wide belt over his shoulder. Then he turned and steeled himself to leave his wife.

Wife.

Naed drank in the lovely picture Raell made with her hand fisted under her chin and her lips slightly parted. Kissable. Oh, so kissable. He bent, kissed her forehead instead. When she stirred and opened sleep-dazed dark gold eyes, he trailed fingertips gently down her cheek.

"Good morning."

"You are going?" She yawned, stretched, and the blanket exposed her perfect breasts, rosy aureoles centered with nipples puckering in the chill air.

Sisters, how he wanted to warm those nipples with his tongue, suck them deep into his mouth, listen to her soft whimpers of pleasure when he did so.

He was hard yet again, a rod straining at his breeches. Thankfully, his undertunic hid the evidence. "Duty calls."

"The assembly," she said with a sigh.

"Sleep. You don't need to get up."

"If Banir has been here, 'tis sure your mother's maid will be close behind." She yawned again. "The silly mouse finds him fascinating, and he returns her interest."

"In truth?" He'd corner Banir later when he could think, when the cloud of her scent didn't grab hold of his belt and tempt him to fall into bed.

Naed blinked. Mayhap her scent played a part, but her hand had indeed caught his sword belt and tugged him closer.

With hooded eyes, the luscious woman warming the bed smiled that cat's smile he'd learned could mean so many things.

"I would spend this day abed with you, my lord husband, but as I've wed a D'nalian and the Prince's Second, I fear I must yield my desires to the greater good."

Grinning, he dove in for a quick, delicious kiss. "You are a minx."

"Come tell me so again tonight, for there be much I'm of a mind to try."

He groaned and unhooked her hand, kissing the back of it before escaping her reach. "'Twill be a wonder if I think of aught else till then."

"I shall be greatly disappointed if you do." She blew him a kiss.

With half a chuckle, half a groan, Naed forced his

feet toward the door. He had to leave while he could still walk. Thank the Sisters the clothing draped over his shoulder gave him some cover. Mayhap the chill corridor would diffuse the heat in his face and disperse the blood pooled in his groin.

Outside, Banir swept him with another sharp glance before falling into step. "Not that tunic today, then?"

"Never again, if I have my wish."

"You need to wash." The dark eyes twinkled. "Else every man's mind will go straight to his cock when you come near."

A long, hot, full-body flush consumed Naed. "Is it that obvious?"

"That you smell of coupling?" Banir smiled, a rare flash of teeth. "'Twas good, aye?"

"Damn you, it was." He grinned. "Better than good."

"So I heard."

Of course Banir had. He'd been standing before the chamber like the devoted guardian he was. "Sisters Three! Did anyone else?"

"The door be thick…enough…mayhap." Banir rocked on his heels, scanned the corridor, then leaned in. "Ignore Grodar and Morys. A bit of coin may've changed hands over yesternight's…performance."

More heat. An internal, infernal blaze of it. At least he no longer had to cover his groin. Groaning, he scrubbed hands over his face.

He was in for it, well and truly, all the crude jokes and ribbing every man of his acquaintance heaped upon the bridegroom the day after the wedding. He'd think it unfair if he hadn't been among those laughing at his brothers' discomfort after their joining ceremonies. "Sisters and the Four Winds!"

Banir bumped his shoulder, a hard, *pay attention* thump. "'Tis envy, no more. Remember—'tis *your* bed your lady warms tonight—and every night you wish for it to be so."

He lowered his hands, studied the man who knew him best, the man closer to him than a brother. "Aye, so it is. Thank you." Raell would be waiting for him tonight. He could get through this day—and every day hereafter—knowing that.

They fell into step again. Until halfway down the corridor when Banir said, "'Tis one thing more."

Naed stopped, brought up short by a stomach-curdling sense of dread. "What has my mother done now?"

Chapter Thirty-One

Raell had settled into the warm depression left by Naed's body when the door opened. This early, she'd hoped for another hour abed, another hour cocooned in this world between worlds, where she'd shed all her earthly trappings but the charm round her neck and the ring upon her finger. She was a new creature now, a woman wed, and her body still thrummed with all it had learned. Why couldn't she stay but a little longer to savor that before the demands of her new station intruded? After last night's festivities, the whole fortress should be barely stirring. But as Naed had been called away, mayhap that was too much to ask from the three women who trooped in.

Gam led, leaning on her stick and shuffling to the bedside. Elda scurried to stir up embers and remake the fire. Lady Vyenne, accompanied by the wolfhound, stood near the foot of the bed with clasped hands and an aloof expression. The dog sat beside her.

Huffing a sigh, Raell allowed Gam to examine her twice-stitched arm. "All is well, as you see."

"Aye." Gam grinned and waggled her eyebrows. "An' more'n well, if those marks upon your neck be any sign."

Raell flushed. She knew she'd gained new bruises; she wished she didn't have to show them to the trio who would pronounce the joining complete.

"We've ordered a bath," Lady Vyenne said. "While you're soaking, we'll change the linens."

Check them, you mean. They'd find the blood evidence they sought. Raell had seen the stains when she'd come back to bed with the cheese. She pulled the blanket under her chin and tried not to scowl at them for doing what was necessary.

"You look...well loved."

Those were the last words she expected from Naed's mother, from this cold column of formality. But, as they were true, she softened her expression, even allowed a small smile. "Aye, so I have been."

"I expect you're sore."

"A bit." Her new mother-in-law looked exhausted, her face colorless and drawn, as if she'd spent another sleepless night. Lady Vyenne wouldn't choose to entertain Lord Wendelmyr till dawn, regardless of D'nalian protocol. *That* man needed no assistance finding entertainment. She tracked the woman to the door, pondering. If not the annoying little lord, what then?

"The bath will soothe those aches," Lady Vyenne said as she directed servants to curtain off a space before the hearth, place a tub within and fill it. The wolfhound trotted between door and tub, inspecting each new person, sniffing—and sneezing—at herbs Gam crumbled into the tub.

Bucket after bucket of fragrant water steamed away the morning chill and frizzed Raell's hair around her face. When the tub was full and the servants had departed, her new mother-in-law stood by the bedside and held out her hands. "Come. Let's get you up and into the water."

That was a surprise. Other than the brief, emotionally charged hug yesterday, had the woman otherwise touched her? What had brought about this new intimacy? Aye, she was wed to Naed now, but was that enough? Pushing back the covers, she grasped hands as cold as the floor beneath her bare feet. She hissed in a breath, stood unsteadily, and discovered a new array of aches as both Lady Vyenne and Elda helped her into the bath.

Water to her chin and knee tops, Raell sighed and closed her eyes while the women examined the bed. The hot water steamed away all her stiffness, leaving her nigh as boneless as Naed's love-making had. Drifting on delicious memories, she ignored the activity until Lady Vyenne positioned a chair behind the tub and drew a comb through her hair.

Raell sat up, sloshing water over the edge. "'Tis not your task, m'lady. The maid—Elda—may do it."

"Elda has gone for her needle to stitch up your shift." A sigh, faint but audible.

Disapproval or resignation? Raell tensed, wishing she could see the woman's face. Reading that would be challenge enough.

A gentle tugging, the comb set down, fingers—still cold—working through a tangle. A murmured, "Young men can be so impatient."

Ah, resignation, with a bit of wistfulness, mayhap. Was she thinking of the man she loved, Naed's father? *How very human of you, m'lady.* Raell opened her hands, willing some of her tension to drain into the water. "We did no harm to the gown."

"Thank the Sisters, for you must wear it again to greet the lords." Another sigh, this gusty enough to raise goosebumps on Raell's damp shoulders. "Elda will do what she can with the clothing we have at hand. Pity you could bring none of your own things with you. Or a maid. Have you someone from Tylus you wish to send for when your belongings are fetched?"

"My belongings?" *Of course. How very practical to think of sending for them.* "I shall make a list, but mayhap my father has already sent them along, m'lady."

The comb set down, firmly, the scrape of chair legs, a face—pale despite the heat of hearth and tub—angled into her peripheral vision. "My dear Raell, as you are my daughter now and a lady in your own right as well as by marriage, we may dispense with titles while among ourselves. Does that suit you?"

Even more unexpected. "Um, aye, of course."

A nod, the woman's face shifted from Raell's view, the comb returned to its task. Logs popped in the fire. The wolfhound, panting, sat beside the tub and stared at the water as if considering a drink. Gam shuffled about in the background, presumably changing the bed linens.

There was a seductive pleasure in having her hair combed while she luxuriated in warm, perfumed water, but Raell would not allow herself to succumb to it. What was that woman behind her thinking? And how the Demon was she going to address her new mother-in-law? *Mother* seemed out of the question and *Vyenne* unnaturally familiar. She'd worked up the nerve to ask when the woman spoke.

"As that blade is lying naked on the table, dare I assume Naed has seen it?"

This again. I thought we'd settled it. "He

understands I am Tolemak and wish to have a means to defend myself."

Crossing before the hearth, Gam poked her head around an armful of linens. "With that lot what's comin', 'tis a fair plan, m'lady. If'n you don't mind me sayin' so."

"These are D'nalians, Gam. Lords and their attendants." Lady Vyenne's voice was stern.

Raell envisioned the regally severe expression that quelled servants and quailed courtiers alike. She needed to perfect that expression for her own use.

The old woman shrugged, evidently neither quelled nor quailed. "Beggin' your pardon, m'lady, but so's them what attacked the master. An' you. The both o' you. None of the folk would want you harmed. If'n the mistress carryin' a blade an' you walkin' with that beast be what protects you, 'tis all well an' good."

Raell's heart sped. "Thank you, Gam," she said before the woman behind her could rebuke what had to be a servant's impertinence according to D'nalian rules. Tolemak rules, too, if she were honest. She should establish herself as mistress in the eyes of the old healer, but not when the concern was genuine and the statement truth. "We appreciate your concern for our welfare and, 'tis sure, it pleases me to know you embrace me as mistress even though I am not what you may be used to."

"'Tis a different world, m'lady." Gam shifted her burden. The steam had ironed twenty years off her face, but the old eyes remained uncharacteristically somber. "Mayhap Druemarwin folk know that better'n most, seein' as we've been at the center o' it."

Lady Aerid. Prince Arn. Naed. Raell's pulse

pounded out the names. So much had begun in this place with the intersection of three lives. Three lives whose interwoven threads would birth a kingdom. And a chance for peace.

The weight of that new world and its promise pressed on Raell's shoulders. She'd put herself squarely into it, chasing a man with a heavy load of misery and a heart full of courage. Could she match Naed's heart? Could she be the partner he needed to ease his burdens, be the face of Tolemak for a people who had good reason to fear her kind? Could she and Naed show how alliances could work between two people who had each other's best interests at heart? She gripped the tub's edge while the wolfhound lapped at her fingers.

"Indeed." Lady Vyenne's voice was surprisingly gracious, as though the old healer's words had struck a chord within her too. "'Tis clear Druemarwin folk have had to endure a great deal, Gam. Yet I fear your trials are not done."

"We'll go the distance for the young master, m'lady. An' for her what's wed t' the Prince. An' for the two o' you. You'll look out for us, you will, an' us for you. Sisters willin'."

Raell thumbed the ring she'd worn for mere hours. She'd carried it about her neck for years and it had never burdened her as it did now, encircling her finger. She stared at the fine gold band—plain, pure, and simple, like the love her parents had shared. Like the love she and Naed shared. Like this fortress and the people in it.

Calm settled over her, and she fixed the old woman with a steady gaze.

"Aye, we shall, Gam. As your mistress, I assure

you, the folk of Druemarwin may count upon me to keep their welfare foremost in my mind."

****

"So it's true!" Alternately muttering and waving his arms, Allyn stormed between hearth and closed door. "What I'm hearing, what they're saying…"

Naed held his seat, gripping the arms. Much as he wanted to hurl himself into his half-brother's path, it would not serve. *Let him rant. Be the lord.*

He could blame this ill-timed visit on his—*their*—mother. After all, her midnight bolt had to have led Allyn directly to Druemarwin. *Where did she think Alwyl would look?* Naed ground his teeth. But the fault was partly his for overlooking her as a player in this drama.

Focus. The current threat was within striking distance, a large, armed, angry man who shared half his blood. That made Allyn all the more dangerous, especially when he was spouting, "Demon's Nine Whores, it bloody well *can't* be true!"

At Banir's insistence, Naed had washed, shaved, laced up chest armor beneath a fresh tunic, and put something in his stomach before allowing his half-brother admittance to his private chamber. Allyn stewing in the Great Hall suited his mood, as did limiting his half-brother's attendants to two.

For this—*this!*—he'd left a warm, willing, naked Raell?

Calm yourself. Be the lord.

That would be so much easier if whatever he'd eaten didn't lay now like a log beneath his ribs.

"What cannot be true?" He assessed the man who, at a dozen years older, had never seemed like a sibling,

292

more like a cousin whose occasional visits sucked up everyone's attention.

"All night they told me...that marsh-mouse of Kassi kept telling me...but I couldn't believe it." Florid with indignation, Allyn looked even more like his father. Barely into his thirties, his lank brown hair showed signs of thinning.

How you must hate that. The thought was unseemly, but damned if it didn't feel good when Allyn was behaving precisely as he had when they'd parted two years ago. Like the spoiled first son.

Naed dug fingernails into the wood. *Nothing has changed. Not in the eyes of Tumin. Yet.*

It fell to him to effect that change. *But not here, now, Demon be damned!* Allyn's appearance threw a stick—belike, a bloody great log!—into the cart wheel of his plans. Mayhap he'd been foolish, naïve even, but he'd clung to the idea he'd arrive in Tumin, accompanied by his allies, and catch the council of lords by surprise.

Play the beads as they've been cast, but turn them always to your advantage.

The Prince did so, and he was soon to be King.

Lay aside your personal feelings and focus on the Kingdom.

Naed willed his jaw to loosen, to unknot so he could ask in a mild, disinterested voice, "What, precisely, do you find so difficult to believe?" He leaned back as he'd seen the Prince do so many times, presenting relaxed confidence in a tense situation. Sisters, but that was nigh impossible when his gut screamed, *Throttle him!*

Allyn swung around, pent-up affronts boiling in his

eyes, and sucked in breath.

No, damn you, you will not speak! Naed cut off his half-brother's retort with a slash of his hand. The Kingdom would have to wait.

"What do you doubt, Allyn?" he said in the same mild but no longer disinterested voice. "Is that I, least among your brothers, am Dranoel's heir? Or are you unable to swallow the idea that I have become a trusted Second to a Tolemak Prince? Or is it so unbelievable that I am now a lord and you are yet the first son still waiting for his title?"

The words, icy calm and dredged from deep within where injuries had festered for years, poured off Naed's tongue with sweet ease. They came so fluently, when the final thought arrived, fully formed from he knew not where, he didn't doubt the truth of it. He simply bared his teeth and plunged it home.

"Tell me, Allyn, is what truly sticks in your gullet the fact you rode here thinking to find a vacant title ripe for a takeover by Tumin only to discover the master quite indisputably at home?"

Face mottled purple, Allyn's mouth worked like a beached fish. He'd taken each accusation like a physical blow, and the last one had shaken him so much he could only spit, "You bastard!"

"Aye! That I am, and 'tis no insult when my father cared more for me than yours ever did. When the man who made me lived and died with honor." He'd drawn blood; Naed could smell it. His innards trembled with the urge to finish this, but he reined it in. *Show power; show mercy.* The Kingdom's goal was to make allies, not enemies.

Puffed up like a threatened bird, Allyn stalked

between his flanking attendants. They were large, stone-faced, and gave him the confidence to retort, "You're a bastard nonetheless, in name *and* deed! Where is the legitimate heir? Where is Dlaniger?"

The wood beneath Naed's fingers was marsh oak; it wouldn't break, but it creaked under his grip. Banir at his side and Grodar at the door were more than a match for the Tumin guardsmen. And he'd expected this line of attack. "The *legitimate* heir, as you call him, was publicly disowned well before I bid farewell to you at Tumin. Dranoel's will, which you are welcome to read for yourself, names me son and heir."

Blinking, Allyn backed a half step, clearly flummoxed, until he gathered himself with a sneer and a two-fisted heft of his belt. "Dlaniger will dispute it."

"Dlaniger murdered his father, something any court of lords would agree renders him ineligible to inherit. As he is dead, the issue is moot."

Shock. Double shock.

Widened eyes offered a glint of white before Allyn struggled for composure, for words.

That kind of astonishment was beyond Allyn's ability to feign. Satisfied, Naed spared his half-brother the need to ask what their mother had fearlessly demanded.

"Rest assured, Allyn. Dlaniger did not die by my hand."

"I didn't…" Face pale, Allyn blinked several times, took stock, cleared his throat. "About Lord Dranoel's death…"

Pulse hammering at his temples, Naed waited. One hurdle, now for the next.

"You…you have witnesses to the act of murder?"

"An entire fortress full of folk saw Dranoel struck down by Dlaniger's arrow."

"And you were...?"

"In full view of all and sundry and unable to do a damned thing to stop it." Nor could he stop the pain slicing into his gut at the memory. All he could do was compress his lips and hold it in, hold everything in.

Something flickered in Allyn's eyes before his shoulders lowered from their hunched, defensive stance. "I'm sorry. No one told us how Dranoel died or by whose hand."

Naed allowed himself a breath. That had sounded genuine, even...brotherly. Still, he had to put down this challenge once and for all. "Do you doubt my account?"

"No."

"Do you dispute my right to Druemarwin's title?"

"No."

"Do you need to examine the will?"

"No, damn it!"

"Then tell me in all honesty why you are here, Allyn. And don't offer me that milksop about wanting to be sure Mother was safe."

"Who the Demon put a bee up your ass?" Allyn blustered now, a shaken man trying to salve his pride. "Letters from Druemarwin came. Mother disappeared. What were we to think but that she'd come here? You've always been her favorite." The last must've slipped out, for Allyn's gaze darted away and color blotched his cheeks.

"And now you know why." Naed unclenched one fist and flexed the fingers. The response—the hard truth of it—diminished his satisfaction. Was Dranoel all she saw in him, all she loved? *Sisters!* His emotions pulsed like blood beneath the fresh, fragile scabs protecting his knuckles.

He raised his gaze, forced his mind to the matter at hand. "When did you find out about my inheritance?"

"I told you—yesternight, from what's-his-name of Kassi."

"Does Lord Alwyl know?"

"Do you think he'd tell me if he did? We all know how close Father keeps things to the breast."

"*Your* father, not mine." Naed hadn't meant to voice that thought, but the bitterness and pain he'd dredged up ate holes in his restraint.

"He bloody well raised you!"

"Sheltered, mayhap, but as to the raising…you've always been his favorite." The food Banir'd made him eat ignited in his belly. He pressed his palm into the burn. Doing so quelled some of the trembling, too. "I was never more than an afterthought."

Naed hadn't meant to say that either, but he said it without heat. Allyn stopped his caged bear pacing. After a moment of stillness, Naed met the eyes studying him. They were father and son's best feature, a steely blue, suitable for lords and commanders.

Arms folded across his well-armored chest, Allyn stood with feet braced apart, looking—finally—like the lord of Tumin's right hand instead of a petulant man-child. "Afterthought or forethought, we've one thing in common, little brother."

Banir tensed, and Naed gave a minute shake of the head. Certain Allyn had seen the exchange, he leaned back and showed his teeth. "You mean, *man-without-a-title*, something besides our mother?"

Puckering as if he'd tasted bitterfruit, Allyn grumbled, "I'd change my birth if I could, but aye, besides that, *m'lord*." He shot Banir a glare, as if daring him to take offense. When none appeared forthcoming, he returned his attention to Naed. "We've both been handed a steaming pile of horse dung. Do you think I don't know Father keeps secrets? Do you think I like it, knowing he doesn't trust me? *Me!* His bloody damned heir!"

Warming to his topic, he ranged the room, circling the long table Naed had placed his chair well away from. "And you! Mother's favorite. All those years she kept you close and didn't tell you, did she? Or you wouldn't be so damned tight-assed about it now. They've buried both of us in the dung-heap of their secrets and lies. And this is what it comes to now, you with your armed guard facing down me with mine. We're blood, damn it, even if our parents aren't!" He slammed both fists on the table, spun, and stomped to the door and back. "We ought to be better than this!"

A show of disloyalty? Unexpected. Is it genuine? Allyn was shrewd enough in battle, a competent leader, but an independent thinker? Still, this kind of emotional response would hardly be sanctioned by Alwyl, epitome of the self-contained D'nalian. Might this be a new cast of the beads? *One way to find out.*

"Do you mean, because we're family?"

"Aye, thick-brain!"

Sisters Three, Allyn, can you not temper your tongue? He saw Grodar fidget in his peripheral vision, saw his loyal guardian's focus narrow, and hoped against hope—all for naught.

"Beggin' your pardon, m'lord." Grodar stepped

away from the door with a scowl. "But should he be talkin' to you like that?"

"I'll talk to my brother any damned way I choose without interference from your kind!" Allyn shot him a glare that would've quailed Tumin men, but the gap-toothed Tolemak only uncrossed his arms and glared back.

Naed lifted his hand a fraction, and both men stilled. His innards burned. How did the Prince endure this kind of tension day after day? How did the man keep his focus when there were so many players in the game, so many possible ways the beads could fall? At least Naed had expected this play. Sooner, in fact. And he was well prepared.

If only his stomach weren't tied in knots and dripping acid.

"Grodar is one of *my* kind, Allyn, as are all Tolemaks, Adanaks, and D'nalians within these walls. And while you are my blood and used to a way of treating me, that way is no longer applicable." His voice was quiet and even. He paused for a heartbeat— or three—while his half-brother absorbed the message. "Get used to it or get out."

He could lay down no clearer challenge. Either Allyn would thunder his way back to Tumin, or he would employ the, albeit limited, intelligence he'd been born with. Naed waited while his half-brother straightened and the steel-blue gaze narrowed.

Finally, you're looking at me as I am now, and not as you remember me.

What would he see?

A jolt of panic jellied his stomach, then melted away. He'd paid no more attention than usual to his attire, which meant he was dressed in clothing he wore like skin. D'nalian-made boots, somewhat battered but of good quality, a Tolemak-made tunic he had yet to return to Toth, a Tumin-made sword belt, much battle-stained, an Adanak knife Grodar and Morys gifted him with after he'd rescued the Prince, and the sword he'd carried with him from Tumin, a blade neither bejeweled nor unique but it fit his hand like the extension it was intended to be. If Allyn were half the soldier his reputation claimed, he'd see this and know it for what it was.

His half-brother gave a short, sharp nod and uncrossed his arms. "You *have* grown up. Two years away and you've made yourself a man. Well and good, Lord Naed. Call off your dogs and let's talk, man to man, about the muck our shared blood has rained down on us."

So much tension drained out of Naed's body, he had to gather himself a moment before attempting to stand. No point in revealing a game leg to a man he wasn't entirely sure he could trust. He pushed up from the chair, found his legs would indeed support him, and stretched his hand toward Allyn when a ruckus erupted in the hall.

"Stand aside and let me in!" The Lord of Kassi pulled open the door. With bloodshot eyes and skin drained of color, the little lord cast a wild gaze from man to man. "There you are, you Tumin bastard!" Rigid with fury, Wendelmyr stalked to Allyn and waved a bloody knife in his face. "A man of mine is dead and you're responsible!"

Chapter Thirty-Two

Raell dusted her hands of crumbs. She'd been surprisingly famished, or mayhap not so surprising. Her cheeks heated despite the chamber's warmth, and she allowed herself a small, secret smile.

How wonderfully refreshing this lovemaking was.

Sunlight streamed through mullioned window panes, washed clean by yesternight's storm. Resting chin upon palm, Raell wondered what matter of importance had drawn Naed away. If only she could wrap her arms around those thrillingly strong shoulders and kiss every freckle decorating them. Sighing, she drained her cup and enjoyed the silence of a chamber finally emptied of servants who'd cleared her bath. Only Elda remained, sitting in the pool of sunlight, head bent to her sewing.

And, of course, there was the woman who lowered her upright carriage into the hard-backed chair opposite and launched into speech. "Given the haste with which you left Tylus and the unrest rampant between here and Tolemak, belike your father is occupied with more pressing matters than his daughter's belongings. Nor is he like to think of sending a maid."

Vyenne folded her hands in her lap, but Raell wasn't fooled. Whenever the woman spoke like this, moved like this, it was all carefully planned. She tilted her head, inviting elaboration.

"While you were dressing and breaking your fast, I took the liberty of asking Ekwul to send us candidates suitable for training as a lady's maid."

That was a kind gesture, but might her new mother-in-law be overstepping? They'd changed places now. The bride-ring on Raell's finger attested to that. "Thank you, but I've done for myself more than not."

A moue of disapproval, removed—not quite quickly enough—from the woman's face. A subtle realignment of hands, signaling, mayhap, a new line of argument?

Raell waited, her own hands curled tight beneath the tabletop. *How long will we dance this dance before you let me be as I am?*

"So you've mentioned. Nonetheless, you are mistress of Druemarwin now and must meet D'nalian expectations. Elda may train whomever you choose." Lowering her head a fraction, Vyenne smoothed an invisible wrinkle from her skirt.

Was that an indication of deference? Raell doubted it. The woman was too skilled at court games to change her manner overnight.

"Cannot Elda do for the both of us? At least until my father can be contacted and a woman from Tylus sent." This marrying a D'nalian was posing more challenges than she'd expected, and she'd expected a fair share. A personal maid when she'd never had to deal with one, a new wardrobe suitable for a host of protocol expectations, and a mother-in-law who, unless Raell was mistaken, would likely remain in residence.

That mother-in-law exuded a carefully modulated sigh. "In the short term, aye. But should the warfare continue as it has, your requested maid may be delayed.

If you soon find yourself with child, 'doing for yourself,' even with Elda's help, will be much more challenging."

Raell's heart banged her ribs. A child—hers and Naed's—she'd thought about that yesternight, before she'd surrendered all ability to think. Her brows knit. Why did the woman have to be so astute? Mayhap she meant well, but this tug-of-war had to end.

Raell decided she could be gracious. For now. "Very well. Let us see if any of these candidates suit."

****

The scent of death hung thick in air already close with the number of bodies crammed into the corridor, but Naed resisted the urge to cover nose and mouth. He'd breathed worse in Vinvinnysee when the city had come down in smoke and rubble. At his right Allyn remained stoically unveiled while on his left Wendelmyr pressed a kerchief to a face gone pasty in the torchlight. Opposite, the captain of the guard rocked on his heels, expression grim.

Banir rose from his crouch and studied the floor surrounding the body. When he lifted a hand, Morys put a torch into it. Guardsmen fell back as he approached, letting him follow whatever minute signs he saw in the rough stone.

Grodar pushed his way into the circle and caught Naed's gaze. He'd ordered all the Tumin guardsmen immediately confined and left Grodar in charge of searching them while everyone else trooped to the storerooms beneath the Great Hall. "Well?"

"We found the man who's missin' a knife, m'lord. No blood on 'im. Says he fell asleep at table, didn't know he'd lost it. Only went out to take a piss when his fellows woke 'im.'' Grodar hooked thumbs in his belt and directed the last at Allyn. "Had a bit too much ale, if'n you ask me."

"No one asked you."

Naed shot his half-brother a quelling glare. "Your men stayed together? All night?"

"My men were not made particularly welcome," Allyn growled. "Of course, they stayed together."

Banir straightened, drew everyone's attention. "Whoever did this was neither ale-addled nor impulsive. Nor, to my way of thinking, a Tumin man."

Allyn puffed out his chest. "See!"

Clenching his teeth, Naed focused on the man he trusted to discover the truth. "Explain."

"He chose a victim he had no need to kill if all he wanted was a purse. There be no sign of struggle. Belike this Kassi man was too deep in his cups to know what his killer was about." He gestured toward the body and the pool of congealed blood beneath it. "Why drop the knife, yet take the time to wipe his hand on the man's tunic?"

"Is the handprint clear enough to help us?"

"Neither over large or over small, though 'tis unlike to be a woman's." Banir shone the torch on the floor. "He stepped in the blood, but so did others after him. See?" Light flickered over a muddle of gleaming prints. "Over here, though, be one drier than the others, but 'tis faint."

"Can you divine aught?"

"A man's boot, to be sure." Banir's face revealed nothing, as usual, but the dark eyes expressed frustration as he added, "Neither over large nor over small."

"How bloody excellent!" Allyn grumbled. "The bastard could be anybody." He swung to Wendelmyr. "'Twas not one of mine. That much is clear, is it not, *sir*?"

The little lord flicked a glance over his kerchief and scowled. "Fine. I was over hasty, but you must admit the evidence—"

"The evidence," Naed interrupted, "was clearly intended to make us quarrel among ourselves, which we will *not* do." He directed the captain of the guard to clear the corridor and supervise the body's removal. Then he led the way back to his private chamber.

Someone who knew his way around the fortress was clearly at work here. If only he could divine who. And why. And under whose direction.

If his gut clenched any tighter, it might turn inside out.

Chapter Thirty-Three

They'd begun with eight candidates, and Raell allowed Lady Vyenne to whittle the field to four. Thus far she could find no fault with her mother-in-law's reasoning: a lady's maid ought to be personally tidy and skilled with a needle, possess hands smooth enough to handle fine fabrics and fingers nimble enough to work tiny hooks and laces, and most importantly be discreet in her manner. The four remaining women ranged from a village girl barely become a woman to one likely to have grandchildren.

"Well?" Vyenne indicated the line of candidates. "What do you think?"

That I don't need another mother figure. Raell dismissed the grandmother with her thanks and regrets. She flicked a glance to see if her choice annoyed her mother-in-law, but the woman merely watched with those cool green eyes. *Do you really have no opinion or are you truly giving me free choice?*

Suppressing a frown, she circled the child-woman and focused on the two near her age. One was pretty in a common, buxom way and should have been eliminated out of hand. Thanks to her brothers' bragging competitions, she knew precisely how much trouble a young, amply endowed lady's maid could get into or cause. Fitting into D'nalian society would be challenging enough without inviting added scandal.

Putting on a gracious smile, she dismissed the woman. No reaction from Vyenne.

Time for my test. She'd left the long-bladed knife on the table, and now she motioned both candidates toward it. "Pick that up, please," she said to the child-woman.

"This, m'lady?" She'd spent the entire interview with eyes downcast, shooting furtive glances at women who clearly awed her. But she grasped the hilt without hesitation. "My father, he be a soldier in the master's service, m'lady. He lets me polish his knives, but he's not got one so fine."

"Indeed," Raell said. "'Tis pleased I am to hear of his service."

The girl blushed and carefully set the weapon down.

That fine line appeared between Vyenne's brows.

Raell suppressed a smile and indicated the second candidate should approach.

Somewhere betwixt twenty and thirty, the woman had a plain face dominated by a too-large nose. She was neither buxom nor thin and entirely unremarkable except for the confidence with which she picked up the knife and turned it this way and that, testing the balance.

"You work in the kitchen." Raell recalled what she'd been told when the women entered. "You must employ knives daily."

"Aye, m'lady, for cutting, chopping, an' peeling." She set it down and stepped back.

Turning to her mother-in-law, Raell announced, "Since you graciously pointed out Druemarwin's lack of suitable maids, 'tis my intention to train both of these women." *You didn't expect me to do that, did you?* Pleased with herself, she faced her new maids-in-training. "You will report to Elda and attend to her every instruction. When I require your services, you will take turns until I decide which of you suits me better. Be that clear?"

"Aye, m'lady!" they chorused. The younger one beamed as she curtsied; the older one's gratitude showed in a slight smile.

Raell considered. Did she want a companion she could read without effort or one who could keep her face a mask when necessary? She'd have to think on that. "What are your names?"

"Mavis, m'lady," said the child-woman.

"Gert, m'lady," said the kitchen maid.

****

Arms crossed, Allyn planted himself beside the long table. Making the most of a slight height advantage and significantly greater bulk, he subjected Naed to a long, unwavering, narrow-eyed scrutiny. "Tell me, brother—pardon me, my *lord* brother—is now the time to ask what happened to your hands, your face? And has it aught to do with that body in the cellar?"

Naed wanted to pace but anchored a hand on the mantel instead. *Steady.* He'd wondered when Allyn would address what he couldn't hide. That his half-brother had waited till now was unexpected, even disconcerting for a man who wore impatience like a badge.

Thankfully, Naed had insisted on privacy before closing himself, Allyn, and Wendelmyr in his private chamber with Banir securing the door. Having apparently accepted the Tolemak's presence as necessary, the two men carried on as if he were invisible. That suited Naed, who relied on Banir as a second set of eyes for this interview. He was fairly certain he could trust Wendelmyr, but how much did Allyn know—or need to know?

Wendelmyr had collapsed into a chair immediately upon entering and, with a wave of his kerchief, saved Naed from deciding how to begin. "Assassins, sir. Did you not see the bodies before the gate?"

"I saw no bodies. I barely saw the gate. If you recall, we arrived in a deluge."

"Oh, aye, so you did." The little lord mopped his face. "Tumin men, some of them. 'Tis why I thought…"

That remark, even unfinished, could trigger the storm that would be Allyn if Naed didn't intercede. "Wendelmyr had reasons for his suspicions, as did I." If only those reasons weren't becoming ever more muddled, thanks to Banir's assessment of events in the cellar.

"Assassins?" Veins pulsed in his half-brother's forehead. "'Tis a serious charge Lord…Wendelmyr makes. Do me the honor, *my lord brother*, of enumerating those reasons."

Closing his eyes to prevent rolling them heavenward, Naed chose to ignore Allyn's renewed digs. They'd come so close to a truce, brothers again…almost…until Wendelmyr had shoved that bloody knife between them.

Damn the man!

Concentrate. Put aside your feelings and focus on substance, on the matter at hand.

The Prince made it look so easy. Did the man experience this same churning of the innards that twisted everything into knots?

Impelled by the need to move, Naed paced a few steps, turned. "Three attacks—now a fourth—in the space of—what? Three days?" He shook his head, scarce believing the number. "*Three days*, Allyn. Two attacks the night before I arrived." He paused, composing himself for the coming ordeal, choosing his words. "You will have to thank Toth of Tylus, Lady Raell's brother, for saving Mother—"

"Mother! What—?"

Naed held up a hand and Allyn wisely clamped his mouth shut. "From thieves, or so we thought, until we recovered the bodies from the marsh and examined them closely. 'Twas not unexpected to find they were led by a disgraced soldier. But, tell me if you can, why would D'nalian thieves living rough in the marsh carry Tolemak weapons and Adanak gold?"

The steel-blue eyes widened, before storm clouds regathered. "And this connects to Tumin how?"

"Patience, and I will come to that." *What shocked you, Allyn? The weapons or the attack on Mother? Or both? Or the fact we know about the weapons, the gold?* Naed's gut burned again. Another turn before the hearth brought him face to face with his half-brother, where he halted.

"The second attack, before dawn, came through the emergency tunnel. Four men. They were looking for me, or so said one before he was killed." He sucked in breath, holding it behind clenched jaws, as if doing so would contain accusations clamoring to be hurled on behalf of Raell and all the terror she'd endured. On behalf of himself, damn it! For all the gut-wrenching fear and helpless frustration. For the echo of both thundering in his blood at the mere memory.

"They had a key," he bit out through gritted teeth, "and the dead man they left behind wore Tumin colors!"

That set Allyn back on his heels. "I…after you? In truth?"

"More came at me upon the parapet the next night. Four at least. The three dead were D'nalians."

"Have you… Three? You have a prisoner?"

Was that hope or fear animating Allyn's expression? Naed rested a hand on his knife and prayed the Three Sisters would provide an answer that didn't require drawing it. One half-brother had already proved an enemy. Would this one?

"I have an assassin loose in my fortress, someone who has employed at least one Tumin man and paid him in Adanak gold. A D'nalian, to be sure, or he would not move so readily among the folk. Do you comprehend now why Wendelmyr and I are suspicious when another death occurs on the night you arrive?"

"When you put it that way," Allyn grumbled. "But this last death, why seek to blame Tumin? 'Twould be a fool who'd cast blame in his own direction. Your own man said as much."

"Aye, 'twould be a fool indeed." Naed resisted the urge to rub his mangled thigh. The trip to the cellar had left it prickling, left him with an all too familiar, crawling memory of impact, shock, and utter disbelief. He squared up before his half-brother. "Or a clever man who trusts such a clumsy attempt would put us off the scent, making us think as you have suggested." Chances of such deviousness were slim, but so were chances he'd be arrow-struck in an ambush by Tolemaks masquerading as Adanaks.

Glowering, Allyn braced his feet apart. "Are you determined to suspect me, *brother*?" His down-the-nose glare made clear the familiar address was deliberate.

"No. I am determined to learn if I can trust you, *brother*. That you, at least, had no prior knowledge of these events."

For heartbeats they stared at each other while the room tunneled and eyes became everything, what they hid, what they revealed, whether truth could be divined from bottomless black pools narrowly rimmed by color. Naed hoped to the Sisters it could.

"Dlaniger," Wendelmyr announced, jarring them from their stare-off.

He and Allyn turned as one to find the man reaching for a pitcher.

Ignoring their daggered looks or, belike, entirely unaware of the outrage directed at his velvet-clad shoulders, Kassi examined the pitcher's contents, nodded, and filled a mug. "I'd put the blame on Dlaniger if you hadn't assured me he was dead. 'Tis the sort of machination he would employ." He shuddered. "Never liked the boy. Not a warm bone in his body."

"Who the Demon cares?" Allyn snarled. "Dead men don't kill people; live ones do."

A chill seized Naed's spine and extended tentacles. The icy probes sucked all blood from his extremities, leaving them tingling on full alert. "Aye," he breathed, "but dead men have friends."

Something in his voice must've drawn both men's attention, for they turned toward him, Allyn with a scowl and Wendelmyr with a quizzical expression.

Naed stood stunned. Why hadn't he seen it before?

Dlaniger must have had a key.

How else could he have entered Druemarwin the day Dranoel was killed? The fortress was surrounded by Tolemaks and stuffed with more. To avoid notice, he must have sneaked in through the emergency tunnel. Either someone within unlocked the door or he possessed a key.

But Dlaniger was dead.

Where was his key? Who let Dlaniger in?

Thoughts tumbling over one another, he spun to his half-brother. "How close were you to Dlaniger? Did you spend time with him at Tumin or elsewhere?"

"He was too young for me, as were you." Arms crossed and still glowering, Allyn eyed him with suspicion. "How, exactly, did Dlaniger die? Not by your hand was all you've said."

He'd known the question would surface. More and more Allyn's timing revealed a brain worthy of Tumin's Right Hand. *I'm not the only one who's matured.* Was that a point for or against Allyn? Naed glanced at Banir and arched a brow. If anyone could follow what had been said, left unsaid, and deliberately avoided, it was the tracker.

The Tolemak responded with a fractional nod.

One more cast of the beads. Sisters, be with me.

"Dlaniger was killed in the practice of his chosen profession, assassin for hire. He made an attempt on the Prince of Val-Feyridge and was struck down by the Prince's man. I was there."

Like a demon unleashed, the memory reared up and assailed Naed. The salt-sweet smell hit first, filling

313

his nostrils. Then the sounds...the fleshy *snick-snick-snick* of blade penetrating skin, muscle. Krenin's anguished screams. The crunch of his own knees on stone as he dropped beside the man he'd tried so hard to warn, to save. The Prince gripping his arm with slick, scarlet hands...

So much blood...

Naed put a hand to his mouth and grasped a chair with the other. Banir came away from the door, but he waved him back. He could handle this, handle the memories, nightmares, emotions pulsing beneath his skin. If he bit down hard enough, he could keep it all contained, keep from flying apart like a pot brought to boiling beneath a too-tight lid.

When a hand gripped his shoulder, he flinched, but the steel-blue gaze that met his held no judgment. The hand remained, flexed, the warmth of it muffling his frayed nerves like a blanket of calm.

"The nightmares come upon me too," Allyn said, voice gentle, muted, for Naed's ears only. "Not so often now, for I've had more years than you since I first went into battle, since the Northern Wars."

"How did you know?"

"Do you think you're the only man to watch friends die? To wish it were otherwise? To relive it night upon night, thinking if only you'd done this instead or made that choice sooner, your friends, comrades would be yet alive?" Allyn inhaled, as if to stem his own memories. Then he blew out the breath and squeezed Naed's shoulder. "The Three Sisters will have what they will, trust me on this. A man dies when his life thread runs out."

Naed studied his half-brother, amazed at how little

he'd known of this man. Blood should know blood, and he hadn't. "Is that-is that what you believe?"

"Aye, I do, when I'm awake and thinking. But my heart would wish it otherwise, and 'tis why we dream what we dream even when we know 'tis naught we can do to alter it."

"I've misjudged you." He had, mightily, and for all the right reasons. But neither he nor Allyn was the man he'd been a scant two years before.

"Aye, so we've made a few mistakes, both of us." With a cuff to the shoulder, Allyn released Naed. "Now, can we put aside this petty nonsense and catch your villain? D'nalian *and* an assassin? 'Tis unnatural! As much a crime against nature as—as pack-hunting, flesh-eating sheep!" He made a warding-off gesture and spat into the cold hearth. "I'll not have Tumin blamed for aught this traitorous whoreson might do."

"'Tis all well and good to see you in league against this villain." The little man whose presence Naed had once more forgotten dabbed his lips with his kerchief. "Unless yesternight's storm has delayed them, the lords you summoned should be arriving one after another about now."

"Demon be damned!" The timing deserved a curse, and he deserved a slap to the head for allowing his feelings, however justified, to distract him. Wendelmyr was as much a player in this game as anyone. While the man possessed little to no battle experience, he was shrewd enough to prosper at the fringe of Tumin's control. Taking him for granted would be a mistake Naed vowed not to make.

"My thanks, sir, for your awareness of protocol. Your experience in such matters is greater than mine, and you are undoubtedly well acquainted with all those attending. Mayhap you would consider presiding over the assembly? That would allow me to better make my case to them."

Wendelmyr's eyes gleamed. "You honor me, sir. Shall I also receive them?"

"By all means."

When the man bustled out, Naed addressed Banir, "Summon the captain of the guard. Have him identify and hold those who might have sympathized with Dlaniger. I'll deal with them as soon as I can."

Once they were alone, a bemused Allyn said, "That was an impressive load of dung you shoveled, brother. Are you sure you're not Alwyl's son?"

"You swear and bluster like a Tolemak, brother. Are you certain you *are* Alwyl's son?"

Allyn guffawed. "I like you better and better, Lord Naed. Will you let me stay another night?"

"What will you tell your father if I do?"

All trace of humor gone, Allyn leaned in. "I know you well enough now, brother, to believe you still suspect a Tumin connection to this villainy. For all Father's secrets, I can't discount it either. Will you share with me what you learn from your captain of the guard?" When Naed hesitated, he added, "Tumin's meant to be mine someday, and I intend to protect its honor with my own."

A reasonable request, it testified volumes about Allyn's character. Having an ally among the northern lords, among his own blood, was a risk Naed's gut told him to take. He nodded.

With the movement, Dranoel's legacy, tangled as ever with Raell's charm, rolled across his chest, and his skin prickled. What would Allyn—and Alwyl—think when they learned what it was he carried so close to his heart, wrapped in his father's will?

Chapter Thirty-Four

Vyenne nodded, smiled, and made appropriate responses to the lords who bowed over her hand. She recognized most—she'd always been good with faces, an asset for the wife of the acknowledged leader of D'nalee—but in her present state, she'd be hard pressed to recall names. It was challenge enough to ignore how they looked at her when they thought her attention was on the next man. Curiosity, suspicion, pity, blatant sexual interest—she wouldn't be distracted by any of it. Her focus was already splintered, what with Naed and his bride to her right, Toth at her left elbow, Beauty in between, nose aquiver at a multitude of new scents. And not ten paces away, blistering her with his stare, the man Vyenne dreaded having to face.

Her breastbone burned, but she curled her free hand into her skirts to prevent rubbing the ache. Calm. Control. Discipline. They would see her through this, as always.

So would Beauty. Exposing the wolfhound to so many new people was a risk, but the dog was well-trained. In truth, Vyenne leaned against the wolfhound as much as Beauty leaned against her.

Dear Sisters! Her pulse ratcheted up, and she inhaled through her nose to calm it.

Naed and Raell were fine. For all Naed's attempts at restraining his emotions, he had his father's inability to be but what he was, an honest man. And his bride, well, if Tolemaks were honest about aught, it was their emotions. Even in her distracted state, Vyenne could see the lords responding in kind.

As to Toth—aye, *there* was honesty. His battered Tolemak face and hawk glare made clear he'd break fingers, or worse, if any lord clung to her hand longer than he deemed appropriate. Vyenne stifled a sigh. If only she could be rid of him.

"Must you stand so close?" she murmured when there was a lull in the line. "You are frightening the lords."

"As is my intention, m'lady. And—" He chin-pointed toward the man glowering at them, "—taunting him gives me pleasure."

Vyenne gaped. "You will *not* be brawling with Allyn."

His mouth curved, straining heavy scabs. It had to hurt, but she spared him no pity.

"Would you deny me? 'Tis nigh two days since I've drawn blood. Mayhap I can wait no longer to do so again."

Her brows rose, then slammed together, no doubt deepening despite her best intentions the indentation between them, that *canyon* marring a face she'd taken great pains to preserve. A vanity, to be sure, but also a rebellion, one small act to show the world Alwyl hadn't deserted her bed because she'd lost her face or figure. Exasperated, she summoned a few choice words to put this irritating, uncouth Tolemak in his place—had he naught to do but shred her remaining nerves with his incessant hovering and bloodthirsty suggestions?— when she caught Toth's expression.

319

Was he *teasing* her?

Sisters Above, was that even possible?

The line moved and three more lords fawned over her hand. She made automatic, polite noises. Two more to receive and this ordeal would be over, but those two were dawdling, one with Wendelmyr and one with Naed. She knotted her hands to conceal her impatience. The sooner they moved on, the sooner she could deal with Allyn.

Or bolt.

Despite the stir it would cause, bolting might be preferable.

She pressed both hands to her breastbone. Sisters, how it burned! A headache throbbed behind her eyes, belike from too little sleep and too much worry. Her stomach gnawed at her spine. When had she last eaten? She could plead illness. Indeed, she felt quite nauseous, even light-headed. She could flee now if this hulking brute of a Tolemak wouldn't dog her every step, even mock her retreat.

"Why must you persist in this unasked for and unwanted guardianship?"

She hoped to drive home a barb, to put a chink in that oh-so-infuriating aura of imperturbability, but all she earned was a mildly spoken, "Mayhap I sense a kindred spirit," that spiked her temper.

"You speak in riddles now? I would expect that from an Adanak, mayhap even a D'nalian courtier, but not from you, sir. Please, employ some of your Tolemak directness and put me out of my misery."

"As you wish." He leaned so close his words warmed her ear. "You are very good at keeping secrets, m'lady."

Vyenne refused to flinch from the unaccustomed intimacy, or the sudden uptick in her pulse. She drew herself ramrod straight, the better to defend, deflect, or deal with whatever he intended to say. "And?"

Her peripheral vision detected his smile, as though he'd noted her preparations and approved.

He bent closer. "So am I."

A jolt of panic snapped her head around. The movement undoubtedly caught onlookers' attention, but she couldn't consider those consequences when she had more pressing concerns. Had she been wrong about Toth all along? Had her ability to read people, to sense their motives, alliances, allegiances been stymied by his Tolemak nature? Was he so foreign to her that she'd...that he'd...?

Her heart shot into her throat and rendered her words a whisper. "Are any of those secrets like to harm Naed?"

Desperate for answers—and terrified of what they might be—she probed those ever so enigmatic gold-brown eyes while he considered. Beauty whimpered beneath her hand, reminding her to breathe, to relax the fingers she'd dug into the dog's ruff.

"I should think not, m'lady," he said at last. "Be assured, 'tis not my intention for them to be used thus. We are family, for good or ill, and that must always be considered."

A shadow fell between them.

"Considered for what?"

Vyenne flinched as if whip-struck. Of course Allyn would choose this moment to approach. She'd expected consequences. The Three Sisters never failed to deliver on those, and promptly too, but she'd hoped, *prayed,* to delay this confrontation till the lords had cleared. If she thought herself dizzy before, her head positively swam now, but she locked her knees against Beauty and faced her son.

****

Naed clenched his left fist. He'd hidden it behind his back, undoubtedly making him appear stiff and standoffish to the men who shook his hand and bowed over Raell's, but that was better than exploding at the seams. How much longer did he have to stand here surrounded by scents wafting off the woman at his side and pretend to be immune? The lords who'd come to Druemarwin with an eye to assessing the new master were clearly succumbing, for without exception they homed in on Raell and fawned over her.

He wanted to bash in their faces.

Mine!

She exuded, as always, an air of fresh white lilies and her own delicate musk, but today he detected some subtle additions. Bath herbs, mayhap? Intriguing enough, but not what made Naed's nails dig into his palm and his molars in danger of cracking. Unmistakable, to *his* nose anyway, was the scent of newly made woman, a sumptuous, devastatingly irresistible fragrance that had his cock straining at his breeches, thankfully hidden under the loose formal tunic Banir had made him put on for this *reception*.

Hah! That was too polite a term for this Demon-be-damned, unending parade of gawkers he had to remember to smile at, or at least not terrify, if he were to fulfill his mission for the Prince.

At this particular instant, he'd trade his soul to be free of it.

If only he had a week, no, a *month* to immerse himself in Raell, to just...*be* with her, to settle into their new roles as husband and wife, lord and lady without the wider world intruding.

An alteration in atmosphere, a murmur of voices, a shifting of heads brought that world crowding back, pulling his focus to the left.

Allyn. Impatient, intemperate Allyn making a scene with their mother.

Naed scowled. More fodder for wagging tongues!

And yet a perfect distraction.

Grasping Raell's arm, he leaned close and surrendered to impulse, to the dark need providing words that formed without thought, bypassed inhibitions, reticence, and restraint, and poured raw from his soul. "I need you. Sisters, Raell, I can't help myself. Do you have any idea how much I want to be inside you?"

He froze, appalled. Had *those* words come out of *his* mouth? A rush of blood scalded his face; its absence so chilled his innards they recoiled into his backbone and shuddered.

The beast was awake, and more than a little hungry.

Before he could apologize, Raell sent him a look beneath her lashes that further torched his skin. "Aye, belike as much as I want you. I've thought of little else. When?"

Naed's heart kicked into a gallop. "N-now?"

"What of your mother? Will she not expect us to stay?"

"Demon take my mother. And everyone else, too."

His tongue should blister for having said that, but

his body would combust if he didn't seize her hand and slip away.

Chapter Thirty-Five

With everyone's attention focused on the Great Hall and courtyard, the man creeping through shadows gambled the living quarters would be nigh deserted. The odds were in his favor, but the Three Sisters—*Fickle, man-hating bitches!*—saw fit to betray him. Servants bustled everywhere.

Tucked into a doorway, he breathed through his nose, taming his pulse. He'd been stupid—*stupid!*—to overlook Ekwul, how the old manservant ruled the upstairs. For all the risk he'd learned nothing useful.

Well, except the bastard of Druemarwin and his bitch were using the old master's chamber.

Had the pompous prick actually bedded her? What in the Name of the Demon would that self-righteous icicle *do* with a woman as lusty as that Tolemak looked to be?

He'd have a go at her himself, if he could. Teach her what a real man felt like. He'd missed his chance with the Adanak witch, but mayhap that was for the best. He shuddered. Who knew with what horrors the witch could've cursed him. Or what poison she might've employed.

Demon and His Nine Whores! He'd gladly drink her poison now if it'd stop this incessant hammering in his jaw, ear, even the back of his bloody head! Weighed against his life and mission, losing a tooth seemed a necessary choice and minor inconvenience. Who knew it would hurt so damned much? He'd packed the hole with linen bits and clove oil charmed from a kitchen maid, but the numbing effects had ebbed hours ago.

Where the Demon was Elthred? Or Gert? He needed more clove oil and linen to chomp on before his skull exploded.

Moderating his breathing, he forced his senses outward, listening until he was sure the corridor was empty. Then he slid from the shadows and walked toward the stairs, following Master Dlaniger's instructions: *Act as if you belong there, and no one will bother you.*

He was congratulating himself when he reached the first landing and collided with Gert.

"Watch yourself—wait! You're not t' be up here!"

Seizing her arm, he propelled her up the stairs, round a corner, and into a door alcove. "Where have you been? I've been through that bloody kitchen so often the cook's giving me the evil eye."

Slapping away his hand, Gert raised her chin and looked down her considerable nose. "I've come up in life, I have. No more hot kitchens an' oil scalds for the likes of me. You're lookin' at the mistress's new lady's maid."

"You're serving that Tolemak bitch?"

"She's the mistress, she is, an' she picked me—me!—t' be her handmaid. 'Tis a chance I'll not be passin' up e'en she be the Demon Himself."

"You worthless, faithless whore! Where's Elthred? She'll stick with me if she knows what's good for her."

"She's not here. E'en she was, she'd not see you but t' scratch your eyes out an' curse you for the babe you put in her. The babe that's swelled her so she can hardly walk, that's made her face a moon full of craters. Gam's put her out in the village, for 'tis sure she's no good t' anyone now till she births that bastard you stuffed in her."

"Bitch!" He backhanded her into the door then drove his fist twice into her face before chatter echoing up the stairwell brought him to his senses. "You're mine, bitch, and don't you forget it!" Drawing his Adanak knife, he flattened the blade on her bloodied cheek. "That body in the cellar? Yours'll be the next if you say a word."

His cock jumped at Gert's round eyes and the fear pouring off her skin. He'd shove up her skirts and pound into her right now, but the place was too open, too public. Leaning in, he pushed his cock into her belly, and she turned white as a Tolemak. Then he slowly scraped his blade across her cheek, gathering a film of blood while she whimpered and shook.

"If I'm caught, I'll say you helped me. Think your fine new mistress will keep you on then? Think anyone will?"

"N-no," she blubbered while that overlarge nose trickled blood and snot.

Demon Below, she's ugly! But she was still useful, mayhap even more so now. Training one ear on the voices around the corner, he backed a half step, withdrew his blade, and made a show of wiping it on her shoulder.

"Tonight, Gert. Mark me, you'll tell me what I need to know, and you'll do what I tell you, aye?"

When she nodded, he thumbed a bit of blood from her cheek and smeared it across her trembling lips.

"That's my good girl." And then he strolled off, toothache all but forgotten.

****

Vyenne braced herself. Allyn was dressed much as yesternight, armored, beweaponed, but dry, his lank hair fastened in a messy queue and his face no longer shadowed with days of stubble. His expression, however, hadn't lightened. If anything, it had grown stormier as his gaze skipped over her and the wolfhound to fasten on the man at her side. Her eldest braced his feet like a man steeling himself.

"I'm told you should be thanked for saving my mother."

Silence…that stretched.

Nearby lords and attendants nodded to each other, tilted heads, cast quick, curious glances over shoulders.

A mortified flush swept up Vyenne's throat. *Speak, Allyn! You cannot leave this hanging.*

Toth hooked a thumb in his sword belt. "Galls, doesn't it, having to thank a Tolemak."

"Sisters Above! Cannot you two be civil?"

As if she hadn't spoken, Allyn swept Toth with a brows-lowered, head-to-toe assessment that deepened his scowl. "Tell me, I beg you, how you came by those marks on your hands, your face. Mayhap you can explain why my brother bears similar marks of a brawl."

Vyenne rolled her eyes. The dogs were at it again, but she'd done all she could. *Bloody, stubborn men!* At least this time *she* wasn't the bone.

Toth remained as he was, neither tense nor braced. His mouth curled up a fraction. "Lord Naed and I had a difference of opinion, but we've come to an

328

agreement."

"Agreement? Is that what you westerners call it when you've had your ass handed to you?" Allyn folded his arms. "Someone pulled him off you, didn't they? Else you'd look even worse."

"Your brother has been to Vinvinnysee and back. I've not had the privilege," Toth said, as if that explained everything.

Not for Vyenne—he could've been speaking in code—but Allyn seemed to grasp his meaning, for his shoulders lowered a little.

"And you and my mother?"

"She took but a groom, a maid, and a dog on her journey. I judged her measures inadequate. After all, we are now family."

"And family must always be considered."

Eyes glinting, Toth made a small nod. "As you say."

"You're damned polite for a Tolemak."

"And you are bloody rude for a D'nalian."

"Are you *quite* finished?" Vyenne scowled from one to the other.

No point in showing her relief at the palpable reduction in tension. How they'd managed it, she had no idea. Men were such a complete mystery.

"Dare I assume you are no longer going to disrupt Naed's assembly with your snarling and—and manly posturing?"

"Manly *what*?" Allyn quirked a brow as if he'd only now noticed her.

"Be assured, m'lady, t'will be no brawling." Toth graced her with an indulgent smile, one she had a sudden, sharp urge to slap away.

"Not today. I make no promises about tomorrow."
Allyn stepped back, aware—at last—he was holding up
the line, and bowed apologies to the final two lords.

Their avid gazes followed him, then darted to Toth
before each pressed limp lips to Vyenne's hand and
murmured platitudes so incoherent she could only stare.
Of course, they weren't paying attention. They were in
too much haste to regale their peers with what they'd
overheard.

Vyenne closed her eyes, gathering the threads of
her composure. Her mortification would be complete if
the lords limited themselves to the truth, but she had
little hope of that. When Beauty rumbled beside her,
she looked to see why.

"Let me be of service, Lady Vyenne." Wendelmyr
stood within intimate distance, mindful of the
wolfhound opposite, but either ignoring or oblivious to
identically fierce glares from Toth and Allyn. "If you
will but allow me to be your champion, I shall see to it
nothing untoward is said in my presence."

"That…that is very kind of you, Lord Wendelmyr."
What was his purpose? No one at court was ever simply
kind.

He bowed over her hand. "We have more
important things to discuss in this assembly, my dear.
As your son has appointed me to preside, I shall
endeavor to assure we do so."

Ah, so that was it. Currying favor with Naed and,
by extension, the Prince he served. Well, she would
expect no less from a man who considered himself as
influential in his own sphere as Alwyl did in all of
D'nalee.

Which of you is the better judge of his own

importance? Her lips curved at that deliciously wicked thought.

He moved on and she took a moment to breathe and settle overworked nerves.

Thankfully, this reception had gone without bloodshed.

Before the lords retired for a couple of hours' rest in pavilions being erected on the green, guests would partake of light refreshment. If she'd learned aught from years at court, now was the time for Naed and his allies to mingle, overhear conversations, assess opinions of those in attendance.

Would talk of finding the lost Crown or restoring the Kingdom be enough to sway them? Or were they too mired in generations of neutrality and suspicion to act?

Vyenne stitched up her composure and turned to signal Naed.

His focus was all upon his bride. Heads bent close, something he said in Raell's ear provoked an *Oh*, and hiked eyebrows, followed by a quick survey of the rapidly emptying reception area. The girl turned and beamed Naed a smile. Vyenne's heart ached.

She'd had that kind of love too, her once-and-forever love, so desperate for each other they'd steal moments wherever they could. If only she'd walked away from her groom, overruled Dranoel's honor and forsworn her vows all those years ago, she and Dranoel could've had years to enjoy what Naed and Raell looked forward to now.

Another exchange of whispers, grasped hands, and the newlyweds escaped the hall.

No! Now was *not* the time to abandon the lords.

First impressions were oh so important, but Allyn stepped to her side.

"Let them go, Mother. I yanked him from his wedding bed far too early this morn. Let them have a few more hours of pleasure before he has to face this nest of vipers."

"How considerate of you." If that sounded waspish, so be it. A minor loss of control was small cost for the opportunity to gather herself, to shift from the needs of one son—who'd proved an inordinate fool, at least at the moment—to the intentions of another, who she would've sworn had been born without a sensitive bone in his body.

She faced her firstborn, his father's favored son, lookalike heir, close confidante and Right Hand, but...oddly, not quite *all* of those just now. Not when he and Toth had moved shoulder to shoulder the way men who were comfortable with each other aligned themselves.

Both watched her, Toth stroking the wolfhound's head, Allyn with arms crossed and a frown darkening his expression.

What had she missed? Not the highly anticipated meeting with Naed this morning. There had been much shouting, the servants eagerly informed her, but not from the master. Mayhap it was the other, equally stormy conference with both Naed and Wendelmyr, the one reportedly provoked by a body in the cellar that had her eldest behaving so strangely.

Naught would be gained with timidity. "As to vipers, do you speak for yourself, Allyn, or are you here in the name of your father?"

That should've been a direct hit, but Allyn let it

hang so long her fingers curled into her aching breastbone.

"I suppose—" He expelled a gusty sigh. "—you intend to refuse to return with me to Tumin."

You'll bring that up now? Vyenne raised her chin. "'Tis naught for me to return to, as you well know."

"Father will be royally pissed."

"Must you be so crude?" Her rebuke was automatic. Futile, aye, but a mother had to try.

"I do it to annoy Father. Forgive me if I forget to mind my tongue around you." He chuckled. "Naed's as much a prig about it as you. I would've thought, being so much in the company of Tolemaks, he'd be used to it."

"Some of us have manners," Toth said in that mild, unperturbed way she so detested.

She ought to be gratified by their truce, but her hands itched to knock their heads together. A Tolemak mother would undoubtedly do so.

Was she fast becoming a Tolemak mother?

Another gusty sigh, before Allyn shrugged as if shedding a heavy pack. "Well, that's done, my mission's been discharged. I found you, I ascertained your wellbeing, and I have your reply." He faced Toth. "Now, tell me about these attacks on my mother and brother."

Both Toth and Vyenne stared at him. Toth recovered first. "Her husband will surrender his claim to her?"

"Don't be daft. I said he'd be pissed, didn't I? I've done what he sent me to do. If he wants her back, he can bloody well come himself." He made a show of dusting his hands. "What she's done is well and truly done, twenty and more years past. You can't change it. But these damned assassination attempts—*that* we can do something about. What do you say, Tolemak? You say we're family now. Will you help me protect and defend my brother?"

The earth shifted beneath Vyenne's feet, and she gripped Beauty's collar to keep her balance. *Dear Sisters, if only the world would choose an axis and stay on it.*

If only she hadn't lost her beloved anchor.

Chapter Thirty-Six

They'd barely slammed their chamber door when Naed spun Raell against the wall and claimed her mouth. If she'd thought him starved that night in his private chamber, he was ravenous now as he flung off weapons, belt, tunic and undertunic while kissing her senseless. She reveled in his hunger, meeting him need for need, stoking the pleasure building inside, the wild, cascading thrill edging ever closer.

Until a tiny ripping noise—

"Stop!" She shoved elbows between them, gasping, "Don't tear the gown. I've naught else fit to wear tonight." One oh-so-subtle chastisement for rough clothes handling was quite enough, and poor Elda's fingers didn't deserve to bleed for their loss of control.

"I can't..." Eyes unfocused, pupils enormous, Naed fumbled with the laces behind her neck. "I need..."

"Shh, my love, I know what you need." Only a blind woman could've missed those scorching gazes at her bodice, at its mere suggestion of cleavage.

Half the lords had likely noticed too. Well, let them gossip. *She* was the one who'd brought their newest member to this state.

Suffused with womanly power, Raell smiled. "My fingers be smaller. Let me."

With gentle insistence she replaced his hands and

unfastened all laces she could reach. Enough to drop the gown off a shoulder and draw his avid attention. Her pulse kicked up—*Oh, yes!*—and her nipples puckered, aching for what those glittering eyes and eager mouth promised.

He shifted, a wolf at the end of his tether, gaze fixed on the fingertips she trailed—ever so slowly—over her collarbone, hot breath fanning her exposed skin, stimulating all the fine hairs, unfurling heat in all the places that begged to be touched, stroked, filled *now*. Sliding her hand beneath the bodice, she lifted out one breast.

With a feral growl, he latched onto it and suckled while her body clenched and wept with readiness. Then his hands were beneath her skirts, sliding up her thighs, grasping and lifting her so she could do naught but wrap her legs around him while he drove himself into her again and again until she came with a cry that echoed his.

They were both still gasping when Raell realized the shoulders she'd dug her fingers into were rigid. He ought to be as boneless as she, so relaxed she'd slide down the wall into a puddle if he weren't holding her up. But the jaw pressed to her collarbone was clenched and breath hissed between his teeth.

"Naed, what…?"

"Can you…can you stand? My leg's locked up and…I can't…"

"Aye, of course."

She touched ground, staggered, and bumped stone hard enough to jar her bruised backside. While her skirts fell around her, he braced an arm on the wall, turned and collapsed against it. Sweat poured down his face. His hands shook while he refastened breeches hanging low on his hips.

Raell preferred he let them drop. Another look, in daylight this time, at that taut stomach, muscled thighs, and tight buttocks would not go amiss. But that was a selfish, unworthy desire when the face she loved was a rictus of pain and misery. Was this more than a cramp?

She was reaching for him when he balled his fist and pummeled his thigh.

"Bloody…damned…leg!"

Shock left her frozen, stunned, before something impelled her to grab his fist, to hang on while he coiled it up, to wrestle it between her arm and body as he tried to shake her off. *Demon's Blood, he's strong!* That flash of clarity knotted her stomach. Once more she'd acted on impulse, committed herself. But she couldn't let go now. He needed her.

"Naed! Stop! That…won't…help."

"What the bloody hell will?" But he gave up the struggle and, eyes closed, thumped his head against the wall. Sweat dripped from his hair and ran between his brows. More brimmed on his lashes.

"Months! It's been months, Raell, and the damned leg still fails me."

Her pulse pounded in her ears at his stricken expression. The last time she'd seen him so wounded and despairing, so dependent on a wall to hold him up, had been their first meeting in the dim halls of Albon. A dark day indeed, with the Prince barely alive, Krenin dead, Val-Feyridge fallen, and what remained of the army fled to Albon. Her skin curdled. What the Demon had happened since he'd left her bed this morn?

She'd find out. But first she'd soothe the obvious

source of pain.

"I can help. I've worked out many a cramp for my father."

She freed a hand to first restore the gown to her shoulder and then slide down his hip, all the while watching for resistance. When none came, she probed lower, finding his thigh a rock beneath her hand. A cramp, aye, but something she could manage.

Kneeling, she flattened both hands on his thigh and gently kneaded. Every so often, she pulled long strokes away, drawing the pain out with the heat and pressure of her hands. Tongue between her teeth, Raell gave herself to the rhythm of her task. Until Naed's fingers threading into her hair popped open eyes she didn't realize she'd closed.

He must have noticed the hitch in her stroke, for he cleared his throat. "That song...I've not heard it before."

What song? Wrapped in her task, she'd apparently been humming. "'Tis old. A lament, I think. My mother hummed it as a lullaby."

"Did she?" His fingers massaged her scalp, sending tingles directly to her womanly parts. "'Twould be calming, I suppose, to a babe, but—"

He shifted, and she became aware of her forehead pressed to naked hip, of tented breeches just beyond her nose, of the musky scent of coupling, both completed and...impending? Mouth dry, she raised her head and found his gaze hot upon her. A smile spread across her face. "'Tis not the usual response to my ministrations, my lord husband, but trust me when I tell you 'tis most flattering."

Naed groaned. "Sisters, Raell! You touch me and I

want you. You work magic on my leg and, beast that I am, I want you again."

"So? You're mad for me, and I for you. Where's the embarrassment in that?" If sating the 'beast'—a thoroughly agreeable activity—relieved his dark mood, even enticed him to talk, well and good.

He coughed out a laugh, face full of chagrin. "You are a minx. You know that, aye?"

She was composing a retort when she found herself upright and wide-eyed, hands braced on a broad, naked chest, nose inches from a mouth looking for all the world as if it intended to devour her. Her heart skittered around her ribs. She was no feather-weight—Toth complained every time she fell on him during sparring practice—but Naed had whisked her to her feet as if she were light as air, despite his aching leg, despite their 'exercise' of moments ago. When he used his strength, thrills shivered down her spine.

"So," Raell said, breathless as much from the sudden move as the steely arms banding her body flush to his, "you'll have me again, will you?"

His answer was a smoldering look from hooded eyes and a slow rotation of hips.

"Well, then..." She trailed her hands down his torso and into his breeches. "Come to bed, my love, and be naked with me."

****

"You do your employer a disservice." The voice came from deep shadow behind a pillar.

The man with the toothache smiled, pleased to finally engage. "You stalk with all the finesse of a workhorse, yet you lecture me?" He'd lured the stranger this far into a dim, deserted corridor of long-emptied storerooms, but the wary bastard refused to close. In truth, he could've pushed the confrontation sooner, but he'd been thinking of Elthred and the babe and the curious sensation of *pride* stuffing his chest.

Focus. Master Dlaniger's voice rang in his head. *A distracted man is a dead man.*

Right you are. Distant torchlight silhouetted him for his stalker but rendered him faceless. Angling his body just so reduced the target and concealed a knife drawn from a hidden back-belt sheath.

"Pray, elaborate. I am all ears."

"Killing a Kassi man, throwing suspicion on Tumin. 'Twas not in your instructions."

He caressed the hilt. Not his Adanak blade, but better suited to throwing. "That was but mischief, to unsettle them. Does my employer object to mischief making?"

"He objects to gold wasted, to risky gambits with short-lived results."

Short-lived? He bit back a retort. The fool thought himself the spider, did he?

Balancing on the balls of his feet, he drawled, "Doubts, once planted, tend to linger...like weeds in a field...I should think your master—my employer—well aware of this." That was a double-edged jibe, truth wrapped in implication and calculated to provoke movement. *I know who's pulling the strings.*

"You were warned not to make this personal. Not to expose your employer to unnecessary risk in pursuit of an immediate, personal gain."

Jaw clenched, pain spiking, he sucked in air. The would-be spider could still sting.

Time to sting back harder, but in the mildest of

voices. "Unless I miss the mark, 'tis indeed *most* personal for your master. Why ever should it not be for me and mine?"

A boot scuff, the squeak of leather. *Ah, there you are.*

"Master Dlaniger was engaged because he knew how to play the long game." Disdain, the voice dripping with it. "There'll be no more gold if you are not committed to the same."

He could make out the shape of the messenger now, could match height, breadth of shoulders, stance to a face in yesternight's crowd. *Are you wearing chest armor?* Knife hidden alongside his thigh, he adopted a nonchalant, non-threatening pose. "Tell me, were you sent to berate me or pay me? Or have you overstepped *your* instructions to merely observe?"

A rustle, a brusque movement, and a pouch chinked to the ground, spilling coins. Two pieces spun, a third flashed as it rolled into the wall and toppled.

"An advance, as requested. But, mark me, there'll be no more till the contract's fulfilled."

"Then tell your master: stay out of my way and let me work."

And mayhap I won't kill you just for the pleasure of it.

****

Vyenne was stifling her third yawn when Allyn herded the last two lords toward the courtyard and pavilions beyond. An hour's rest before the assembly, time alone to restore her balance would be a Sisters-sent blessing, but with host and hostess fled to engage in—

Well, she needn't envision *that.*

After condoning, mayhap approving, Naed's desertion of his duties, Allyn surprised her by stepping in.

What was his game?

No, she had to stop thinking like Alwyl, seeing ulterior motives in everyone. Allyn was her flesh and blood, like Naed.

But he was half Alwyl's too.

She pressed fingers to her temples. Hammering at both sides trapped her mind in a churning whirlpool.

Sleep. Barring that, a little food, some drink might break the cycle and allow her to surface. Vyenne turned. For all Toth's hovering this never-ending day, he could be useful and fetch a bit of sustenance, but a clatter of hooves beyond open courtyard doors stopped her mid-motion.

All those invited had arrived. Who was this? She glanced at Allyn near the door, whose profile showed…surprise? Alarm scraped her nerves.

Not Alwyl. No, please, not Alwyl.

"So, this be Druemarwin, the hope of D'nalee," rang a voice clearly meant to carry. "Seems a bit…less than imposing, aye?"

Two men stood silhouetted by the lowering sun. By his cocky pose, Vyenne attributed the remark to the leaner, evidently younger man.

Not Alwyl.

Thank the Sisters!

Not D'nalian either.

Bristling with affront—much easier to manage than fear—she set off toward them. *How dare you—*

Fingers curled around her arm, pale-skinned, freshly scabbed fingers that had become all too familiar. Vyenne gave an unladylike jerk and spun. "Sisters Above, will you not—!"

Toth halted her with a look so fierce her abrupt inhale sucked her mouth dry. She recognized that look from the marsh, and from the night he and Naed had bashed each other senseless. Her stomach crawled into her ribcage.

Releasing her, he signaled the wolfhound to stay and strode into the sun.

"Ah, look!" The younger newcomer flapped a hand in Toth's direction. "We've found him, we have." He laughed, elbowed his companion. "And here, 'twas in my mind you meant to lose me in that bloody marsh."

The older man mumbled something, turned and executed a neat sidestep as Toth, without altering stride, put all his momentum behind his fist.

Chapter Thirty-Seven

A collective gasp…before Allyn's "What the bloody hell!" unfroze everyone.

Beauty bolted for the door, barking and snarling.

"Stay!" Vyenne grabbed for the wolfhound's collar, missed, caught scruff and dug in her heels. The dog bee-lined after Toth, evidently having foresworn both training *and* allegiance to defend a Tolemak.

Dragged by a great, slavering beast was a wholly undignified way to make an entrance, but Vyenne damned well didn't care—as long as no throats were ripped out. Wrestling the wolfhound to a halt, she seized Beauty's collar and locked fingers around it.

"Foolish beast! He'll break your heart." She glared at the dog, who managed to look both chastened and thwarted. "They always do."

Pulse rat-tat-tatting at her throat, Vyenne shoved that disconcerting thought away and focused on the scene: Toth, fists clenched, at the portico's edge, the newcomer three steps down, sprawled in the much-trampled dregs of yesternight's rain.

"Bastard!" Toth spat. "Lying, word-weaving, serpent-tongued bastard! Rot in hell!"

He spun on his heel, made a curt nod to Allyn and Vyenne, and ground out, "Forgive me. 'Twas a Tolemak matter and needed to be done." Then, white-faced and straight-backed, he resumed his accustomed

344

place at her elbow.

The wolfhound—*Traitorous beast!*—tracked him with dark, liquid eyes and whined.

Fury poured off Toth in waves. Whatever was molten within clearly still seethed despite the eruption. But her hand extended of its own volition—*not a traitor, merely concerned*—and laid light fingers on a rigid forearm. Comfort or caution, it mattered not what she intended nor how he took it as long as some of the tension eased in muscles strung tight as a lute string.

Calm, control, discipline. She'd applied the first two, and they were holding—for now.

Allowing herself a breath, Vyenne restored her garments, smoothed wayward hairs into place, and prepared to overcome Druemarwin's disastrous first impression.

The younger man sat in the courtyard muck, hands to his face and cursing. Vivid red oozing between mud-stained fingers contrasted sharply with pale skin and dark, wavy hair.

Clearly a Tolemak, and one who should have better manners, considering the quality of his clothing. So should the man who stood off to the side, splatter-free and chuckling.

"Stuff your whining and get off your ass." He hitched a belt over a midsection as broad around and solid as a log, despite gray-salted stubble and hair. "'Tis time to greet your hosts afore they take you for the snot-faced whelp you are."

"My nose, he broke my damned nose!"

"Aye, and 'tis grateful you should be to have that pretty little thing bent. 'Tis the mark of a proper warrior, that."

The man turned, a bold, hooked beak bearing testimony to his claim. An array of battered armor and wicked weapons hanging from his substantial but not tall person eliminated any remaining doubts as to his authority on the subject.

He homed in on Vyenne, as undeterred by Beauty as if the great beast were no more than a lapdog. Extending a heavily scarred hand, he lifted her fingers to his lips. "Ah, m'lady with the fine, fiery hair, 'tis a pleasure." Gold-brown eyes twinkled at her. "Lord Naed neglected to mention he had a sister."

"He does," she responded, distracted by rough whiskers tickling her knuckles. "Two, in fact. Twins." It was the oddest sensation, despite the hundreds, mayhap thousands of times her knuckles had been bussed in thirty-plus years at court.

Blinking, she snapped her gaze to his face and stiffened her spine. "My daughters. I am Lady Vyenne, Lord Naed's mother." She swallowed 'of Tumin' with a small stab of regret. The words no longer applied. "This is my eldest, Allyn of Tumin, son and heir of Lord Alwyl." She didn't add 'my husband.' Let this twinkling-eyed Tolemak work out the scandal.

Pointedly withdrawing her hand, she gestured toward the youth who'd regained his feet. "Will you not grace us with your name and that of your…son?"

He guffawed. "That?" He wiped a laugh-induced tear from one eye. "That useless spawn of a Bedian goat's not mine. This strapping lad is." And he enveloped Toth in a hearty, one-armed hug.

Toth grimaced but returned the gesture with a fierce squeeze.

Words passed low between them.

"A wedding?"

"Aye, yesternight."

"Consummated?"

"Beyond any doubt." Toth colored as the men separated.

A look flashed across the elder's craggy features and vanished, but not before Vyenne noted it. Her breastbone ached, recognizing it as any parent would—profound relief—but why?

"Pardon my father's poor manners, m'lady," Toth said, normally pale cheeks fever red.

"'Tis naught to pardon." Resuming control of the situation, she filed away that cryptic exchange to examine later. "You've made quite clear how dearly the house of Tylus regards family." She shot a quick, quelling glance at Allyn. Despite looking alternately dumbfounded and bemused, he remained silent and let her handle the protocol.

Conjuring a gracious smile, she returned to the newcomers. "Welcome to Druemarwin, Lord Tylus. And your companion is?"

"Companion, hah!" Tylus snorted. "'Tis a delivery, no more. Safe passage for Lord Belac's brat—"

"You call this *safe*?" The young man waved a bloody hand at his face, clothes. "I'm assaulted—"

"'Twas my charge to bring you through the gate. What happens after be none of my affair."

A moment's daggered glare, then the youth shifted his focus to Vyenne. "Forgive my manners, m'lady." He executed an abbreviated bow involving bent knees and an awkwardly up-tilted, pinched nose. "I am Bennin of Nye, and I should very much like to be taken to your healer."

****

Raell woke to a golden glow that matched her mood. This love-making of an afternoon might be scandalous in D'nalee, but she would happily repeat it tomorrow and endless days thereafter with the man sprawled on his stomach beside her. She smiled. Sound asleep Naed was, a rest much needed if she'd judged aright the strain he labored under. With a feather-light touch she smoothed hair from his face. When not confined in a queue, the copper strands kinked and curled in a most endearing, un-D'nalian disorder.

Resisting the urge to run her fingers through it, she slid carefully out of bed and located her gown. Despite a stretched seam, everything was intact, thank the Sisters. A few shakes and careful draping over a chair back would smooth the worst wrinkles. That done, she padded naked about the chamber, marveling at the shambles. She plucked her slipper off the table, stretched to retrieve a stocking dangling from the bed canopy, and located her shift crumpled under a chair.

A tentative knock followed by the slow lifting of the latch panicked Raell into yanking the garment over her head. "Who comes?"

Mavis poked her face into the chamber. "Beggin' your pardon, m'lady, but 'tis late an'…" Sidling around the door, the girl shut it on insistent male voices. She took a step, found her path barred by discarded weapons, and halted. A flush crept up her cheeks. "The master's man, he says to tell you 'tis late an'…I'm to dress you."

So much for waking Naed slowly and prompting him to talk. Raell heaved a sigh. "Very well, but I thought 'twas Gert's turn."

"Aye, but…" The girl pointedly avoided looking toward the bed.

Raell refused to peek. She'd left Naed decently covered. Unless he'd turned over—

"She's had an accident, she has. Took a fall on the steps an' bled somethin' awful. Old Gam made her rest."

Who? Oh, Gert. "How unfortunate, but Gam has the right of it. Now, take yourself outside and tell Banir the master and I need a few moments to ourselves."

When the girl sidled out, Raell crossed to the door and threw the bolt, something she wished she'd done sooner. She plucked at her shift, discovered it inside out and backwards. *Bloody hell!* She wrestled it right-side out.

"What was…?" Yawning, Naed sat up and scrubbed hands over his face. "Did you say…Gert? The kitchen maid, Gert?" Bedding pooled at his hips, exposing a wide expanse of corded belly muscle.

Her insides clenched. She fought the temptation to hop into bed and run her palms over those delicious ridges. What was it he'd asked? *Oh, Gert.*

"Aye." She pulled the shift over her head and stuffed her arms through. "It seems I require a proper lady's maid, so I've engaged Gert and Mavis to train with—"

"No."

Raell froze. That was a word she'd not often heard from him, and certainly not delivered in that flat, brook-no-arguments tone. Mayhap she'd misunderstood? "No…to what?"

He planted both feet on the floor and leveled a frown in her direction. "Not Gert. Train Mavis. Her father's a good man, loyal. Send Gert back to the kitchen."

He regarded her in a most un-husbandly way, rather like the lord and commander who expected to be obeyed. Gooseflesh arose on her bare arms. That golden glow she'd so enjoyed moments ago lost its warmth. Was this a test of their new relationship?

Well, she was neither soldier nor servant to be ordered about. "Why? She possesses the right skills."

Either her logic or defiance caught him off balance. While he floundered, she cocked her head and added the clincher, "Your mother approved her."

That shot him off the bed with a heated, "My mother doesn't know her!" Snatching up his breeches, Naed stuffed his legs into them. "She's not fit...to serve you so...so intimately."

He blushed, but the line of his jaw was as obstinate as ever she'd seen it. She fisted hands on hips. "Tell me what you know. Is she not discreet?"

"No! Not when it comes to men." Face fully scarlet, he fumbled with the fastenings.

Tapping her bare foot, Raell waited, but he refused to meet her gaze, instead hunting up his boots. "A woman of her age, 'tis no surprise she'd have lovers—"

"She's a whore, Raell!" He'd spat the words, looking more flustered than yesternight. "She and Elthred, they'd lift their skirts for any man who asked. Together or singly, in the storerooms, the stables..." He trembled with palpable disgust. "Even if he didn't ask."

Ah, so *that* was it. A rush of tenderness thickened her throat. "She offered herself to you, Gert and this...Elthred, aye? When you were but a Free Sword?"

Color drained from his face. He clearly hadn't

meant to lead her to that conclusion, but as long as she'd arrived…

Assuming a severe expression, she folded her arms. "I trust you refused."

His horrified look confirmed it. Not that she'd doubted him or yesternight's profession of innocence. Honor and propriety meant far too much to her proper D'nalian husband. Her heart swelled and her pulse beat heavily at her throat. *Poor soul.* No wonder the mention of Gert moved him to such anguish.

Nonetheless—she inhaled a fortifying breath—her new husband needed a lesson in *partnering* with a Tolemak wife.

Raell palmed his face and offered just enough pout to engage his full attention. "Mavis it shall be, then." An easy concession, all things considered. Rising on tiptoe, she kissed him, pressing her belly to his before she drew back and added, "Now that I understand."

He apparently didn't, staring at her in wide-eyed bafflement even as his color improved.

Winding her arms around his neck, she employed her tongue so thoroughly he still leaned in when she broke the kiss to trail her hand down his torso. "And your leg…how does it feel now?"

"Uh…" Naed's gaze had followed her hand. Now he looked up, blinked his pupils back to normal size, and eyed her with growing wariness. "Is there magic in your hands, Raell?"

She beamed her most benign smile. "No magic, merely a desire to keep my lord husband healthy and happy. 'Tis easy, aye, and far more pleasurable, when I am made privy to what troubles you. Such as—" She walked fingers up his abdomen. "—whether 'twas your

351

brother or aught else that brought you to such a state you required my comfort."

He colored, a sign he'd caught her drift at last. "Forgive me, Raell. I'm not used to confiding in anyone. 'Tis not a D'nalian practice, at least not at Tumin court."

"So I've gathered, if your mother be any example." She traced a finger over the charm she'd given him. "Among Tolemaks, however, 'tis the mark of a strong bond, one blessed by the Sisters." She gazed up under her lashes. "So what must I yet know about the dead Kassi man? Did a Tumin man indeed kill him?"

"What? Does the whole fortress know?"

"Servants and soldiers talk. A wise mistress takes care to overhear."

"So she does." Heaving a great sigh, Naed dropped into the deerskin-lined chair and pulled her onto his lap. Tenderly, he tucked a lock of hair behind her ear. "You are wise, my lady wife, as you've shown me more than once. I promise to be more mindful of that."

Warmth unfurled in her chest. Although they were half-dressed, in nigh intimate contact and surrounded by the scent of recent love-making, her husband focused on her face. On meeting her eyes with that intent green gaze she so loved, the one that hid nothing and pretended nothing. He'd gifted her with his attention; now she had to show herself worthy. She caught her bottom lip between her teeth, stifling the tiniest whisper of unease before it spoiled the moment.

With both hands Raell smoothed hair from his face and twisted it into a loose queue before returning her hands to his shoulders. "There be much you have to be concerned about, my love. Let me help untangle it. Tell me what troubles you most about this death, this day."

"Very well." Naed inhaled as if steeling himself to speak words that would name his fears, give voice to what lurked so far only in dark dreams. There would be no going back once he'd done so; she knew that well enough.

She curled her hands into his shoulders to lend him strength. His fears were her fears, too, but they would face them together.

"Someone is clearly trying to disrupt the assembly if he—or they—cannot murder me." The words rushed out, a dam breached. "It feels personal, Raell, but he who stood to gain the most is dead. I saw him die."

Ah, the Prince's would-be assassin. "This...Dlaniger, aye? Has he friends? Allies?"

"Most of Druemarwin's folk knew him, but few liked him. This was made plain to me when I came to serve in his stead."

"Still, there were some?"

"A few..."

He'd gone into his thoughts, so she sat quietly. Wrapped like this in his arms, the lowering sun hazing the chamber, his thumb absently stroking her forearm, she was tempted to press a kiss to his cheek. The worst of the bruising had faded, although the visiting lords had taken note, some unable to hide their shock. How many of them had real battle experience? This far south, few would've been inclined to take up arms in the Northern Wars. This assembly of soft-handed, soft-bellied lords was unlikely to provide Naed the allies he needed.

Unless Tumin treachery would galvanize them.

Shifting in his arms, she ventured, "Be there a

connection between your brother Allyn and this Dlaniger?"

"Beyond the fact they're both my half-brothers? And cousins to each other?" He huffed out a breath. "Allyn denies any other connection. Seems as shocked as my mother over Dlaniger's activities."

"Do you trust him?"

"Aye. No. I want to, but I don't...entirely." He faced her. "You've only just met him, but...what do you think?"

Her heart gave a little leap. A direct request—that was what she desired, wasn't it? Why then did it curdle her stomach to offer her honest assessment? Raell swallowed and returned his gaze with all the gravity he'd bestowed upon her. "Fierce but...not to be feared. Rather like Toth."

He expelled a half laugh, half groan. "Sisters, I do believe you've pegged him." Pulling her closer, Naed sighed and spoke into her hair, "And that's why this feels...more vicious than he alone would concoct."

"Who else bears a grudge against you?"

"Krenin, but he's dead too, and everyone knows we settled it when I went to warn the Prince about...Dlaniger..."

His body tensed and his eye movements quickened. She sat very still, sensing he'd latched onto something important.

"Gert," he said. "And Elthred. And...Yormoc. I wonder..."

"Who is Yormoc?"

"A Free Sword here who should've been senior, but then I came."

"Was he jealous?"

"Aye...and he knew Dlaniger, trained with him. Knew Dlaniger killed Dranoel. Sisters, Raell!" Naed thumped her onto her feet, sprang off the chair, and flung on his tunic. "*He* was the one who told me so!"

He snatched up his weapons. "Stay away from Gert. Don't go anywhere alone, understand? I have to find what's become of Yormoc."

The chamber door slammed behind her husband, leaving her open-mouthed and staring. She ought to be gratified she'd helped him to a critical insight. That had been her goal, hadn't it? So why did she feel so...what? Unsatisfied? Underappreciated? Abandoned?

Before she could decide, the door opened again to admit Mavis.

"M'lady, your father's come, an' he's asked to see you."

Papa's here! A rush of pure joy lifted her, weightless, for an instant before a tidal wave of panic crashed onto her shoulders. Her knees buckled, and she grabbed the chair with both hands.

"Who...who has he come with?" came out as a croak.

"A young man. Oh, 'twas ever such a scene, m'lady. Your brother broke his nose, he did! Right in front of Lady Vyenne an' Master Allyn."

Raell slapped a hand over her mouth to stop the hysteria bubbling up, but a laugh escaped anyway, a strange, half sobbing sound. She'd have given gold to witness Bennin laid flat, but it changed nothing. Her father's promise had caught up with her. She collapsed into the chair.

Bloody, bloody hell!

Chapter Thirty-Eight

"What do you mean, Yormoc's disappeared?" Naed shoved both hands through his hair and cursed. He'd lost another queue thong. A petty irritation but easier to expend emotion on than the nightmare scenario battering his defenses. Easier than blaming himself for another hesitation, another mistake.

Banir proffered a strip of leather. No comment. No judgment in those dark eyes.

His fists clenched with the desire to beat that bland Tolemak face into revealing something. "I gave you orders to imprison him months ago." Aye, blame the man he'd left in charge of Druemarwin, a brave alternative, that.

Not a flicker of reaction. "He fled afore he could be found. Mayhap he used the key."

"Sisters and the Demon!" Naed ripped apart his tunic collar. A better use of both hands than violence. He hated—*hated!*—this ridiculous insistence on formal attire. Protocol could go to the Demon! He wanted clothing that *fit*, that moved with him like skin. If that made him less of a D'nalian, so be it. He sucked in breath to quell volcanic forces within.

Banir again offered the queue thong. "Punch me if 'twill make you feel better."

It would for a moment, until shame set in. "Damn you! I'd rather peel off Yormoc's face. Find him so I

356

can."

Snatching the strip, Naed flung it around his hair and yanked tight. His scalp protested, but he welcomed the throb. Anything to distract from the inferno that was his gut. If only he'd personally stuffed Yormoc in a cell that night, if he hadn't underestimated the bastard's jealousy, if he'd had an inkling how pervasively Dlaniger's poison had spread...

But he hadn't. Instead, he'd rushed to warn the Prince.

So much blood...

The corridor tunneled. Phantom steps opened along one wall, propelling him leagues away, months backward. A cold wind iced his sweat-drenched torso. Disoriented, he pitched forward, catching himself with a bone-jarring stagger. And the corridor snapped back, flat again and solidly Druemarwin, while his pulse hammered out, *Too little, too late. Too slow, too stupid,* and fire needles stabbed his thigh.

Sisters!

He'd failed then and he was failing now, indulging base desires—wild and wonderful though they were—rather than courting the lords. Wallowing in the emotional pit that was his family rather than advancing the Kingdom. He had a mission to accomplish, one far more important than Raell, his mother and brother, or even Yormoc. He curled fingers into his tunic, assuring he still carried Dranoel's legacy. That had to take precedence over all else.

Did it?

Last winter when he'd hurled himself into saving the Prince, into advancing the Kingdom, he'd have shouted *Aye!* But now, when he'd moments ago left the bed of the woman he loved, when her scent lingered in his nostrils, clung to his skin?

Now his heart wanted to cleave itself in two.

Stop the assassin. Rally the lords. Protect Raell.

He closed his eyes. Here was a task for an army. What did he have? A motley handful of battle-tested warriors and devoted allies. Well, it would have to serve.

Stiffening his spine, he locked gazes with Banir. So much of what passed between them was unspoken. Damned irritating sometimes. Like now, when his emotions jangled like an exposed nerve. But reassuring too. Banir might let him fall, even fail, but the devoted Second would be there to pick him up afterward.

"Set our own men to searching. If Yormoc's here, if he's dared come back, someone among the folk may be hiding him or spying for him."

"Aye, but…there be one thing more."

Naed halted, steeled himself. "What in the Name of the Sisters is it now?"

"Lord Tylus has come, and not alone."

****

"Your hand—it's dripping blood!" Vyenne snatched a cloth from an empty bread basket and thrust it at Toth.

Allyn had escorted the injured stranger to Gam while she'd led father and son to what remained of the lords' welcoming refreshments. The servants had cleared all but one table, so she sent them scurrying below stairs till the latecomers finished.

Protocol—it would restore normality to a situation teetering on insanity.

While Lord Tylus made straight for a pork platter,

his son dropped onto a bench and planted both fists on the table. He sneered—*sneered!*—at the cloth she waved at his face.

Vyenne's spine snapped so tight her body vibrated. She didn't need this. Heavens above, she did not need to care, but she couldn't stop herself. She marched around the table and flung the cloth at his father, who made a startled grab for the thing. A stripped rib bone arced up and plopped at her feet. Beauty dashed from under the table and snatched it. Vyenne scowled at the wolfhound, who slunk away with her prize.

"Your son's knuckles!" She flapped a hand toward the glistening appendages. "He's opened them again. See?"

"'Tis naught, I said!" Toth growled. "A Tolemak matter."

"Oh, indeed!" Not for one minute did she believe that tripe.

Again, she rounded on his father, who recoiled a half step, scattering bread crumbs down his tunic. She must've looked like one of the Demon's own Nine, her fury out of proportion to the provocation. How could he know what had passed between her and his son these past days?

His son, *not* hers.

She damned well didn't need another; her own were quite enough. But she found herself advancing on Tylus.

"Do you know what he means or is it a Tolemak practice to assault guests?"

The fierce warrior, all bent beak and scarred visage, retreated, this time bumping the table. Putting out a hand, he blindly connected with a tankard, risked a glance at its contents, and grinned as if he'd found salvation. With a flourish, Lord Tylus stretched across the table and poured ale over his son's hand. Then he tossed the cloth over Toth's knuckles and drained the tankard.

"'Twill be fine." He suppressed a belch. "'Tis a clean cut. Cleaner now."

The gesture, at once dismissive and consummately, stupidly male, shredded Vyenne's temper. All afternoon she'd held the threads, like the reins of a galloping team, spooked and barely under control. Now they'd taken the bit and pulled loose.

"Do you take me for a fool?" With a hiss of frustration, she stalked around the table and slammed her hand inches from the pool of ale-diluted blood, inches from Toth. "You assured me your secrets would not harm Naed, but I suspect one of those has most definitely come home to roost. Do you deny it?"

Furious gold-brown eyes locked on her. "'Tis none of your affair!"

Staring down a hot-tempered young man—how many of these matches had she won over the years? Every single, teeth-grinding one. She leaned in, spoke softly. "Oh, but I think it is."

Silence stretched, broken only by bone-crunching sounds beneath the table.

They might've come from Toth's fists for as tightly as he clenched them. With a snarl rivaling Beauty's, he punched his bloody, cloth-covered fist into the other and broke eye contact.

Arms braced on the table, Vyenne waited. That puzzle she'd sensed earlier was taking shape.

"Forgive the lads, m'lady," Tylus offered in a

placating voice. "They've known each other since they were born. 'Tis a boys' grudge, no more."

No, it was not. She'd seen boys' grudges played out. This was something much deeper, darker. 'Twas almost as if Toth and...*Bennin*?

No.

Her skin curdled. That was not possible. Was it?

She assessed the staring-straight-ahead eyes, the set-in-granite jaw. *Dear Sisters!* If it were so, that would explain...everything.

Lord Tylus grazed the table. Despite his apparent interest in all things edible, the eyes under those bushy brows watched her. Did he know? Did Raell?

More to the point, did it have anything to do with why Lord Tylus had come?

Protocol be damned. She needed answers.

"One of you had best tell me what this is about. Because, mark me, I *will* find out."

****

If her life was about to go to the Demon, Raell would damned well do her best to stop it. She was undeniably wed now, and out of Tolemak. That ought to be enough.

In case it wasn't...

Trailed by Mavis and Naed's man Morys, she sped down stairs and through corridors. An unpleasant and increasingly pungent herbal bouquet indicated she'd found Gam's domain. She swept inside, saw the man she sought perched on a stool, nostrils packed with linen and protesting while the old healer swabbed, none too gently, at his bloody chin.

Bennin! She'd hoped—desperately—her fears were groundless.

361

Allyn blocked her path, asking, "Lady Raell, should you—?"

Fierce, but not to be feared. Her own assessment. It had better be true.

Chin raised, she presented her most imperious glare. Not quite up to Vyenne's but sufficient to inject doubt into her new brother-in-law's scowl.

"Master Allyn, I thank you for your concern, but young Master Bennin and I have a long acquaintance. You may step outside for we have…family matters to discuss." Amazing how calm she sounded, how unperturbed, when her insides shivered like jelly.

"Oh, he's a sight, he is, m'lady." The old healer studied her patient, then tweaked his nose to the left.

Bennin yowled.

Gam cackled. "'Tis as straight as I can make it, young sir. Keep it packed till tomorrow." Throwing her rags into a basin, she shambled out.

Raell shooed an objecting Mavis and Naed's man after Gam. "You may watch from the corridor with Master Allyn, if you must. I'll leave the door open."

After a territorial D'nalian-Tolemak stare-off— ended by Raell's, "*Now*, all of you."—Allyn, Morys, and the girl obeyed. The men, arms crossed and brows lowered, took up stances directly outside. Mavis, between them, bit her lip and quivered.

Not far enough, but it would have to do. Raell trained her imperious glare on the man on the stool.

"Keep your voice down. 'Tis my wish to keep this private."

"And 'tis a pleasure to see you, too, Lady Raell." A blood-red gaze took her in, head to toe and leisurely back again. Despite the poultice he shifted to the other side of his nose, his face was rapidly purpling. "I must say, though, you look better in armor. 'Twould please me if you wore it every day."

'Twould please me to see you gone. Seeing him with two black eyes by dinner and breathing through his mouth would have to do for now.

"Why are you here, Bennin?"

"Doing my father's will, of course." He cocked his head. "Does your D'nalian insist you dress 'properly'? How tiresome for you."

"Lest you've not noticed, I am a woman. It pleases me to sometimes dress as one."

"More's the pity." He heaved a sigh. "When we were children you thought differently. Such a pest you were then, my lady, in tunic and breeches every day, chasing Toth and me everywhere, wanting to play with the boys."

Damn you! She remembered those days all too well, how she'd yearned to join their games, to fight and ride and hunt with them. Most times they'd run from her and hide, or mock her mercilessly, then decide it might be amusing to let her spar with them. If she chanced to win, they'd gang up on her only to run off laughing.

That was then, before Roines and his bloody campaign drove a wedge between friends and turned allies into enemies. What it couldn't change, though, was one's essential nature.

Sweat trickled down her back. *Sisters Three, let me be right about that.*

"Why, Bennin? Since when do you do your father's will when 'tis so contrary to your own?"

An instant's narrowed eyes—*a score!*—promptly

blinked away. "Since becoming Lord of Nye has begun to look far more attractive, if and when your fine Prince destroys Roines. The man's become unhinged, turning on his allies."

"Your father should've thought of that afore he allied himself with the man who carried out Yinnad's scorched-earth purges."

"Ah, well, hindsight." He shifted the poultice again, eyed her steadily. "Your father made a promise, as did mine. Who are we to stand against an oath?"

"Who are *we*?" She flung up her hands. "Why, only the ones most affected! The ones ne'er informed, at least on my part. The ones who, if we'd been told, would've laughed in their faces. Indeed, you have no more care for me than I for you."

"That's untrue. I find you, at present, quite uninteresting. You, on the other hand, actively dislike me." He thrust out his lower lip and half turned.

Argh! She forced her fingers away from her sleeve dagger. Slicing that pretend sulk off his face would be deeply satisfying, but she reined in her temper. Any further bloodshed was Toth's to deliver, if aught remained between them. She'd never understood Bennin's appeal—*Cold, sarcastic son of a Bedian goat!*—but she'd come to terms with her brother's interests. They weren't uncommon in Tolemak, or even unaccepted among men who spent months at war. If only he'd chosen someone else!

"That's unfair," she said when her voice wouldn't betray her seething innards. "'Twould suit me to merely *ignore* you were it not for this ridiculous situation."

With slow deliberation he rotated to face her, all pretense gone. "How unfortunate, for we cannot simply ignore it, can we?"

No matter how innocuous, whatever he said always needled under her skin. At least he'd provided an opening. Unclenching her jaw, Raell stared down her nose. "Nor can we ignore the fact I made my commitment to Lord Naed afore I knew of this...arrangement. Or that the marriage he and I contracted has been consummated. Indeed, 'tis very like I'm already with child."

Hah! Respond to that!

His mouth, upper lip puffed to double size, pulled into a grotesque smile. "Well and good." He chuckled. "'Twould save me the trouble of getting my own heir. Mind you, 'twould be less of a chore if you wore breeches and armor. At least till the task was done."

She gaped. Her stomach heaved, threatening to add its contents to the filth decorating his boots and breeches. "You are a bastard!"

"No!" Heat flashed in his eyes. "The man who's stolen my betrothed is a bastard, well and truly."

By sheer force of will, she limited her recoil to a half step. "You can't be serious, Bennin! To commit yourself to a sham—"

"I have to, Raell! 'Tis the only way to keep close what I love."

The naked desperation in his voice stunned her. Steeped in her own dislike, she'd never credited Bennin with humanity, much less feelings. Now they stared at her from hollow eyes. *Damn and blast!*

"Toth won't come with me." A weak argument, but the best she had left.

"Aye, but he will." The familiar smirk she detested returned. "Neither the Prince nor your father will give you o'er without one of your own to see to your safety. They distrust my father, you see. And well they should."

Bloody hell! He'd thought this through—far more than she had. Well, she wasn't done.

"Lord Naed will fight for me. You'll see."

"A D'nalian fight *against* honor?" He guffawed, rocking back on the stool and slapping his knee. "Don't be a fool, Raell. You've dishonored *him* by making him complicit in your betrayal of me, my father, and yours."

She jerked as if lightning struck. The flash lit up her brain, shocking it with the truth she'd known, deep down, but simply ignored, thinking she could outrun it. Hoping if she left Tolemak, crossed the border, it would never call her to account. Deluding herself with the idea there was a place—*any place*—she and Naed would be safe and free and together.

Daft fool! The Three Sisters spun and wove, and if a thread chanced to work free, it would eventually be found, for nothing escaped the Sisters' plan.

She loved Naed *because* he was honorable. How could she ask him to kick out his very foundation, to betray his core belief?

She couldn't. Not if she loved him.

Raell stumbled for the door, waving off the men's hands, speaking words that must've satisfied them. All the while her body quaked from the inside out, and bile burned her throat. *Sisters Three, have mercy on me, a fool a thousand times over!*

What the bloody hell was she to do now?

Chapter Thirty-Nine

The Three Sisters had betrayed him again—*Fickle bitches!*—but he couldn't blame them entirely. It was only a matter of time before he was recognized, named, and connected.

"Yormoc!" echoed man to man, servant to servant in the corridors he slunk through. "You remember—the Free Sword."

Oh, Yormoc remembered. How his hard-earned command position had been leap-frogged over by the bastard of Druemarwin, how his years-won reputation at arms was eclipsed in Adanak by the Sisters-kissed exploits of a mere youth. How he'd been forgotten by all but Master Dlaniger, who understood what it was men like him desired: gold and revenge.

His pulse drummed at his temples. He'd been stupid for thinking Gert still had value. Beating her felt good, aye, but slitting her throat, belike, would've done the same.

Emotion, that was the enemy.

Leaning against the wall, Yormoc forced his clenched fists open, willed his jaw to relax. Master Dlaniger had the truth of it when he killed his own father. The mission was everything.

Stone at his back cooled his blood, calmed his thoughts.

I'm not out of options. Or allies. The gold he'd

collected this morn confirmed that. *Time to see what they're willing to do.*

****

Breathing hard, Raell flung open her chamber door and rushed inside. "Tunic and breeches, Mavis. Find the ones I wore when I arrived."

"M'lady?" The girl hovered in the doorway, the uncertain look she'd worn since leaving Gam's domain turning more apprehensive.

"Someone must've washed and mended them by now. Go, girl! Fetch everything."

Mavis bolted. Raell slammed the door on her guard's worried face. She considered throwing the pin, but that would leave her all the more trapped. She couldn't stay, couldn't face Naed's rejection. How soon would he find out? Minutes, she had minutes to grab her belongings and escape.

Escape the humiliation. Escape the alternative, a sham political marriage to a man who loved her brother.

Shoving down an urge to vomit, she yanked at her gown and froze. Changing now would make her intentions obvious. If she bundled everything into a blanket, she could say it was laundry and no one would be the wiser. She'd head for the stable, change there, saddle her horse and sneak out the gate. Among the visiting lords and attendants, one anonymous rider wouldn't be noticed.

Strung tight with the need to flee, she flew around the chamber, gathering cloak, boots, armor, weapons, leftover bread and cheese. The sword she'd conceal in the folds of her skirt. The rest she tumbled into her cloak, then forced breath down a constricted windpipe and paced.

Now, Mavis, hurry!

Long minutes later, Raell slipped into her mare's stall. Murmuring soft assurances to the sleepy animal, she dumped her bundle into the manger, reached for her gown's laces, and cursed. The bloody thing fastened all in the back.

She pulled out her dagger and—

"Don't you dare!"

With a little shriek she blundered into the mare, who flung up her head, squealed, and kicked the stall. Grabbing the halter, Raell soothed the beast while her heart returned to her chest. Naed's mother was the last person she expected to see standing outside the stall door, braving heavy scents of last year's hay, musty straw, and ripe manure.

"Have you no sense?" she demanded. "Horses startle easily."

"So, apparently, do you," Lady Vyenne retorted. "When you're caught doing precisely what you shouldn't."

First Lady Aerid, now Naed's mother. Raell was heartily tired of meddling women, whatever their intentions, blocking her escape route. She glowered at the woman standing ramrod straight, arms crossed, dainty slippers undoubtedly ruined.

Don't you dare blame me for that!

She scooped her dagger from the straw and slammed it into her sleeve-sheath. "Mavis told you," she grumbled, kicking off her own utterly impractical footwear.

"Elda did. She encountered an agitated girl asking after your—" A moue of distaste. "—men's clothes and came straight to me."

You'll never let that go, will you? Eyes stinging—*Damn and blast!*—she spun, located her breeches and pulled them on under her skirts. She would not cry over what this damned woman thought. "'Tis clear I was never good enough for you." That slipped past her guard anyway. "You should be pleased I'm leaving."

"Aye, I should, for the colossal mess you've hauled out of Tolemak with you! And don't think I don't know. Your father saw reason and told me everything."

Bent over her second boot, Raell froze, afraid to move while the world, along with her stomach, dropped from under her. "You can't know…everything."

"About Toth? 'Twas a shock, I admit, but not out of the realm of my experience." The woman inhaled through pursed lips. "But we can deal with that later. *After* you march back inside and explain yourself to Naed."

"I-I can't." Swallowing down more threatened tears, she put on her most determined expression and turned. "I won't."

Lady Vyenne's brows collided, before her chin ratcheted up and her shoulders stiffened. "You disappoint me. I thought you had courage."

If the woman had been wielding knives, she couldn't have cut more deeply. Raell reeled. *How could you? I was beginning to…like you.*

Stone-faced, Naed's mother measured her with a flinty gaze. "Evidently I was mistaken to assume it took courage for you to tramp halfway across two lands, with no more escort than your brother, to reach Naed. Or that 'twas brave of you to race into battle with those villains in the marsh when the prudent choice was to stay hidden. Or that it took nerve to kill a man on the ramparts to save Naed. *Sisters*—" Her voice cracked.

She flung up her hands, startling Raell and the mare. Color saturated her cheekbones while tendrils escaping a carefully bound braid waved wildly about her face. She looked...out of control, if that were possible, spearing Raell with fiery eyes, making her back-step.

"You-you've defied me at every turn, a task even my daughters couldn't manage. And now—*now*—you choose to run?"

Aye. Because I am *a coward, just as you said.*

Raell buried her face in the horse's mane while that truth burned behind her eyelids, etched itself into her soul. Best if it blinded her so she'd never again witness that awful shock and disappointment in Lady Vyenne's eyes. The woman was *not* her mother, no matter how much it seemed she could've become like one, mayhap...someday.

"'Twas only my life I risked then," she murmured. "Not my heart."

That heart was breaking now, splintering along the fault lines of her foolish—and cowardly—efforts to protect it, each fracture a tiny explosion that rocked her body. If facing Naed's mother flayed her so close to the bone, how could she endure facing him?

"Why should I stand before Naed when naught I say will change what he must do?" she whispered. "'Tis my fault his honor will be called into question. He must rid himself of me to clear the stain."

"I see." Two words, heavily frosted, chilling Raell to the marrow. "And how will you clear the stain upon *your* honor if you run away now, without explanation, without apology?"

"Are you-are you determined to humiliate me?"

"No. I am determined the two of you deal with what is between you so it does not fester, so if there is to be a break, it will be clean and final."

Clean and final, like death. Raell shuddered. To go inside, face Naed, witness those beloved green eyes look at her with revulsion, disgust, hatred, would kill her. Far better to console herself with how she'd last seen them, filled with love and admiration. That small memory—illusion, mayhap—might allow her to survive the dark days ahead.

She inhaled a shallow breath, fighting ribs that refused to expand despite the now hollow space where her heart had crumbled. "What if-what if I write it down? What if I make my apology in a letter?" She turned a pleading gaze on Naed's mother. "'Tis on me, all the fault, I know. Have mercy on me and let me go with some small piece of my dignity intact afore…afore I must lose it all to Bennin."

That appeal seemed to resonate.

Lady Vyenne spread both hands over the stall door as if to touch it, then reconsidered, clasping them together instead. "Very well. I'll bring you ink and paper, and send for your father."

****

"Ah, m'lady, have you lost your way?"

Vyenne recognized the man immediately. Not by form or face, but by the pricking of her nape and the cold, congealing knot in her stomach. The assassin had materialized in the stable doorway while she—fool that she was—fixed eyes on her footing and her mind on the difficult conversation ahead.

Mistake.

Fear spread tentacles up her spine. Was he alone? How much had he heard? Did he know he'd effectively cornered both of Naed's women?

Calm, control, discipline.

Bluff.

"Mayhap, 'tis you who are lost." Best to assert command, speak in her usual voice and hope it carried to the back of the dim stable. Hope that headstrong girl had sense enough to stay hidden or find an escape route. "Your master, Dlaniger, was my nephew. My sister's son, blood of my blood."

If aught would stay his hand, save either or both of them, that horrible truth should do it. She'd vomit later, attach leeches, cut off a limb—*anything!*—if it would purge whatever in her bloodline had birthed such a monster.

Standing eerily still, the assassin absorbed her meaning. Neither tall nor wide, of Allyn's years and garbed as a Druemarwin guard, with his hood up he'd have drawn little notice. Now, despite the fading light, Vyenne's gaze zeroed in on the misshapen, blood-crusted slash that served as mouth.

Her nostrils flared. *First blood!*

Raell had drawn that blood. *Brave girl!* Savage gratitude flooded Vyenne's system. She stepped forward. "Stand aside."

He stretched an arm across the doorway, blocking her exit by leaning on the frame. A thin smile pulled at those grotesquely swollen lips. His tongue flicked out, a quick taste of oozing scabs, while flat viper's eyes pinned her in place.

"I shouldn't be so trusting of a blood relationship, m'lady. Dlaniger—your nephew—killed his own father."

Dranoel. My love.

He'd meant to flatten her. Already her innards had seized and muscles gone rigid. She ought to have closed her eyes, swayed, even fallen, while pain gutted her. But Vyenne ground her back teeth and fisted the hand gripping her skirts. She refused to flinch while the snake itself watched, testing the air for a scent of weakness.

Pain burned, white hot and piercing. An endless, all-over-the-body oil scald. A Demon-be-damned agony more intense than when she'd first learned of her beloved's death.

Because now she knew *how* he'd died. And *why*. And *who* had ripped the heart from her body, the life from her soul.

Her hands curled into claws as her focus tunneled to the venomous creature before her. *And you, you bloody bastard, helped him!*

Two strikes, lightning fast, and she'd ripped claws across his face. Tore his wounded mouth apart. Gouged at his eyes, his throat, spraying blood across her fine lace cuffs while a high, keening rage bellowed from her lungs.

Chapter Forty

Glowering at the men standing about his private chamber, Naed sat rigidly still, fingers clenching wooden chair arms. He'd prefer to crush the windpipe of whoever next spoke. That wouldn't do. Not in the heart of D'nalee. Not even for one so provoked. Especially not for someone already regarded as a Tolemak sympathizer.

Even the Tolemak avoided such overt violence.

Damn the Tolemak. Damn the Prince. Damn the bloody Kingdom, too!

It was all a lie anyway. All the promises of friendship and trust and loyalty—lies! Lies told to keep folk like him from questioning the motives of those who wielded power, to keep their naked ambitions hidden and his people in line! D'nalee, always in the middle, always trampled on, its rights ignored, people belittled, land destroyed at the whim of others.

Hearts destroyed.

No! Naed refused to think about Raell. Whatever she'd done or known was not part of this discussion. This was about the future of D'nalee, and Dranoel's legacy, and what the bloody hell he would do once he got at the truth.

Because no one, not lords, lordlings, or witnesses, was leaving this chamber until he was satisfied.

His gaze skipped over Wendelmyr, wringing his

hands behind the table and as far from danger as possible. A scowling Allyn claimed Naed's right. Banir, silent and watchful as ever, protected his left.

The evidence—three men—formed a loose triangle several strides away. The nearest looked as if he'd been handed a dish of bitterfruit and commanded to eat.

The Tolemak's obvious discomfort gave Naed a small measure of satisfaction.

"Let me see if I understand you correctly." He pinned Lord Tylus with a blistering gaze. "In order to maintain my allegiance, and the potential allegiance of D'nalee, the Prince allowed—indeed, encouraged—me to pursue an alliance with your daughter, to make a marriage and consummate it, all the while knowing she was promised elsewhere?"

The man he'd expected to look upon as father-in-law had the grace to redden. "To be fair, 'twas not known to the Prince until *after* you departed Albon."

"But before Lady Raell departed, aye?" He'd steeled himself to say her name, but it still burned like salt in a wound.

A cleared throat, a jerked nod from the Tolemak.

Guilt. As much an admission as the spoken word.

Naed shifted a fraction, flexed his fingers to withdraw nails embedded in wood once he was sure he wouldn't lunge for the man's throat. He'd always pegged Tylus as an honest, plain-speaking man. *At least you're not lying to my face. Yet.*

"As I said..." He paused in case anyone else objected to the truth as it was becoming brutally clear. "With the Prince's full knowledge—and yours—she, along with her brother, was sent to me in order that I would complete this marriage contract without suspecting it was fraudulent, aye?"

"No!" Tylus squared up before him, brows a fierce V over his bent nose. "I resent your insinuations, sir." Hefting his sword belt, he planted his boot on a chair. "Much as I accept what fault be duly mine, I'll not be saddled with more. 'Twas not meant to be a fraudulent contract. Belac of Nye voided all such promises when he allied with Roines. 'Twas never in my mind he'd offer to change sides and make it contingent on fulfilling my old promise."

Truth. Whenever the grizzled warrior assumed that position, he was deadly, honestly serious. *And honorable, damn it.*

But it changed nothing except, mayhap, to elevate Tylus from belly-crawling slug to something with four legs and a tail. Something that nonetheless colluded with the Prince in this underhanded ploy to keep the allegiance of D'nalee while attempting to splinter Roines' support.

"I thank you for your candor, but whatever you *meant* is moot, for the Lord of Nye has indeed made the claim." Naed sucked in breath, seeking to redirect the fury boiling beneath his skin. Tylus deserved some of it, make no mistake, but more targets abounded.

His gaze landed on the raccoon-eyed Tolemak lounging—*lounging!*—against the wall. "And this—" He barely refrained from spitting the words. "*This* is the intended groom?" They were of an age, although a freshly broken nose distorted the man's features.

The youth had sense enough to stand up straight and incline his head. "Bennin of Nye, m'lord." If only he hadn't smirked as he said it.

Entitled little prick! I'll rip your fingers out by the

root if you dare put a single one on her!

"Shut up, fool!" Words from Toth, and a daggered glare, confirmed who'd put fist to that arrogant nose.

If Naed weren't so furious, he'd thank Toth. Then cuff him upside the head for too much restraint. *I'd have gone straight to blades, filleted Bennin of Nye like a fish.*

Too true, but not wise. Killing a Tolemak lord's heir who was a guest in his home would, mayhap, be a greater stain on his honor than this debacle was shaping up to be. The way his innards churned, he was sorely tempted to defy D'nalian values and find out.

But he wouldn't. Those values held the civilized man in his chair and prevented him from butchering whoever interfered with his desires.

Honor! Naed ground his teeth. *Bloody damned honor!*

No matter how his body screamed *Mine!* at the thought of Raell with another. *Any* other! No matter how her scent, the musk of their recent, and repeated, joining steamed from his overheated skin, it stood as nothing. Not even the very real possibility he'd planted his child in her could change the stark truth.

She was not now and never could be his.

Bile clawed at the back of Naed's throat. What little he'd eaten threatened to follow.

He had no right to Raell when she was—had always been, apparently—honor-bound to another. He'd taken her to his bed, she whose virginity was promised elsewhere. He'd done so unknowingly, aye, but that changed naught. However much the fault might lie with the house of Tylus and the Prince for deceiving him, what he'd done could not be undone.

Honor dictated he would have to give her up to—

"You cannot abide this," Allyn said.

"I know very well what I can and cannot abide! I do not require a late-coming *brother* to inform me!"

If the rebuke offended Allyn, so be it. No one was lord and master of Druemarwin but he, damn it! Naed dug in his fingernails, holding tight to that certainty while the rest of his world spiraled out of control. It had been tilting all year. He'd journeyed east to Adanak and west to Tolemak, saved his uncle/father only to lose him, traded his D'nalian heritage to pledge his sword to a Tolemak, and thought he'd come to terms with most of it, only to have his legs cut out from under him again.

Sparks exploded before his eyes. He needed to breathe but…he couldn't…get…air in.

I've been a seven-times fool to trust the Prince after he burned me with Aerid. Tolemaks always do what is best for Tolemaks.

Did that include Raell? She'd been so…*warm* when he'd left her, so soothing, so eager to help untangle the threats they faced. Did she truly love him? Or had she merely used him to escape an unwelcome marriage?

His gut blistered. If he clenched his jaw any tighter his teeth would crack.

Sisters! Was there anyone who hadn't plunged a knife in his belly? Or wished to?

The chamber door banged open and Grodar rushed in.

"Beggin' your pardon, m'lord—!"

But it was the figure behind him, a bizarre man-woman in muddy leggings and chest armor half fastened over the shoulder and red-stained skirt of a once-fine blue gown who absorbed all Naed's focus. And his fury.

Until those honey-gold eyes, round with terror, locked on him. "Your mother's been taken." Then she fled.

****

Eyes blurred with tears she refused to shed, Raell blundered into the Great Hall. Servants stopped lighting torches to stare. The assembled lords turned like a startled flock, faces shifting from interest to surprise to shock.

Horror would come next, once they noted the blood on her hands, her skirt. She bolted for the courtyard doors before that horror could infect her. Smelling the blood, slippery between her fingers was enough to comprehend. She had to get out, get away, crawl into a crevice until her mind stopped flashing over and over what couldn't be but was...

She'd been halfway to the stall door, sword drawn, when her brother's words from that night in the marsh stopped her.

Think first! And look!

How could she think when her instincts screamed at her to intervene, to save the creature whose agonized howls raised all the hairs on her body?

Because it's a trap and Lady Vyenne has sacrificed herself to warn you.

Shouts, squealing horses, thumps, thuds, and curses. And one voice screaming, "I'll kill you! Bloody crazed bitch! I'll teach you to claw me!"

But it was the second voice, the one commanding, "Hold!" that iced her to the marrow. "My master would prefer no harm come to her." A pause. "Well, no further harm."

An inhuman snarl, the crack of breaking wood.

"Your master is a fool! Dlaniger would've killed his mother!"

"Then it is fortunate Dlaniger is dead, for my master has very specific aims. Aims your repeated missteps have failed to advance. Now, all of you, quickly! Find the Tolemak girl."

The rest was a blur. She'd killed one, mayhap two. She remembered slicing a throat, her stroke defensive, wild. Her mare rearing, kicking, trampling while Raell jumped into the manger, found a hole, and wormed her way into the loft. The hay mow door ajar, winch rope dangling, a palm-burning lifeline to the ground...

She'd escaped, as Lady Vyenne intended, but she hadn't done a damned thing to stop the bastards!

All she had was a patch ripped from the dead man's tunic. The patch she'd meant to deliver to Naed...until they'd locked gazes across his chamber.

An instant, mayhap two—less than a heartbeat—and she'd seen all, seen enough. A beloved face consumed by rage, eyes full of hate, and a voice, if she stayed to hear it, that would spew all manner of condemnations upon her.

Raell sucked in breath, forcing unshed tears to scald her throat. "Bloody, damned fool!"

This was what she got for falling in love instead of marrying the man her father chose for her. If she'd been the demure little lord's daughter preferred by these D'nalians—and her own people, too, damn it!—she wouldn't be standing on the courtyard steps with her heart sliced in two and a bloody wad of cloth fisted in her hand.

A bloody wad of cloth taken from a villain who'd taken someone she cared about.

She stared at her fist while cool, evening air bathed her face and her stomach curled into a tight, hard knot. Toth's words mocked her. *You want to fight, Raell? Then you* kill *the bastards. Anyone who hurts you, you kill. Understand?*

Aye, she understood. Warriors didn't cry. And they damned well didn't give up.

A hitched breath, two, before she wiped her nose on her sleeve and straightened. She could still help Lady Vyenne, but she couldn't do it alone.

Her heart beat a fierce tattoo, and her muscles shivered like jelly.

And she couldn't do it by running away.

Not this time.

Chapter Forty-One

Naed flew across the threshold before anyone else reacted, shoving aside Grodar and flattening a guardsman who'd been shouting…something. He moved without thought, impelled by Raell's stricken look and his own panic.

Blood! He'd seen the splatter on her face, scented the tang in her wake. He homed in on it, following the trail of shocked faces and pointing fingers through the Great Hall, running pell-mell while his heart hammered *Mother!* and fear buzzed everything from his mind but the need to pursue Raell.

At the courtyard doors, he stopped, stunned to find her on the landing.

Pale as death despite the torch glow, she faced him with arms hugged across her midsection. Naed's every impulse screamed, *Go to her! Touch her!* Her abrupt out-thrust fist rooted him in place.

"Raell…" His mind blanked. Moments ago he'd had questions, demands pushing at his throat like flotsam at a river bend. Now, not a whisper dared take voice when every inch of her trembled on the edge of flight.

She swallowed, visibly gathering herself. "Your mother…I couldn't stop them."

"You tried." That came without thought, a rusty statement of truth. He leaned a fraction closer, holding his breath, scanning for wounds in rapidly dimming twilight. *Nothing, Sisters be thanked.*

She swallowed again, throat working with the effort, and dashed her other hand under her nose. "It was…it was that Yormoc…and others…"

Running feet pounded behind him, voices bayed.

"M'lord!"

"The stables!"

"Stay back!" He threw both arms wide, refusing to turn, holding her in place with his eyes, that oh-so-tenuous thread of connection.

Banir, voice calm, authoritative, contained the pack well out of sight.

No matter how Naed wanted to focus on the two people who mattered most, he couldn't ignore his responsibilities. "Bar the gate. Secure the lords. Search the damned stables!"

Orders were given sensibly, not shouted. Pounding feet dispersed.

One set of footsteps approached, slowly. "Raell, girl…" Tylus cajoled when he drew abreast.

Her brave face crumpled, and she whispered, "Papa."

Her father enfolded her in burly arms, stroked her hair, kissed her forehead and made comforting sounds, all the while glaring at Naed.

Mine! The response was raw and primitive and impossible to ignore. It bared Naed's teeth, fisted his hands, and filled him with an overwhelming urge to rip them apart and claim his mate no matter how many times his mind shouted, *Traitor!* But he could do naught. Only stand while the beast within growled long and low against the bonds of honor and propriety and all things D'nalian.

Tylus must've heard the growl, for his glare altered, and he gave a small, barely perceptible nod.

Naed's brows shot up. Overlapping shadows—dusk, dark, torchlight—must be playing tricks on his perceptions.

Raell's abrupt separation from her father was no trick—of the light, at least. Expression grim, she stuck out her fist, palm up. "I took this from one of the villains in the stable."

He focused on her clenched fingers, pried the sticky, stiffened thing free and attempted to flatten it.

A burst of salt-sweet death assaulted his nostrils, and the beast howled till Naed's innards shook with the strain of keeping it contained. He set his teeth, held on. Raell was alive, she was unharmed; this was not her blood. Logic demanded he concentrate on evidence at hand, this clue to whoever had taken his mother.

Bringing the scrap closer, he tilted it at uncertain light, ran fingertips over raised stitching. A design took shape in his mind, a tunic patch, one so unaccountably...bone-chillingly...*familiar* even the beast went silent.

Naed's stomach dropped to his feet, and most of his blood with it. This insignia could not be whose it was.

Dizzy with dread, he forced his gaze to her face. "Is this—?"

"Aye." She approached a half step, her voice low, urgent. "Don't turn your back on—"

"The lords are secure," Allyn's voice boomed, his strides approaching. "Forget the lying bitch! Where the bloody hell is Mother?"

Raell's hands jerked. Naed blinked, and the impression she meant to draw a weapon was gone. She stepped back, ghostlike, whispering, "Don't turn your back on anyone. Please."

His legs turned to jelly and the earth, he could swear, heaved beneath Druemarwin, beneath D'nalee, beneath all he held dear.

She faded toward her father, inches away yet impossible to reach, as if a chasm opened its great maw and split the courtyard. It gaped at Naed's feet, separating her from him, Tolemak from D'nalian, the Kingdom and all its potential from Druemarwin.

Leaving him isolated at the precipice, a solitary figure marooned on a chunk of stone in the middle of his own court, wondering who in the Name of the Sisters meant to stab him in the back because Tolemaks, for all their faults, looked a man in the eyes when they meant to kill him. They did not kidnap a man's mother, attack his bride, and send assassins into his very home.

No, these villains hired D'nalians to do that, D'nalians with no conscience and no honor.

And no sense of blood loyalty.

Something coiled around Naed's heart and squeezed. He had to breathe, but there was no breathing until Dlaniger's poison was excised, the gangrenous limb on his family tree amputated.

How deep did it go?

He stared at the fabric between his fingers, wishing it away, praying the toxin hadn't somehow seeped from it into his skin. The urge to throw it down, stomp on it, was nigh overwhelming. But damning as it was, the thing itself wasn't the viper.

Dear Sisters, who?

He pivoted, and there was Allyn—arrogant, ignorant, interfering Allyn—a clean, unstained, *matching* patch emblazoned on his chest. Naed's focus narrowed, reddened, shot from damning patch to man while his innards, the rage so tightly wound within, exploded.

"*Tumin*, Allyn!" He thrust the bloody patch at his brother's face. "What the—?"

He was jerked forward, hurled off his feet by something that tore through his collar. Another something whipped past his cheek, stinging. And then he was falling, off the precipice, into that chasm, down, down, with no time to—

****

Vyenne lay still, absorbing sounds echoing in the stable. The whole side of her face was numb, only her nostrils registering straw pokes and the musk of hay, horse, and manure. She could see enough to know they'd left her alone, for now, and she'd bled into the straw. Heard enough to know the blood had been well spent.

Run, Raell.

A rustle. Above. A handful of hay cascading gently into view.

That better not be a rat. She'd scream if a rat fell out of the loft, all teeth and whiskers and scrabbling feet. Moving only her eyes, carefully, Vyenne looked up.

Not a rat.

A round, terrified, sweating, *familiar* face gleamed between slats.

Humbert!

Vyenne's heart slammed into her throat. *Dear Sisters, don't let him do anything rash.*

She stared at her groom, desperately messaging with her eyes, moving her head a fraction. *No!*

Humbert blinked rapidly, shifted, triggered another shower of hay, and slid something between the slats.

The knife landed with a soft thud.

Oh, you dear, smart man! Vyenne grasped the hilt. Her arm hurt like the Demon—*Bastard!*—but it still functioned. Gritting her teeth, she carefully threaded the blade into her sleeve. Not as well concealed as her daughter-in-law's, but it would serve. All she needed was an opportunity.

She made another movement with her eyes. *Go. Get help.*

****

Naed smacked the ground, bounced, saw stars. Then he was grabbed, tumbled across stone, and shoved into a wall.

"Stay down!" Raell's breath whooshed across his face while his head spun and his senses registered time and place.

"On the parapet! North tower!" Banir shouted.

"Cover him, you flat-footed fools!" Tylus bellowed. "Quick now!"

Naed pulled his nose from Raell's chin, glimpsed the courtyard. A mass of men huddled beneath shields while Tylus, Toth and others pulled a body toward shelter.

Allyn!

His heart seized. "No, no, no, *no!*" *Sisters Three, not again.*

Pushing at Raell, he peeled her off and staggered to

his feet. His pulse hammered ineffectually at his throat, unable to move blood upward, unable to clear the vision of Dranoel—*Father!*—struck down before this well. Dranoel had fallen just there, arrow-struck in the back, the Prince beneath him, wounded. Dlaniger meant to kill the Prince then, but Dranoel had moved, and Naed had inherited and—*Oh, Dear Sisters!*

He bent over and vomited. It was embarrassing and unmanly, but he couldn't stop. Raell rubbed his back, crooning under her breath, until he'd purged himself. Shaky and sweating, he wiped his mouth and straightened. Her hand fell away, and he missed it acutely until he stumbled. She grabbed his arms and propped him against the well.

"Stay!" In the torchlight, her face shone white beneath the grime and—*Sisters!*—was that fresh blood?

Naed touched a finger to her chin. "Are you hurt?"

Her eyes flashed. "No, daft fool, *you* are. Chin and cheek and..." She peeled back his collar, scowled, tore a fragment from what remained of her skirt and stuffed it into his tunic. "Scratch," she muttered, fisting bloodstained fingers against her hip. "Sisters be thanked you put on your armor." Her voice shook, and she clamped her lips together.

She was terrified, his fierce Tolemak bride, but she'd flung herself at him and saved him, just as she'd saved him on the parapet. That she'd done so—*twice, no less!*—left him feverish *and* chilled. Whatever she was, she was no traitor. He couldn't keep her, the reminder burned like acid, but damned if he wasn't grateful for her right now.

"Raell." He groaned and pulled her into a crushing embrace.

She gulped a sob and hung on as if she'd squeeze herself into his skin. They stood, hearts pounding against each other, while guardsmen raced around them. After a moment Naed sensed Banir's discreet approach. He lifted his head, saw the dark pool marring the pavement—*more* family blood—and gathered himself.

"Allyn?"

"Took two. Chest and shoulder. Armor blunted both."

"Alive, then." He released the breath he'd been holding. Destiny would *not* repeat itself on these cursed paving stones. Not today, at least. He faced Banir, who nodded. If any man understood the emotions coursing through him, the Tolemak did. Understood, validated, and moved on.

"Four arrows loosed. Belike Master Allyn took arrows meant for you, but to my way of thinking, 'twas no accident he was stuck."

"But those men who took Lady Vyenne—" Raell looked from Banir to Naed, "—they wore Tumin livery. Aye, and they told that bastard Yormoc he's to do their bidding. I heard them." She'd anchored an arm around Naed's waist with a fistful of tunic, but her expression said, *I don't understand.*

Neither did he—yet—but his focus was all on her, on how her heat along his body galvanized him. He palmed her fist, wishing he wouldn't have to peel her fingers away. She was in danger here, no matter how he yearned to keep her close.

No matter how determined she seemed to stay.

"Raell—"

She lifted her chin, that stubborn, scraped and

bloodied chin he longed to cradle against his chest and protect from further harm. "They hired Dlaniger too, aye? Who else but Tumin would do as much?" Some color had returned to the face she presented now to Banir, and her voice no longer shook. "Yet, 'tis sure, Master Allyn's men wouldn't dare risk harm to him."

She was astute, this woman. Naed squeezed her hand. How had he ever thought her a traitor?

Banir included her in his gaze. "Aye, m'lady, if they all be *his* men."

Naed went rigid. All this time, had he been looking in the wrong direction? Or at the wrong person? With disorienting speed, formerly discrete pieces abruptly rotated and clicked into place. His skin crawled at the emerging picture.

"Explain."

"Why wait till Master Allyn approached to loose arrows? 'Twas plenty of time afore that to strike only you." Banir held out the patch. "Besides, 'tis not the first we've seen this."

The villains in the marsh and Raell's attacker.

Sisters Three, would the ground never stop shaking?

Naed gripped Raell, the only solidity in a landscape turned to quicksand. "And well before my brother arrived." Demon be damned, how could he have been so blind? Everything had turned on its head.

Again.

Brow furrowed, honey-gold eyes full of concern, Raell turned her face up to his. "*Not* Tumin?"

He blinked, and she came into focus, as did her question. "Oh, most definitely Tumin." He squeezed her shoulders, cupped her chin, kissed those lips pursed to ask what the Demon he meant. His gut knew; his brain still absorbed the message.

He pressed a hand to his heart, to Dranoel's legacy resting there. This—*this* was what it was all about. Someone had worked out the secret. And that someone was more than willing to kill for it, no matter who stood in the way. No matter whose blood he had to shed.

"The stables be empty," Toth said, jogging up to the well. "Two dead, a blood trail. Can Beauty follow a scent?"

Naed hauled his mind fully into the present, noting the leashed wolfhound straining at the grim-faced Tolemak's side. Fury, sharp and acidic, bit at his nerve endings, as eager as the dog and the man to hunt, to find and slaughter the human wolves who'd wreaked so much havoc among the people and place he loved. His duty was to defend them. Even D'nalee, for all its vaunted restraint, gave a man leave to use any means necessary in pursuit of that duty.

He had plenty of means. They were arrayed around the courtyard, torch-lit faces awaiting orders, Tolemaks and D'nalians alike.

"Set Beauty to it." He stepped out of Raell's arms. "Go to your father. He'll protect you."

A snap of his gaze to Grodar brought the gap-toothed Tolemak to attention. "Tell Lord Tylus to keep the lords safe in the Great Hall. Morys is to protect Master Allyn at all costs. The captain of the guard will stuff every man wearing a Tumin patch into the cells until this is over. Then assemble a detail and systematically clear every nook and cranny of this place, starting with the tunnels. I want these bastards cornered."

The Tolemak bounced on his heels. "Can we kill 'em, m'lord?"

D'nalian values taught that a wise man displayed mercy to those who could be redeemed. The Prince had taught him its corollary: Only a fool offered it again.

"They deserve no less, Grodar. Have at it."

"'Twill be a pleasure, m'lord!"

Yes, indeed. Adrenaline flooding his veins wasn't precisely pleasure, but fuel for a sense of absolute rightness. Restoring himself to order after that tumble across the courtyard required only a shrug to realign his armor, two yanks on his forearm guards, and a twist of his sword belt. He had clear targets now, and one of them was within these walls.

Banir waited at his shoulder. This man had been as close to him as his shadow, a devoted guardian, a better brother than blood. But now Naed needed him elsewhere. "Go with Toth. Find my mother."

"And you? What will you do?"

"Settle a long festering score with a man I once, *very* briefly, looked up to."

Naed scooped a discarded shield and fitted it to his arm. The action, so familiar after a year of war, calmed his nerves, narrowed his focus to the task ahead. His men would do what he'd asked so he could do what he'd ask only of himself. Inhaling a deep, fortifying breath, he stalked into the open, into a bright pool of torchlight.

"Yormoc!" he bellowed to the walls. "You gold-grubbing turncoat! I'm coming for you! I've shut down your tunnels, closed the gates, and killed every man you've sent after me. Face me like a man and let's be done with this. You don't give a damn whose side you're on. 'Tis me you want. I've always bested you, and I'll do it again. Or are you too much a coward to meet me man to man?"

Chapter Forty-Two

Raell shivered without Naed's body pressed to her side. He'd moved away, as she'd known he would, known he must, to take charge. This was his home, his family, his folk that were threatened. She was only— what the bloody hell was she?

Wife? She twisted the ring on her finger. *Or scorned bride?*

Moments ago he'd embraced her, listened to her, even kissed her! She'd saved his life, the daft fool! And she *still* didn't know what she was to him. Instead, he'd set her aside and carried on giving orders as if he'd forgotten her.

As if he'd forgotten the whole disaster that was Bennin.

A tremor rattled her teeth. Raell hugged herself, rubbed her arms to ward off the shaking. Aftereffects of danger, nothing more. Her brain knew that, but her body...

Why the Demon did it *feel* like so damned much more?

Toth's voice broke into her misery. "You left these in the stable." He shoved a shield and helm into her hands. "Good thinking, getting into the loft."

Nonplussed, she blinked at her brother, who proceeded to yank her chest armor into place and none- too-gently fasten the straps. Was that...*praise*? Her scrambled brain searched for a response. "Use whatever's to hand—"

"—or to foot. Father's first lesson—I know." He glowered at her, all bent nose and thunderous brows. "You killed two. 'Twas good, you daft, spoiled girl, but keep your head."

More praise? And from the brother who never said anything nice but loved her fiercely just the same? A lump clogged Raell's throat.

"I will if you will." When his brow ticked up, belike at the tender-hearted sound of that, she summoned a scowl. "Ass."

He grinned, pinged a finger off her helm, and turned to go...just as he'd done weeks ago, before they'd begun this journey. Weeks ago, when they'd been so, so much younger. And safer.

Her stomach lurched. So much was at risk.

"Bennin loves you, you know." She had to say it, now, before he went to fight an enemy that hid in shadows and wore disguises, before he lost the chance to acknowledge whatever was between him and Bennin, before her brother died or was injured and she hadn't told him...

Toth halted, stiffened. Eyes dark with emotion pinned her in place despite her body's urgent desire to step back and away from the response she'd triggered. The response she didn't think would be this *intense*.

"And you love Naed, aye?" He slashed a hand toward the man who'd sent a challenge ringing off the walls, a challenge designed to bring that very enemy down upon them all. "What of it?" Seizing her fingers, he thumbed the gold band. "Deal with your problem, little sister, and mayhap I'll deal with mine."

Raell gaped, glared, and yanked her hand free. How dare he tell her what was true! "Go! Save Lady Vyenne, you bloody great ass! And-and watch yourself, aye?"

She was shaking again as he trotted off with Banir and the wolfhound, a great, full-body quaking. But this was anger, not fear. *Never fear, damn it!* Not for Toth; he could handle himself. Not for Lady Vyenne; Toth and Banir together would rescue her if that formidable woman hadn't already rescued herself. Wishful thinking, mayhap, but it settled some of the trembling.

A few deep breaths settled more. Now she could focus on Naed, on how he stood alone in the torchlight, armed and battle-ready, his very stillness daring his enemies to come at him again, to take another shot now he knew who they were. His profile had gone flint hard, brows low, gaze intent on what lay ahead. He'd given his orders, sent his men to their tasks, left the most dangerous one for himself.

It was why she loved him. *Daft, daft man!* And why he made her so blindingly furious.

She shoved her helm onto her head, snagged some hair, and winced. *Bloody hell!* Her eyes stung, but she would not cry.

Nor would she be pushed aside, left behind—*forgotten* even!—like some proper D'nalian female.

"Go to your father, hah!"

Her father could take care of himself. The one who needed protecting was the selfless idiot determined to face death alone.

"Deal with *my* problem?" Raell huffed. Damned men, thinking she couldn't take care of herself and those she loved.

Drawing her sleeve knife, she sliced off her skirt above the knees. Not exactly a tunic to cover her breeches, but now she had freedom to move and full access to all the blades about her person.

"I'll show you how I'll deal with *my* problem!"

****

"That was stupid! Foolish!" Yormoc spat blood. The bitch had gouged him like a bear, her bastard brat was calling him out, and he was surrounded by idiots.

"Two birds, one stone." The Tumin man shrugged. "Your precious Dlaniger's arrow attack was worth a try."

"Dlaniger's attack scored! All yours did was give them a rallying point!"

"No, I split their attention, gave them two targets." He smiled, smug, superior. "They know about you. They'll be wondering who's aligned with us."

Yormoc wiped more blood from his face, using the moment to rein in his fury. So, that was the way the beads fell; he was to be their scapegoat while they slunk away. He eyed the man opposite, assessing. Two could play that game.

"Your master may have grown up with him, but I trained him, watched him learn from those Tolemak savages. Naed—" He gagged then coughed to cover how the coming words burned like salt in a wound. "Naed is not the green lad he remembers."

"So, finish him as you were hired to do. We'll keep the hostage."

A bargaining chip, no doubt. Well, let them have the bitch. He had intimate knowledge of the place, all the escape routes, while they were strangers here.

"Damn yourselves, then. Give me my gold."

****

Tunnels or battlements? Naed rocked on the balls of his feet. Yormoc had shown a fondness for dark places months ago, but Grodar's search below stairs would be thorough. And deadly, given the Tolemak's eagerness to bash something.

He understood that need, that blood lust. So much energy sizzled in his veins he'd explode if he didn't find Yormoc soon.

Let me think first.

The turncoat rat had been seen above ground in the stables a short time ago. Naed's gaze shot in that direction. His pulse, already fast, skipped and skittered. His ears rang and his throat closed up.

Damned panic!

He fisted his hands against it, clenched his jaw, but the impulse to charge the stables and rescue his mother battered him anyway. Emotions—love, hate, fear, rage, guilt—stormed his judgment, pelting him with hailstones of doubt. Any normal, loving son would go to his mother's aid. What son would leave the saving of his mother to friends?

One who was not the son he thought he was, who'd grown up in a court of weasels and vipers, thinking they were his family.

A bastard who knew damned well it was a trap.

He sucked in breath, enduring. If he was wrong, if any harm came to his mother, it would kill him.

And he would deserve the most gruesome death.

But he wasn't wrong. His gut, when emotions weren't drilling holes in it, agreed with his brain. Toth and Banir and the wolfhound would run to ground those villains who'd taken his mother. But Yormoc—*the self-*

serving bastard!—he'd find a way to desert his cohorts and save his own skin.

After all, he'd come virtually unscathed through the Adanak campaign.

Unlike me.

Naed flexed his thigh, wishing away the crawling sensation the whoosh of arrows always triggered. That hollow, fleshy *thunk-thunk* striking Allyn hadn't registered at the moment, but the sound reverberated in his brain now. Sweat broke out along his hairline, and his pulse ratcheted up again. A dull ache radiated from his thigh bone.

No. Stop.

He grit his teeth, bit down on the memory. This was a phantom ache, nothing more. Aerid had done her best to make him whole. And he was whole. He had two functioning legs. He was fit and determined. He would find Yormoc and end this threat to his family, his home, his life.

Where would you go to meet me?

His gaze shot to the nearest tower, and his gut tightened another notch. *Up, of course. Make me climb the damned stairs because you know I'm lame.*

Only he wasn't as lame as he'd been when Yormoc last saw him. And he hadn't run the stairs at Albon merely to pass the days.

Nor would he be last up them this time. Not if he were the only one climbing.

Sweat bloomed on Naed's upper lip. He'd failed that day, miserably, but never again. No one else need die because he was too damned slow.

Banir understood. The Tolemak had taken a long look before going with Toth.

Naed drew his sword and let his hand settle into the familiar grip, let doubts fall away and focus fill him. How different from a warrior's skills were those required of an assassin? He knew Yormoc's moves from all their sparring sessions, but those had ended months ago. What had Yormoc learned since? What had he learned from Dlaniger?

Everything deadly, Naed had to assume, or he'd never awake to Raell's hair strewn across his face or her soft backside curved into his groin.

He flinched, scrubbed that thought from his mind. She was promised elsewhere. And he had a viper to hunt.

****

Play dead, play dead. The sing-song reminder kept Vyenne limp even as the Tumin man's bony shoulder dug into her abdomen with each jarring step. Thinking her unconscious, he'd slung her over his shoulder when the villains fled the stable. They'd argued somewhere in the darkness; she'd long ago lost her bearings. The one she'd gouged, that snake Yormoc, had broken with the Tumin cohort. She'd thank the Sisters, but he'd gone after Naed.

Be safe! Oh, please be safe!
And don't come to save me.

That would be the height of stupidity, considering what she'd overheard. How could her bloodline have spawned another like Dlaniger? It was almost too much to take in, the treachery, the absolute betrayal of all she'd thought true.

But she couldn't think about that now or it would consume her. Humbert and Raell must've found help. Someone had to be coming.

Sisters, help them find me!

A deep-throated baying reverberated between close-set walls.

The villains pulled up short, turned. The baying thrummed in the blood. Vyenne's spirits soared and the man carrying her cursed.

"That's the bloody wolfhound!"

"Go to the garden! Go!"

The villains scrambled in the narrow passage, weapons clanking, shields scraping, all pretense at stealth abandoned.

Vyenne fumbled for Humbert's knife. Her injured arm had gone numb, a mercy at first, but now she had no idea if her fingers would grasp the hilt, much less find it amid all this jostling. If only she could *see* a little...

She bit back a sob, regrouped. If she could get the knife into her left hand, wrap those fingers around the hilt, she could stab her abductor in whatever unarmored flesh she could reach—hip, thigh, buttock—and make him drop her. But she had to do it at the right time, as soon as Beauty got close enough. Too soon and the villains would snatch her back and she'd be weaponless.

Sisters Above, help me!

****

Raell ran up the tower stairs, following the sound of footsteps. Naed had sprinted off like a demon was at his heels, and she'd been caught flat-footed. *Daft man!* The demon was surely ahead of him, lying in wait. If only she could catch him before he burst onto the parapet.

If only the stairwell weren't so damned dim, so

bloody narrow, so dizzyingly *circular*...

She stumbled onto a landing, banged her shield, and teetered backward.

"Bloody hell!"

Heart in her throat, clinging to the wall, she gave herself a moment to breathe. And become aware of silence above. Naed must've reached the parapet while she was crashing into walls.

"Argh!" Shield forward, sword in hand, she charged up the stairs.

"Naed! Wait!"

She burst through the tower door, slamming it on its hinges. Something whistled at her head, and she flung up her shield against it.

Strike. Block. Strike. Block. Everything she'd trained to do without thinking until—

"Raell! What the Demon?" Naed stared, white-faced and panting. "I heard someone on the stairs. I thought—" Color rushed his cheeks, and he slammed sword into scabbard. "Demon be damned, Raell! I could've taken your head off! What in the Name of the Sisters are you doing up here?"

She'd shaken him; that was clear from the way he huffed and stomped around, pounding his fist into his shield. Well, he'd bloody well set her heart to racing too.

"Daft man!" She shoved her sword into its sheath. "Have a death wish, do you? Only a bloody great fool goes off on his own when he's no idea of the danger!"

"I *know* the danger! I know Yormoc, damn it!" He swung about in his pacing and froze. Surprise—mayhap even shock—widened his eyes as he took her in from helmeted head to the shield fitted to her arm.

Then he swore, and her brows shot up. Clearly, her proper D'nalian had learned more than blade skills from her Tolemak brethren. Not that she was offended; she'd heard worse from her father and brothers. Why did he employ them now? While she considered that, she fastened her helm strap.

"Oh, no!" He seized her wrist, yanked her onto her toes. Sweat sheened his thunderous expression; his eyes smoked with some kind of wild, white-eyed fury. "You're to march back down those stairs and go straight to your father! Wherever the Demon you got that armor, you take it right back!"

Stunned, she sucked in breath, rocked back onto her heels. Hadn't she been wearing chest armor and carrying a sword in the courtyard moments ago? Hadn't she saved his bloody damned life—*again!*—precisely because she'd been armed and armored? Oh, she could allow he was upset—she'd startled him, after all, made him raise a sword against her—but this was beyond the pale.

She jerked her hand free and thrust out her chin. "'Tis mine, all of it! 'Tis Tolemak I be, not some fancy D'nalian female who waits by the fire while her man goes haring off by himself. Or have you forgotten who you wed yesternight?"

He reared back as though she'd slapped him. No, as though she'd plunged her sword into his belly and twisted it.

Face ghost white, he rasped, "Raell, I have no right to you. That *raccoon* is your intended."

"Not *my* intended, thick-brain!" She didn't want to stomp her foot like a petulant child, but she couldn't help it.

He was so damned honorable. And ass stubborn.

"I *told* you all yesternight! I knew naught of some old agreement betwixt my father and Nye. When I gave you my promise, 'twas free and unencumbered, to the best of my mind, anyway."

It was the truth, and he'd accepted it yesternight, because he'd lain with her then and made her his. Just as she'd made him hers, because they'd both come to the marriage bed with no experience of another. They'd made public vows to keep unto each other, and they'd meant them. At least she had.

A lump swelled her throat, shorting her air, forcing her to swallow hard. Surely, what was done and said couldn't be changed, wiped away, forgotten when they'd both been irrevocably changed by it. How could he turn his back on the vows they'd made, the child they might have conceived?

But that was then and this was now. The earth had somehow split between them, yawning wider with each thud of her heart. Soon it would be too wide to leap. She'd run at it now, hurl herself to his side and shake sense into him, but it would be no use. The gap was in his mind and of his own making. It was his to cross.

Throat tight, ears buzzing, she waited while desolation sank into Naed's eyes and her hope melted away with it.

"He came after you, Raell. Bennin of Nye came after you."

Dear Sisters, she was losing him. Losing him to that D'nalian sense of honor she so loved. It would be her undoing—if she let it.

Not bloody likely!

She had one cast of the beads left. His honor would

either save them or doom her, but she'd be damned if she wouldn't take the risk. Steeling herself for all or nothing, she poured her love into her eyes, softened her voice, offered her hand palm up.

"When I fled Albon—and flee I surely did—'twas to keep my promise to you, made in all good faith. As yours was to me."

"Raell, I never should've...I can't..."

Argh! Just the sort of slump-shouldered response she'd expected to the soft approach. He'd sunk too deep into his own misery for aught but throwing herself at his feet and begging to penetrate that fog. She blew out a breath, sucked in more, and stiffened her spine. A daughter of Tylus did not beg. Fighting for what mattered, for what was right—*that* best suited a true Tolemak.

"Look at me, Naed. Look me in the eye and listen."

"Raell, now is not the time—"

Aye, it wasn't. They stood in torchlight on an open parapet while assassins stalked them, but this might be the only chance she'd have to press her case, to reach him across that precipice, to secure the future they were meant to share. Gathering her courage, she spoke what was in her heart, what had propelled her on this journey to this man to whom she'd given everything.

"Does *my* honor mean naught? When weighed with D'nalian honor, is mine lesser because 'tis a woman's honor? Or because 'tis a Tolemak's honor? Be honest and tell me that."

The world had gone silent, or so it seemed, because Raell heard nothing over the rush of blood in her ears, the terrible heavy beats of her heart while she waited, dizzy with fear, breathless with longing, for the man she loved to respond with a word, a look, even a blink. Even a shift of his gaze she'd take as a sign he'd at least listened, mayhap begun to consider—

"Yes, be honest, *Lord* Naed."

A voice she'd heard but once, a voice that raised all the fine hairs on her body. Her innards contracted into a cold, tight knot.

"Tell us both how much honor means to a bastard who's betrayed his countrymen and his blood."

Chapter Forty-Three

Another turn, a sudden earthy dampness, a hint of lightening ahead—*the garden!* Vyenne had to act now, before the villains reached their goal.

She wrenched the knife free and with both hands stabbed, stabbed, stabbed until her abductor screamed, bucked, and she flew, weightless for an instant, into stone.

Pain! It sucked the breath from her body.

Her arm came to life screaming with it.

A bloodcurdling shriek—not hers; her lungs hadn't refilled. Something—a body—fell across her legs. She kicked at it, pounding with both heels until she was free and fetched up against a wall, gasping while pandemonium filled the darkness.

Clatter, crash, shouts, grunts, screams, Beauty's ferocious snarls, and over it all the relentless *thud-swish-scree* of blades.

Then, silence, broken only by men's harsh breathing and her wildly pounding heart.

Friends or foe? Vyenne curled onto her side, prepared to slither away, when a dark shape materialized beside her. "Touch me and I'll cut off your fingers!" She'd lost Humbert's knife, but the villain needn't know that.

"M'lady, 'twould suit me to keep my fingers, at least till we've dispatched all the villains."

Toth! Vyenne's muscles collapsed into jelly. With a little sob, she fell against him. "Thank you."

He gathered her and she let herself be held close like a child, enveloped by steam pouring off him, letting it warm her shivery nerves. A hiccup—a giggle?—slipped past her lips at the irony of it all. She'd been carried off and terrified by men of her own kind—Tumin men, no less!—and rescued by 'the enemy.' Another hiccup-sob escaped.

"Shh, m'lady mother-bear," Toth murmured, standing. "'Twas a fine, fair fight you put up. 'Twould do a Tolemak proud."

"Hah!" At least it was a word this time, not something bordering hysteria. "Do not pander me."

More armed men clattered around the corner, some bearing torches. Light seared Vyenne's eyes, flashed over Toth's face, gleamed on a blood smear from hairline to chin. He stared at her with a sober expression and those intense eyes.

"Hear me, then: *you* do me proud. There be little I remember of my mother, but 'tis sure I am she'd be no more fierce."

Vyenne blinked. She didn't need another son; blood was unreliable, traitorous even, as this day was proving. What she needed, what she'd never had, was a friend, someone she could trust. The Three Sisters in their often unfathomable wisdom had given her this fierce, tempestuous Tolemak who'd taken it upon himself to assume the role.

A wave of gratitude welled in her chest and stung her eyes. Tears would be embarrassing now, and entirely unnecessary, so she swallowed them. "Dare you imply I 'mother' you, Toth of Tylus? For if I do, 'tis for your own good and entirely against my will."

He guffawed, a full-throated laugh that shook her in his arms. Her lips curved despite her best intentions and insistent pain raging along her arm.

He must've detected her flinch because he sobered immediately. "What hurts?"

"My arm, 'tis wrenched."

He swore, two vehemently spoken, graphic words for which he made no apology.

Another Tolemak face appeared at Toth's shoulder.

Banir, Naed's man, gave Vyenne a sharp, assessing look. "M'lady, how many? We've four here. Be that all?"

"No." She shuddered, trying not to magnify, multiply shadows in the dark. "More. Two or three at least. And that Yormoc, he wasn't among them." She gripped Toth's tunic. "He's gone after Naed."

The men exchanged a look. "Aye," Toth said, "he knows."

Vyenne's stomach clenched. "Tell me he's not facing that monster alone."

Another look between the men. "Not alone," Toth said, a grim set to his mouth. "Raell followed him."

****

Naed barely recognized the man who emerged from the shadows. Fresh claw marks gouged his face, and his mouth was grotesquely swollen. Even his hair, normally slicked into a tight queue, had partially escaped. Despite that, stance and sneer marked him for who he was.

"Yormoc," Naed said while ice chilled his veins.

Two or three shadows moved beyond the torchlight. One rounded the tower just past the open door and behind Raell. *No, no, no!* He'd been too stupid, too damned slow—again! His brain was too fear-struck to do more than push out her name.

"Raell—!"

She'd been staring wide-eyed at the man who'd wrought so much terror in so short a time, but she must've sensed movement—or heard his gasp—for she spun and kicked the door.

Clang! The villain stumbled back, cursing. Yormoc laughed.

Breathing hard, Raell backed to Naed's side, shield up, sword at ready. "At least I'm armed this time," she muttered. Her blade trembled ever so slightly.

Naed drew his sword, slowly, so as not to trigger an attack while he engaged his brain. He'd meant to meet Yormoc, and he'd guessed the viper wouldn't be alone. But Demon-be-damned he hadn't meant to endanger anyone else, least of all Raell.

And certainly not after she'd ripped the earth out from under him.

"Stay behind me." He angled his body across hers while his heart triple-timed.

"Not on your life!" She flashed him an incredulous look. "Why the Demon do you think I came after you? 'Tis four against two."

"Mayhap five." *Or more.* The tower blocked his view on one side, a guard shelter on the other. Dear Sisters, this was bad.

Raell ought to have been terrified. He was, for her. But she elbowed her way alongside.

"'Twas four against us afore, me with no weapons and you with no armor. *They* died." Her mulish expression told him she was going nowhere. "Trust me.

'Twill be no different tonight."

Time stopped. Between one heartbeat and another, the truth struck Naed square in the chest. He did trust her, always had, even when he denied what his bones and his gut told him because he feared once more being betrayed, of giving his heart to someone who wanted only his allegiance, his friendship, his sword and not the fragile thing that was his love.

"I love you." He spoke without thought, a whispered confidence straight from his soul.

His blood fizzed with the truth of it, with the certainty she would—and effectively could—defend him to the death. *Sisters Three, let it not come down to that!*

"Aye, so *now* you answer." She flicked him a quick, tremulous smile and shining-eyed glance.

A wild, absurd joy shot through his body. "Will you follow my lead?"

A nod. A promise from honey-gold eyes and determined chin.

He inhaled, shifted his focus, steeled his nerves. They would survive. They had to. He wanted a lifetime with this woman.

A few feet away Yormoc laughed, twirled his sword like a street performer, and sauntered forward. "You never could manage a woman, could you? That Adanak bitch danced you a merry jig, all the while whoring behind your back with your beloved bastard Prince. This one looks to do the same." He cast a hooded glance down and up Raell and licked his oozing lip. "But time is short and I've a bag of gold that wants your blood to make it mine before I attend to your bitch."

Fury surged through Naed. And fear. He needed a stall to give himself a little space, to adjust his grip on his sword, to think of something while sweat dripped into his mouth and his pulse beat raggedly and Raell stood beside him with more confidence than he deserved shining in her eyes.

Yormoc caressed the money pouch hanging from his belt, and Naed's brain lit up. From first he'd met the man, everything for Yormoc came down to gold.

Naed straightened, rearranged his face into a sneer. "Is that all the gold they gave you? Rolnar of Roines offered 200 coins to whoever killed the Prince. Surely I'm worth at least half that. Or are those skinflints in Tumin taking a cut?"

"No one takes a cut from me," Yormoc snarled. "'Tis here but half my take for killing you and bringing them that cord you wear round your neck."

Thank you for confirming the Tumin connection. Dranoel's legacy stuck to his skin as he breathed. Did the villains know what it was or were they only guessing? He'd have to survive to find out. He hoped to the Sisters Raell understood what he was doing.

"But you have to share that reward, don't you? And with Tumin's dregs, no less." He dismissed Yormoc's cohorts with a jerk of his chin. "Unless you kill me yourself. Then the gold is all yours." Would that tip the scales toward risk?

Yormoc twirled his sword again. "Do you think I'd deny myself that pleasure?" He licked a bloody dribble and spat it at Naed's feet. "But I won't make it quick. You'll die hearing your bitch scream." He grinned.

Naed suppressed a shudder, as much at the ghastly state of Yormoc's mouth as at the threat, but he leaned on his sword, just as he'd seen the Prince do when he wanted to aggravate an opponent, prick his pride with a show of careless indifference.

"Yormoc, poor Yormoc, you never could accept the fact I surpass you. By birth and by blade, 'tis the truth. Why, I'm lord of this place, and you—you're not even a Free Sword anymore. You think you're an assassin, Dlaniger's heir apparent? Hah! You're a mere pawn in service to those puppet masters in Tumin, just as he was."

The Tumin men shifted, casting glances between Naed and his opponent. How loyal were they, how willing to die?

Yormoc's ghastly mouth clamped into a tight, red line.

Naed surreptitiously flexed knees, fingers, toes. "Tell your lackeys to stand down, and let's see who learned more about swordplay on the road to Vinvinnysee."

At his elbow Raell shivered delicately, but her face gave nothing away. *That's my girl.*

"Come at me man to man, Yormoc. Your men have us cornered; let them watch you prove you could've earned my honors if you'd had the same chances."

There was a torch a few steps beyond. He could use that, mayhap. He'd danced on the parapet before, between stone wall and wooden rails, and survived. The risk lay in provoking Yormoc. Fury made a man both strong and stupid.

Sisters Three, I need him stupid. Please.

Eyes on the target, Naed gave a one-shouldered shrug, making it look careless, disdainful. *Time to push.* "That bag of coins still looks thin. Belike they'd have paid Dlaniger more. Tell me, did you ever collect what he was owed for that bungled attempt on the Prince?"

Yormoc's face blotched scarlet. "Whoreson! His blood is on your hands!" He charged.

****

Raell followed Naed? Vyenne huddled in Toth's arms while he and Banir spoke, something about Beauty, but she couldn't attend.

If Raell went after Naed, that would be both good...and bad. The girl could fight; she'd proved that more than once. But that put both in harm's way. And she was not prepared to lose either one.

Vyenne rubbed her breastbone. All those years with Alwyl, guarding her emotions, restricting her intimacies—eliminating them entirely—must've stiffened her heart. These last days contending with this trio of young people and all their mad passions had stretched that organ beyond its cage.

Dear Sisters, she *hurt*! For all of them, the danger they faced, the loves they shared, the fearless way they threw themselves at obstacles. No small number of which her bloodline had created. She winced. This had to come right. She didn't see how yet, but she would do all in her power to make it so.

Banir and Toth must've decided something, for Naed's man turned away, but another Tolemak shoved into his space.

Vyenne started. At least she thought he was Tolemak. Two purpled eyes and a red, swollen nose clashed gruesomely with white skin and dark, wavy hair.

Toth's brows plunged. "What are you doing here?"

Bennin of Nye's puffy gaze took in Toth's face, the

blood smear. If it were possible, he paled. "What do you think?"

Ill-fitting armor thrown over a tunic spoke to Vyenne of haste and, mayhap, concern? She'd thought him odious upon first meeting, but what she'd learned since gave new shape to that impression. The way he and Toth stared at each other told her much, much more.

Toth growled. Vyenne doubted he was aware, but evidence of frustration vibrated beneath the arm she'd wrapped around his neck. He tore his gaze from Bennin and bent to her.

"Banir needs Beauty to track."

The wolfhound circled Toth's legs, whining. At her name, the dog looked up; devotion shone in those dark, liquid eyes.

"And she'll do it for you. I understand." Every last villain had to be hunted down, or they'd never be safe. And even then—

No! Deal with the immediate threat. What she'd heard, what she feared was as yet unconfirmed— however much she believed it to be true.

Get through tonight and then think about tomorrow.

"I'll be fine."

One brow ticked up, but he faced Bennin. "You want to help me? Take m'lady to the healer. And *don't* come back!"

Before Bennin could do more than drop his shield, Toth passed over Vyenne, whistled up the wolfhound, and strode off.

"I could walk," she said, clinging awkwardly to strange arms.

"And make him madder than he is?" With one last glance after Toth, he shifted her into a more secure hold. "Don't be daft."

A moment later Beauty bayed discovery of a new trail.

Vyenne sent a prayer for Toth's safety, for all their safety, and girded herself to make at least one thing right. "He doesn't mean it, you know."

Bennin snorted.

Rude, spoiled brat! She'd have to overlook that for Toth's sake.

"He's angry because he thinks you've thrown him over for his sister."

"What?" He stopped, stared, narrowed his eyes. "What the Demon are you to him?"

Clearly, one of your betters.

"More importantly, what is he to you?" While he gaped, she raised her chin and looked down her nose in the way that quailed servants, sons, and courtiers alike. "I have eyes, Bennin of Nye, and the two of you are fooling no one except, mayhap, yourselves if you persist in this pursuit of Lady Raell. Whatever your reasons, weigh them carefully before you take any other action."

He flushed redder than she'd thought possible for one so pale. "You are one bloody meddling bitch!" he sputtered.

"And you are an utterly repugnant and obnoxious excuse for a lord's son. Still, if you are Toth's choice, I can only wish you will do right by him and prove me wrong." Vyenne waved an imperious hand. "Now, either move forward to the healer or put me down so I may walk there myself."

Chapter Forty-Four

Raell recognized Naed's tactics, saw how his insults riled the man called Yormoc, but the flashpoint was a lightning bolt to the senses, a blur of sudden, savage energy that stopped her breath. She'd never seen men move so fast, heard such thunder of struck blows. It was mesmerizing and terrifying and—

Thud. Clatter.

"Bloody hell!" She'd backed into a barrel of torch oil and knocked the lid off. Bad enough, but she'd roused the attention of the nearest villain. She'd made him wary with the kicked tower door, so instead of immediately engaging, he alerted his compatriot. That man spat a curse but never shifted his gaze from the combatants. The first man returned a rude gesture, glanced at the fight, then focused a scowl on Raell.

Her throat clogged. She desperately wanted to watch too, but these villains weren't likely to stand by for long, and certainly not if—*when! Absolutely!*— Naed gained the upper hand. Her task, which she'd all but demanded, was to keep them off his back. Oil fumes teased her nostrils while she flexed fingers gone numb around the sword hilt. She could handle one man, mayhap two, but she had no idea where the third had gone or if he still lurked on the far side of the tower.

Her foot nudged something—the barrel lid—and her brain sparked. *Father's first lesson.*

Electrified, Raell passed her sword into her shield hand and dove for the lid. She came up with it by the rim, swung the rough-hewn disk across her body, across her shield and, before the nearest villain could shout a warning, flung it.

A shield would've flown higher and truer, would've smacked the chest of the man she aimed for, but the warped wood took a sudden dive—straight into the far villain's legs. He flew up with flailing arms and landed square on his back.

One down. While the near man gaped at his stunned comrade, Raell charged. He turned, not soon enough. She crashed shield to shield with enough force to send him stumbling backward...into his downed partner. More flailing, this time against the rampart railing, which cracked ominously.

"No!" He dropped his sword, scrabbled for a hold.

He'd grab the weapon again if she gave him a chance.

No time to be squeamish. "Hang on then." She kicked the splintered rail.

With a shriek that brought bile up her throat, he tumbled over the side.

Don't be sick! Don't be sick!

The other man had recovered his feet, if not his weapons. Before she could turn, he flung arms around her.

"Got you, bitch!"

****

The shriek dragged talons down Naed's spine. He and Yormoc froze, turned heads as if by mutual compulsion. Naed absorbed the broken railing, took in Raell grabbed from behind, and his innards seized. A

419

blur of motion, a heartbeat's warning before Yormoc's heel drove into his thigh. "Hah!"

Crunch-snap!

Naed screamed, smacked the stone with shoulder, hip, hand. If the fall hurt, he couldn't tell; his leg was on fire, a volcanic mass of blistering pain that sucked up all his focus, hazed the world, dragged him so far into himself only one thought—*Raell!*—kept him from surrendering to its pull. Clawing at the edges of consciousness, he hauled his shield over his body and curled beneath it.

Sisters...help...me.

****

Raell's assailant bear-hugged across her shield and sword arm, thinking she'd be immobilized.

Fool. She dropped her sword, raised her knee, and pulled a knife from her newly made boot sheath. A lightning slash at his thigh, another at his hand and she was free.

He may have lost fingers; she neither knew nor cared. She slid free of her shield straps. A risk, but it left him howling and clinging to a dead weight while she shoved him down and slashed his neck. Blood sprayed.

Two down.

The third man rushed around the tower.

Choking back vomit, she snatched the fallen villain's shield and flung it. It caught her attacker in the chest, knocking him on his heels long enough she could recover her own shield.

Then jerk with such terror she almost dropped it.

Naed!

All her instincts told her the scream that body-slammed her was his. She backed a step, half-turned, and lost all power over her knees. Her ears roared with blood that had nowhere to go because her heart stopped.

Naed! Down? He lay curled under his shield while Yormoc danced around him like a gloating demon.

"No!" Where she'd found breath, she had no idea. Mayhap it was the sting of a blade slicing her upper arm that jolted her to sensibility.

And action.

Strike! Block! Strike! Block! Everything she'd trained to do without thinking propelled her toward her attacker with a roar. "Not my bloody damned arm again, you half-assed bastard! If you've torn Gam's stitches, I'll slice you to ribbons!"

And she would have...if the tower door hadn't crashed open and knocked him flat. Raell stared at the groaning villain sprawled at her feet then at the man filling the doorway.

His round face ran with sweat, and the pitchfork in his white-knuckled grip shook, but Humbert squeaked out, "M'lady, I-I came to help."

Her adrenaline-fueled brain told her he was both familiar and safe. "Aye, so you did."

Pulse still pounding at her throat, she backed a step and kicked the fallen man's sword away, then kicked him in the jaw because she couldn't stop herself, so much energy crackled in her veins.

Raell sucked in air and danced on her toes. "Kill him if he moves." Then she turned to save the man she loved.

****

Naed clung desperately to consciousness while Yormoc danced around him, laughing, spraying bloody drool.

"You're weak! You hear me? Weak! You can't even stand and you'd claim to best me?" Yormoc halted, panted, hands on knees. "Killing you would be a mercy. Pity I'm not feeling merciful." He chortled, chin-pointed toward the tower. "Your Tolemak whore's putting up quite the fight. Mayhap she'd like to watch me slice pieces from you. Those barbaric friends of yours always enjoy a good dismemberment."

This will not end...so soon. Naed dredged himself up from the pit.

Change the dance. The words echoed in his brain.

The Prince himself had bested him, and he'd not died. He'd fought Krenin bare-handed and survived. He'd taken on a Lancer on foot, armed only with a sword, and lived to tell about it. He'd be damned if he'd succumb to a puffed-up former Free Sword on his own bloody parapet when all he had to do was *change*...something.

He'd lost his sword...somewhere...and his vision doubled the nearby torch, but he'd always been able to sense his opponent's location: inches away, where the original stone walkway had been extended with wooden planking. He gripped his knife. There'd be one chance, and he had to take it now...if he could mute the pain and aim true. With a feral snarl, he flung his arm out and the knife down with all the force he could muster.

He didn't wait for the sickening crunch or high-pitched howl to tell him he'd driven the blade through Yormoc's boot. Instead, he heaved his body over and slammed his shield onto the knife hilt, pinning the man's foot to the wooden planks.

A screaming, cursing Yormoc slashed at him,

dropped his shield, yanked at the knife.

Naed's head swam, his eyes refused to focus, but he gritted his teeth and coiled up his good leg. "See how you like being lame!"

He drove his foot into Yormoc's trapped kneecap and savored the *crunch-snap-snap* of splintering bone. The man collapsed like a felled bull, with an inhuman bellow to match.

"They put horses down for less than that." Rolling to his side, he crawled out of Yormoc's reach. "Pity I'm not feeling merciful."

He found his sword and used it to lever his body into a sitting position. His entire left leg throbbed like a limb three sizes larger, but it was still properly aligned.

Not so for Yormoc. His leg twisted at a grotesque angle, and his kneecap looked utterly smashed.

Naed's lips pulled back from his teeth. A good D'nalian would feel remorse, and mayhap he would later, but at the moment his pulse pounded with pure savage satisfaction.

The sight of Raell—his woman, his wife, his *partner*—alive and safe and running toward him filled his heart near to bursting.

Chapter Forty-Five

Vyenne sat beside Allyn's cot, her good hand clamping his wrist whenever his curses rose in volume. Her arrival relieved Morys, who happily traded Allyn-minding for joining the guards at Gam's door. The old healer promptly manipulated Vyenne's arm, pronounced it sprained but unbroken, tucked it into a sling, and offered a sip of evenroot to dull the pain.

A secure support provided some relief, but Allyn's profanity, Bennin's pacing, and that poor kitchen maid's moans—*Gert, was it?*—combined to tempt Vyenne to a second sip. Nonetheless, she declined. Until the danger was over, she needed her wits about her.

"Tis naught to fear, Mother," Allyn grumbled. Again. "I've had worse. Those bastards must die for harming you."

As shocked as she was to see Allyn in Gam's care, she quickly ascertained his injuries were nonlethal. That quieted some of the skittering within. The rest was manageable because she believed—no, *trusted*—in Raell's ability to warn and defend Naed.

Now *this* hard-headed son needed to listen to and heed what she'd learned.

"Toth, Banir and Beauty are quite properly avenging me as we speak. I suspect Raell and Naed will do the same. You are to stay here and let Gam tend you."

He made another attempt to rise. "Naed needs me."

She dug what remained of her fingernails into his big bones. "He needs you safe, thickbrain."

Allyn blinked, and his jaw went slack.

"Aye, you heard me. Those arrows were meant for both of you. 'Tis a Tumin plot to deny you and Naed what comes to you by blood and birthright. That monster Yormoc is not merely acting to avenge Dlaniger, he is also fulfilling Dlaniger's contract with Tumin."

"Contract...with Tumin?" Although he gaped, rapid eye movements showed wheels turning in that not-so-thick brain. "With...Father?"

Outrage tightened the muscles beneath her hand. *Sisters, help me make him understand.*

"I cannot rule out Alwyl's participation," she said in a neutral tone. "Dlaniger's role in targeting the Prince goes back at least a year, and both he and Alwyl had motive to harm Naed when Naed inherited."

So far so good; this rigid mountain of grown man, her firstborn, listened without comment. No doubt he was thinking her animosity toward Alwyl colored her perceptions, and therefore he might discount or minimize what she told him. She couldn't help that; Allyn's mind was his own to change.

Vyenne's body was strung so tight, her shoulder throbbed. *Get through tonight and then think about tomorrow.*

This was the hard part, the betrayal most personal, the one she was heart-achingly, miserably certain of. The truth that poisoned all her memories and stood to contaminate all future relationships. Allyn could repudiate her for telling it, but his life would be in danger if she did not. Better to lose the regard of a living son than to mourn at his grave. She'd buried Elwyn; she could not endure that kind of grief again.

"As to the plot against you—" The words blistered her tongue. "—I suspect it may have been recently added by the one most likely to benefit. The one closest in age to Dlaniger."

Allyn went white, then red, then white again before he whispered, "Fennyn?"

Her third-born's name spoken aloud—*made public!*—hit Vyenne like a body blow. She swayed, clamped her lips together. *Why does it have to be this way?* She'd borne six children and one—*damn him!*—was a murderous traitor to his bloodline. She sucked in a ragged breath and plowed ahead.

"Do you think I enjoy accusing my son of plotting against his brothers? Fennyn is my flesh and blood too! But I was 'not to be harmed' by Yormoc because the villains' master did not wish his 'mother' harmed. With you and Naed targeted, there is but one other living son I am mother to. How can I not conclude it is he?"

Uncoiling her fingers from Allyn's wrist, she pressed them to her breastbone. No amount of rubbing would mend the rip in her heart, but she had no other way to soothe the scalding pain. Her murdering, traitorous *son* didn't want to harm her, *his* mother. *Well, Demon be damned to that!* He'd already flayed her flesh with each attack on Allyn and Naed.

She'd retreated within her grief, and facing Allyn would only add to the sense of overwhelming loss, so she spoke to his feet. "Do what you will with what I've said." Then rose.

The hand beneath her elbow was unexpected. And surprisingly gentle.

"M'lady," was all Bennin said.

A commotion erupted in the hall. Toth burst into Gam's chamber. He was panting, sweat-stained and blood-streaked, but his eyes shone.

"Safe. Raell and Naed, safe."

She'd have sat down hard if Bennin and Toth together hadn't eased her landing. Blinking away useless tears, she squeezed Toth's bloodstained fingers with matching ones. Tumin blood. Would what they'd shed be enough? For now, it would have to do. "Thank you."

He nodded, but his attention had shifted to Bennin, and the two stared at each other. A world of hurt and yearning shone in that gaze. Vyenne heaved a sigh past the lump in her throat.

"Talk," she said. "Stop being asses and talk to each other." It was the least she could do and all her broken heart could manage.

****

"Take me into the Great Hall," Naed insisted. "The lords need to see me, see both of us."

Raell wiped her eyes. He'd said that twice since their immediate, bone-crushing embrace, as if she hadn't heard the first time. She avoided touching his leg, remembering that horrible scream when he'd fallen. At least it looked intact, not fractured, bent or bleeding. Not like the mangled mess attached to the villain nearby.

She purposely hadn't given Yormoc a second look, not since guardsmen took charge of the others and Humbert, pitchfork at ready, positioned himself between her and that vicious, venomous snake. Not looking kept her blades sheathed, kept a lid on that still sizzling urge to mow down all threats. His fate was Naed's to decide.

"What of that…Yormoc?" She spat the name.

"Leave him to the guardsmen. Live or die, he's finished. But have that fellow with the pitchfork fetch the Tumin gold he was flaunting."

"Aye, but first…" She concentrated on wadding up remnants of her skirt to fasten over every source of blood she could locate on Naed's person. That Demon-be-damned monster had sliced at least a dozen gashes, most not deep. *Thank the Sisters!*

"Daft man," she choked, tying off another wound, "you need to see Gam."

"Aye, soon, but humor me first, my love." He brushed tangled hair from her forehead and kissed her again.

Gah! She had to taste like salt and blood. *He* did. Or was that all her?

Pulling back, Raell wished she hadn't embarrassed herself with tears. *Warriors don't cry.* Yet she couldn't stop the leaking. Relief had flooded her with such intensity her throat was thick with it. Naed's reverent expression as his gaze took her in didn't help. Her face had to be blotchy, tear-stained and blood-spattered, but his eyes said he'd never seen anything so beautiful.

More embarrassment torched her face. They sat on cold stone and damp wood, in bloodied and torn clothing, surrounded by dead and wounded after surviving a fight for their lives, and all the addle-brained man could think about, besides overlooking her obviously wretched physical state—*was going down to the bloody Great Hall!*

She shot him a fiery glare. "You would show yourself to the lords to prove all is well. I understand." She did, truly. Confidence had to be restored after so vicious an attack, but— "'Tis a wise move, I admit, but not at all to my liking."

He chuckled, winced, laid a hand on that poor injured thigh that had to be throbbing.

She bit her lip, wishing she could take his pain upon herself, then wondered what the bloody hell was so funny. "Can you stand?" she growled. "'Twill do you no good to appear less than upright."

"I can stand—" He sucked in a deep breath. "—but only if you help me."

He cupped her chin, gently urging her to meet those green eyes that had captivated her from first glance. They'd turned deep as a shadowed pond and equally solemn.

"Sisters, be thanked, I am a man most blessed. My beloved is a warrior, a woman most passionate, an ally most fierce. I can ask for no one better as wife than you, Raell. Please forgive me for doubting your promise."

She choked back another threatened flood. "Do you have to near die to make up your ass-stubborn mind?"

He laughed, but his eyes shone. "Mayhap—if it means you'll stay. I'll be damned if I give you over to anyone, least of all that raccoon-eyed Tolemak. Your father can suffer for his own promises. I intend to honor mine."

Lord Tylus choose that moment to appear. Raell suspected him of pacing nearby, awaiting just such an opportunity. Smiling broadly, he knelt and threw arms around them.

"Well done! Well done indeed!" He bussed Raell's cheek, beamed at her, then thumped Naed on the shoulder. "You left me with a virgin sword, sir, but mayhap I can do you one good turn this night." Laying hands on his thighs, he assumed a chagrinned expression. "Aye, for all the grief my arrival's caused."

"You *heard*." Raell glowered at her father. *What the Demon are you up to?*

"So I did, but first, sir, your mother be safe. Toth, too," he added, before she could ask. He beamed again, as if they were prize pupils and he couldn't contain his pride. "'Twas a fine rout. All dead be villains and so too most of the injured."

Naed nodded. He looked dazed, as though relief sapped more of his strength than the injuries. Her heart pinged, but before she could express concern, he quirked a blood-streaked brow and said, "About that good turn, sir…"

Tylus grimaced. "You may not think it so at first, but hear me out. Not far behind me and mine be a force from Tumin."

All color drained from Naed's face. "Alwyl."

Raell's stomach clenched. They'd just fended off one attack; how could they deal so soon with another? Naed was injured and she was terrified.

"And you said naught? Papa, how could you?"

The hawk-beaked warrior shrugged off her panic. "*Said* naught; did much." He jumped up like a man half his age, strode to the wall, pulled out a lit torch and waved it three times back and forth. After a moment of peering into the distance, he nodded and returned, grinning.

"Do you think I came alone, girl?" He jerked a nod toward the far woods. "Fires be lighting now, and men will be showing around them, enough men to cow a small force from Tumin. Mark me."

Raell closed her mouth. When he trailed a calloused palm over her cheek, she caught it and kissed it.

"Thank you, Papa."

His bewhiskered cheeks reddened. "Don't fuss, girl."

Hitching up his sword belt, Tylus knelt beside Naed and leaned in. "Between you, me, and the Prince what sent them, 'tis but a force of Adanak walking wounded returning home." He winked. "None but we here need know that, aye?"

Despite his ashen skin, Naed's grin spread like sunshine over his face. "You, sir, are as wily as a long-lived fox, and I thank you."

"'Tis the least I could do for my daughter's husband." He cast them a meaningful look. "The marriage bond, 'twill keep between you, aye?"

Raell gripped Naed's hand and looked him in the eye. "Mark me, no one is taking this ring off my finger."

A distant trumpet blared. Druemarwin's bell rang.

"Stand me up, wife," Naed said. "We have company to greet."

He'd given her one more besotted look, and though Raell rolled her eyes, her heart warmed and expanded nigh to bursting with the pleasure of it.

Chapter Forty-Six

Naed refused a change of clothing, even a wash of his face. These southern D'nalian lords had avoided war so thoroughly and for so long, he meant to shock them with its bloody reality. The Kingdom was coming regardless of their wishes, and it would be a rough birth. Nowhere was safe, as events this night ought to have made clear to the most stubbornly reclusive. They must take sides or be trampled.

His task, the mission the Prince had set upon his shoulders, was to drive home that point...in direct confrontation with the most powerful man in D'nalee.

The man he used to call *Father.*

Who now, very likely, wanted him dead.

Naed's heart thumped double hard.

If only it weren't past midnight and his muscles jangling from expended adrenaline. If only Yormoc hadn't cut him in so many places every twitch made him want to scream. If only his emotions weren't as knotted as his innards.

He drew a shaky breath. He was alive; he was whole; he was not alone. He'd pushed his body to the limits before, and he could do it again for the sake of his friends, his folk, and his true father.

"'Tis time you took your rightful place," the Prince had told him on that cold, crisp morning weeks ago.

He'd carried Dranoel's legacy for the better part of

a year; this was the time to embrace it.

All of it.

At Raell's urging—"You cannot afford to appear weak. Save your strength until you need it."—he entered the Great Hall from the back, close to the table and three chairs he'd ordered set apart to force Alwyl to come to him, to establish in all minds who was master of this domain.

Because she scowled over his injuries, some still seeping blood, he agreed to be carried, mostly upright, by Banir and Toth through the shadows until the lords sighted him. Then he walked, step by agonizing step, keeping his face blank while his insides shuddered. When he finally sat, undertunic plastered to his skin, it was with increased respect for the Prince and all the times the man had shown himself to allies and enemies alike after a grievous wound.

Those prospective allies stood wide-eyed and gaping as Raell, fierce in armor, weapons, and bloody cloth wrapped around her arm, stepped to Naed's right. Banir took his left. Toth, half his face a bright red smear, elicited gasps as he and the leashed wolfhound joined Grodar, Morys, and Lord Tylus in standing around the long table. Even that raccoon-eyed Tolemak sidled toward Toth with an I-dare-you-to-toss-me-out expression.

Oh, I dare. But he'd see to that later. For now his mother, with bruised face and arm in a sling, walked slowly with a heavily bandaged Allyn to take the only other chairs, positioned to Raell's right.

Naed bit down a blast of rage. Killing Yormoc would be justified for all the havoc he'd wreaked, but Naed had no taste for it. He'd put all his anger and fear and vengeance into that one crippling, bone-crunching kick. What simmered now was directed at the man striding into the Great Hall with fury and suspicion contorting his features.

"Who are those men in the forest? Why am I allowed only two of my personal guard? What in the Name of the Sisters is going on here?" Alwyl of Tumin thundered.

The lords scattered like sheep before him.

Naed stifled a sigh. His task was nigh impossible, but he'd hoped for a more auspicious beginning.

At least the lords knew better than to be trampled.

"Welcome to Druemarwin. Please, take some refreshment." Summoning a bland smile, he indicated tables along the wall. "Our offerings are somewhat depleted as the staff have been occupied elsewhere for much of this night, but I trust you can find something."

Alwyl halted before the table separating them. Despite mud-splattered travelling garb, he commanded the room's attention. If two years had altered the Lord of Tumin, it showed only in the gray liberally salting his whiskers. For a man scrupulous about his appearance, that he'd not shaved or washed before making an entrance spoke of supreme confidence or considerable urgency. Either was dangerous. Both, together, might be explosive.

How far will you go to maintain control of D'nalee? Yormoc's pouch and the bloody patch lay on the table between them. *How far* have *you gone?*

Eyes narrowed, Alwyl took in surroundings he must've merely glanced at before. His stormy gaze stayed on Raell nearly as long as it surveyed Naed, before it dismissed the Tolemaks. If he noted Vyenne and Allyn, he gave no sign. A curl of the lip accompanied his sweep of the lords, who'd reformed into a loose knot, before he faced Naed.

"You called an assembly!"

"Of the southern lords," Wendelmyr piped from the front of the group.

Whether he thought the announcement mollifying or defiant, Naed couldn't tell. Either way, the Lord of Kassi stood his ground when Alwyl fixed him with a baleful glare.

Naed intended to keep Alwyl's focus, hoping to protect the lords from blame should his gambit fail, but he had to commend Wendelmyr for nerve. The man would need it going forward.

"So I did."

After a year of war, months under Tolemak command when death was but a mistake away, that fierce frown Alwyl leveled in his direction was not nearly as intimidating as Naed remembered.

"Allow me to introduce my bride, the Lady Raell, daughter of Lord Tylus."

Tylus made a polite nod in Alwyl's direction, but Raell bent not a bit. Chin high, spine straight, she met Alwyl's glare with her own blistering one.

Naed's heart swelled, and even more when Alwyl blinked.

"You wed a Tolemak," he sneered. "I confess to being *not* surprised." He waved a hand toward the lords. "Now, as to this…assembly—"

"Do you not offer them congratulations, best wishes?"

Oh, Mother. He needed all these witnesses. If only he could muzzle them.

Lady Vyenne sat as composed as ever despite her obvious injuries, but her gracious smile didn't reach the eyes she'd fixed on her husband.

Alwyl clearly did not want to engage her, but she'd forced his hand. Courtesy was a basic D'nalian tenet.

"Of course." He offered a placating gesture, but his jaw looked sewn together. "I wish you much joy of each other."

If lies were truth, I might believe you. Naed flattened fingers he'd dug into the chair arm.

Several lords scowled as if they shared his thoughts. Two in the back leaned heads together and whispered.

"Do you not greet your wife, your son?" Allyn spoke in a strong but raspy voice.

More lords shifted as Alwyl shot his heir a furious glare before spinning to Naed.

"Enough! Do not pretend to be what you are not. This is not a social call. We have business to conduct, and it must be done in private."

Naed leaned back in his chair, carefully. His entire leg throbbed as if under a smith's hammer, but he dared not flinch, wince or grimace. Alwyl would press every advantage he perceived. This display of temper, though....

Either Alwyl was spooked by a few questions and a circle of frowns and whispers, or he was so confident in his power and position, he could ignore the good will of those he considered beneath him.

You have made a bad cast; now it is my turn.

"No. Everything we have to say to each other shall be said right here, right now." Naed steepled his fingers and bared his teeth. "Let's begin with what you think I pretend to be."

Alwyl's lips clamped together.

They'd avoided calling each other by name, title, or relationship, a fact the lords now seemed to notice. More murmurs permeated the room.

The Lord of Tumin's hands curled into fists, held, then opened. "I presume this assembly is about that pretender you serve. You want to turn the south against us, against the north, and put them in league with a Tolemak."

Alwyl had a grip on himself, and Naed had to tread carefully.

"True. False. And true. I am the Prince of Val-Feyridge's chosen emissary. 'Tis not my—or his—intention to turn anyone against anyone else. As to putting D'nalians in league with Tolemaks, that is indeed my aim, as I have made plain to Lord Wendelmyr and the others."

Wendelmyr squared up before Alwyl though doing so brought the man only to Alwyl's chin.

"Have you heard naught?" he said in clear voice. "The Prince has found the lost Crown. 'Tis real, this dream of what once was and can be again. The *Kingdom*, sir, a unified land."

More murmurs then a rising cascade of exclamation shut down at Alwyl's glare. Bunching his shoulders, he bore down on Wendelmyr.

"Indeed? And to bring this fanciful *dream* about, are you willing to pledge allegiance to a Tolemak?"

To Wendelmyr's credit, he gave but an inch. "Mayhap, if he will provide me with more security than I currently receive from a distant council of lords."

"Aye, that's the truth!"

"Well said!"

"Hear, hear!"

At the chorus Wendelmyr stiffened his spine.

"If Adanak and Tolemak make peace, 'twill be an end to such horrors as the Northern Wars. Are you not in favor of such a peace?"

Silence. Would Alwyl dare say no?

Wendelmyr rose another notch in Naed's estimation.

The Lord of Tumin's gaze scoured the room, before his mouth quirked up. "Tell me, any of you. Have you even *seen* this Crown?"

Naed's gut clenched. That was a clever cast of the beads, but not unanticipated.

"I have."

All turned to him.

"Prince Arn recovered it from a tower in Vinvinnysee, and the Crownkeeper acknowledged him as rightful heir. The Crown traveled separately out of Adanak. It was here at Druemarwin late last year. I had care of it, briefly, before it went on to Tolemak."

There was a collective gasp.

"What does it look like?"

"How big is it?"

"Is it true the princely stones are gone?"

"Be quiet, you fools!" Alwyl bellowed. "Would you take the word of a Tolemak lover, a cuckoo in my family nest, a bastard I raised as my own only to discover he has turned against all things D'nalian and sold our security, our independence, even our very existence to our mortal enemies?" He stalked left, then right, a figure of full-blown, righteous indignation. "Think! D'nalee has prospered all these years under the council of lords and our tradition of firm neutrality. Would you throw all that away on the word of this-this *traitor* who surrounds himself with not our own folk but these white-skinned barbarians, these blood-thirsty savages?"

Gasps. Panicked glances at the Tolemaks, who fit the image so deliberately invoked.

The blood show had been a gamble, and Alwyl was shrewd to try turning it to his advantage. What he didn't know, what Naed gambled on now, besides the vaunted Tolemak discipline, was a brave, mayhap foolish hope the lords would remember for whose protection that blood had been spilled.

For a long moment, nobody seemed to breathe.

When the 'white-skinned barbarians' remained stone-still, the lords turned to each other. Murmurs arose, gathering in intensity and outrage.

Directed at whom? While Naed exhaled, the lords looked over their shoulders, circulated, conferred furiously.

A smirk crossed Alwyl's face as he nodded to his two attendants. The Lord of Tumin had made a powerful argument, based on the truth as he saw it, and acted as if he'd scored.

Sweat beaded Naed's hairline and trailed leisurely beside his ear. Too many torches burning for too long sucked all freshness from the Great Hall despite thrown-open doors. Too much fear and uncertainty pouring off too many bodies added to the stew. Late-night air curling around his feet brought only a damp chill that kept his undertunic glued to his skin. Dranoel's legacy rose and fell with each breath. No storm brewed in the stillness outside, but the atmosphere within required only a spark to combust.

What he carried would ignite a firestorm.

All faces turned to Naed. This was what the Prince had asked of him: to face a charge of treason and find a way to answer it. For weeks he'd pondered. All those generations ago the Kingdom had broken because Prince Adan stole the Crown from the rightful heir, Prince Tolem. And the middle son, Prince D'nal, refused to take sides in the ensuing war. However much his descendants praised his commitment to neutrality, D'nal had failed to right a clear wrong. Was it treason to want to right that wrong now? Especially for a people who claimed to be morally upright and honorable?

On my honor, it is not. Naed leaned forward.

But it was Allyn who spoke first.

"Mayhap they take his word already, sir, since my brother has been frank with them—and me—about all this and more." He rose with visible effort. "Mayhap it is he they trust."

And not you.

As clearly as if they'd been spoken, the words rippled through the assembly. Men who'd only watched now began to nod.

Lord Alwyl flinched as if whiplashed, swung about then quickly rearranged his face into an expression of concern.

"What in the name of all that's holy has this treasonous bastard done to you, son?" He advanced a step before Allyn froze him with a stare.

"More to the point, Father, what has Tumin done?" He braced himself on the table, and his mother covered his hand with hers. He seemed to draw strength from that.

"Tumin, Father. Against all that is honorable and right, someone from Tumin engaged Dlaniger—my cousin and your nephew—as an assassin to stalk the Prince of Val-Feyridge. 'Twas Dlaniger, these lords know, who killed his own father here, in the courtyard, in front of all the folk and the Tolemak army."

Naed stared at his half-brother. He'd expected Allyn to provide only silent support, not stand up to Alwyl on his behalf.

But Allyn paused only for breath. "That alone were enough to damn Tumin, but 'tis more. Against all that is proper and D'nalian, someone from Tumin engaged Dlaniger's associates to stalk my brother and mother and me. You think my brother Lord Naed has harmed me? Think again, because the men who attacked us this night were Tumin men, men that *someone* sent to accompany me here while ordering my own guardsmen elsewhere."

Face ghostly pale, he gestured toward the table. "There lies proof and payment." Then he collapsed into his chair.

Raell pulled a dagger from her sleeve, startling two nearest lords and raising Alwyl's brows. She sliced open Yormoc's pouch and, with the dagger's point, shoved three coins and the bloody patch across the table.

"Tumin insignia, Tumin gold." Her expression dared him to deny it. "Blood money."

Naed touched her arm, prompting her to sheathe the weapon. No need for blades yet.

More murmuring, louder, accompanied by dark glances.

"Murder!"

"Attempted murder."

"No, treason!"

"How can you claim treason when your own hands are not clean?"

The last made Alwyl bunch his shoulders, but he gave the items only a cursory glance.

"Your claims are absurd: a dead man who cannot speak for himself; a bag of coins, common currency; and a patch torn from a tunic anyone could obtain." Head high, he swept the assembly with a scathing glare. "You would accept this as proof?"

"Mayhap not," Wendelmyr said, hitching up his sword belt, "had events this night not produced two of the assassin's henchmen. With your permission, Lord Naed, might we call them forth?"

Inclining his head, Naed signaled the captain of the guard. The sheep were becoming men. It was a heady moment, but nowhere near time to relax his vigilance, no matter how his body clamored for sleep or the torches wavered at the edge of his vision.

Yormoc was brought to the fore in a wheelbarrow, his ruined knee and distorted face triggering mass recoil and horrified gasps. Prodded alongside him was a Tumin guardsman, bruised, bloody, and in chains.

Clearly enjoying his role, Wendelmyr sauntered over and pointed to Yormoc. "That one belongs to the assassin Dlaniger." He rotated a half turn. "And that one belongs to you, my lord."

A roar of outrage echoed around the Great Hall.

When it faded, a stone-faced Alwyl deigned to glance at the prisoners. "Dlaniger was not engaged to kill his father; that death is entirely on him." He drew himself up and cast a defiant glare around the Great Hall. "The council of lords thought it best to stop the pretender Prince of Val-Feyridge by any means possible. You should be grateful for our attempts to keep you safe."

Scoffing noises broke out. "What—do you think us *children*?"

Arms raised, the Lord of Kassi reclaimed the floor. "We here did not and do not condone the engaging of an assassin. If not outright treasonous, 'tis against all things D'nalian, no matter how you or the council might justify such an action."

"Hear, hear!"

"Aye, that's the truth!"

"Why should we follow you when 'tis clear you've no respect for us, for our wishes?"

"How dare you make such decisions without consulting the whole of D'nalee, without consulting us!"

Ignoring the outbursts, the Lord of Tumin dismissed the prisoners a look of disgust. "As to these two, I know naught. The council of lords paid no one other than Dlaniger. Where that Tumin gold came from or who employed these two, I have no knowledge."

Something inside Naed loosened its grip. The man he'd long thought of as *Father* traded in half-truths, innuendo, and misdirection but never outright lies. This declaration smacked of truth, or as close to it as Naed had known him to go. Alwyl, at least, hadn't plotted to kill him.

"Of course, you have no knowledge." With a resounding slap of the tabletop, Lady Vyenne stood. "Having *knowledge* would require you to *do something.*

Well, my lord, here is your chance." She thrust an accusing finger at the Tumin man. "Surely, *he* knows who employed him. I heard him say his master did not want 'his mother' harmed. *Ask him* if you would know whom he meant."

Head high, spine straight, she skewered her husband with an expression of utter disdain. "You are worried about a cuckoo in your nest, my lord, when 'tis clear you should instead be looking for a cold-blooded murderer."

Alwyl staggered as if she'd struck him a body blow.

Someone dropped a goblet.

Oh, Mother. Naed gaped at the avenging fury who'd borne him. She'd struck masterfully, accusing without naming, sticking in the blade of a truth Alwyl would immediately comprehend.

Naked fear flashed in the Lord of Tumin's eyes before he lunged for the shackled man.

Yormoc was faster. The guardsmen hadn't tied him; he couldn't flee. Producing a thin dagger, he flung it into the shackled man's throat. Blood sprayed Alwyl, the prisoner collapsed, and Yormoc laughed like a man possessed.

"You'll never know who now, will you? Not for sure, you privileged, pompous pricks!" He spat toward Naed while guardsmen grabbed his arms. "They paid me to get that thing you wear about your neck. What the Demon's so special about it?"

"Get him out of here!" Naed half-stood before pain reminded him he couldn't.

"'Tis all about that thing!" Yormoc shouted as guardsmen hauled him away. "Make the cowardly bastard show it!'"

A panting Alwyl wiped blood from ashen cheeks. He looked stunned, a man adrift from his moorings.

Wide-eyed lords glanced from him to Naed, pointedly ignoring the body and what pooled beneath it. What they couldn't ignore was the hot, salt-sweet tang. Some coughed, others wrinkled noses.

"This thing he speaks of." Wendelmyr carefully stepped past the dead man. "'Tis Lord Dranoel's will, aye?"

Naed's heart hammered against Dranoel's legacy. This wasn't how he'd hoped to introduce it, but Yormoc—*Damn his eyes!*—was right.

"Much as I hate to agree with a bloody-handed villain, that 'thing' is indeed what all this is about. That and more."

He withdrew the cylinder, pulled the plug, and dumped the contents onto the table. "If you would, my lord."

Pursing his lips, Wendelmyr approached. He separated the items with the care of a man upon whose shoulders a momentous task has been placed. "Here be a letter and something wrapped in cloth, a polished gemstone. The letter, 'tis addressed to Lord Naed from Lord Dranoel. I recognize his hand." He held it up, squinting, until candles were fetched from the far tables. "I read here that Lord Dranoel acknowledges Lord Naed as his son and…names him as his heir in place of Dlaniger—" He cleared his throat as though the words tasted foul. "—the assassin."

"Aye, see?" Allyn thumped the table, some of his color having returned. "'Tis all as my brother told us."

"And the stone?" someone said. "What means

that?"

Several lords leaned in. One said, "'Tis no diamond, ruby, emerald or aught else precious, aye?"

The aforementioned stone glinted a warm golden brown in the candlelight. It was faceted, rectangular cut, and traced with darker brown streaks—just as Naed remembered from the one other time he'd seen it. On that day he'd buried Dranoel and had his life ripped inside out.

Lying there now, the stone called to mind the soil he'd heaped over his father's grave.

The soil into which D'nalee sank its roots.

Home.

His brain lit up, his skin tingled, all exhaustion fled. The Prince had indeed sent him back for a purpose. He'd thought it merely to rally the lords, to advance the Kingdom, but the man intended so much more. Naed was to acknowledge his blood rights and claim his destiny.

He was to set down roots and grow a new D'nalee.

Raell leaned close. "You offered that to the Prince, months ago," she whispered, honey-gold eyes full of awe. "He didn't take it?"

Naed grasped her hand, kissed it. "He saw another, better purpose for it, my love." Warmth flooded him at the prospect of a future with this woman in this place where he well and truly belonged. "Can you be at home with me here, make a life away from all you know?"

"Daft man." Her smile beamed like the sun on that fruitful D'nalee soil. "From the moment I saw you, 'twas clear to me I would."

Alwyl edged closer to the table. "That isn't…" He paled further.

"The D'nal Stone." With reverent fingers the Lord of Kassi unfurled the wrapping cloth and read, "*Let he who finds this care for it as I have. 'Tis the D'nal Stone, treasure of D'nalee.*"

"Sisters Three!" Someone gasped.

"Lord Dranoel was Keeper of the D'nal Stone?" exclaimed another.

"Do you know what this means?" Wendelmyr breathed.

"Indeed, I do." Naed looked from the gold-brown gaze of his beloved to the stone of his forefathers and beyond to the assembled lords. "Dranoel's line was blood heir to D'nal, and therefore so am I."

A beat of silence.

"Sisters and the Demon!"

"Bloody hell!"

"Sisters be praised!"

"I do not accept that!" Alwyl sputtered. "It cannot be. This is a forgery, some kind of trick perpetrated by the pretender prince."

Wendelmyr of Kassi faced him. "I will swear to the authenticity of these documents, my lord. Upon my honor as a D'nalian and my long friendship with the deceased, I will vouchsafe the D'nal Stone has been found, and we are truly in the presence of D'nal's heir."

Chapter Forty-Seven

"Stop looking at me as if I've grown another head," Naed growled.

He and Allyn climbed—haltingly, as befitted two invalids—the gate tower. The morning was half gone, and sweat dripped off Naed's nose despite the stone's chill. His thigh complained. Groin to knee had bloomed hideously blue and purple, but something had cracked with Yormoc's kick and the deep, persistent ache was gone. Gam, having stitched and salved into the predawn, said belike scar tissue had broken. He'd arisen stiff but hopeful.

If only Allyn would stop pestering him.

"But you're a prince now, little brother. Or you should be. How does it feel?"

Naed grunted. He'd slept just enough to leave him sore all over and grumpy. Plus, he'd awakened alone. Raell had guests to attend as lady of the place, and she'd sent Banir to help him dress, but damned if looking forward to her naked astride his hips hadn't sustained him through all Gam's poking and prodding.

And there remained that raccoon-eyed Tolemak.

Banging the tower door onto its hinges was petty, aye, but took some of the edge off. Deep breaths of mist-born Druemarwin air calmed the pulse at his temple. *Be civil. Allyn's only blathering.* "D'nalee's future is far too unsettled for such talk."

If he sounded harsh, so be it. The Three Sisters seemed bent on dropping such *gifts* onto his shoulders. Unclenching his jaw, Naed crossed to the wall overlooking the drawbridge. He refused to chase what promised to be more burden than gift, no matter how attractive it might appear upon first glance, or to onlookers.

"I'm no more nor less than I was before. And the Kingdom will decide if the principalities return."

"Modesty, modesty…it's always become you." Allyn shrugged, then hissed, "Damned stitches!" Cradling his wounded shoulder, he faced Naed. "Father's convinced you'll take the title. Did you note how he bolted as soon as Kassi proclaimed you D'nal's heir? I'll wager he's halfway across that bloody marsh already, determined to protect his precious council of lords and cover his ass with them."

He grinned, more full of good cheer than anyone had a right to after yesternight, especially someone who'd taken two arrows in an assassination plot engineered by his brother. "And he gave up Mother as if he'd forgotten all about her."

Naed scowled. True, but hardly worthy of such glee. "He has more than the Kingdom and Mother's dowry lands to concern him, and well do you know it."

He surveyed the pavilions and the men hustling about, preparing to strike them. The lords were gathered in the Great Hall, hammering out details of their new alliance. Already riders had been dispatched to spread the news and bring others to the table. With Lord Tylus representing the Prince's interests, Naed saw no reason to interfere. The lords had taken ownership, and that was more than he'd hoped for when the Prince set him on this journey.

Forearms propped on the wall, he clasped his hands. This vantage point provided a view of Druemarwin's stone cairns, some so old as to be grassed over or sunken, one bare but for a few tentative green shoots. He'd laid Dranoel there. Someday— *Sisters willing, a long, long time from now*—he'd be laid beside the man who loved him.

Father and son. Family. At last.

His throat thickened, as he suspected it always would when he thought of his father, of what might have been.

But what might have been didn't make the future. Only the living did that. And the man beside him, despite his inordinate cheerfulness, had a living father to fear for. Time to broach the subject he'd taken his half-brother here to discuss.

"What do you think Alwyl will find at Tumin?"

Allyn hemmed, tugged his collar, adjusted his sling. "I doubt Father's in danger. Yet. And you've put him on his guard." More fidgeting, another tug. "He's no fool. He'll find a way to turn this to his advantage. He and our dear, deadly brother have that in common. Mayhap he'll admire Fennyn's audacity. After all, Father had no qualms about hiring Dlaniger to do his dirty work."

Naed risked a side glance. That was a raw nerve for both of them, and a Tumin father-son alliance was a too likely scenario. At least on that they were in accord. Unclasping his hands, he offered palms and hoped for more agreement.

"What will you do now?"

"I've been thinking. Not my strong suit, I know,

but hear me out." Allyn frowned into the distance where mist rose over the forest and sun slanted beams through it. "Now she's free, Mother's dowry lands need oversight. Mayhap I should take my men—my loyal men—there to protect her interests. Aye, and yours and mine, too. The bloodline goes from her late sister to her and, with the marriage now voided, ultimately to us."

Naed gave his half-brother a long, assessing look. "You *have* been thinking."

A flush crept up Allyn's throat. "Aye, well, in case you haven't thought that far, being occupied leading armies for the Kingdom and such, you inherit Dranoel's share; 'tis what Father wanted to secure when he sent me to recover Mother. With Dlaniger dead and you branded a bastard and a traitor—well, 'twas what he hoped, anyway—Dranoel's rights would fall to Father."

His half-brother was right; Naed hadn't thought that far. And certainly not about property...and land...and the possibility of secure footholds for the Kingdom beyond southern D'nalee. His pulse ratcheted up. "And that means?"

"Once Father comes to his senses, he'll realize 'twas bloody foolish to give up all rights to the lands. Belike he'll make a claim, move on them."

"And 'tis in your interests to defend them because, by your account, you'd inherit a share of Mother's portion."

Allyn's flush deepened. "Divided with you, aye." He gripped the stone and turned sober, steel-blue eyes on Naed. "When the council of lords acts—and act they will, I promise you—you'll need more allies than these, little brother. Do you trust me to bring men to your side?"

Naed scrutinized the man who shared half his parentage. Blood was indeed a contradiction: unreliable at the best of times, traitorous at the worst. Allyn had every reason to look after his own interests and put them first. But informing Naed of his rights directly conflicted with Allyn's best interests. That counted for something.

"You realize Alwyl will likely disown you now you've stood beside me."

Allyn dipped his head, stared at the stone. "Better disowned than dead, but I don't think it'll come to that. Father's too shrewd." He straightened. "As long as I remain heir, and well out of reach, Fennyn will have no incentive to remove Father."

They studied each other for a long moment.

"I never liked you much growing up, but you'll make a good Lord of Tumin, someday," Naed said.

Allyn barked a laugh. They stood in companionable silence while the mist cleared and the sun shone full on their shoulders.

****

"Yormoc's dead!"

Raell stared at the harried-looking captain of the guard. *Sisters be thanked*, leaped to her lips, before a commotion in Gam's chamber made her reconsider. Someone inside laughed like a crazed woman.

"Tell me."

"'Twas Gert, m'lady. She took one of Gam's knives and stuck it in his throat." The man swiped a hand over his mouth. "So fast she was…afore we knew what she was about." He stood, panting. "Not that I'm sorry he's dead, m'lady, but what do I do?"

Raell turned to her mother-in-law. Despite dark

circles under her eyes, bruised face, and arm in a sling, she'd partnered Raell all morning as they oversaw meals, beds, cleaning, and anything the assembled lords required.

"Yormoc beat her," Vyenne said, expression grim. "I saw how badly."

"Aye, he did." Raell tapped the blade strapped to her thigh beneath her newly altered gown. If she'd taken her sword to Yormoc on the parapet, Gert wouldn't have acted. "She defended herself from a monster. A bit late, aye, but listen to her, Captain, she's out of her mind."

The crazed laughter muted under Gam's murmurs, but a low, uncanny keening issued from the chamber now. The sound raised gooseflesh on Raell's arms. Beside her, Vyenne shivered. The captain of the guard swiped his face again.

"I'll leave her to Gam, then, m'lady, if 'tis your wish."

"Say naught to anyone for now."

He looked at her askance.

"For Gert's sake. I'll tell the master."

The man nodded with evident relief and excused himself.

"What will you tell Naed?" Vyenne said moments later as they climbed to the Great Hall.

"That the monster is dead and we're well rid of him." Raell stopped, stared at nothing, felt...nothing. No sense of victory at an enemy destroyed. The cost, paid by Gert, was too high. A creeping frustration remained.

"If Yormoc had aught to tell us about his cohorts, he meant to take it to the grave. You saw how he murdered that Tumin man to thwart us."

"We know enough, nonetheless." She startled Raell with a hand on her arm and a meaningful look. "That poor woman...I feel for her, truly. But I thank the Sisters a thousand times over neither you nor Naed poisoned yourselves by spilling that villain's blood."

Raell blinked at the vehemence in those words, at the honest, frank expression of concern. Lady Vyenne was a study in aloof self-containment; that she'd unbent this much chased all gloom from Raell's heart. She squeezed her mother-in-law's hand. Belike, they'd never again speak of yesternight's events, but neither would they forget what each dared do for the other, and for Naed. Because of it, they'd begun the day in silent accord, prepared to make a fresh start based on mutual respect. She might live to regret this, but she had to make the offer.

"You'll stay here with us, aye? Now you're free?"

Vyenne's lips curved. "Don't be too hasty to welcome me into your household. You are mistress here, and I shall find it difficult to resist interfering."

"Aye, but we Tolemaks are a hard-headed lot, and well do you know it." She grinned, feeling ridiculously light and energized.

"Indeed I do." Humor, and something equally unusual—warmth—sparkled in the older woman's eyes. "If your similarly hard-headed husband agrees, I shall stay—at least until I have someplace else to go." She tucked her arm into Raell's. "Now, if you'll permit me to interfere, I've an idea about this Bennin of Nye."

****

"The lords are gone, finally." Naed sank into his chair with a gusty sigh.

His leg throbbed, eyes scratched, stomach rumbled. Barely sunset and all he wanted was food, bath, and bed—in whatever order they could be obtained.

"For now." Tylus accompanied him into his private chamber and prowled the dimness.

He found two goblets, sniffed at pitchers, chose one, and poured. "You'll have a week, mayhap six days afore the first of 'em return to be trained, made fit to fight in this army you're building." Handing one cup to Naed, he raised his own. "To the future of D'nalee. May it come fast and clean, without bloodshed."

"Sisters willing."

Naed accepted the toast although it was wishful thinking. D'nalian obstinacy—that was the true challenge. How to convince those accustomed to power to surrender some of it for the sake of something bigger than themselves and their own interests.

He stared into his cup as if it could provide answers...and heard the Prince's voice: *A battle, my friend, is never merely about brute strength.*

Aye, it wasn't, or the Lancers with all their armor would've won before Vinvinnysee, and Rolnar with his massive forces would've won at Albon fields. If brute strength always prevailed, Alwyl of Tumin wouldn't have fled empty-handed when confronted by Naed and his ragtag, untried allies.

He sat up. A battle—indeed, a war—was about hearts and minds and numerous small but consequential steps that turned potential enemies into possible friends. It was about men like his half-brother Allyn, and Wendelmyr and the other lords who, at great risk to themselves, defied those with power for the sake of a future in which they might have a voice. Indeed, the

Kingdom they wished for was even now present in numerous alliances already made.

Tylus chuckled. "I see that gleam in your eye, sir, and I applaud it." He toasted again, drained his cup. "'Tis true, the Kingdom be well on the road to the future. But 'tis like to be a long, hard road, and there be much yet to do afore we celebrate." He thumped Naed's shoulder and winked. "That said, take yourself off to my daughter and make me a grandfather. With my lot all grown, I'll be wanting a lad or two to train. Aye, mayhap a lass too, knowing Raell."

Heat blazed up Naed's face, but before he could choke out a response, much less formulate one, Tylus, still chuckling, strode out and Mavis slipped in.

The girl peered into the darkening room, head cocked, one brow raised—she couldn't detect his blush, could she?—before bobbing her head.

"Your pardon, m'lord, but your lady says there be hot food and a bath, if'n it please you t' come upstairs."

By all that's holy, it most certainly did. And not just to make Tylus a grandfather, although indulging in the process topped Naed's priorities. More heat suffused his skin. 'Twas only natural between a husband and wife; what was unnatural was her father talking about it. He tossed down his wine and hoped Mavis would take it for the cause of his flush.

"Tell her I'm coming." Envying the girl her light-footed scamper, he shoved himself upright and prepared to follow.

The Great Hall, site of frenetic activity these past days, stood steeped in shadow, silent and deserted except for two figures who sat close together before a solitary lit fireplace.

Naed halted, recognized Toth and that raccoon-eyed Tolemak. His gut churned. There was still that to deal with.

Side by side they appeared to be talking—until Toth pulled the other into a one-armed embrace. Heads leaned together; the other man's head lowered to rest on Toth's shoulder.

Another kind of heat flamed up Naed's face. *That wasn't—it couldn't—what the bloody hell?* He swallowed, turned away, glanced again, confirmed what his gut told him.

One foot lifted to stomp over and demand what in the Name of the Sisters that bastard thought he was about with wanting Raell when sense intervened.

If that was the way the wind blew, the threat wasn't the man but the politics. And that—Naed's mouth spread into a wide, toothy grin—landed the mess squarely in Tylus's lap.

And out of mine.

Snatches of song and an urge to hum accompanied him to his chamber door when something prompted him to look back. *Sisters Three!* He'd climbed stairs without once thinking of his leg. Mayhap Gam was right: he *was* healing, finally. Lightened in body and mind, he lifted the latch.

Clad only in her shift, Raell was drying her hair before the fire as Naed entered. When she turned and smiled, light outlined her body through the thin fabric.

Desire, like a bolt of lightning, shot through his system. *Mine.* He strode across the room, hauled her into his arms, and plundered her mouth.

"A-a bath?" she breathed when he slid his lips to her throat.

"After."

"Well, then." She licked into his ear, took the lobe between her teeth. "You've too many clothes." And her fingers went to work unfastening laces and buckles.

Later, Naed luxuriated in a not-too-cool bath while she scrubbed his scalp. "Shall I expect to be bathed like this from now on, wife?"

Raell slid her hands down his chest and thumbed his nipples. "If and when you deserve it."

He caught her arms and considered pulling her in, but the tub was too small, so he settled for a kiss and palmed her breast, leaving her shift deliciously transparent. He grinned. Two could play at the mischief game.

A slight alteration in her demeanor pulled his gaze from a tantalizingly peaked nipple. "There be several things I must tell you afore we do aught else."

Gooseflesh prickled Naed's shoulders. 'Twas too early to know she was with child, wasn't it? He eyed her askance and waited.

"Yormoc is dead. Gert stabbed him. She's out of her mind, poor woman, so I thought it best we let the folk think he died of his wounds. Do you mind?"

Not at all what he expected. "Of his wounds," he echoed while his mind wrapped itself around the idea of Yormoc dead, finally, and not by his hand. "Well, if that's all, good riddance." He picked up a pitcher, rinsed his hair. "Will Gert recover?"

"Mayhap, in time. Gam's hopeful." Raell handed him a drying cloth.

"That's one thing dealt with." He rubbed his scalp, hoping the rest would be that easy. He had plans for that nipple. "What else?"

She licked her lips, pulled a face. "Bennin of Nye. Your mother's had an idea."

Oh, Mother. Shivers shot across his skin. Pushing himself out of water gone cold, he climbed from the tub. At least he'd had some forewarning about this issue.

"It's Toth, isn't it?"

"Toth…" She stared while he padded toward the fire to dry himself. "But how…?"

"I saw them together, just now, in the Great Hall."

Her befuddled expression provoked a spurt of satisfaction. He'd put her off balance, something he suspected would not happen often, if their relationship thus far was any indication. Best enjoy it while he could.

But not too long as her brows already inched together. She had beautiful, expressive brows, blessedly easy to read.

Throwing on a robe, Naed trailed a fingertip over one brow and down her cheek. The matter was serious after all, and he'd expended a fair amount of energy considering how to gut the bastard.

"This Bennin, he was never truly after you, was he? Not in that way."

"I-I didn't know how to tell you. I thought, being D'nalian…"

Ah, that. "Being D'nalian, we don't do such things openly but 'tis not unheard of." There was a great deal they had yet to learn about each other. He looked forward to the next surprise.

"'Tis what your mother said."

Anything but that. More goosebumps prickled. He tossed another log on the fire and poked it into place.

459

"My mother has sharp eyes and a sharper wit."

Straightening, he cast Raell a sideways glance. Her dampened breast stood out from her shift, round and full and perfectly sized for his hand. A serious temptation, but they had all night.

"I hesitate to ask, but what idea does she have for this Bennin of Nye?"

"Well, if Belac insists on an alliance between Nye and Tylus, Father should present him with the one that already exists, and has done for years. As to a blood heir, Bennin must provide that elsewhere as I am well and truly wed."

Demon be damned. Leave it to his mother to sort this solution out of something so tangled. The woman was both a treasure and a curse. Crossing to the bed, he sat and heaved a sigh. "Belike you'll now tell me Mother intends to stay at Druemarwin."

Raell beamed a cajoling smile. "Not forever. Only till she has elsewhere to go."

"Wonderful." *Heal fast, Allyn. Mother needs to go north.*

Raell approached, knelt, and ran her hand up his bruised thigh. "You move better," she murmured, stroking feather-light over black, blue, and purple skin, "since yesternight."

Her touch set off a riot of sensations. "I am better." He gripped the bedding while his body tightened. "Healing," he said gruffly.

She flashed him a thoroughly mischievous look, then bent and pressed kisses to his thigh. "I'm of a mind to test that."

"You are a minx." He groaned and shoved hands into her hair, but she'd already parted his robe and risen to push him onto his back.

Much later, when the fire was but glowing coals and she lay sprawled across his chest, Naed voiced a niggling thought. "Was that all?"

"Mm?"

"You said you had several things to tell me. I counted two." Tucking a hand under her chin, he raised her sleepy gaze. "Have you another?"

Raell yawned, crossed her hands, and propped her chin atop them. "Aye, but I wanted you all warm and satisfied first." She wriggled her hips, causing delicious skin-to-skin friction.

He arched a brow. "Forgive me if I think that sounds somewhat ominous."

Laughing, she planted a kiss on each corner of his mouth. "Daft man. 'Tis only that I've a plan to train the women to handle weapons. Why should half the folk be armed when all can learn to defend themselves? Aye, even your mother agrees there's a need. You should too, after these last days."

Naed dropped his head to the pillow. His skin crawled at images of his mother in armor, wielding a sword nigh as tall as herself. But the memory of Raell, fierce and competent, fighting at his side restored his pulse to normal.

Or nearly normal. Nothing in his life would ever be normal again, not as long as this woman was in it.

And that was exactly as it should be.

Helen C. Johannes

List of Places and Characters

Tolemak

Tolemak: western land, rugged and mountainous

-Albon: winter sanctuary for the Kingdom's forces

-Val-Feyridge: fortress of Tolemak princes

~

Arn: Prince of Val-Feyridge in Tolemak and heir to the Kingdom

Aerid: healer of Adanak birth, wife of Prince Arn

Krenin: Arn's deceased Second

Gorm: Master of Horse

Lord Tylus: in charge of defending Val-Feyridge fortress

Raell: Tylus's daughter

Toth: Raell's brother

Lord Rolnar of Roines: leader of eastern Tolemak lords opposing Prince Arn

Lord Belac of Nye and son Bennin: formerly allied with Rolnar of Roines:

~

D'nalee

D'nalee: middle land, a marshy and low place

-Druemarwin: a fortress in southern D'nalee

-Kassi: a fortress near Druemarwin

-Myrinnen Marsh: near Druemarwin

-Tumin: center of power in D'nalee

~

Lord Dranoel: deceased master of the Druemarwin fortress

Dlaniger: Dranoel's deceased son

Naed: new Lord of Druemarwin, illegitimate son and heir of Dranoel

Yormoc: Free Swordsman, friend of Dlaniger
Elthred and Gert: kitchen maids
Mavis: Raell's maid
Ekwul: lord's personal servant
Old Gam: healer
Banir: Naed's Tolemak Second and best friend
Grodar and Morys: Naed's Tolemak personal guard

~

Lord Alwyl of Tumin: head of the Council of Lords
Lady Vyenne: Naed's mother, Alwyl's wife
Allyn: Alwyl's heir, Naed's eldest half-brother
Fennyn: Naed's younger half-brother
Elwyn: deceased half-brother
Elda: Vyenne's maid
Humbert: Vyenne's groom

~

Lord Wendelmyr: master of Kassi fortress

~

Adanak

Adanak: eastern land, fertile and rolling with mountains in the north
-Vinvinnysee: walled city in central Adanak, center of commerce, defended by Lancers

~

Gaelwynn: Master of the Guard and formerly keeper of the Crown of Tolem

A word from the author...

An Army brat with a yen for travel and a fascination for history, I majored in German and English and have taught creative writing and composition. I have lived in Germany, studied in London, traveled in Japan, Scotland, Ireland, and the Caribbean, and proudly dipped my fingers into the waters on the east and west coasts of both the Atlantic and the Pacific, yet my roots are solidly Midwestern.

Growing up, I read fairy tales, Tolkien, *The Scarlet Pimpernel*, Agatha Christie, Shakespeare, and Ayn Rand, an unusual mix that undoubtedly explains why the themes, characters, and locales in my writing play out in tales of love and adventure.

My other books with The Wild Rose Press include *The Prince of Val-Feyridge* and *Bloodstone*.

If you enjoyed *Lord of Druemarwin*, please leave a review at your favorite book retailer or reader website.

http://helencjohannes.blogspot.com/